P9-DTP-320

PLOUGHSHARES

Fall 1993 · Vol. 19, Nos. 2 & 3

GUEST EDITOR
Sue Miller

EXECUTIVE DIRECTOR
DeWitt Henry

MANAGING EDITOR & FICTION EDITOR
Don Lee

POETRY EDITOR
David Daniel

ASSISTANT EDITOR
Jessica Dineen

FOUNDING PUBLISHER
Peter O'Malley

ADVISORY EDITORS

Russell Banks
Anne Bernays
Frank Bidart
Rosellen Brown
James Carroll
Madeline DeFrees
Rita Dove
Andre Dubus
Carolyn Forché
George Garrett
Lorrie Goldensohn
David Gullette
Marilyn Hacker
Donald Hall
Paul Hannigan
Stratis Haviaras
Fanny Howe

Marie Howe
Justin Kaplan
Bill Knott
Maxine Kumin
Philip Levine
Thomas Lux
Gail Mazur
James Alan McPherson
Leonard Michaels
Sue Miller
Jay Neugeboren
Tim O'Brien
Joyce Peseroff
Jayne Anne Phillips
Robert Pinsky
James Randall
Alberto Alvaro Ríos

M. L. Rosenthal
Lloyd Schwartz
Jane Shore
Charles Simic
Maura Stanton
Gerald Stern
Christopher Tilghman
Richard Tillinghast
Chase Twichell
Fred Viebahn
Ellen Bryant Voigt
Dan Wakefield
Derek Walcott
James Welch
Alan Williamson
Tobias Wolff
Al Young

PLOUGHSHARES, a journal of new writing, is guest-edited serially by prominent writers, who explore different and personal visions, aesthetics, and literary circles. PLOUGHSHARES is published three times a year at Emerson College, 100 Beacon Street, Boston, MA 02116-1596. Telephone: (617) 578-8753. Phone-a-Poem: (617) 578-8754.

STAFF ASSISTANTS: Barbara Lewis and Stephanie Booth. FICTION READERS: Billie Lydia Porter, Karen Wise, Barbara Lewis, Maryanne O'Hara, Holly LeCraw Howe, Christine Flanagan, Michael Rainho, Tanja Brull, Phillip Carson, Sara Nielsen Gambrill, Erik Hansen, Kimberly Reynolds, and David Rowell. POETRY READERS: Barbara Tran, Linda Russo, Tom Laughlin, Mary-Margaret Mulligan, Tanja Brull, and Jason Rogers. PHONE-A-POEM COORDINATOR: Joyce Peseroff.

SUBSCRIPTIONS (ISSN 0048-4474): $19/domestic and $24/international for individuals; $22/domestic and $27/international for institutions. See last page for order form.

UPCOMING: Winter 1993–94, Vol. 19, No. 4, a fiction and poetry issue edited by Russell Banks and Chase Twichell, will appear in December 1993 (editorially complete). Spring 1994, Vol. 20, No. 1, a poetry and fiction issue edited by James Welch, will appear in April 1994.

SUBMISSIONS: Please see back of issue for detailed submission policies.

BACK ISSUES are available from the publisher. Write or call for abstracts and a price list. Microfilms of back issues may be obtained from University Microfilms. PLOUGHSHARES is also available as a CD-ROM full-text product from Information Access Company. INDEXED in M.L.A. Bibliography, American Humanities Index, Index of American Periodical Verse, Book Review Index. Self-index through Volume 6 available from the publisher; annual supplements appear in the fourth number of each subsequent volume.

DISTRIBUTED by Bernhard DeBoer (113 E. Centre St., Nutley, NJ 07110), Fine Print Distributors (6448 Highway 290 East, Austin, TX 78723), Ingram Periodicals (1226 Heil Quaker Blvd., La Vergne, TN 37086), Inland Book Co. (140 Commerce St., East Haven, CT 06523), and L-S Distributors (130 East Grand Ave., South San Francisco, CA 94080). PRINTED by Edwards Brothers.

PLOUGHSHARES receives additional support from the National Endowment for the Arts, the Massachusetts Cultural Council, the Lannan Foundation, and Business Volunteers for the Arts/Boston. Major new marketing initiatives have been made possible by the Lila Wallace–Reader's Digest Literary Publishers Marketing Development Program, funded through a grant to the Council of Literary Magazines and Presses. The opinions expressed in this magazine do not necessarily reflect those of Emerson College, the editors, the staff, the trustees, or the supporting organizations.

CONTENTS

Ploughshares · Fall 1993

INTRODUCTION
Sue Miller 5

FICTION
Janet Desaulniers, *Never, Ever, Always* 10
Jonathan Wilson, *From Shanghai* 24
Laura Glen Louis, *Fur* 37
T. M. McNally, *Insomnia* 61
Wendy Counsil, *Other Wars* 75
Michael Dorris, *Shining Agate* 87
Mary McGarry Morris, *A Man of Substance* 105
Fred G. Leebron, *Lovelock* 118
Ann Packer, *Nerves* 140
Robin Hemley, *My Father's Bawdy Song* 162
Eileen McGuire, *The Life of the Mind* 173
G. Travis Regier, *Crooked Letter* 186
Elizabeth Tallent, *Kid Gentle* 201
Peter Gordon, *Photopia* 224

CONTRIBUTORS' NOTES 233

ABOUT SUE MILLER 235

BOOKSHELF
The Pugilist at Rest by Thom Jones 241
Talking to High Monks in the Snow by Lydia Minatoya 243
Hurdy Gurdy by Tim Seibles 245
The River at Wolf by Jean Valentine 246
Not Where I Started From by Kate Wheeler 248
The Paper Anniversary by Joan Wickersham 249
Beloved Infidel by Dean Young 250

POSTSCRIPTS 252

PLOUGHSHARES

Patrons

Introduction

It is perhaps the height of optimism to try to structure an issue of a literary magazine around some single subject or theme. There is clearly the notion that, floating around out there, waiting to be beckoned, are the requisite ten or twelve or fourteen fine stories which will exactly fit, which will make an anthology, rather than just Volume something, Number whatever, out of this edition. And perhaps it's symptomatic of a kind of ingratitude, too, or so I've always thought. After all, shouldn't you be happy enough—ready to weep with joy, one would think—to find the requisite ten or twelve or fourteen stories about anything under the sun that you truly liked?

And so when DeWitt Henry suggested *time* to me for the Fall fiction issue—because he had noticed, he said, that it seemed a preoccupation of mine, the way the impact of an event or a situation played itself out over time—I was a little reluctant. Probably no more than I would have been at any other suggestion. But it seemed at the moment more a limitation set on what I was looking for than a promise of what I might get.

Well, fine, I said. Time, okay. Yes, I supposed it was a kind of preoccupation, at least some of the time. At least in some of my work.

And then, of course, as can happen once you've heard an idea and played with it, you begin to embrace it. *Time.* Of course, time. Inevitably. DeWitt was exactly right about my own work. And I began to see that all the short stories I'd cared most about used time in an integral way, as a structural element, really. And so when Don Lee, the managing editor, called to ask me for a little help—what, exactly, was I looking for, what did I *mean* when I said time as a structural element?—my conversion had already been accomplished, I was able to offer examples in enthusiastic abundance. Nearly any Alice Munro story, I suggested, but "White Dump," let's say, in particular, in which the alteration of the chronology of events as well as the jumps in perspective are almost impenetrably baffling until you realize that what Munro is presenting fictionally is the sense of inevitability: the seeds of this event contained in that, the result of another event implicit already in the way it begins to play itself out.

Or the Chekhov story "The Student," in which Chekhov steps outside the narrative frame near the end to comment on his self-important main character forgivingly, "He was only twenty-two"—and thereby makes us complicit in a particular way of seeing time's passage: foolish optimism and innocence ending, the inevitability, with age, of disillusionment and betrayal; but perhaps also the possibility of the very understanding that allows for the forgiveness Chekhov is expressing.

Or "Across the Bridge" by Mavis Gallant, which leaps forward several decades in the last sentence and offers us the remarkable, unexpected outcome which makes us want to reread the whole story to see how it could have contained this unnoticed possibility.

Anything like those, I told Don, with the optimism of the convert.

And slowly the stories began to arrive in the mail, two or three to a package at first, then in heavy envelopes of ten or more, trailing me around as I traveled this spring. Some, as it turned out, had been submitted earlier to another editor who had liked them but didn't have room for them, submitted with no notion whatever of satisfying my thematic or structural requirement. And some were from people who'd never inquired about whether there *was* such a requirement, simply thought an editor might like their stories. Some were aimed right at my issue, the writer claimed, and some explained how. Sometimes Don would note on a submission, "I think this is exactly what you're looking for." Sometimes there'd be the equivalent of a shrug. Implied: maybe you can make the *time* connection here that I can't, but meanwhile, I think you might like this.

And the truth was that in each category of submission there was about the same percent of stories which seemed to have anything on their minds at all that had to do with time. But what was striking to me as I read and reread my way through all the stories was that DeWitt's intuition had been correct—I was most drawn to, most interested in, those stories which might fit into this time-centered issue, different as those stories were one from another, different as their ways of connecting to our theme were.

Some, in fact, did use time as a structural element in the story in some way close to the way I'd envisioned. At the end of "A Man of Substance," for example, Mary McGarry Morris takes a leap forward into a world beyond the main character's life and presents us an appalling revelation of its meaning to others. "My Father's Bawdy Song" and "From Shanghai" both jump years in time in their narrators' lives at the end, to offer—explicitly or implicitly—a more adult perspective on the meaning and events in the story. "Photopia" moves backward in time at its close to give us the surprise of a completely unexpected remembered event, and the comment which that makes on the nature of memory itself. And "Other Wars" moves forward in time so that the narrator can be openly speculative about what she has recorded in the story, and about what the true meaning of that recording—even perhaps of the nature of fiction—might be.

"Nerves" by Ann Packer and "Crooked Letter" by G. Travis Regier are both stories centered around memories, and main characters whose relations to those memories change in the course of each story. Janet Desaulniers's "Never, Ever, Always" offers at its start several events from the narrator's past whose import is woven into the present of the story and gives it a deeper meaning.

In two other stories there's a nearly dizzying confusion about time and sequence, about what's memory and what's happening in the present of the story. In "Kid Gentle," this is brought about by Jenny's solitude, by her need to make sense of her life in that solitude; in "Insomnia," by a powerful combination of alcohol and obsession.

In "Fur," Fei Lo lives surrounded and immobilized by the past. During the course of the story he comes to painful terms with the present, indeed with the future, with his own age and needs. "Shining Agate" works thematically in nearly the opposite way, its glib anthropology student coming to understand and appreciate something about the way the past lives on in the present among the people he's observing.

And there are two stories here whose characters seem to live in a kind of timeless suspension: "Lovelock" by Fred Leebron, whose main character, West, coming from nowhere, going to nowhere, stops and retraces his steps in the story, commits an act of conscience, and so enters time; and Cecilia in "The Life of the Mind," who feels that her past as Andy imagines it is more interesting than her own life.

But every one deals somehow with time, every single one.

And yet, surely any one of these writers could argue with me that, more than making use of their time structurally or thematically, he or she is making use of some other element—voice, say, or sexual need. Cultural differences, or the acceptance of death.

Of course, that is true, too. Having been anthologized myself as a "New England writer," as a "writer of the new American family," as a "writer of the erotic" (and as a *Ploughshares* writer, several times), I've felt the impulse to argue with however I'm being categorized, even as I'm grateful to the category, or to the accident of fitting into it—whatever, so long as I'm published.

But it's not just a matter of resistance to categories. As with any group of fine stories, these stories *are* more different than like. In fact, the way they deal with time is, in many cases, quite incidental to a story with primarily other concerns. But the sometimes almost accidental presence of time as an element, however marginal it may have seemed to the writer, gives all these stories a weight and authority, a sense of consequence, if you will, that comes more or less directly from that presence. Because they are all also dealing with another kind of consequence: with what follows closely, necessarily, on something else. We're made who we are over time, these stories argue. By the things we remember, by the memories we try to push aside. We live in time, with the consequences of our histories, of our behaviors and choices. Sometimes the story suggests that we need to be open to the past; sometimes it seems to be saying that we must recognize the implications of the present, that we must understand where we are going in the future. Several seem to deal with the experience of a kind of weightlessness, timelessness—but even these are stories which take note of that, rather than just reproducing it: they watch a character shift, marginally, into a life of consequence.

They compare a character's insubstantiality with the imaginary substance of a screenplay, or a falsified memory.

Can I make a rule, then, that stories which encompass time, structurally, thematically—however—necessarily carry this authority, this weight? I suppose one objection might be that all fiction makes use of time. There is always the earlier *now* of the story as opposed to the later *now*. There is always, at least implicitly, the *then*.

The difference, I think, lives in the will of the writer to subordinate one *now*—one *then*—to another. It seems to me it was likely Hemingway who introduced into American prose the lack of subordination, even in sentence structure, that has become the trademark of what might be called the affectless new fiction. But of course, in Hemingway's fiction you got to see, with varying degrees of explicitness, the source of the anomie, the wounding moment that accounted for the carefully and beautifully balanced neutrality of the shimmering prose.

And certainly the more artful of our fiction writers manage to suggest a source, too. But there has grown up virtually a school of writers who seem to work in this way tonally and structurally without having asked themselves what such a tone or structure might imply; who have found a voice without thinking about what it is they're already saying by using that voice; or what it is they'd like to say, period. And a characteristic of this school is the numbed, undifferentiated *now-ness* of their narration, a *now-ness* which doesn't point beyond itself to any source, any origin, any deeper meaning.

To move beyond this present-tense recital of events—as these stories do—to selectively shape a presentation of events playing out over time; to point to the connections, the results, the meaning, is to deal with consequence. And, I'd argue, to make consequential fiction. It seems to me, then, that in so casually accepting DeWitt's suggestion, I guaranteed myself stories with a certain *gravitas,* a certain moral seriousness. This would have been a far more difficult thing to ask for—certainly more pretentious—than for stories that somehow made use of time. I'm as grateful, then, for the accident of happening on this theme as I did, as I am to the experience of reading these fourteen powerful stories.

Never, Ever, Always

My husband often traced what he called the minor flaws of my character to Kansas City, Missouri—a city he placed in the dead middle of the Midwest, a "stunningly homogeneous" town, he liked to say, where it must have been horrifyingly easy for me to grow up believing untruths about the world. Often enough I agreed with him about my hometown. I grew up there the overprotected and only child of a doting, widowed mother, and I grew up there a Catholic girl. The way I remember it is as a nine-year-old in the back of Sister Mary Benedict's catechism class, as a girl tall and smart and timid enough to be trusted back there, out of Sister Mary Benedict's reach, left to my own resources.

In Sister Mary Benedict's catechism class, we mainly discussed sin—sins of omission and commission, venial sins and mortal sins. We were twenty-five girls preparing for the sacrament of penance. On Good Friday we would line up outside Father Lucardo's confessional and bare our souls for the first time. Sister Mary Benedict wanted us to feel, in those last few days, the privilege of our own redemption. She urged us to imagine a flock of white birds mired in sticky tar suddenly breaking free and clean.

Pretty girls who sat in a cluster near the coat rack tried to charm Sister Mary Benedict with claims that they had no true sins, none that mattered anyway, none that weren't eased by something as simple as the confiteor recited at daily Mass. Someday they might commit sin, they told her—it was possible that someday they might commit even mortal sin—but when they were grown, when they were *women*. They shifted in their chairs at the word. They rolled their eyes at one another. Watching them, I saw that the idea of womanhood embarrassed them— much the way the idea of sin embarrassed them—sin and womanhood both distant, querulous predictions. I had to raise my hand a long time before Sister Mary Benedict noticed me.

"Sister," I said, standing next to my chair. "Suppose I had committed a sin, but then I was deeply sorry in my own heart. And suppose I was *on my way* to the church to confess when a milk truck ran me down."

In a black-and-white movie my mother had watched on Saturday afternoon while she combed out my hair, I'd seen a man run down by a milk truck. He had been on his way to tell a woman that he loved her. The woman was a beautiful invalid. She loved him, too, but out of pride or misguided kindness, she had never told him. In her wheelchair, she took the news of the man's death stoically while my mother's tears ran down my bare shoulders.

Sister Mary Benedict was a tall nun, heavy and hard except for her long, milk-white hands. The weathered skin around her eyes pinched into furrows at my question, and the pretty girls quieted. I stood waiting next to my chair. Two white bows held my hair away from my face, which then was the blank, open face of a girl in a movie, the face of a girl who thought runaway milk trucks were about the limit of injustice in the world. "God would still welcome me, wouldn't He, Sister?" I said. "He'd open His arms, right?"

Sister Mary Benedict tucked her hands inside her habit and arranged them secretly at her waist. I watched her and thought, oddly, She's a woman inside those clothes—like my mother or the invalid that man died trying to reach. A flush spread under her cheekbones, and I worried for a moment that she'd known my thoughts, that she was angry. When my mother was angry, she opened her pocketbook and threw things—tubes of lipstick, car keys, crumpled tissues—but Sister Mary Benedict stood still and dire as a beam of light, her eyes only on me. I saw then the answer to another question I'd once pondered alone back in the far corner of her class. That question had been: Why would she do it— give up men, cars, cologne, colors, and desire? I saw then that she'd done it to become what she was at that moment—a woman in black about to pass on cruel facts to a stupid, winsome girl.

"God would not welcome you, Nora." She spoke quietly, lowering her eyes when she said my name. Then she looked at me again. "You would die alone and outside His love."

The pretty girls smirked at me as I sat down, but I thought,

Okay. All right. I believed her. In my mind, God was a man, and though I had never really known any men outside of Father Lucardo, I had seen him often enough—sitting in Sister Mary Benedict's chair, asking each girl to stand as he read aloud in stentorian tones the grades from her quarterly report—to understand that some part of a man's stature or his calling or of manhood itself must allow him or require him to be merciless.

That night after my bath I sat again at my mother's feet in the soft light of the TV while she put up my hair. She dipped a wooden wide-toothed comb into scented water, ran it through my hair, then wound sections up in strips of soft flannel. I leaned my cheek against her solid knee. She was watching her favorite variety show. On it, three girls in elaborate wigs sang a sad song about all the trouble they'd had after they'd gone out into the world and forgotten what their mothers told them. They'd lost their shy and happy homes. They'd lost their pasts. They'd lost their hearts, they sang. I sat up between my mother's knees. The girls blinked glamorous, affecting tears under their mountains of hair. They sang words like *never, ever, always.* I believed them, too.

"Gullibility is not a victimless crime," was what my husband liked to say. He said it was no wonder I grew up to be such a strange, long-suffering woman, frightened of my own needs, inordinately interested in doing the right thing. My husband married me more gently than his opinions implied. When we met, he was a tough, suspicious, hair-trigger sort of man—easily angered, quick to push back his chair and walk away—but in my presence, he quieted, he settled, and he listened as I rambled through a set of stories I believed must represent the central confusions of my life. "You know, you think too much," he told me once across a table in a crowded restaurant. "You study your life like it's an equation, like you expect an answer." When he said it, I knew he was right, but I was not ashamed because I also knew he was a little mesmerized by and a little protective of the frailty of my hope. Standing to leave the restaurant that night, he took my elbow gently in his hand, and I felt him feel, perhaps for the first time, the delicacy that underlies any true authority. He looked at me for a moment, and then he steered me out of the restaurant.

So it was lightly that my husband eased me away from home and church, from my mother, from many of my qualities. There were times I admired him more than I did myself. He had been, before he met me, an adventurer. He'd gone places. He'd done things. Once, on a bluff overlooking a cornfield where we'd stopped to rest coming back from a day trip to the country, he told me a story about waking up from an opium sleep to an earthquake in Burma. Hanging in a hammock, he'd been dreaming, he said, of a deep rumble, the sound of a plane touching down. When he opened his eyes, he saw the treetops above him shiver eerily in no wind, and when he sat up, the ground rose with him and then bowed away from him, undulating in a slow wave that carried a small shed at the edge of his clearing down a ravine. There was no one around—the man who had rented him the hut lived half a day's walk through the jungle—and there was no sound but the rumble and the crack of falling trees. My husband, though, felt a strange calm. Finally, he said, he'd gotten far enough away from all he'd been and known. There didn't seem to be anything he could or should do. He watched a huge tree fall slowly to crush a line of smaller trees, and he sat still, waiting for what would happen next.

I took his hand after he told me that, and I drew closer to him. Giving myself to a man might finally have a purpose, was the wish I was making. I'd been in love by then often enough to have noticed that my passion for any man coincided pretty neatly with the urgency of my need to escape my own character. I'd seen myself eat calamari, wear elaborate lingerie, claim to enjoy incoherent plays. Yet here was a man who had escaped himself long ago, on a clouded day in Burma, while trees fell around him and the ground grew supple and undulate. I don't think anyone who has ever wanted to feel the world as frankly as a stand of corn or a common bird would not have taken the chance I took.

We ended up in Chicago, where he had a friend who was storing a trunk for him. In that trunk was the money my husband had made during what he called his "invisible time." After high school, he sent away for a book called *Your Right to Privacy,* which explained how to live outside government, how to remove your name from birth records and social security rolls. He lived for ten years like that, traveling the world, avoiding the draft and taxes, and after we were married we moved the trunk from his friend's apartment to ours.

"I feel criminal," I said, next to him in the car that day, the trunk wedged into the back seat. I was remembering something my mother had said before we left Kansas City: You don't marry men like him, she told me. You carry their pictures in a locket. You keep their letters at the back of a lingerie drawer. "I feel like we're moving a body or something."

"Don't," he told me. "No one in the world knows about this money except you. If it makes you nervous, you only have to forget about it. That's about as gone as anything gets."

On that day, which was a cool summer day with a breeze off the lake, I looked out at the skyline of Chicago, the long towering line of apartment buildings that edged the shore. Still new to the city, I was moved by how many people lived there, and I felt a stranger to myself, as though I could forget everything. He turned the radio on low and I rolled down the window. The breeze lifted my hair off my neck and then settled it again. I leaned back against the seat and closed my eyes. When I opened them again, we were home.

Even the baby was not a surprise. He wanted her, and after a childhood during which I'd been led to believe that even my good intentions could not save me, I wanted a baby who would grow up with him as father. While I was pregnant and full of extravagant feeling, I dreamed her—a rangy girl with tangled hair running over hills along the African coast, part of a graceful, long-legged herd of children that zagged toward the water like gazelles, then eased smoothly inland in a sudden shared choreography of will.

We named her Willa as a kind of testament to that dream. She was a long, lean, blond baby with delicate fingers, quick eyes, and a serious mouth, and she was a baby of considerable will. From the day she was born, she hated sleep. She'd struggle upright out of anyone's arms, bolt screaming out of sneaking dozes as if someone had thrown a blanket over her head. At some point we noticed that she closed her eyes easily only in clamorous and well-lighted public places—restaurants, El platforms, the Sunday afternoon beach—as if she needed hearty assurance of the world even as she slept. So nights at her bedtime we spread her quilt on the living-room floor, turned on all the lights and the TV, and talked over her until she drifted off.

One night, when Willa was thirteen months old and still struggling against being weaned, the three of us watched a documentary on the westernization of China together. The insistent monotone of the interpreter's speech combined with the strange swallowed cadences of the Chinese to please Willa in some way. She lay on her back, very still and alert, her eyes open, her thumb in her mouth. I could see that she was happy. Though she wasn't looking at me, I smiled at her and then over my shoulder at my husband on the couch. He was watching the screen. He looked as happy as she did.

"I've got to get there before I die," he said. My husband had been so many places in his life that he spoke of far-off corners of the world the way I spoke of the dry cleaner's down the block. "Just up the beach from Montevideo," he'd say, or "about a kilometer outside Toowoomba." Now he was a computer specialist, a systems troubleshooter for a huge corporation that sat far out in the suburbs on sixty acres of land, but China, open and in front of him, sat him up in his chair. He patted his pockets for his cigarettes and leaned toward the set. "Watch this now. This is one of the world's last mysteries."

On the TV, peasants swamped a group of American tourists shooting sixty-second film. The tourists shot their Polaroids frantically and tossed pictures into the crowd. There was a close-up of a man holding a snapshot of his child as it developed. His face reflected first a kind of simple, nodding good cheer, and then, as I imagined he began to recognize the features of his own child, a reverence. He pressed the snapshot to his chest and looked up into the filmmaker's camera. What his face showed then was gratitude. "Look at that," I said. "Look at that face. It makes me want to go over there with whole crates of cameras."

"We'd become millionaires."

"Oh, not to sell," I told him. "I'd want to give it all to them." He looked at me sharply. I thought perhaps Willa had stirred, but she was curled up now on the quilt, sleeping. "What?"

He lit another cigarette, then threw the matchbook down. It skidded across the coffee table and fell to the rug. "Nothing," he said. "I just hope that's your hormones talking. I hope that isn't you."

"Of course it's me." I stretched away from Willa to reach the matchbook. "Pay attention." I tossed the matches back at him. "I'm your wife."

He snatched the matchbook out of the air, slipped it in his pocket, and smiled. "I recognize you," he said. "You're my wife, all right."

I looked back at the TV.

"Hey," he said until I turned around again. "All I meant is you can't just give things to people. You murder your own chances, and you murder theirs. Any good missionary will tell you that. Besides, what those people love about Americans is not all our stuff. What those people love about Americans is how we got all our stuff—buying and selling, putting our own needs first."

"Don't get all tough-guy, citizen-of-the world with me. It's a TV show. We're watching TV."

"Right." He nodded and looked back at the TV, still smiling. "Let's do that."

I lay down next to Willa, who did stir then. She gave up her thumb and began to pull at my clothes, fretting to nurse. I slid her across my lap and patted her hard between the shoulder blades, which occasionally calmed her. Then I looked back at him. "And don't talk to me about hormones when I'm weaning our child."

"Give me that baby. How can you expect her not to need you when you're right there next to her?"

I handed him Willa and he laid her on her back next to him on the couch, settling one hand on her chest. He didn't stroke her or pat her or try to ease her, and this benign neglect worked. She watched him for a while, fiddled with his fingers, then found her thumb again. I looked back at the documentary. The interviewer was examining a farming couple on the nature of marriage. They sat before him in identical chairs, wearing almost identical clothing, and they appeared to be equally embarrassed by his curiosity. "I'm wondering," the interviewer said, "what provokes marriage here. What sorts of needs are fulfilled by it? Is it love, production, procreation?" The Chinese farmer cocked his head. He appeared actually to wince under the weight of this question, while his wife's uneasy smile grew more distant and fixed. I knew they weren't going to answer, but I sat up anyway and paid strict attention. Like the interviewer, I didn't know much about marriage. Even after three years with my husband, I still had the sense I was making myself and the two of us up as I went along. The Chinese couple exchanged a quiet glance, and as I watched them, some part of me held out hope that marriage meant two people resigned in good humor to their own poor characters. I realized then that I still believed in redemption—even for Americans— that someone or something might come along someday and show me my need by meeting it.

Not long after that night in front of the documentary, my voice began to change. Willa noticed first, and it was the change in her behavior—her constant demands for me to talk to her, sing to her, tell her stories—that alerted my husband. "Something's different," he told me one day at breakfast. "Your voice is younger— breathier or something. It's different somehow. She hears it." I worried for the two weeks it took to get an appointment with my doctor, but when he saw me, he said I was okay, he said I was fine, it was only nodes—a lot of them, but benign. Then he referred me to a surgeon.

In the recovery room, I woke to someone slapping my forearm. "Open your eyes," she kept saying. "I need to hear your voice." There was a slim possibility that my vocal cords, encrusted in the nodes, had been damaged, though I trusted the surgeon, a cancer specialist accustomed to far more delicate and taxing surgery than mine. I opened my eyes. The room was tiled white and cold as an icehouse. Suddenly a woman's face, fleshy and florid under her surgical cap, was above mine. "Are you trying?" she said. "You're not, are you?" Under her gaze, I felt puny and dissolute. I wanted to ask her for a blanket or for something to make me sleep again, but I could hear how busy she was. I knew she wouldn't bring me anything, that she'd listen to me choke on a syllable, then disappear.

"I can see you're awake," she said, "and I'm going to stand here until you say something." I closed my eyes then. I felt a deep, delicious stubbornness.

A few days before, I had taken Willa out to buy a new aquarium for her turtle. We were going to throw away the plastic thing with the miniature palm tree and do it right. At the pet store, I shopped capably, choosing a modest but spacious tank with a built-in sunning ledge, and Willa helped carry a bag of colored rocks up the steps to our apartment. "Bobo is going to love all this," I told her. "He's going to stop feeling like a dime-store attraction. He's going to feel like a real turtle when we're done."

When I opened our front door, I saw my husband kissing a twenty-year-old girl who sometimes messengered his reports around his office complex. They were in the dining room. My husband had the girl pressed up against the table. Her back was arched and both his hands were involved in her long hair.

I pushed Willa behind me. "Okay," I said. "That should do it."

She was a raw-boned girl, with fleshy, full thighs and large breasts loose under her T-shirt, but at the sound of my voice she straightened herself silkily. When she looked at me, her eyes were still dreamy.

"Get out," I said. "You get out of my house."

My husband drew Willa from behind me and guided her down the hall and into her playroom. "Show Bobo his new pebbles," I heard him say. For a moment, the girl and I were alone together. She stood still, not looking at me, then tucked her T-shirt into her jeans. My husband came up the hall. He reached behind me to push the door closed, then stood between us. "Do you want to sit down?" he said. "Do you want to talk about this?"

I saw that he meant to create out of this chaos some sort of civilized and complicated event. I wouldn't have expected that from him. The girl relaxed at the sound of his voice. She drew her hair up in both her hands, then dropped it over her shoulders. "Just try to be fair," she said.

I think even before she spoke I had decided that I could not bear to hear her voice in my house. "You realize, don't you," I said to her, "that you're a lower form of life. That the damn house plants are laughing at you."

She squinted at me. "Your husband doesn't seem to think so," she said. We both looked at him. He put his hands in his pockets and shook his head lightly at the floor.

"I guess we can't be too sure of what my husband thinks, can we?"

She picked up her bag, a ridiculous cloth pouch held closed with a safety pin, from under the dining-room table. "Well, I'm leaving," she said, looking my husband in the face as she passed him. I reached behind me to pull the door open, but only enough so that she had to slide through. Then I eased my weight against it until I heard the click of the latch.

My husband and I looked at each other then in a new way, in the strange new light of my sudden authority. "I'm sorry. It was stupid," he said. "It was unseemly. I've insulted you, and I'm sorry."

I pulled a chair away from the dining-room table and sat down. "I always thought you wouldn't lie. You might run off to Bogotá for six months, but you wouldn't lie."

"I'm not lying now, Nora. You know what she is. You nailed her. Don't pretend you don't know what happened here. Don't pretend you don't know how insignificant she is, because I'm not going to pretend she's more than that."

"I know what happened here," I said. I looked up at him. "I just want you to know there's going to be a problem for us now, and I'll tell you what that problem is going to be. That problem is going to be that I needed to believe that you would not do this, that you would never do this."

He sat down across from me, looked out into the living room for a time, and then back at me. "I didn't ask you to believe that," he said. "I wouldn't have. You believed that on your own. If you'd asked me, I would have said, 'Never say never, Nora. One, it's sentimental. Two, it's dangerous. And three, it's always a lie.'"

In the recovery room, it occurred to me that it might be useful to be mute. I have large, expressive eyes. I could drive him mad, never offering him a word.

·   ·   ·

Outside an elevator, as the gurney on which I lay was rolled down a hallway and then nudged up against a wall, I woke to the scent of my husband's cigarettes and the wool of his good sports coat. Then I felt his presence next to me. He touched my hair and ran the back of his hand across my cheek—odd, stylized gestures that I could not quite appraise. I kept my eyes closed. I thought of my mother. She had called the day before from Kansas City and asked to speak with my husband—something she had never in the three years of my marriage asked of me. I had told her about the young girl, and so I hesitated. "You're my only child," she said into the pause. "Now put that man on the telephone."

I held the receiver out to him. "My mother," I said.

He spoke to her in clipped affirmatives. Yes, he would, he said. He knew that, he said. He was sure, he told her. Then he handed the phone back to me.

"He says he'll be there for you," my mother said. "Will he be there for you?"

"I think so," I told her.

"Well, I suppose this could be good. He should take care of you for a while. He should remember his responsibilities." Slower then, with less certainty, she said, "I suppose this could be to your advantage."

"I suppose."

"So I won't come, then."

"I guess not," I told her.

Next to my gurney, my husband stood still. I knew he was staring down at me, though I did not open my eyes. I think I believed that my pain and deep fatigue would offer a clearer sense of the genuine than anything I might see.

"Your wife?" I heard a woman say.

"Yes."

"One of Dr. Scranton's patients?"

"Yes," my husband said again.

"So am I. So is half this ward," the woman said. "His work is a miracle, you know. Even the nurses say so. You keep that at the front of your mind now. You hold on to that." I realized then that she believed I was a cancer patient, and in the quiet that followed her remark, I knew my husband had realized that, too. I heard, in the silence, his confusion. It pleased me. "She's very young," the woman said.

"She is." My husband paused again, and then he said, "We have a one-year-old daughter." The woman gasped a little at this new and deepened sense of my tragedy. I came ferociously awake, feeling a little like Willa as I opened my eyes. The woman took a step back. My husband removed his hands from the side bar of my bed and put them in his pockets.

Two nurses came then, and pushed my gurney into a room. They arranged rolled towels on both sides of my neck to immobilize it, wrapped my sheet tight around me like a shroud, then slid me off the gurney onto a hospital bed. Over their heads, I watched my husband hang back in a corner of the room. After they left, he came to sit on the edge of the bed. He fingered a corner of the sheet, then folded it over the shoulder of my gown. "The doctor said it went well. He wants you to try your voice."

"You son of a bitch," I mouthed at him.

He stood up from the bed, running both his hands through his hair, moving toward the door; then he turned back to me. "What would you have said to her, Nora? 'My wife's not dying and I'm sorry if you are?' Is that what you would have said? For six hours"—he pointed behind him to the door—"I have been sitting in a goddamn surgical waiting room." Leaning closer to me, he spoke through clenched teeth. "What is it you think people imagine in those rooms, Nora?"

I felt my eyes fill with tears and so I closed them. After a time, he said, "I need to pick up Willa. I'll be back tomorrow."

I opened my eyes.

"After lunch," he said. He laid one hand on mine. "Try your voice, Nora."

I shook my head lightly.

Bending to kiss my forehead, he whispered, "All right then, don't."

After he left, I wondered what sort of sin it was to imagine the death of your wife, and I wondered, had he imagined my experience of it—the pain, the terrible slipping into loss—or only his own experience, only the absence?

Twice in my hospital bed I woke up confused. The first time I saw outside my window a low grove of trees on a grassy hillock, and I believed I was home, in Kansas City, in a downtown hospital where, when I was sixteen, I'd been kept in quarantine for scarlet fever. My mother had been allowed to visit me then only for a few nervous minutes each day, and since she wasn't at my bedside, the doctors must have felt they could speak their news directly to me. So they worried aloud—formally and gravely—over a weakening valve in one of the chambers of my heart. I had believed they meant I was dying. Outside my window then a narrow park rolled up another hill and on it sat a tower in memory of war dead. Sixteen years old, in my closed room, a window away from a sunny morning, I felt something more kindred than age and inequity with the boys memorialized by that tower. I felt the pure, hollow loneliness of doom. That hospital had been a Catholic hospital, and each day, just after dawn, a priest came to my room wearing a surgical mask and carrying a chalice covered by a linen napkin. He touched my shoulder to wake me, and when I opened my eyes, he whispered, as if we were on sacred ground, "Child, would you like to receive the Holy Eucharist?" Each day I told him no.

The second time, I woke to a swoon of pain as a woman I believed must be my mother removed a drain from the incision in my neck and then arranged a new dressing over the wound. She nursed me the way my mother had nursed me as a child—with a light, tender touch that felt quickened by fear. I reached out for her hand, and she leaned close to whisper, "Don't move, honey. You don't want to feel how sick you'll be if you move." When she slid open the heavy drape, I was confused by the sunlight. My mother had only touched me that way in the middle of the night, as if her love and dread ranged wilder in the darkness. Outside my window I saw the low trees again, and though this time I knew I wasn't home, the scene outside my window felt closer to home than I was, offered a promise, a contiguity. If I walked over that hill, and then kept walking, I could get there. I closed my eyes and slept.

When I woke again, a woman stood in my doorway—the same woman who had spoken with my husband yesterday, the woman who believed I had cancer. Her face, anxious and tentative, still held the memory of what my husband had told her. I tried to raise myself in bed, but I moved too suddenly and a searing pain tore through my throat. Then, with horror, I felt the nausea the nurse had warned me about. I reached out to the woman in the doorway. "I'm going to be sick," I said in a voice grainy and guttural, but familiar. Fingering the dressing over my throat, I said, "Oh my God, don't let me be sick."

The woman rushed to my bed and took my hand. "You won't," she said. "Lie very still. Breathe through your mouth. You won't be sick, dear. You won't be."

I did what she said and slowly the nausea subsided. I sank deeper into my pillows, exhausted then, and I closed my eyes. She stayed at my bedside, smoothing a blanket over my shoulders, gently pressing the rolled towels closer to my neck. "I shouldn't have startled you." Her voice was low and hushed. "I only meant to peek in, say a good word." She patted my hand for a moment. "You're all right now, aren't you?" she said.

I was just at the brink of sleep when she said it, but I felt myself called back lightly into consciousness—the way I'd felt since Willa was born, when I would linger briefly each night on the edge of sleep and wonder if I'd tuned her radio to an all-night station, latched her crib rail, done all that I needed to do for her. I opened my eyes and saw that she was an older woman with thinning, frowsy hair and a kind face, an earnest face. She still held my hand in hers. "I'm not really dying," I whispered to her.

"Oh, of course you're not, dear." She squeezed my hand firmly between both of hers. "Of course you're not," she said.

From Shanghai

The advice note, dropped on my father's desk in the first week of September 1955, lay unread for a week. My father was away from home, resolving a dispute over burial sites in Manchester. He was a synagogue troubleshooter, the Red Adair of Anglo-Jewish internecine struggles, and it was his job to travel up and down the country, mollifying rabbis and pacifying their sometimes rebellious congregations. It was only when he returned to his office in Tavistock Square that he learned that a package awaited him at London docks. My father was a little confused. The note had come from the Office of Refugee Affairs, a department, now almost defunct, that he had little to do with. What could possibly be sent to him, and why?

During his lunch hour, he traveled to Tilbury, emerging by the loading dock on the river where bulky cargo vessels lined up beneath towering cranes. It took him a long time to locate the appropriate office, and even longer to find the right collection point. But my father was used to bureaucrats, and patient with them, and he chatted amiably while the papers he had brought with him were perused and stamped.

In the warehouse, he was presented, not with the brown paper parcel that he had imagined, but with two enormous crates, lowered to his feet by a man on a forklift truck.

"What's in them?" asked my father.

"No idea, guv. They're in off the boat from Shanghai."

"I see," said my father, utterly bemused. After the usual delays and indignation, a crowbar was provided, and my father, with the reluctant aid of the forklift driver, pried open one of the wood slats on the side of the crate. The driver, his inquisitiveness aroused, tore through some thin paper wrapping.

"Looks like books," he said.

"Books?"

"Yes, mate, books."

"But who from?"

They searched the surface of the crate; the bill of lading indicated only "P.O. Box 1308, Shanghai."

"Well, I've got work to do," the driver announced, remounting his forklift and starting the engine.

My father reached into the crate and dislodged one of the books. It was a German translation of *The Collected Tales of Hans Andersen*, strongly bound in blue linen. He took out another book; it was written in a language he couldn't understand, Japanese or Chinese. The third book was, again, *The Collected Tales*, but this time in English. He tugged out five more illustrated, English-language versions of *The Fairy Tales of Hans Andersen*. My father returned to the Far Eastern text and flicked through the pages. Sure enough, there were the telltale drawings: a duckling, a nightingale, three dogs with eyes as big as saucers.

Over the next few months, more and more crates arrived, each one adding to the Andersen collection. My father arranged to have them held in a warehouse near the docks. My mother was less than pleased with the extra expense imposed upon our family by this storage of books from nowhere. After all, we had only recently been freed from the restrictions of wartime rationing: filling the larder was her priority, not the unasked-for freight of a phantom dispatch agent. But my father reacted in his usual light-hearted manner, as if we had all entered a fairy tale. From out of the blue, a gift had come our way. Who could possibly guess what the magical consequences might be?

By the end of the year, we had some twenty thousand books in storage. One winter morning, under a cold blue sky, my father took me down to the warehouse with him to view the crates. It was like a trip to the pyramids. I ventured cautiously into the dark alleyways between the wood containers, piled three high, as if these mysterious monuments held an ancient power. What on earth had we come to possess? Of course, my father had written to the P.O. box in Shanghai, but so far he had received no reply.

As we walked away from the docks, the ships grew smaller and smaller in the distance, until they looked like the curios at the fun fair that you could snatch up with the metal jaws of a miniature crane. I asked my father, as I had heard my mother ask him in a moment of frustration and anger, why we didn't sell the books. "Because they are not ours to sell," he replied.

It was Sunday, and we were both free, for the only day of the week, from the dual constraints of work (homework, in my case) and synagogue. We walked all the way to Tower Bridge. A small crowd had gathered in an open area on the wharf. Nearby, on the river, a brightly painted houseboat, *The Artful Dodger*, had been moored.

A small, muscular man, with a shaved head and an ugly tattoo inscribed upon his forearm—barbed wire entwining a naked woman—was passing round a set of heavy chains for the crowd to inspect. Shortly he bound himself up. My father, who appeared more captivated than most, was selected to turn, and then pocket, the key of a massive padlock that secured our escapologist. The Artful Dodger then asked my father to gag him. After this, a giggling woman from the audience helped the escapologist step into a burlap sack, laid out on the flagstone next to him. This accomplished, the woman waved to her cheering friends, and tightened the drawstring with a flourish.

Behind the writhing sack, the black Thames flowed hastily. Two swift Sunday-morning scullers, who had taken my attention, disappeared behind a chugging tugboat. By the time they emerged, our prisoner was free. I wasn't surprised. I knew his trick. I had read all about Houdini in a school library book. I knew that our man had swallowed a duplicate key before the show, and then regurgitated it while in the sack. But, to my astonishment, I found myself no less impressed. Escape, however it was accomplished, was the glittering thing.

In the spring, my uncle Hugo arrived from Shanghai. He wasn't really my uncle but my father's second cousin. He brought with him his wife, Lotte, and nothing more than the clothes on their backs. At first, of course, he was simply a stranger who walked into my father's office one day in March, and announced that he had come to claim both the Andersen books and a relationship.

My father took Hugo Wasserman for lunch, by which I mean that they went to a nearby park, sat on a bench, and shared sandwiches. It was one of those transitional spring days, when it is warm enough in the sun but still very cold in the shade. While they sat, side by side, lifting their faces to the pale medallion in the sky, Hugo told his story. He had been expelled from his home in the Austrian Burgenland in 1938. Like many others, he had fled, in desperation, to the International Settlement in Shanghai, the only city in the world he could enter without a visa. A gentile friend, Artur Jelinek, a philatelist, had forwarded the Andersen books to China with money left for the purpose by Hugo. He had lived in Shanghai for fifteen years, working as a technician in a hospital laboratory. By profession, he was a biologist, he had written a botanical treatise on mushrooms; by inclination, he was a bibliophile. In Austria, before the war, through penny-pinching, perseverance, and resourcefulness, he had accumulated what he believed to be the world's second largest collection of Hans Andersen books, exceeded only by the corpus owned by the Danish royal family.

My father listened. There had been, of course, a thousand refugee stories in wide circulation in the London Jewish community in the previous ten years; most reported greater hardship, some less. Hugo had escaped early. He was lucky. Of course, his life had been terribly disrupted, but he was alive, he was here, his collection was intact.

"But how did you get to me?" my father asked.

"Your cousin, Miki, the one who..."

My father nodded before Hugo could proceed. He already knew the details, and wanted to spare himself the pain of hearing them repeated.

"Well," Hugo continued, "before—that is, some months before he was taken, when I was about to leave, he gave me your name. He told me that you were an administrator for Jews. The address of the office I discovered in Shanghai."

"But why," my father continued, "didn't you reply to my letters?"

"Arthritis," Hugo replied, and held his misshapen hands out for my father to inspect. "I cannot hold a pen."

"But surely..." My father stopped. Sometimes, he told me later, an excuse, given for whatever reason, simply has to be accepted.

Hugo had met Lotte in Shanghai. Like him, she was a refugee from Hitler's Europe. But, unlike him, she was vivacious and energetic. Partly this derived from the fact that she was twenty years Hugo's junior. Although Hugo was only in his mid-fifties, he was, to my eyes, an old man, with his shock of white hair and deeply lined face. It was Lotte who enchanted me. She would arrive for Saturday night dinner in a fox-fur stole (borrowed from her neighbor) and chain-smoke through a long cigarette holder. She liked to sing, and after supper she would call my father to the upright piano in our dining room. He would accompany her in feisty, throaty renditions of songs in German that I couldn't understand, but of which both Hugo and my mother appeared to disapprove. I would stand near Lotte, in the aura of her rich, heavy perfume, and take deep breaths.

Lotte's family, miraculously, had survived the war and were now dispersed all over the world. Her parents were in America with her sister, Grete; one of her brothers was in Buenos Aires, the other in Israel. Sometimes she would bring me the latest post-cards and letters that she had received, and together we would sit in the kitchen, soak the stamps off, and carefully catalogue them in my album. You might have thought that this kind of activity would have been more up Hugo's street, but he remained remarkably indifferent to me, almost cold, until the day that my father gave me the present.

Two evenings a week, my father took art classes at the adult education program of St. Martin's School of Art. The works that he produced provoked a great deal of hilarity in our household. He generally painted nudes. The teacher, not rich in imagination, seemed to demand two poses of his models. The first, a dull, straightforward, upright seated position in a high-backed chair; the second, a "sensual," provocative draping of the body over a velvet-backed chaise longue. My father, an admirer of Matisse but not a great colorist himself, would bring home to us strange light brown figures, twisted, not altogether intentionally, into expressionist poses. He would line his canvases up against a wall in the hall. My brother and I would collapse in laughter. My mother, busy with supper, barely gave the works a passing glance. To his credit, my father took our cruel responses very well. For two nights a week, he seemed to enjoy playing the part, not of the overburdened synagogue administrator, but of the lonely artist struggling in a hostile, philistine world.

Perhaps in order to establish for himself evidence of the duality of his personality, or perhaps, in some unconscious way, to sanctify the graven images that he created, my father initialed all his paintings in the bottom right-hand corner, but with *Hebrew* letters: a serpentine *lamed* and squarish *vav* that served to represent the artist, Leslie Visser.

After the arrival of Hugo and Lotte Wasserman, I thought I began to detect something new in "Lamed Vav's" paintings (my brother and I had taken up the initials as sobriquet). I may have been mistaken, but it seemed to me that the faces of the nudes were coming more and more to carry Lotte's features: her full lips and unmistakable green eyes. But whether this was the result of my fantasies or those of "Lamed Vav" has never been clear to me.

My father had a friend at the art class, a man named Joe Kline, who worked as a salesman for the publishing company of Eyre & Spottiswoode. One night, my father came home with a small cardboard box packed with four hardback books. "More?" said my mother, who was suspicious of all transactions involving bound volumes. We were still defraying the costs of the Andersen storage until Hugo and Lotte could "get on their feet."

"These are a gift," my father responded, "from Joe. They're remainders, out of print, but in mint condition. It was really very nice of him. There's a book for every member of our family, including you."

The novel for my mother was *My Cousin Rachel,* by Daphne Du Maurier, while my brother received a how-to guide to safe chemistry experiments in the home. My book was, well, a brand-new, very nicely illustrated edition of *The Collected Tales of Hans Andersen.* "Coals to Newcastle," said my mother scornfully.

I was twelve, a little old for Hans Andersen, I thought, although secretly I still liked the stories, and soon became quite attached to one lavish illustration in particular. It showed the beautiful princess from "The Tinder Box," asleep on the giant dog's back, a low-cut dress revealing the cleavage of what the illustrator had decided would be disproportionately large breasts. This color print fed into the fantasy connected to Evelyn, the fourteen-year-old girl whose bedroom window faced mine across the two

29

postage stamp–sized lawns that abutted our homes. Recently, I had removed a round mirror from my bicycle, bolted it to a long stick, and attached it to one of my bedposts. In this way I was able to watch Evelyn Boone undress in her room without being observed myself. Unfortunately, most of the time, Evelyn took what was the conventional precaution in our enclosed neighborhood of drawing the curtains before disrobing. So far, I had not seen any more in my magic mirror than had already been granted to me by Eyre & Spottiswoode's dubiously inspired illustrator.

From the first time he laid eyes upon it, Uncle Hugo wanted my book. In the wide world of desire, there is little that exceeds the covetousness of the collector. From a distant, unconcerned relative, Hugo was suddenly transformed into a charming, wily confrere. I was not immune to the bribery and seductiveness of adults, nor was I invulnerable to the parental cajoling that began when my father (my mild-mannered father!) decided to join in the fray and persuade me to hand over my book to Hugo. Indeed, I might have given in, were it not for the fact that what Hugo was asking for constituted, however bizarrely, a piece of the puzzle of my erotic life, one that I was unwilling to relinquish. Lotte, who seemed to have a sense that there was more than stubbornness and obstinacy to my refusal, took my side.

"You don't have enough books?" she asked her husband. "So you have to steal from a child?"

"It's not stealing," my father interposed. "Hugo has offered Michael an extremely rare and valuable first edition in return for his book. We are talking about a swap here. An exchange in which Michael will come out the winner."

The two men pressured me for a month, but I held my ground.

"Why can't he buy the book from someone else, if he wants it that badly?" I whined to my father, after Hugo had left the house one day.

"Because it is unavailable in bookshops, and Uncle Hugo does not steal from libraries. What is more, buying books costs money, and, at the moment, Hugo and Lotte are trying to *save* money. You're not too young to understand that. Joe Kline tells me that they only printed a thousand copies of your edition. It didn't do well. Too many competitors on the market. It isn't valuable, but

Hugo would have an impossible job tracking one down. To you, it's virtually worthless, but to Hugo, as part of a collection, it means something. Has it sunk in what Hugo is offering you in return? You could own a book worth, maybe, fifty pounds!"

Fifty pounds to give up Evelyn Boone's breasts? For, yes, I could no longer distinguish her teenage bumps from the more developed forms that belonged to the princess in the illustration. Out of the question!

For reasons of domestic propriety (perhaps my mother had noticed the Lotte heads on the naked bodies, too), the Wassermans had, some time during the summer, been switched from Saturday nights to Sunday afternoons. Hugo and Lotte had bought a car on the HP, an old Singer with seventy thousand miles on the clock. In this distinguished vehicle, Hugo at the wheel, Lotte making hand signals because the left indicator did not work, they negotiated a slow, careful way to our house each weekend. When they pulled up at the curb, my father would look out of the window and say, "Here comes the Rolls Canardly, rolls down one side of a hill, can 'ardly get up the other."

Hugo was now a fully incorporated member of something my father called the Cheesecake Club. This organization now boasted four members, men from the neighborhood who gathered weekly to overpraise my mother's patisserie and discuss the contemporary scene. One of the men, Sidney Oberman, would arrive with the week's newspapers under his arm. It was his responsibility to select and underline topics for further discussion. The group's heroes were Winston Churchill, the late Chaim Weizman, and Dr. Armand Kalinowksi, a brilliant Jewish panelist on the popular radio show *Brains Trust*. In deference to this invisible mentor, the members of the Cheesecake Club each sported a bow tie, symbol of decorum and high thought.

Six weeks after Hugo had first held my book in his hands for examination and quiet evaluation, the Wassermans arrived, as usual, late for Sunday tea, and, as usual, in the middle of an argument. The general cause of their altercations was "The Collection." The Wassermans were poor. They lived in a tiny two-room flat in Willesden Green. Hugo had looked for laboratory work, but, he said, his strong German accent made prospective employers uneasy. The Wassermans' small income accrued from Lotte's piano lessons offered to neighborhood children in their own homes, and from piecework (advice on fungus and fungicides) that Hugo performed as assistant to a local landscape gardener. According to Lotte, if Hugo were only to sell his books, they could live like royalty. On the other hand, if Hugo ever tried to unpack his books in her home, he would have to find another wife.

Lotte's scorn for Hans Christian Andersen and his work knew no limits. Fairy tales! What nonsense. A collection of Goethe or Tolstoy she might respect, although, in her present crisis, she would still want to sell it. But a grown man straining his eyes poring over "The Emperor's New Clothes" in twenty different languages. What a terrible waste.

When Lotte spoke this way, Hugo flushed deeply; he would look around to see if my brother or I were in earshot. When his eyes met ours, we would try to look distracted and hard of hearing. On this particular occasion, their argument appeared to have peaked shortly before the ring on our doorbell, and what I overheard as I opened the door ("You want us to remain poor all our lives." "Is this all you care about, money?") were their last tired shots, the blows of a boxer whose arms are spent, and legs wobbly.

Lotte moved shakily toward the kitchen. "I need a glass of water," she said. Hugo carefully removed his jacket and searched our hall cupboard for a hanger. Were there tears in his eyes? I wasn't sure, but suddenly I felt sorry for him. Perhaps it was the look of deep exhaustion on his face—a look I had seen before but not really registered—that softened me, or maybe it was simply the fact that, for the first time since we had begun our battle of wills, he did not say to me, "So, have you changed your mind?" Whatever the reason, I hovered around until Hugo had hung up his jacket, and then I said, "I'll swap."

The ceremonial exchange of books did not take place for more than a fortnight. It was mid-August, and time for our annual holiday. My parents would book us into some quiet, respectable boarding house in Margate or Swanage or Southbourne, making sure to order vegetarian meals in advance, in this way anticipating and surmounting problems that might arise with *kashrut*. Off we would go, packed snugly into our old Ford Prefect. After a long eighty miles or so of traffic jams, carsickness, and back-seat fights, we would arrive at someone else's house, not too different from our own, ready to read indoors while the rain fell in sheets; play crazy-golf in light drizzle; and venture out on the three or four fine, warm days that nature seemed to guarantee us, to swim the cold sea and shiver.

This year, however, we were doing something different. We had *rented* a seaman's cottage on the beach in Folkestone. High, choppy waves thundered against the retaining wall behind the little dwelling. When I lay in bed at night, I felt as if my bedroom were a ship's cabin, pitching and rolling in the summer winds. In the mornings, my brother and I explored the dunes near where the ferry came in from Boulogne. The sandy knolls and hillocks were still dotted with concrete pillboxes. We clambered inside these dry chambers, peered through their narrow window slits, and pretended to be gunners scanning the Channel for approaching German aircraft.

At the end of the first week, my father was suddenly and mysteriously called back to London. All we knew was that Lotte had phoned one day in a state of high excitement. My father had a few whispering sessions with my mother. But, after he had departed, she claimed, and she seemed to be telling the truth, that my father had told her only that Hugo and Lotte had a real emergency, not of a medical nature, but serious enough to warrant his returning home for a couple of days to help them out.

It rained for the duration of my father's three-day absence. We visited a shop that held demonstrations in toffee manufacture, went to the pictures to see Danny Kaye in *The Court Jester,* and attended a children's talent contest in the local town hall.

When he returned, late one night, my father appeared anxious and disturbed. In fact, he was so agitated that I allowed myself to imagine, for one brief flicker of a thought, that he and Lotte had perhaps, well... no, it was inconceivable.

The Prince of Denmark, we learned eventually, had sent an emissary to Hugo. The royal family's librarian wished to review the collection. There was genuine interest from Copenhagen. If Hugo would not agree to sell it whole, perhaps he would permit the collection to be split up?

Lotte had called on my father to help her persuade Hugo that this was a once-in-a-lifetime chance. They could escape their dreary lodgings and dead-end jobs. They could move to Golders Green; better, to Hampstead! If he wished to pursue his "hobby," Hugo could open an antiquarian bookshop. My father had spoken to Hugo, but he was powerfully resistant to the idea of selling.

"Leslie, you don't understand," he had said. "I have to hold it together. The collection has to be protected."

But then something happened. Here, my father paused in his narrative, as if to gather strength. My mother poured him a cup of tea. Hugo had received a letter in the mail. He had not let Lotte see it, but after reading it, he had rushed out of the house. He had gone missing for a day and a night, and when he returned in the early hours of this morning, hatless, soaked through, with his teeth chattering, he had simply slumped in a chair and refused to explain himself. My father had visited the Wassermans' for lunch. Hugo had been polite, but withdrawn. He did not want to discuss the collection anymore. Perhaps, after all, he would sell, he only wanted to be left alone and given a little more "time to think."

"Well," said my mother, testily, when my father had finished speaking. "I think they've got a nerve. Interrupting a person's holiday, and then behaving in this outrageous fashion, when you— and only *you* would do this—went up there to help them." My father didn't reply. Outside, the sea swelled and surged, spraying droplets of surf against our kitchen windows. I thought, in my ignorance, that my mother had a point.

When we returned to London, my father immediately had to deal with a crisis at work: for the first time, a woman had been elected to the Board of Management of a North London synagogue, and now the entire spiritual staff—rabbi, cantor, beadle, and choirmaster—was threatening to resign. "This is the beginning of the end for Judaism," the rabbi had written back to headquarters, and added in parentheses, " 'A foolish woman is clamorous: she is simple, and knoweth nothing' (Proverbs 9:13)." My father was dispatched to calm everybody down.

The school holidays were drawing to a close. I had to buy a new blazer and stock up on those sweet-smelling essentials: an eraser, a new exercise book, blue-black ink, and a fountain pen. In the subdued excitements of anticipation before a new school year, I almost forgot about Hugo and Lotte.

One evening, when an autumn chill could already be felt in the air, they turned up on our doorstep. Lotte was transformed. She was wearing a white crepe de Chine blouse and a knee-length black satin skirt. Her hair was dressed in a chic new style. She was brimming over with joy. "He's going to sell!" she announced even before she greeted us.

Hugo followed her sheepishly into the house. It seemed that Lotte had jumped the gun. Her emphatic expectation of great wealth had led her to spend, in one brave day, the little savings that they had managed to accumulate in the previous six months of struggle and hardship. "Yes, I will sell," said Hugo. "But who knows what I will get."

Late in the evening, Hugo pulled me aside. "Come in the other room," he said. "We need to talk." I had been expecting him to approach me, and wondering why he had delayed. "Listen," he whispered, pushing his face close to mine. I smelled alcohol on his heavy breath. "I am going to give you a book. I don't want *them* to get it. It's very valuable, but it's worth nothing. I want you to keep it. You can't sell it."

The bars of our electric fire turned on for the first time in four months, glowed bright orange, and gave off a pungent scent of burned dust. Hugo raked his white hair back with his fingers. "You must," he said, taking me by the shoulders. "You, above all people, must forgive me." Despite the heat that was moving in waves up my back, I felt a chill go through me. He was weeping now, sobbing, his shoulders heaving as if he could never stop. Suddenly, Lotte and my father appeared in the doorway. They rushed to Hugo, put their arms around him, and led him back into the kitchen.

That night, my parents sent my brother and me to bed early. But, as was our custom when this happened, we crept halfway down the stairs to eavesdrop on the grown-up conversation. We sat in our pajamas, hugging the banister. In the brightly lit kitchen, Hugo began to speak, in low tones, and with a halting voice. At first we only caught words and phrases: "wife," "son," "arrangements," "waited and waited," "betrayed," "not even

Lotte." Huddled on the stairs, we heard, clear as train whistles in the night, sharp intakes of breath around the kitchen table. Soon we grew used to Hugo's broken, hoarse whisper.

If, at any point in Hugo's story, my brother and I could have returned to our beds, we would probably have done so. But curiosity had called us to listen, and now we were trapped.

After ten or fifteen minutes, Hugo paused for a moment. My father got up and switched the lights off in the kitchen. It was a strange thing to do. Perhaps he wanted to take the harsh light of self-interrogation off Hugo. Now, Hugo's voice came up to us out of darkness. "The collection," he said, "the collection came to Shanghai, but not my family." There was a long silence. "Soon after the war, I received a confirmation. My wife. Someone from the woman's camp who was there. I received a letter. But my son, of course, unlikely—all right, impossible, but even so. Two weeks ago, a letter comes. You know. Sixteen years. An official letter: the place, the date." Hugo began a muffled sob. "My Hans, Hans Wasserman, Hans Wasserman." He said the name again and again.

It was thirty years before I opened the edition of *The Collected Tales* that Hugo had given me. My nine-year-old son's teacher had invited parents to come to school and share their favorite children's story with the Nintendo-obsessed throng. I thought for a while before settling (of course!) on Andersen's "The Tinder Box." My old, illustrated copy of the tales had long since been lost in some chaotic transfer from home to home. But I had managed to hold on to Hugo's gift. It was an ordinary-looking book, with a slightly torn blue binding and faded gold lettering on the cover. The early pages were spotted with brown stains. The frontispiece proudly announced "A New Translation, by Mrs. H. B. Paull." I flicked through the pages; they appeared unmarked. I turned to the Contents: a faint circle had been inscribed around "The Brave Tin Soldier." I found the story, and read it through. In the last sentence, two phrases had been thinly underlined in pencil: "instantly in flames," "burnt to a cinder."

Fur

Fei Lo noticed the new clerk right away, a persimmon in a basket of oranges. Three letters on a gold-toned plaque spelled out her name. So as to make no mistake, the old gentleman wrote it in his notebook, FUR. He liked to know the names of all the women tellers, as he flirted with each in turn; he had even when his wife was alive. The clerks indulged him, they treated him with deference, they called him *Ah Goong,* Old Grandfather. Behind his back they said, without derision, *Fei Lo,* Fat Man.

Fei Lo tipped his hat.

Fur said good morning, and she called him Ah Goong.

"Your name, very pretty."

She smiled. "I chose it myself."

Her mother had named her Four Fragrance. When American-born Chinese made fun of her nonsense name, she changed it to Fur, something she coveted more than any perfume. She tried first Mink, then Sable, but never Chinchilla, since it had too many syllables for Chinese. She finally settled on the all-encompassing Fur, and while it made no more sense than Four Fragrance, the other tellers let it go.

"Yes. Fur. Very distinctive."

Fur gave the old gentleman her full attention.

Fei Lo smiled, too.

He would offer a proposition. She only had to wait. "Something I can do for you today?"

Fei Lo could tell by the shift of her weight that she had stepped out of her shoes. He tapped his breast pocket where he kept his deposit.

"Guess," he said. "Guess the amount of my deposit, within ten percent, and I will sign my check over to you."

Fur pressed her bunions back into her shoes, she rolled her tongue over her teeth. The clerks on either side stopped in mid-motion but did not look up.

Back-room eavesdropping had told her about the rotund flirt, his large appetites and even larger deposits—monthly totals of some $20,000 in Hong Kong rents, shack storefronts, three dollars a square foot. She quickly calculated the ten-percent error and added a chunk. She did her best imitation of shooting in the dark.

"$23,199!"

Fei Lo's eyes narrowed. He glanced about. The other women made busy. He did some calculating himself as he pulled out his check.

"Pretty good guess. But you are off about fifteen percent. Still, pretty good guess."

"No! So close? Let me see!" Fur examined the front and back of the check as she stamped it. "Maybe next time I'll be more lucky." She grinned.

"Hmmm. Maybe."

The next time Fei Lo came into the bank, Fur timed her transactions to coincide with his arrival at the head of the line. "Ah Goong, you are a traveled man. You ever been to Las Vegas?"

"Oh, many times. But Tahoe is nicer."

"Better than Vegas?"

"Umm. Like gold is better than paper."

"You win?"

"Win! Of course, win. Even when I lose, I win. Consider our hotel, very reasonable, very nice. Dining room—out of this world. Menu thick like a book, and every dish ready at your fingertips." He passed his hand over the counter so elegantly Fur lifted up on her toes to see. "Lovely pink crab, prime rib, five different ways to eat potatoes—"

"Any desserts?"

"On a table of their own! Meringue pies, sweet cream cakes—"

"Chocolates?"

"Ah, chocolates." Here he reflected. "Yes, chocolates. Even on your pillow, chocolates."

Fur framed a smile and lowered her eyes. She could even blush on demand.

"Twelve dollars," he said, staring straight at her. "All you can eat."

The bank clerk and the old man regarded each other. Between them, the tellers' counter laid end to end with food only they could see.

"I don't go anymore."

"Why not?"

"Wife died. She didn't like to go."

"Oh, sorry, Ah Goong. I didn't know." Fur knew. She had read his entire file. "But Goong, what's to keep you, now that you are a free man?"

"No. Can't. It's no fun without her."

Fur nodded. "Yeah, yeah, I understand."

Fei Lo reached into his breast pocket. He tried to keep it light. *"Neih seung mhseung heui?"* You want to go?

"Seung!" she said. "You bet. I'm going, yes, I am." The bank clerk tilted her head towards a sign promoting the opening of new Certificates of Deposit, $1,000 minimum. "Twenty new accounts and I win a free trip." She winked. She drummed her fingernails, red painted over chipped.

Fei Lo turned away long enough to read the large print. "And how many you have so far?"

"Nineteen," she said, as if giving her age. He laughed out loud. The clerk on her right shot a glance, the one on the left har-rumphed.

He pulled out his deposit and pushed the check towards her. She saw his knowing smile.

"Oh no, Ah Goong, you get much more interest if you add this to your existing account. Oh, but you are such a kind man. Really, I mean it. Don't worry, before the day is over I will get my trip to Las Vegas. I'm a good salesman."

Fei Lo was thrown. "Hmmm."

Fur punched in his account number, then stopped. "Ah Goong, you want me to be happy?" She tapped the check on the counter.

Ah, he thought, here it comes after all. "I want all you young women to be happy."

"You have been so kind to me, since the very first day. I want to take you to lunch. Will you let me, please?"

. . .

The bank clerk herded the fat man into the most expensive restaurant in Chinatown, one with valet parking and a doorman. Her eyes worked the room, studying, memorizing the choice of wallpaper, the recessed lights, the antique screens—scholar on a donkey, painted silk in a teak surround.

"Oh no, Ah Goong." She pulled the paper insert out of his hand. "No rice plate specials for you today. It's my birthday and we are having only the finest food on the menu. *Oh! Yin wo!*" She lay her hand on his arm. "I've never had Bird's Nest Soup. Can we have that? I mean, would you enjoy it?"

Fei Lo glanced at her hand. She removed it and giggled.

A fiftyish woman in a wool crepe suit bumped Fur's shoulder and made a point of apologizing. Fur never had a lady apologize to her, and this woman was deft. She managed within the same breath to greet her friends three tables away, tossing her hand in an effortless wave. As she passed, Fur caught the surprise of her shoes, faux leopard with an open toe, the flash of red, as if a woman's power and every secret resided in the feet. Fur rubbed the top of her own pump against the back of her other leg, a quick, dry polish under the table.

Fei Lo was staring at her. "So, how old are you today?"

"Oh! How old do you think I am?" She crossed her legs and leaned forward on her elbow. She giggled. She swung her free leg carelessly.

Fei Lo got a little warm. He giggled, too. He steadied his hands on the menu and studied. He tried to consider balance and contrast, spice and subtlety, texture, methods of preparation, a soup, a fish, a fowl, some green vegetables to cleanse. He peered over his bifocals at her.

She flipped back and forth in the eight-page menu, her eyes scanning down the right-hand column as if doing addition. She smiled. "Remember, it's my treat."

It's my treat was repeated three more times during the meal. They ordered as if for a wedding banquet. Fei Lo was smitten to finally find a woman not afraid to eat. He didn't know Fur had not eaten since breakfast the day before, but he had already guessed that she couldn't afford such a meal on her salary and that, in the end, they both expected him to pay. By the time the oysters arrived, sizzling, practically leaping off the hot cast iron plate, he also deduced it wasn't really her birthday.

Fei Lo parked his Lincoln Continental next to the chapel, got his things out of the trunk, and started up the hill. He enjoyed the approach to the gravesite and didn't want to rush. He liked the walking, the tulip beds in spring, the tall stalks of summer, grass that stained the hems of his pants, proof of his participation. He liked reading the names on the house-like tombs, miniature temples adorned with columns. He, too, owned one of these stone houses, enough space for an extended family, guarded by an iron gate. If he drove up to the site, he might feel compelled to drop off the flowers and just go. Soon he might not come at all. Their children rarely came—at Christmas, her birthday, maybe Mother's Day, in alternating turns that smacked of arrangement.

He set his things down and used both hands to open his folding stool. He unlocked the gate and opened it wide, letting into the crypt every possible ray of sun. He hung his coat on the gate and said hello to his wife. "Hear that?" The crunch of leaves fueled his appetite. "Indian summer," he sighed. He sat down on the folding canvas.

From a plaid thermos he poured some fragrant hot tea. He fanned himself with the Chinese daily. When the tea cooled, he unwrapped the towel he used as insulation and untied the string around the square pink box, enough *dim sum* for a family: parchment chicken, pink shrimp in translucent dresses, sweet rice studded with three treasures and bound with shiny *ti* leaves, sweet black bean paste in a golden seeded pouch. From the tens of offerings from the *dim sum* tray, Fei Lo always chose those that came wrapped up like gifts.

The sun warmed his back and he did not sweat. Fei Lo chewed his toothpick into a flat pulp. He didn't look at his wife's grave. With effort he could get through the entire visit without mentioning the bank clerk's unusual name, or the number of times they'd had dinner since the "birthday" lunch.

He held the newspaper upright and turned a bit away from the gate. This was not the way he had imagined it, him sitting here talking to her. The vision that had come most frequently to him, in the years before her death, was of her, her approaching with plants and flowering shrubs, working on hands and knees, she, who would finally discover in widowhood the meditation of horticulture.

"Young Woo died last week," he relayed.

Young Woo was the seventy-three-year-old son of Old Woo, who was still living, in his own home, in his own bed. Young Woo had built from a corner stand, selling hand-knotted brushes, a chain of hardware stores stretching up and down the peninsula. He made Old Woo very comfortable. His last act was to step on wet dog excrement. Young Woo saw the droppings as he was taking the wheelchair from the trunk, and he was very careful while helping his father sit down. A car double-parked behind him and banged his bumper. In his excitement, Young Woo let go of the wheelchair. It rolled, he lunged, he slipped, and broke his hip, from which he never recovered. Young Woo had built from nothing, yet this the ladies at the bank would soon forget, as quickly as they would forget his name, recalling only a man who was killed by dog droppings. Fei Lo unbuttoned his vest. He knew what men feared. Men feared acts of foolishness. Women had no trouble with this. They only feared being unvalued.

The air chilled. The widower lifted his head just in time to see the last of the fall sunset, a pulsing ovoid tangent to the Pacific, the sky seared orange and red. As on recent days, he thought he could see with his naked eye, even at this distance, ribbons of fire eject from the surface, streamers from a departing vessel. She burned, his sun, day and night, witnessed or not, she burned.

"What a fine view we have. A splendid view. Splendid."

And, as he did at the end of each visit, Fei Lo watched until the colors bled from the sky. Then he slowly packed up to go.

"I'm looking for investors."

They had warned him she would ask for money, it was just a matter of time. Fei Lo wanted to give it to her. Whatever she asked. But his son said, *No.* His daughter said, *No.* They said, *We don't want it, Dad, but you need it to live on. And why would you want to give it to this woman with no family?* Fei Lo had wondered how he could have raised such children. And yet, when a certain woman had asked Young Woo for a loan, Fei Lo had offered similar advice.

Fur laid her chopsticks across her rice bowl, she nudged her plate aside. She had barely eaten.

"Ah Goong"—she spaced her words—"I'm not a clever person. Some people have good ideas every day. Me, I only have so many good ideas. Not every day. This is my good idea. A beauty shop for hair. No permanents. No color. No nails. Just wash and cut. Look, look at our beautiful hair."

Fur whipped out her drugstore compact and shoved the mirror under his nose. Fei Lo had a view of the top of his head, spare gray strands parted low on one side and combed over to the other.

"Thick, straight, and black. The most desirable hair in the world. Why make it something different?" She snapped the compact shut and tapped it on the table. "Wash and cut." She amended as she went. "More than a cut, a shape, a frame for the face. A high class." She inhaled with care. She looked him in the eye. "Partners. Fifty-fifty."

He stared at her, chopsticks poised. The rice was getting cold.

Fur wet her lips. "You like my idea, yes or no?"

Fei Lo hated talking business over food. He wished she had asked for fun money. He gladly would have given that, even a monthly allowance, whatever she wanted, for a little silk scarf, a sumptuous dinner, car payments. But this was an investment, and while the actual dollars might end up being the same, or even less, he had to think it out. Real estate he knew, but not shop-keeping. He asked himself, Is it good business? Does she know about hair? Has she any talent?

As if from behind his ear the bank clerk pulled out a card, the name of a salon, someone else's salon. "I'm there Thursday nights, all day Saturday and Sunday until four." Whenever she wasn't at the bank.

Fei Lo considered Fur's own hair, which was chemically curled and had never struck him as anything special. But then he was not a judge. He tried to calculate how many women would want their hair cut by her. Would his wife have gone to her? Would the ladies at the bank? And there came to him a startling realization. "Women don't like you."

He spoke with such carelessness, as if comparing coats in a store window, that Fur, too, saw herself with detachment. "That's right. Women don't like me. I don't fit, do I? But men like me fine. And men get their hair cut three times more often than women."

Fei Lo nodded. "Then what you really want is a barbershop."

"No, no, no. No barbershop. *Beauty* shop. Barbers charge a fraction what hairdressers charge." She marked off the tip of her index finger with her thumb to indicate how small a fraction she had in mind. "Barbers don't wash. I wash. I wash very good, very gentle. Men like that. You come sometime, I show you."

They stared at each other.

Fei Lo thought about more shrimp, salty, crusty, pan-fried little devils in their bed of lettuce.

Fur let her gaze wander about the room. She tinked her glass with her chopsticks. When the waiter approached, she got up to go to the restroom.

Fei Lo caught her eye. "Let me think about it."

She nodded once and smiled, knowing that he wouldn't.

The bank clerk made a detour by the bar and talked to three different men, men she knew well enough to touch their shoulders. There was laughter, eyes that did not move, glancing hands, codes he had long forgotten. When she continued on to the bathroom, the men watched through half-closed lids. Heads inclined in her direction. Someone made a joke. They all laughed.

Fur took her time returning. Fei Lo stood up and held out her chair, but she did not sit. She took her jacket in one arm and said, "I should take you home now. It's a long drive for me back to Fremont."

"But I can take a cab. Please, sit down, we haven't finished our dinner."

"Oh, no, I couldn't let you take a cab. You are my dearest friend. I'll wait. Please. Sit down. Eat."

She sat and did not look about, did not eat, did not fidget. She was more silent than even his wife had been on her most quiet days.

Fei Lo lost appetite. He didn't ask for the leftovers.

They drove, and the silence sat between them like cold fat. Chinatown blurred into downtown, blurred into the lakefront, manmade, polluted, and fringed with high-rises. A wall of glass separated them from a dinner party halfway up a building, sparkling stemware, red wine and white. A family ate in silence. Another tasted from cartons passed back and forth. Others were locked down for the night in front of TVs that etched them in a pulsing blue light. On the top floor, darkness, except for one low light, a night light. As their car rounded the bend, Fei Lo could make out a form. A child too young to stay alone pressed her palms into the glass and kissed her own reflection.

"Is it true, what they say about your father?" And as soon as the words came out, he regretted.

Fur tapped the brakes. "Who, they? What do they say?"

"The women at the bank. They say—" Fei Lo blushed. "They say your father had two wives."

The women had circulated a story about young Four Fragrance, some said twenty, some said eighteen. One woman said she was barely fourteen, with a dead mother and the address in America of a father she had never met. They spiced it up with his car, all fins and angles, his quick drive up to the curb, a hand that extruded only to slap her face, the motor running. They iced it with his parting line: "I have no daughter. Don't call me again."

Fur said nothing, and Fei Lo wondered if she had heard him. She drove straight to his house with no instruction from him. She pulled right up the curved driveway, as if she did it every day, and parked behind his garaged Lincoln Continental. She killed the engine and looked out at nothing in particular.

"Rumors, Ah Goong, are like the bamboo. Planted and left alone they will multiply into a forest that blocks out all light. They weave a root system you cannot destroy. The tiniest splinter can cause unbearable pain. And every day the bamboo sways, it bangs one into its neighbor. It wails its song, it clanks its tune, and makes you deaf to all other music." She turned and smiled at him. "Or so my mother used to tell me. You believe this?"

They sat some. The windows frosted.

He asked, "You want to come in?"

She didn't answer, but when he came around and held open her door, she got out.

Fur sat cross-legged on the bathroom carpet, reading outdated decorating magazines. Her eyes stopped on an advertisement of metal spiral staircases. She tore out the page and tossed it with other torn sheets, ragged ideas for a dream salon.

Fei Lo was a few steps away when he thought he heard something rip. He tapped the door. "Is everything all right?"

She didn't answer.

He unlocked the bar and set out his favorite liqueurs, substituting brandy for port and French for domestic until he felt he got it right. He went back and asked if she would like a drink. She turned a page and said without shouting, "I can't hear you. I'll be out soon."

When Fur finally emerged, the TV was on. Fei Lo had fallen asleep, his head hung on his chest. A fire raged in downtown San Francisco. Glass exploded. A barefoot woman half in flames stumbled from the building. The fire seized her like a jealous husband. Fur nudged the old man with her finger. His lips fluttered.

She walked along his mahogany bookcases, dragging that same finger along the shelves. No dust. Even now, though *she* was dead, no dust. Not many books, either. Some statement in simplicity. But each spare shelf was anchored by an object, things she probably picked out.

Above the bar were a pair of lions, one facing east and one west, carved from jade so rare the stone was almost white. She picked one up and almost dropped it. Much too heavy to slip into a pocket. On another shelf—arranged so precisely as to discourage touching—what looked like shoehorns. Fur flipped one over. They *were* shoehorns. Here, in the front room. Carved ivory, no two alike, untouched by human feet. A pair of this, a dozen of that, nothing was collected singly, as if Fei Lo's wife had been shoring up against a day of enormous need. Fur understood that urge.

Here, sterling bowls, graded to nest, so shiny with polish they sang. The hollows of each were lacquered a different color—ruby, emerald, sapphire. Fur pulled a bobby pin from her hair, bit off the coated tip, and ran the sharp end against the ruby hollow of one. She was surprised that it did scratch. She glanced at Fei Lo, then wet a finger with saliva and tried to repair the damage. She shrugged, picked up another.

This bowl was filled with chocolates, individually wrapped in foil and molded into assorted sea shells. Fur put a fat fistful in her pocket and continued her tour of Fei Lo's house, saving the master bedroom for last.

From the dim hall light, Fur could see her, Fei Lo's dead wife, captured as a young woman of forty, sitting in the shade of a backyard tree, framed for all eternity in sterling. Even seated, the woman looked uncommonly tall. Fur flopped down in the middle of the bed. She wondered what kind of woman would wear a suit in her own backyard.

Two doors flanked the oversized bed. One led to Fei Lo's closet, the other to an enormous walk-in, perhaps once a study or a nursery, and finally refitted as a temple of adornment. On either side of the door, identical dressers, gloss white with cut-glass pulls. Opposite was a matching cabinet for shoes, shoes for every season and social occasion, including shoes in which to be alone in the house. Handmade of glove leather, not one pair would redefine the toes, or hinder flight from a difficult situation.

Fur stepped in. She opened drawers, she fingered lingerie several sizes too large. Around her neck she wound a rope of pearls.

On the vanity lay an engraved silver tray filled with everything a woman needed to enhance, mask, or preserve. She picked up a crystal atomizer and misted behind each ear, then tried to fan away the sticky perfume. *Luster, Bedazzle, Remembrance*—lipsticks that gave no clue to their color but attested to some state of mind—*Promise*. She wiped off her own lipstick and drew a new mouth. The vivacious pink favored by older women barely covered lips stained dark red. The corners of her mouth where the tissue had missed formed sharp little brackets around her smile. She looked all wrong and told herself it was lovely.

Initials were carved into the matching brush. Fur tossed her hair. *One, two, three…one hundred strokes a day for a dazzling shine.* In the dusty gutters between the bristles, the hairs of two women matted into a loose felt. Fur rested her forehead against the mirror. It refreshed. When the glass beneath her warmed, she rolled her forehead to the next cool spot. A little breath escaped. She opened her eyes. Pink lips, so close to her own, they almost touched. She leaned, a small but deliberate move, and much less effort than holding the distance, she pressed her lips against the glass.

When she turned to go, she saw it.

In the back of two long racks of dresses—a zippered cotton bag. Dark brown hairs poked through the neck, their glisten subtle but distinct. Fur walked over. She unzipped. There it was, Fei Lo's dead wife's coat—mink, past the knees.

The gold paper was stamped with a pattern of ridges and spines, a miniature nautilus wrapped around dark, imported chocolate. Unlike cheap candy that clawed and irritated, this confection slipped down the throat and satisfied.

The gold paper was subtly textured, and, like fine damask, when angled just so to the light, it revealed secret designs—diamonds—iridescent and intermittent. Opened flat, the foil was about a three-inch square. It never failed to amaze Fei Lo how boxes and bags could be knocked down to a flat piece of hard paper with notches and missing corners. But the spines that formed this shell design could not be flattened. They were hot-stamped into the paper almost permanently, giving the wrapped chocolate its crisp elegance. Fei Lo turned the foil over. A shard of chocolate fell free from the crease. He stared at it before knocking it into his mouth.

In the restaurant, he would watch his daughter fold the long, flat envelope her chopsticks came in, first twice along its length, then diagonally across one end. She would turn the paper over, and fold, turn, and fold, butting one crease up against its neighbor, a process that gave the translucent paper thickness and integrity. Then she would hook the ends together and make a ring on which to rest her chopsticks. She made one for him and one for herself, her fingers busy while they discussed the menu. He had watched her do this many times, and still he could not duplicate the process.

He tried it now with this square of gold foil, knowing the proportions were wrong and his fingers no longer deft. He inhaled, his breath whistled, but he refused to breathe through his mouth. Only children, asthmatics, and dying dogs breathed through their mouths. He also refused to talk to himself. He would not do that. So it was largely in silence, broken by this whistling breath, that he folded and refolded the gold paper, patiently trying to transform a flat square into a standing ring, as he waited for Fur to call.

It was Thursday when he found the foil, almost two weeks after their last dinner. The gold paper lay scrunched in the hallway outside his daughter's old bedroom, a room last used by his wife as her private refuge. She could have sat in their raked rock garden, or in the living room overlooking the creek, but she preferred to spend her afternoons in her daughter's old room, which faced east and was cool. What she did in there he never asked, and she never volunteered. He occasionally passed the door just after she went in. If he shut his eyes, a pattern of sound would return: the flap of a shade, a book scraping the shelf, a lamp switch at midday.

He wouldn't have stopped outside the door, but there was this piece of litter, this scrap of gold. He bent over, and from that stooped position he could see light under the door to a room unvisited except by the housekeeper.

Fei Lo opened the door.

It wasn't the overhead, but a table lamp in the middle of the room. He walked over in such a hurry to walk out again, he was already turning away as he reached for the switch. The hot socket stung. He recoiled and slipped on something slick—opened books, half shoved under the club chair.

"What the goddamn."

Afraid of moving his feet, Fei Lo leaned on the table, setting his considerable weight on his forearm. He turned the light up another notch. More books lay on the carpet, almost as if arranged.

Fur.

In here. She had been in here—here, where his child used to sleep. Fei Lo spun as if he heard a thief. Not just in here. No. She had gone into each of the twelve rooms of his house. He could imagine her, nosing around, touching everything, her eyes eating up whatever they wanted, greedy, hungry animal, while he slept, while he snored, the indignity. What had she ever wanted that he had not given? He wanted to ask, he wanted to know, What kind of girl you are you come into my house and look while I sleep? He dialed. Her phone rang, rang, rang. Had he slept with his mouth open? He angled his watch face to the light. Ten p.m. He hung up and redialed. Hung up again. Call the police. He laughed. And tell them what? That she ripped up some magazines? That she dared to sashay in here in her, her *sa chahn* way, here where his wife always shut the door? Fei Lo took out his handkerchief and wiped his forehead. Robbed. He was sure of it. His son had been right. His daughter had been right. Surely, she had taken something.

He walked around until he was standing where he imagined her sitting. But he was mistaken. Photo albums, not books. He traced the trail back to the bookcase, shelves tight with albums, a rack as high as a hatted man, as wide as a marrying couple.

The old man slumped into the overstuffed chair and just as reflexively jerked his feet back, as if at the last moment he saw her sitting here, cross-legged on the floor, her skirt inching, inching, surrounded by these musty photographs—birthday parties, horses, a succession of bigger houses and better neighborhoods. And when her legs became numb she had stood up and stretched. While he slept in the front room, she had kicked off her shoes, tucked naked legs under, and sat, in this same chair, in this very room where his daughter shut the door, where she talked in hushed tones with girlfriends, where his wife used to nap, where the two of them brushed each other's hair while his son wheeled around on his tricycle, head back, hair flying behind, caught forever in the streak of being two years old.

Funny, Fei Lo did not remember his son having a tricycle. But every child had a tricycle.

He got out his glasses. He pulled the lamp close and sat down. The album was edge-stitched with brown yarn. Roy Rogers waved from his horse and smiled the *So long* smile. Fei Lo wiped the cover with a handkerchief, sneezed, and turned the page. A square of foil slipped out. And another. A cascade of gold.

He dropped the book.

He stood up faster than his blood could recover and he lumbered across the room. The doorframe boxed him. Seal it up. Let the housekeeper tidy it. He slammed the door. It popped open again. Fei Lo steadied himself in the dim hall, willing some cooperation between heart and lung.

In time, the eye adjusts. Pupils dilate. A table lamp and a comfortable chair were what he saw. Together they defined a space and scale for intimacy. Yes, he could imagine them here, his daughter, his wife, even Fur. Nothing had happened. She had been looking, only looking. It could just as easily have been like that.

Fei Lo thought about cold chicken and *jook,* thick rice soup, hot and cleansing. He thought about bed and forgetting. But the widower went back in, as if his life depended on it.

If there were ten albums on the floor, there were another eighty or ninety still on the shelves, no two alike. The books on the top shelf documented the youth of his wife, until she married; then she almost disappeared. There were few pictures of him or of the two of them, fewer yet of the entire family. And what pictures there were of the four of them showed events he could little recall, as if his participation had been aural and after the fact.

Here—something familiar. On their wedding day, his mother had broken her toe and brothers jostled for the privilege of carrying her. *Her* mother was relieved to find for her gangly daughter a decent and equally tall husband. He turned a page. His bride could not believe how skinny he was, coming from such ample parents. And after she had gotten used to skinny, she could not believe how quickly he could grow. With each return trip to Hong Kong, he would multiply their wealth, hers, and come back displaying it to the world around his middle. That day, she had loved him handsome in a top hat, and said he should own one. With that passing remark, she had inspired in him a taste for acquisition as a measure of his feeling for her. That day he had kissed her for the first time.

Fei Lo had to close his eyes, had to. For just a moment.

Over the years he had perfected the habit of falling asleep in his chair, to awaken refreshed after everyone had gone to bed. Then, in the company of other people's sleep, he would pad about the house, eating whatever he wanted, wherever he wanted, admiring figurines he suspected were new, thumbing through textbooks lying about, arranging the shoes at the front door into tidy pairs.

After the children left and after his wife died, he was at liberty to roam the house. He stayed up later and later, to bed at dawn, to table at three. Soon he could not distinguish night from day. He feared a tumor. His doctor laid a hand on his shoulder and said it was grief, and would pass.

Christmas, 1962. His wife posed in her new ranch mink, the top of her head cut off, her eyes red from the flash, making her seem alien. He had admired her coat when she came to pick him up. *"You like it? Just a little something I bought on my way home from the airport. Perhaps it could be my Christmas present."* Each year, he returned three, four times to Hong Kong, to inspect their properties, to visit their mothers. But he only ever missed that one Christmas.

He thought he saw his wife last week, in San Francisco, going up the alley-like Commercial Street. Or rather, her mink coat. A woman walking away, in a fur coat, and on a fairly mild day. The warm weather and the coat's vague familiarity distracted him, because the walk he knew very well. He had spent many evenings watching Fur walk away.

Fei Lo slipped a finger beneath his bifocals and rubbed. He didn't have to go to his wife's closet to check, he knew.

A fur coat. She wanted a fur coat. For a damn coat she made herself into a thief.

Dinner, she had written. *Next Saturday. Someplace new. All you can eat.* Then she had kissed him before leaving. He could just taste her lipstick when he woke.

Fei Lo pushed himself up from the chair and made his way to bed, overcome with the fatigue of a hiker who realizes, as he reaches the peak too late in the day, that his rest will be inadequate, and his descent will have to be made mostly in the dark.

· · ·

Dusk and the lighting of the city appeared hand in hand. Thousands of amber lights came up in the special stillness that occurs only in dead winter. The city shimmered.

Of all the views of this city, Fei Lo loved best this one, at night from Treasure Island. From the island, the city's spires seemed to rise straight out of the Pacific in defiance of gravity. These buildings were set upon precious square footage and thrown up to the skies, maximizing the total number of rooms that could command rent. Under these towers lay a scattering of human-sized buildings. One of them was new and sprawling, built in flagrant disregard of cost.

With reluctance, Fei Lo got back on the bridge and continued on to San Francisco. He arrived and drove three times around the same blocks until a street spot opened up, half hoping for failure and an excuse to go home.

A single restaurant occupied the entire new structure, a building so flat an expanse it spread out like a stain, this restaurant launched by a Hong Kong entrepreneur eager to reinvest, eager to put both the Empress and the Mandarin to shame. Every lavishness had been pursued. That was the talk. And to guarantee good fortune, the owner had staged a parade, he hired a dragon, he chose a name of promise and called it The Forbidden Palace.

Fei Lo hated this kind of restaurant, where overplush carpets absorbed all gaiety, where autographed pictures defined who you weren't and men felt more at ease without their families. Gloved waiters served with discretion. Deals were negotiated in a subtle mélange of tranquility and artful consumption. Right hands clasped, left hands remained on the table. Why come to a restaurant if not to eat? Fei Lo could not comprehend. Yet he had attended the grand opening and returned each subsequent Saturday night, arriving early, staying late, eating, drinking, hoping for a glimpse, a chance encounter to set Fur straight.

But opening night belonged to the wife, the mother of the owner's sons. The following Saturday, to the owner's favorite mistress, not the youngest, but the most ruthless. With each succeeding week, Fei Lo had felt both a petty victory and some small embarrassment for Fur, whose one claim in the hierarchy was to be novel.

Tonight he should have stayed home. Or gone to the Economy Cafe in Oakland—run by a Chinese granny in constant sport of very dark glasses to filter out what the grill on the windows could not. For a fraction of what he would be leaving here for a tip, he could have had a fine bowl of granny's *jook*. The rice soup soothed as it meandered through one's system, happily carrying away with it all impurities. His stomach was in need of rest.

Fei Lo arranged and rearranged his utensils. From a deposit slip, he tried once again to fold a paper ring, ignoring the ceramic one that matched in design the plates and bowls and the solid brass door handles. He canted the ubiquitous chopsticks—here, ebony.

He was tired and was contemplating leaving, going home to lie down, just getting up and going, now, before the waiter arrived, when Fur finally walked in.

She was preceded, however slightly, by the men in tuxedos, the owner and his towering guards. Fei Lo knew S.K., a man of questionable alliances on both sides of the Pacific. During the Japanese War, he had tried to buy up a quarter-mile section of Tsim Sha Tsui, including property once owned by Fei Lo's wife.

S.K. conferred with his men, his eyes swept the room. He pointed with discretion and the young men nodded as one. The group began to move on, having forgotten Fur. Very soon she was standing all alone. And yet she continued to wait for one of the men to come back, to help her out of her coat, to hand it to the checker, this fur that had belonged to an Amazon of a Cantonese and that she clutched to her breast as if it protected against some as yet undiscovered element.

Fei Lo went past the bar, past the bank of telephone booths, past several doors marked PRIVATE and down the broad, curving stairs, following arrows that pointed the way. On the door to the men's room was a hand-lettered sign: *The management regrets... Please, use the Ladies' Room.* Fei Lo could hear voices, arguments about specifications and fulfillments punctuated by banging pipes and gurgling water. He added percussion of his own as he turned away—his shoes squished the carpet.

The door to the ladies' room was propped open. Fei Lo hesitated. His intestines beckoned. Inside, two more doors faced each other. One led to a washroom. He turned to the other and was startled to see a sickish old man, equally startled, staring back at him. It was himself, reflected in a mirror. He was standing in a generous powder room faced with enormous sheets of silvered glass, ceiling to floor and wall to wall. Relief came where one expanse of glass was sheared by a slab of peach-veined marble. Fei Lo was now supporting his gut with one hand. He shouldn't have ordered for two, shouldn't have then tried to eat it. Some men came out of the washroom after first allowing a woman to pass. It seemed all right to go in.

He rushed through the washroom to the toilet room and locked himself in the first free cabinet. Despite the warm tones and textured wallpaper, he still felt the chill, the damp.

By the time the old man finished his business, the washroom had emptied out. He removed his jacket and hung it on a gleaming hook.

The hall door creaked open and swung shut.

"Don't turn around."

Someone was standing in the powder room. While she herself couldn't be seen, her reflection could. His heart contracted.

The old man worked the pink soap into a lather. "Don't turn? Why not?"

Fur tried to make it light. "I have to fix my slip."

Without her coat, he could see she had lost weight. He missed her fleshiness, the suggestion of abundance. Her smart black sheath and stilettos only emphasized her gaunt frame. She looked worn, as if from the strain of standing erect.

"Are you well?"

She waited until he looked up again before answering. "Why didn't you stop me?"

He purposely misunderstood. "But you were with your party."

Fur arranged and rearranged a wayward curl. "He's asked me to marry him."

"Congratulations."

Neither of them mentioned the golden anniversary wife, the litter of mistresses.

"Do you love him?"

Her smile was a fine line in her face. "Did you marry for love? What do you and I know about it? You've been in America too long."

The old man leaned heavily against the sink, seized by sharp pains in his stomach. He paled. Fur started to go in, then stopped. She wasn't used to helping. She didn't know where to begin. When he straightened up, she busied herself with the contents of her purse.

She finally blurted out, "What about the coat?"

The old man cupped some water to his mouth. "Your fur coat? It looks very nice on you."

"Don't be a fool. It's not *my* fur coat."

He had to laugh.

"Aren't you going to call the police?"

"And say to them what?"

"Your wife's coat has been stolen!"

There. She had said it. Almost. But where was the satisfaction?

Fei Lo wet his handkerchief and applied it to the back of his neck. His convulsions had almost subsided. "To call the police I would first have to go home to my wife's closet, where I never go, and discover that her fur coat is missing. If the coat is not missing, what will the police do for an old fat fool?"

In the other room, Fur's eyes darted here and about. Everywhere she looked she could see only herself. "You won't go into her closet?"

It had never before occurred to him that his death could be sudden. He could very well die tonight. Even right here, down in S.K.'s basement toilet. No one would remember the fortune he had built, from nothing, shacks. They would remember only another old man who died without his family.

"In order to find the coat is missing I would have to violate my wife's sanctuary. I would have to think of my friend as a thief. And I would have to consider myself indifferent to a life I can't fully comprehend. That would be the cost to me." He looked for the towel dispensers and found in their place monogrammed linens. "And the gain? I might get back a coat my wife can't wear, a coat my daughter won't wear. A political coat, she says." He tossed his used towel in a basket. "Besides, it's not the coat that I miss."

The hall door opened. A young man filled the frame. He glanced at Fur. She was drawing a generous outline around her lips. The man continued through the washroom with keen dispassion. From the toilet room came the snap of heels, the bang of doors. Down the aisle. Back. Fei Lo managed to produce a comb. Fur was filling in her lips with a sable brush, an even darker shade of red than she used to wear. She puckered. She blotted. The young man paused at the door.

"Five minutes," he said, and he left without haste.

Fur was flushed with color, as if the threat excited. All these weeks Fei Lo had mistakenly thought his desperation to find her was to chastise.

"Fur, you are the boss. Of your own life, you are the boss." If only they were in the same room. "Please, learn to make better opportunities."

"Opportunity! Always the deal! You and he were torn from the same womb, you think I'm a deal to be made?"

"Please. I meant no disrespect." Fei Lo shook his head. He wanted to sit down. "A man cannot change the eyes through which he views the world. Opportunity, it's just my way of speaking. What do I know of fancy words? I just want for your happiness."

She tossed her tissue and kissed the air in front of her. "Maybe it's not just *my* happiness that concerns you."

Fei Lo blushed. "Oh! You are an impossible girl! S.K. will ruin you. Without regret!"

"I have a top-floor apartment, a view of the Golden Gate so wide I have to turn my head to see it all. He visits two or three times a month. I regret nothing."

"And your name is on the deed?"

She gave no answer.

"You have a driver? Wherever you go, he goes?"

"I live like an empress."

"An empress is *protected* by those who watch her."

"And with you, life could be so different?"

"Yes! Of course different, because *I* am different."

"Here's how you are different. You hang on to all those shacks in Tsim Sha Tsui when you could have bought in Victoria, like S.K., be a millionaire many times over."

His color deepened. "Anyone can take valuable property and turn a profit. Where is the challenge in that? I have taken what others discard as worthless and made that into something valuable."

"I am no chunk of land to be improved. I am not worthless. I will not be discarded."

"No. Of course not." Fei Lo hung his head. He went back over their times together and pondered all the things he might have done differently, knowing that the course of a person's life is all but unalterable. Yet he was unwilling to give up hope, or the desperate optimism one can acquire in increasing abundance the nearer one gets to the end of life.

As if she could read his mind, she said, "Nothing you do will change things."

"What I do is of no consequence, you are right. But what you do can determine the rest of your life."

"Mine is a good life, Ah Goong. No better." She spoke with little conviction.

He nodded. "I fear you will beat me to the grave." From an abundance of names, *ga jeh, mui, gu ma, biu jeh*—precise nouns that left no ambiguity as to whether a sister was older or younger, a cousin was male or female, an aunt was single or not, related by blood or marriage, and on which side of the family—from the hundred names which evoked the exact relationship between two family members, he could find not one that might describe what he felt about her. And he had come to think of Fur as family. "We could have had something fine, something that honored us both, a relation not unlike what I had with my wife, or daughter, or sister, or even my mother. Something quite—fundamental."

Fur rolled her tongue over her teeth. She snapped her tiny clutch.

Fei Lo flinched and made no move to hide it.

She avoided his gaze, steadfast and genuine, but she could not avoid the ring of his words: mother, sister, daughter, wife. Something fine, he said. Something fundamental. Something, she felt, completely foreign to them both. He might as well have invited her to jump off the boat. For what?

The minutes ticked. Four, five.

Mother, sister, daughter—if she could hold still for just a moment, the brilliance would surely fade. The beckoning would pass.

Her voice was barely audible. "I'm a good girl, Ah Goong. You believe me?"

He nodded, with conviction. She did not see.

"I was a fool to take the coat. And you had invited me into your home."

Fei Lo's heart caught.

Fur stepped out into the room, a little unsteady, as if on first-time legs. Her determination remained, but not the steel. He could imagine her in the center of other cold rooms, awkward, young, toughing it out, coached from the side by a mother who wanted her child to practice standing alone.

Fei Lo shifted to turn.

Fur held a finger to her lips, at once kiss and admonition: *Don't...turn.*

He ached to turn, to speak to her, face-to-face.

She moved decisively towards the door. He struggled. She hesitated. The hall door squealed open. Fur stepped through.

He would not remember going up to the street. Nor would he remember the people he passed, any more than they would remember him. He would recall instead the lightness of her steps.

Fei Lo climbed the stairs and walked through the restaurant, stopping only when he reached the sidewalk. The stars seemed especially bright and plentiful tonight. Not a wisp of cloud in the sky. Not one.

He had to laugh. All these years he had been gazing at the skies at the wrong time of day, so dazzled was he by the sun, so thankful for its warmth on his back. All those nights he knocked about his house while his family slept, he could just as easily have stepped outside his door, and looked up. *Bak Dou Chat Sing, Sin Hauh Choh,* the Big Dipper, Cassiopeia, the stars were the same no matter what they were called, constant in the firmament, whether or not he looked, there to give definition to the space that could be seen, and hint at what could not.

Fei Lo shielded his eyes from the streetlights, and he counted, taking special delight in the faintest sparks, stars that might indeed be small, but could just as easily dwarf his sun while being much farther away. So far away that some already may have burned out, even though their light was just now reaching his eyes. So far away that numbers were incomprehensible. So far away that faith was prerequisite.

He counted all the stars that he could see, and when he was finished, he felt confident that if he stood there a bit longer he would spot another. And another. The price for such clarity was just the cold, the pure cold of a clear night. Fei Lo paused to savor its kiss and sting.

Insomnia

He thinks about the water often: sitting in traffic; in a chair in his office; in bed with his wife, Jeanette, who is now asleep. Together they live the life of the city, Phoenix, where the smog blisters the horizon and the swimming pools are treated by experts. Byron, his brother-in-law, runs a pool cleaning business. Byron drives from home to home in his sky blue pickup truck, *Byron's Pool Service,* measuring the pH, the need for chlorine and acid treatments. He has recently hired two graduates from Tempe, has bought each a truck and supplies; next year, he'll be hiring another, business is swell. The college graduates are tan, and one of them, the blond, deals cocaine.

"It's a great job for a kid," Byron said, earlier this afternoon in the driveway. He stood in the sun, his long arms resting on the roof of his truck. "You drive around a lot. You get to listen to the radio, get a tan. And get laid by all those lonesome housewives."

"That's a myth," Tom said.

"Myth, my ass. Just ask old snowhead next time he comes by. Ask him if *he's* getting any."

"Drug dealers," Tom said. "It's not the same."

"Kids," Byron said. "Kids. You ask Jeanette sometime. Sometime when you're feeling lonesome. Kids these days—they're like bunnies. Like bunnies and monkeys," he said, wagging his finger. "I'll give 'em this, though. You can't call 'em lazy. They just ain't lazy."

"It's the nature of the drug," Tom said, and he knows Byron thinks he's lazy. All accountants, according to Byron, are lazy. Ever since the calculator. Byron resents him his wife, Byron's sister. At thirty, she's still a vision—all skin and hair, and now, while she sleeps beside him, while he watches the clock, the luminous patterns which read 3:37, he thinks about Jeanette sitting outside in the sun, drinking her iced tea, reading a book, and watching the pool man. The pool man is just a kid skimming orange blossoms across the surface of the water—the pole in his hand a sword. A foil, he thinks. The kind you have to point with to do any real damage.

Since the advent of the repeating rifle, nicotine, like other drugs, has become decreasingly popular. When he smoked, he would handle his cigarette like a pointer—a hot, burning tip, punctuating the rhythm of his sentences and ideas. And while he still carries his cigarettes, he no longer smokes them. Not for three months. To celebrate the event, March 17, he picked Jeanette up at the library and drove to the airport. There they caught the first flight leaving for St. Louis.

To quit smoking he had to face his addiction. Whenever he felt the urge, the first shivers of nicotine withdrawal, he would put a cigarette in front of him. He would focus on the cigarette until the shiver passed and he began to think about something else. If he could think about something else, then he didn't want a cigarette. Even at dinner, over his coffee, which he kept, and his Scotch, which he also kept—even then he would reach into his pocket and remove a cigarette, and set it before him, standing end-up. Increasingly, he became less conversational and more stoic. "No one," he would argue, "wants to be an addict. You name me one who does. A drunk, a junkie—a Twinkie nut. I don't care what he's using, no one wants to be an addict," and then he would stop talking, focus on his cigarette, a monument of self-discipline, and feel stronger about himself than ever before. "Just one," he might say. "Just one," and by now he knew that he was beyond the danger of addiction, that addiction was something you need not be afraid of if you face up to it. He was smart enough to know he didn't want just one.

This is what he thought about on the plane, as he sat in non-smoking, a window seat where he sat holding his wife's hand. He had smoked a particular brand of cigarettes, one which advertised cowboys and wild horses; Jeanette told him for the first time in years he smelled really nice. Once in St. Louis, they rented a car, found a motel near the airport and bought a bottle of Jameson's. It was, after all, St. Paddy's. They drank whiskey from plastic cups and watched television until he passed out. In the early morning, he woke to find Jeanette sitting on a vinyl chair, staring out the window. She sat watching the lights and the planes land, which he pictured as he closed his eyes, turning into his pillow, the planes falling into his mind—the edges blurred by the light on their wings.

"They're so pretty," she might have said.

In the morning, dressed, she did say, "I want to see the arch."

"I don't want a cigarette."

"Yes you do."

"You're right," he said, flexing, reaching for the Tylenol. "I want to see the arch."

She had of course been raised in St. Louis. "When I was a kid," she told him, "they were building the thing. To celebrate Jefferson. The Louisiana Purchase. They kept building it, and every weekend we'd drive downtown to watch the progress. And then Dad got a job in Detroit, and we moved. They still hadn't connected the top—it wasn't complete. I want to see it complete," she said, and he had promised someday they would, and now they were in St. Louis and this was something he was remembering: their vacation, on Oahu, the place of his birth. They had married in Phoenix and flown across the ocean and for two weeks set themselves up in a condo which belonged to friends of his parents. Normally, the friends got three grand a month for it, but his parents knew people, it was a small island, and it was then, while treading water in the Pacific, that she told him about St. Louis, and the arch she never saw complete, and the way when you looked up at the arch it always looked the same. What was different, she explained, was the sky, and he felt himself drifting on the water, wondering what it would be like if the sky never changed, if only the things below it changed, like trees. Like plants and all those people who planted them and all this water.

Because he cannot sleep, and because he does not want to think about not sleeping, he decides it is time. He rises from the bed and walks through the dark halls of his house; in the kitchen, he reaches under the sink, where he knows there is a half-bottle of gin, a gallon of Chablis, and a full liter of Scotch. He bought the Scotch last weekend and it is still in its bag. He bought it at a liquor store downtown, off Van Buren, the type that caters to the hookers and johns—cheap beer, soda-pop wine. The whiskey bottles were covered with dust, behind the counter, where a man sat watching a television. Beneath the counter Tom knew the man had a gun, it was that kind of place, and the bottle is still dusty. He rinses it under the tap and locates a glass, his whiskey glass, the one with a picture of the Howard Coleman Library stenciled onto the surface. Once before, when he used to worry about Jeanette worrying about his drinking, he had tried to quit: he had tried to face it the way he would later face his addiction to nicotine. He'd pour out a glass of beer, or Scotch, and set it down in front of him and stare at it. But while he stared at the glass, he would want what it held, and so he would drink it—smoothly and in one pleasant, lingering rush. Addiction, he reasoned, wasn't addiction when you wanted it. It was need.

In the mornings, Jeanette always took a swim. "You've got a problem," she might tell him someday, shaking the water from her hair. Maybe reaching for the towel.

"Really?"

Of course it's all in the blood: a treasure to be passed down the genetic line, like blue eyes or hemophilia. In your weakest moments, something to be proud of. Usually, it begins at the elbows, a sudden, nervous little twitch near the joints, really, on the inside—the tender part. From there it spreads equally up the biceps while the fingers grow nervous and clumsy and the brain, ever on the alert, begins to send signals elsewhere: the gut, the ankles—the hamstrings, even, which tighten up as if being choked: the way you lock in a drill bit, by choking it. By now the brain is foggy, its logic unpredictable, caught in the undertow of need. What once seemed clear is now less so. Your sentences become confused, *post hoc,* and what you're thinking is what, simply, is going to stop you from going through this one more time now?

A swallow, you think. Just enough to swallow yourself full.

After clarity comes love. Sweet, feckless love. Eventually the flesh begins to soften, around the eyes at first, and then the mouth, into the neck and arms and flanks until, one morning over coffee and juice, you realize the flesh you have is not necessarily the flesh you want. Last Christmas in Hawaii, with his parents and Jeanette, and Byron, who'd wanted to come along—"What kind of swimming pools they got over there?"—there they shared a room with Byron, there one night, in bed, Tom had wanted his wife, Jeanette, and she had said, "No, Tom. Byron."

"So?"

"So wait," she said, sleepily. "Wait until morning."

And after a while he had fallen asleep. In the morning, he walked on the beach in a T-shirt. Byron slept in and woke late to fix eggs. Jeanette went shopping with his mother for a swimsuit in Waikiki, and his father changed the oil in their rental car. But on the beach, in his T-shirt, while walking along the white sand, he came across a couple. The boy was in a wetsuit, and the girl, a young girl with short blond hair, lay on her back, the top of her bikini curled loosely in her fist. She lay on her back and smiled up at Tom, as if to say *Morning, Dad,* and he had wanted to tell her to watch out, this was a public beach, the cops patrolled it with helicopters, but instead Tom had looked at the boy, his skin swollen with fine, perfect health, and of course at the girl, and then Tom had walked on. He could feel the boy's eyes, following him, and he thought never again would a woman look at him the way he had wanted to look at her—in sweet, gentle admiration. He thought about Jeanette, telling him to wait. To wait until morning.

"You know what I think?" Byron said later. They were sitting on the porch, drinking beer, watching the birds inside his father's pigeon coop. The coop had burned down once years ago. Neighbors said you could see them flaming, the birds, flaming as they tried to beat out the fire. Some of them escaped into the sky.

"No. What?" Tom said.

"I think if a man wants to screw around on his wife, he should let her screw around, too."

"You've never been married."

"I think if a man screws around on his wife, it better be worthwhile. I've seen plenty of those housewives, let me tell you. They sit out there by the pool, wagging their tails. Loyal as goddamn pups, bud. Pups!"

"Never," Tom said. "I've never cheated on Jeanette."

"Meaning? Meaning what, bud?"

"Meaning, why are we talking about this?"

Just then Tom's father came through the gate, holding a fan belt in his hands, the knuckles of his right hand bloody and skinned. He stumbled through the gate, reached into the cooler for two beers, and stepped slowly into the house.

"If you ask me," Byron said, pointing to Tom's father, "I think you better start keeping an eye on your wife. I think your old man's about half-lit."

His father had enjoyed the study of our American heritage and raised homing pigeons. Once, his father sneaked a dove on a plane and flew to the Big Island. There, he let the bird go, and by the time he flew back on a plane, finding his car in the parking lot, driving over the Puli, and arriving home late for supper, there she was, sitting on the coop, roosting. His father would tell the story often.

But now outside on his driveway, under the floodlights, it's time for glory. The basketball is dense, in need of air, and after pumping the ball, filling the yellow-orange ball full of air, he's ready to go. The ball in one hand, the drink in another, Tom forces the net, lofting the ball. After the ball goes in, as planned, he turns to face the crowd which he can't see for all the floodlights. Still, he hears it, and he knows it admires his grace—this basketball player with the lovely wife, Jeanette.

"I had a good coach," he's telling the crowd. "The finest coach in college basketball today, Gene Tummings." He turns to the crowd and waves, sipping from his drink. "Gene," he says, nodding. "Gene, you taught me everything I know."

His next shot from the free-throw line sails onto the roof; he can hear the ball rolling across the length of the house, and what Gene Tummings taught him, specifically, was how to run suicide sprints. Running those sprints had taught Tom how to measure his endurance, how to break through the barrier of pain into the promise of a second wind. Once into the second wind, that wind which emerged from all of this pain, he was invincible. And Jeanette would watch him from the bleachers, running his sprints, and he would be oblivious, running.

"My wife," he tells the crowd, smiling, pointing to where she might be seated. "She's a vision."

Now, setting down his drink on the free-throw line, he looks down the length of the driveway. The mailbox is a hundred yards, easy. As easy as making a dash, which he does, but along the way he stumbles, sliding onto his belly into a cholla. When he rises from the pavement, he understands that his arm and cheek are full of needles. His belly is going to raspberry, and he can't feel a thing.

"Wait," Jeanette said in bed, with Byron just four feet away. "Wait until morning."

Meaning, Tom thinks, that she knew in the morning Byron would be too caught up in his sleep to notice. Meaning, Tom thinks, that this is the voice of experience. And what he wants to know, here and now, standing in the doorway of their bedroom, watching his wife sleep—what he wants to know is where she learned to wait. Where, and with whom?

Most mornings she preferred to swim naked alone. And naturally Tom had not wanted to wait, and Jeanette had slid under the blanket, receiving him with considered affection. There, she labored under the blanket, and what he thought about, with Byron next door—next bed, actually—what he thought about was what she must look like, there beneath the blanket in the same room with her brother and her lover and all this experience. What he thought about was what this meant, this waiting for morning, which she might as well have done. And later, after Jeanette would rise from the covers, spooning him, later the next morning while Jeanette went into Waikiki looking for a new swimsuit, he would know that she was not going to talk about this. He knew she was going to tuck it into the back of her mind, quietly, the same way she had tucked him into her mouth, waiting for him to either come or fall asleep.

Whence comes this experience? The needles in his face belong to the cholla which grows along the borders of his driveway. In the bathroom, with Jeanette's tweezers, he plucks them from his skin.

The needles are barbed and he is careful not to break them, but even so they break, still under his skin, his hands large and uncooperative. The roots of these needles will remain lodged in his skin until they begin to fester; he will need to dab at the roots with turpentine, or nail polish, he can't remember which. On the beach, when you ran into a man-of-war, the most immediate cure was urea. You'd ask a friend to piss on you, and now, after he takes a leak, he rubs at the blisters along his arm and face. Eventually, he rubs his hand along the skin of his belly and picks out the small pieces of gravel; sooner or later, things are going to start beginning to hurt. Meanwhile, he stands here, in the doorway, watching his lovely wife sleep.

Wait till tomorrow, he's telling himself. *Wait.*

If Gene Tummings had been his father, instead of his coach, Tom might have become someone else, and vice versa. Because he cannot sleep, Jeanette must be sleeping with someone else. Tomorrow, things are going to hurt like hell.

But he's sensible enough to know there's a way to put that off; he can't remember where he's put the basketball. The whiskey is on the kitchen table, where it belongs, and he grabs the bottle and glass and returns through the garage to his driveway. Because he can trace the first, faint stirrings of dawn, he decides to turn the floodlights off. The switch is located behind a rake, a three-foot-wide rake he uses Sunday mornings to groom the granite lawn, and when he reaches for the switch, the handle of the rake falls forward, striking him in the face. Pissed, he takes the rake and hurls it across the garage. The rake bounces off the wall, landing on the hood of his car—a fully restored 1968 Pontiac station wagon. A family car with an enormous engine just beneath the painted hood. In the morning, he will have to check the paint for damage. Above him, propped on the beams of his garage, rests his stepladder.

After he thinks about the basketball long enough, maybe he'll remember where he's put it.

Love is for the timid and the damned. In Phoenix, the water becomes necessary, the whiskey supplies him with regret. What if he had reason to be someone else? His wife, he tells himself, is sleeping with someone else, and his father never taught him how to dribble properly. This much is clear, the ladder is unsteady, and as he ascends, bottle in hand, he knows what he is doing. He is climbing onto the roof of his house. Once there, he realizes the need for furniture. He descends, removes a lawn chair from the porch, and returns to the ladder, climbing once again. When he swings himself onto the rooftop, the chair swings with him, disrupting his balance and spinning him full circle—the chair striking the ladder, the ladder falling slowly. When the ladder finally hits the ground, there is a loud, awkward noise, leaving Tom alone on his roof to consider recent events. Simply put, the ladder has fallen to the ground, and the tar paper is sticky with grit; his father never meant a thing to Gene Tummings; perhaps basketball could have been a way of life. He unfolds the chair by the air-conditioning unit and leans back into it. After a while, he recognizes the basketball, across the roof, sitting in a puddle of stale water over their bedroom. Jeanette could possibly be sleeping with the pool boy, or maybe someone else he doesn't know. Usually she waits until morning when it is safe. Any minute, he thinks, looking into the sky. Any minute now and the sun is going to break.

In St. Louis, there on the lawn beneath the arch, St. Paddy's Day weekend, he thought never had he seen anything so impossibly big. The ocean was big, but not as big as the sky. The arch stretched across the sky, and looking up at it, he realized he was no longer looking up at anything. Rather, he was looking down at something larger than himself and his wife combined—the promise of good fortune, a homestead. Land for the taking and enough space for a man to milk his cow in. Clearly the possibilities were enormous.

"It's so big," Jeanette said. "It's bigger than I remembered."

The air was brisk, washing over the arch and the shape it described. They stood on a large, dead lawn, and Jeanette shivered inside her coat.

"A veritable wonder of the world," he said, taking her arm. "Let's go inside."

Inside, underground, with the lawn overhead, and the sky above that, they talked to a woman about tourist attractions—a newly constructed mall, the local riverboat rides. The woman asked if they were on their honeymoon.

"No."

"You're so young. And pretty," she said. "You really should go up inside. You can see the whole city!"

Tom wondered if the woman had ever been on a honeymoon; he felt like a tourist, and realized that he was. A visitor in a foreign land. The Louisiana Purchase, which Tom knew Jefferson had been allowed to buy because Napoleon had got his ass kicked in Santo Domingo. Napoleon was on another continent, no longer a threat. His navy was locked in ice. A long time ago, before he began training doves, Tom's father had undertaken a correspondence course entitled Our American Heritage. His father had often encouraged Tom to learn from the past and to help him study.

Waiting in line, Tom thought about his father, and cigarettes, his head racing while Jeanette read to him from the brochures. The air was hot and still, museum air, and Tom pretended not to listen. Growing up in Oahu, Tom had learned to hate the tourists. He watched a family from Arkansas, or Missouri, standing before them: three overfed children shoving each other, sucking on their Cokes, their parents standing stiffly, equally overfed and uncomfortable. He wondered what type of car it was that they might drive.

"So why?" Jeanette said.

"Why what?"

"Why now—'68. Why build the thing now?"

In 1968, Tom was watching television and learning to surf. His father was in another detox unit on the mainland, someplace near Portland, and Tom was made responsible for taking care of the birds; his mother was afraid of lice and she wanted to go back to school. She wanted to protest the Vietnam War, expand her horizons. For the very first time, Tom realized that maybe she wanted to leave him.

"It's a symbol," he said to Jeanette. "It makes the future seem bigger than it is."

Tom watched a man standing by an ashtray across the room light up. The man took a drag from his cigarette and, exhaling, blew the smoke away and up into the ceiling.

"You know," Jeanette said, taking his arm and kissing him, briefly, on the neck, "I'm so proud of you."

"Just don't leave me," he said. "Promise."

If he hadn't played basketball in college, taught himself to slam-dunk, Jeanette might have never fallen in love with him. He holds the basketball on his lap, watching the sun rise, thinking the basketball is round and in about the same shape as the world. If it weren't for gravity, he'd keep slipping off, and when he holds the ball up to his finger, he thinks maybe he can still make it spin. He can make the ball spin and balance on the point of his finger, only when he does so, when he gives the ball a spin, it doesn't stay in place. He takes another drink, reaching instinctively for a cigarette. He has a pack of cigarettes in his toolbox, on the shelf over the washer-dryer, but even now, were he there, standing in front of the washing machine and looking at his cigarettes, even now he knows he wouldn't smoke one. He has too great a discipline; smoke is a matter of the will. Jeanette, who's sleeping with someone else, is proud of him. The sun is filling up the space on his roof, and now, when he spins the basketball on the tip of his finger, the ball remains: facing him, spinning, turning him giddy with relief. He still hasn't lost his touch.

Before his father returned home from the mainland, Tom slipped outside. It was night, and late, and still very warm. He slipped into the backyard in his shorts, all white and lit up by the Hawaiian moon; he slipped into the coop and rearranged the straw. Then he took a match and set the birds aflame. To this day, it remains secret, this source of unexpected fire in his childhood backyard. His father came home later, sober, and wept for days. Sometimes Tom wishes he could tell someone. Sometimes, when he cannot sleep, he stays up thinking about other things he's done. Maybe Jeanette wants to tell him what she's done?

Because when he cannot sleep, she must be sleeping with someone else. Wait, she said. Wait until morning. In the morning, they rode up through the tunnel of the arch with the family from Kentucky. The family wasn't from Arkansas or Missouri, after all. The family talked nervously in the small space of their car, and Tom had to duck to keep from bumping his head against the low ceiling. He sat silently as the family talked on and the car shifted, corresponding to the angle of their ascent, keeping them level. Next year, the family was going to go to Florida; they'd been planning the trip for years, since the birth of Jimmy Roy, who was too young yet to come along. Jimmy Roy was at home with the in-laws, and back in Phoenix, Byron was taking care of Tom and Jeanette's pool.

Jeanette was smiling at the couple, being polite. "I grew up here," she was saying. "But I've never really seen it."

"That's a shame," said the woman. "That's a real pretty shame."

Briefly, the man reminded Tom of his father. They had the same faces, and Tom realized the man was a drunk. You could see it in his eyes, and he wondered if the woman knew. He wondered if she'd leave him if she knew.

Once at the top, they followed a narrow metal stairway leading to the center of the arch: the observation room. It was the last section to be installed, the final piece of architecture Jeanette had never seen. And now they were here, all together, standing in its center—an integral part of the construction and design. The metal floor was carpeted, and they could feel the wind buffeting the walls of the arch. The floor was unsteady and they found themselves leaning uncertainly against a window, looking out over the western frontier, industrialized and full of smoke. They leaned into the view and rested the weight of their bodies against the vibrating monument.

"What I said," Tom said. "Down there. That's not what I meant."

"Tom," said Jeanette, "I'm not going to leave you."

"What I meant was, if you want to leave me, then I want you to. I mean I want you to do what you want."

"I love you."

And standing there, leaning against the window, he knew it was going to be dangerous. Here, where there were no longer any Indians or buffalo. Here, where there was only the future and all the wrong ways you could turn, wandering through that space reserved especially for you while you went looking for a river, hoping the water clean. Avoiding disease. It was a place, finally, you had to travel into alone, West, where the land was big enough for a man to get drunk for a living. If you kept living long enough, the land eventually turned to water. The history you knew you were going to have to go through—even without a lover, or a wife, it was enough to keep a man up at night.

"I feel like I'm falling," he had said. "I feel like I'm falling and I don't know where I'm going to land."

"It's so pretty," she said, taking his hand. "It really is pretty, isn't it?"

Basketball is a team sport, five men on the court; today, a woman is even free to join them; without a coach, you may as well be without a team, which you always are. Alone and on the court, who is there left to judge? By seven, though he doesn't know what time it is, he knows he's in control. He knows things are right and going to be okay. Okay, he tells himself. Everything's going to be okay.

From the roof he sees Jeanette opening the sliding glass door of their bedroom. She is walking through the doorway carrying a pink towel, preparing to take her morning swim. Each morning, she does this even before brushing her teeth; something more than merely habit, he thinks. The way things wake you up like that. Jeanette is walking over the deck, up to the ledge of their pool.

Tom stands and says, "Morning."

"Tom?"

"Nice view, from up here."

"You scared me! What are you doing?"

"I'm watching you. That's what I'm doing. Best to wait until morning, so that's what I'm doing. And watching, of course."

"Come down," she says. "Come on down from there."

"You're beautiful," he says, and looking at his wife by the pool, he feels an unexpected relief. She loves him. Some people just don't know any better, and looking at her here in the still early dawn, everything is inexplicably clear. He is a man, standing over the roof of his house, looking at his wife and the pool they have built together. The pool is blue as the sky and full of clean water, and he wonders why he never thought of doing this before. He holds the ball up and lofts it into the pool, where it lands dead center, waiting to be recovered.

"Watch," he says, removing his shorts. Afterwards, he stands almost perfectly still, eyeing the distance.

Jeanette lets go the towel and lifts up her arms. "The ladder, Tom. Wait."

"Watch," he says, and looking at the water below, he knows there's no going back. There's only going gracefully and following through.

"Tom!"

"No, wait," he says. "This'll be good."

Other Wars

This is my tale about the Vietnam War; at least I think it qualifies. This story, however, comes no nearer to Phnom Penh than 10,000 miles: blame this lack of action on my year of birth—1954—and blame it on my gender. A muddy river does appear later on in this story, and you'll see a few guns, and on a marshy bank, wild grasses will whip at my bare legs, but there will be no leeches, no shrapnel, and no one in this story will be called Charlie unless it is his mother-given name.

I got my first menstrual period on the same day that Lyndon Johnson was reelected. I remember this date clearly because my mother was working as a poll-watcher for LBJ's campaign, and when I came home from school at noon, bleeding from my genitals, I had a hell of a time searching for the new sanitary belt that I knew Mom had bought for me and hidden somewhere in the bathroom. This was back in the days of sanitary belts, back in the days when not many women entered the military for reasons such as—if I understand the military mind correctly—the existence of sanitary belts.

I spent three hours bleeding onto wads of Kleenex that I crammed into my underwear, and was much relieved when Anna, my eldest sister, came home from her last class at the commuter college that was the only place my folks could afford to send her. But when I opened my mouth to ask her to give me some help, she brushed by me, slammed the door to her room, and burst into loud, wailing tears. I retreated to the room I shared with my younger sister, Lynn, distracted from my own trauma by Anna's uncharacteristic outburst.

My sister Kathleen, the second oldest, came home at 4:15 after pom-pom-team practice. She helped me find the pads and belt, though the whole setup was so bulky and awkward that I soon reverted to using wadded-up Kleenex. Kath avoided the room she shared with Anna—they didn't much like each other, and they still don't—after I told her about Anna's tears.

"She never cries," I said.

Kath shrugged. "It might do her some good, then."

"Maybe you should check on her," I said. "Make sure she's not dying or something."

She shook her head. "I'll get supper started." Dad always got home at 5:15, and so we always ate at 5:20. With Mom gone, Kath became the cook. Anna was hopeless in the kitchen.

I was always closer to Anna, anyway, so I finally found the courage to knock on her door and ask to come in.

She was lying on the bed, crossways, wiping her face on her pilled cotton bedspread, which had once been white. Its color now was an uneasy compromise between yellow and gray. She sat up, no longer crying, but red-eyed, puffy-faced, and miserable-looking.

I sat down on Kath's bed and shoved my bare toes down between the bedframe and box springs. Now that I was here, I didn't know what to say. We weren't a very demonstrative family; we didn't talk about our sorrows with each other; we never hugged. We were half-Dutch Methodists, and at one time I thought that might be the reason why we didn't act anything like the gushing TV families that had been popping up on prime-time shows. But by this age, I knew that our next-door neighbors—the ones we liked, the ones with kids—were melting-pot Baptists and they didn't act any different than we. So it wasn't religion or lineage that made me just sit there dumbly and pick at my cuticles.

"I broke up with Danny," Anna finally said. Danny was the bass player in a local rock band she followed. He had a Fender bass and shining black hair that hung over his eyes so that I couldn't even tell what color they were. He never said anything to me when he came over.

"Oh," I said.

"He thinks I was talking too much with Mark."

Inside the bedframe, my toes were going numb. I liked the feeling. I was one of those kids who spent hours spinning around in circles just to make myself dizzy. "Who's Mark?" I asked.

"He's the drummer of this other band, Blackie Z."

"Oh," I said. "Is he cute?"

"Mark?" The fake-innocent way she said his name made me think that Danny had been right to be jealous. "I guess so." The way she said *that* made me sure of it.

It was less than a month later when Mark first came over, and I considered him a real improvement over Danny. He talked to me, for one thing, like I was a real person. I could see his eyes, for another. He came over more often, too, and sometimes he brought a few of his brothers with him. I was his favorite—other than Anna, of course—in our family. Eventually, I got to go with the two of them out to Mark's hometown, riding in a battered Chevy that smelled strangely sweet all the time, an odor I would later be able to identify as low-grade, home-grown marijuana.

Mark had grown up on a large farm about fifty miles from our town, in German immigrant country, next to the river. Berger Township had forty farm families, one Catholic church, and just two paved roads that formed a single intersection known to the locals as "in town." On every corner of the crossroads stood a tavern, each with Anheuser-Busch beer on tap, each with an old, round-topped jukebox and nicked-up tables that sat empty. "Don't sit there. Those are saved for the euchre players," Mark told me. He could bring a ten-year-old kid sister into the bar with no problem—he himself was only nineteen, but still got served because he was a local boy.

He was blond and blue-eyed behind thick glasses, and broad-shouldered. All his seven brothers looked just like him, except the even-numbered ones had perfect vision and no glasses. There was Mark, then Matthew, who would be the first of them to go to Vietnam. Bobby, John, Michael, Peter, Luke. And James, who was Lynn's age, and who was born missing a finger from each hand. They were wild boys, rough boys, boys who had borne up through farm accidents and fights. They all liked each other in an unrestrained and rowdy way that my sisters and I never would have been allowed to duplicate.

The Vietnam War began to escalate soon after Mark and Anna met. I knew of the war mostly from television. I knew, too, that Mark changed his major to engineering to get a draft deferment and dropped out of his band to keep his grades up. I knew that his brother Matthew joined the Marines as soon as he turned seventeen and went off to some Southeastern state to train, and then to Asia. I heard about body counts on television. But those weren't facts that affected me. They were background noise, part of the voice-over to my childhood, like the endless reports on the ups and downs of Elizabeth Taylor and Richard Burton's relationship.

What I did know—personally—about the Vietnam War was this: I spent dim winter Sundays with Kathleen, fixing boxes to mail to "our boys"—really just some anonymous platoon number she'd picked off a list at church. I helped her bake chocolate chip cookies. Kath knitted mittens, and tried to teach me how, too. I fumbled my way through one pair, then went on to popping batch after batch of popcorn to use as packing material. The address that Kath printed on the finished package was like no address I had ever seen. It seemed to be in some secret code.

Anna didn't take part in Kath's baking projects. Anna was a member of the commuter college's White Panthers unit, though the most radical thing they did was listen to MC-5 records while planning to bomb the Oakville Post Office, which was the only federal building in town. They were all liberal arts majors, however, so none of them knew how to build a bomb. They all knew how to talk about it, though.

The first time I went out to Mark's family's house itself was almost two years after he came into our life. Anna didn't go with us—maybe she was at a White Panthers meeting. It was just me and Mark. I forget how we got to be friends, and I see now that it must have looked funny to some people that he was hanging out with his girlfriend's little sister, but there was nothing but innocent liking between us. We both liked shooting pool. We went fishing together. We both liked football. His parents disliked my sister, as they disliked all their sons' girlfriends, but had no reason to let that spite slop over onto me.

The farmhouse had once possibly been yellow, but it had faded to about the same non-color as Anna's bedspread. Rickety steps led up to an aluminum back door. Inside, the little house had a sour smell, of spoiled milk and urine, that seemed to come from everywhere.

I sat huddled in the corner of the dilapidated sofa, holding a jelly glass of lemonade Mark's mother had handed me wordlessly before disappearing back into the kitchen, like a rich person's maid. While Mark talked with Luke, I watched seventeen-year-old John and his father exchange words. A tiny black-and-white television set droned on in the corner.

Their father, Clint, said, "It's time to bring the cow t'barn, son." He swigged a can of Bud. He had an enormous beer belly.

From his spot in front of the television set, John said, "Oh, Pa, that cow can find her own way home."

Clint got to his feet quicker than I would have given him credit for. "Don't you sass me, boy."

"But I'm right!"

The old man slammed down his beer, sloshing some onto a veneered end table. He picked John up off the floor. John was a strong boy, a guard on the varsity football team. Without any apparent effort, Clint tossed John into the wall. A cloud of white plaster dust puffed out around the boy's shoulders. As he struggled to his feet, I could see a new crack in the plaster next to the doorway. The ugly room swam in focus for me: suddenly there was meaning in all those other holes in the walls and doors, messages in the drooping door hinge, in the splintered rocking-chair arm.

Mark's mother didn't come running into the living room. Mine would have. I gripped my glass more tightly and refused to meet anyone's eyes. On the TV, a special on the war began, and Clint sat down to watch it. John left to—I assume—bring the cow in. I couldn't help but notice that none of the GIs on TV were wearing mittens. To be honest, it looked a mite warm in Southeast Asia for mittens. I wondered if they'd ever gotten the cookies we baked, if whoever opened the boxes ate the popcorn or just threw it out.

On the drive home that night, I said to Mark, "I was surprised about John and your father."

"What about them?"

"The argument they had about the cow."

"Oh. Yeah," he said. "Y'know, John was right."

"Huh?"

"That dang cow has been led back to the barn every night for the past fifteen years. She'd have made it back on her own just fine."

That wasn't the point I had meant to make, but I just let it pass. I knew I had just visited a foreign place, a house where no one acted anything like any family on TV, a household with a difference that went way beyond that between Methodists and Baptists or Catholics. I wondered if they ever made popcorn at the farm-house. I wondered, for the first time, how Matthew was getting along in the war.

I never got a chance to ask. He was killed in combat that same winter.

When the draft lottery was next picked, Mark's birthday came up 107. He signed an employment agreement with an aerospace firm in Seattle, an agreement that included a guaranteed draft defer-ment. He proposed to Anna, and they were married right after he graduated. I cried at their wedding.

His brother Bobby's birthday had been drawn as number two in the lottery. I suppose he could have gotten out of the draft somehow—perhaps because of Matthew—but either he didn't know how or didn't want to try. Bobby came back from basic training to be best man at the wedding, laughing and grinning throughout the whole evening, having a boisterous good time. Later, Mark learned that Bobby hadn't been given leave, that he'd gone AWOL to make it to the wedding. Bobby also saw his girl-friend that weekend and got her pregnant.

At the reception, Clint bragged on Bobby. Standing there in his white shirt and clip-on tie, looking about as natural as a cow wearing a tuxedo, he also talked about Matthew as if he were some damned saint. I remembered Matthew as being a lot like John—and I remembered the night that Clint had hit John.

The week after their wedding, Anna and Mark moved to Seattle. The next year, Kath eloped with a boy from high school who was in the Coast Guard in Maine. I grew up and took a lot of drugs, which was at least as much fun as spinning around in circles until I got dizzy. My mother got elected County Clerk, and Dad learned to eat dinner at 5:40. My little sister, Lynn, ended up being an okay kid—we did drugs together every now and then until she got arrested for possession, and then we both pretty much quit.

The war ended, the U.S. slinking home with its tail between its legs like a whipped dog. Nixon resigned the summer between my high school graduation and college. I went to the same commuter college as Anna had, and majored in Government. There I met professors—all men—who were passionate about the subject of the Vietnam War. I got into a lot of discussions with them about "isolationism" and "self-government" and "imperialism," and I never thought to contribute to the conversation by mentioning Matthew or Bobby—who Anna said had come home in one piece, but "weird"—or Kath baking cookies or my mother's stint as poll-watcher for Johnson in '64. None of that seemed as though it had anything to do with the war, or with the grand political theories that my professors espoused.

In my senior year of college, Anna and Mark moved back from Seattle, Anna saying, "I hope I never see another fucking cloud for as long as I live." Mark started working on his master's degree and we began to hang out together again.

On a muggy Saturday just after I graduated, Mark took me to the family farm again, to hunt for morel mushrooms. At dawn I waited for him on the front porch of my rented duplex. The sun was just a vague gray light tucked into the hollows of the hills to the east. Mark picked me up in his old Chevelle and drove me out to the country, over the river, and to the farm. He steered the Chevy through weathered gates and on behind the farmhouse, now painted a peeling white. I waited in the car, spinning the radio dial and hearing nothing but static.

Mark came out of the back door with his nephew, Bobby's son, here for his custodial every other weekend. He was named Matt after his dead uncle. The boy carried a shotgun. Bobby trailed behind, empty-handed. I barely recognized him. He wore jeans and a short-sleeved plaid shirt. His blond hair was so dirty it looked almost brown, and it was stringy and long. It clung to his thick neck and slipped down inside the collar. He walked stiffly, his eyes tracking any motion around him on an oddly delayed schedule, as if his brain were processing everything he saw a bit too late. Watching him gave me the shivers.

His son helped him get into the back seat, and the boy greeted me politely—he had obviously learned his social graces somewhere other than here at the farm. Bobby said nothing. I don't think he knew me.

Mark drove us back to untilled acres of the farm, where the brothers had once grown their marijuana. He had brought his good shotgun along and his old over-and-under for me. Why hunting mushrooms required a gun, I didn't know, but I took the damned thing, though I held it awkwardly, as if it were a snake. Bobby had no gun, and I was glad of that.

We made for a thick stand of trees. I imagined sneaking up the brush-covered rise, pausing, pointing, shouting, "There's one of them suckers now!" and—blam!—blowing the mushroom heads to kingdom come. Spores would flutter down over the hapless brown squirrels cringing on their thick tails.

We split into three groups—Bobby and Matt stuck together—and Mark briefly described the mushrooms to me. "You just gotta learn to see them," he explained: this was the whole of his advice to me. I scuffed along, alone, scanning the ground, looking for odd, tiny objects that I'd never before seen. I learned to see the woods—really see—that day for the first time. I remembered, as if from another life as a tracker, about tiptoeing between dead sticks. I saw the layers of brown rot blanketing the ground. The wet smell from young birches filled my lungs. Touching a vine here, bracken or lichen there, I tracked the killer mushrooms through the quiet wood.

I was the first of us to find a patch. "Beginner's luck," Matt said, disgusted. The three of us filled paper lunch sacks with the tall, striped dwarf-caps of fresh morels. Bobby stood back and stared with a vacant look.

When we got back to town, I phoned Anna. "Why didn't you tell me?"

"About what?" she said.

"About Bobby! Christ, what a ghoul!"

"I forget," she said. "It's something we're not supposed to talk about. My in-laws pretend like he's completely fine."

Two weeks or so later, Mark asked me to go back to the farm with him to fish. I hesitated, thinking of Bobby, thinking, too, that I was having a bad menstrual period and cramping something fierce, but at last I agreed. The next morning at dawn, he drove us down the curves of Old Frankfort Road to a tiny bait store. After parking the Chevelle in the gravel driveway, he led me inside.

The bait shop was a smelly, dirty little place. Mark loved it. He stood and traded lies with the beefy, red-faced owner while I peeked into the row of aluminum bait tanks. They looked like a giant's ice cube tray. Some had chicken wire over them, to keep chirping crickets prisoner; some were filled with water and such a dense concentration of writhing minnows that I wondered how they could stay alive. Other cubes were topped with cardboard; underneath was dark loam threaded with worms. There were two sizes of crickets, two of minnows, four varieties of worms, from the tiny red wigglers up to fat, sluggish night crawlers. I rested my hand on my aching belly and watched the glittering movements of the minnows, considering how they and I were connected on the food chain. I needed them, it seemed, but they could easily do without me.

We escaped the wet chewing-tobacco smell of the shop with two little Styrofoam cartons. Mark had selected the bait with some sixth sense: some days were just red wiggler kind of days.

We parked at the farmhouse, and Mark ran inside for a quick hello while I gathered up our gear. We walked down a hill to the equipment barn and rode a flaking green tractor over the rough ground to a pond. We passed Bobby, who walked the grounds like a ghost.

Mark picked the pond: Long Pond today instead of Little Pond. His decision depended on the stock, who had fished it recently, the rains for the past week. He always knew which pond to choose. I knew by now that he spent hours on the phone each week with his father and brothers discussing fishing and hunting conditions, but as a kid I had suspected he had some kind of arcane talent, like ESP. Bobby's eerie presence must have made me remember that.

Mark showed me, for at least the fifth time, how to slip my hook under the spine of the minnow just so. "Now twist," he said, "and you'll have him." I tried. The minnow was wet, slick. I stuck him on the hook, wrenched him around a bit, then cast. The weighted line flew southeast, the minnow northeast.

When I finally got the hang of it, I cast as far as I could. Twice, I hooked Mark on my backcast. He never once yelled at me for it. I caught less fauna than flora. "Moss bass" is what Mark called the hunk of green I kept peeling off my line. Why couldn't my hook like minnows the way it liked weeds?

I bottom-fished because it kept me busy. I cast, felt that click deep in the reel where I never had bothered to untangle an impossible monofilament knot. In the mirror of Long Pond, the sinkers dropped through the sky, rippled the reflected trees. I slowly—*slowly*—ratcheted the line in, taking care to keep it just taut enough to feel a fish-sized tug. How long could I spend reeling in a single cast? That was the sport for me, not catching fish. Over and over: cast...crank slowly, fighting boredom...then giving into it, hypnotizing myself with the country rhythms.

When my line was hit, I was jolted, had forgotten I was fishing at all. Mark let me keep whatever I was willing to clean. There are no game limits when you're on your own land.

We both caught a fair amount of bass—pulled from the water with their eternally indignant expressions—and flat blue gill and sunfish. I cleaned the fish on an old board that I set on the wet bank. The weeds scratched at my legs. I decapitated each wriggling fish, wondering as I did so if it felt any pain. Scaling fish required the same skill as peeling potatoes. As I scraped the serrated blade over the headless fish, scales flew into the air, stuck to my fingers, my face, my bare feet. I looked as if I was covered with glitter, I'm sure. It was as close to wearing makeup as I'd ever come.

As I was cleaning the fish, Bobby came along, holding a pint bottle of bourbon. He stared at me for a while. Then Mark walked up and began to talk to his brother.

"How's the old man?" he asked. I didn't hear Bobby say a word.

But Mark went on as though he'd been answered. He asked about the milo crop, he said Matt was turning into a good little hunter. I glanced at Bobby once, and he was looking down at the ground, digging his toe into an ant hill, rubbing the back of his neck with a corner of the whiskey bottle.

"All finished," I said, standing up.

"Want a ride back up to the house?" Mark asked Bobby. His brother gave a little shake of the head and Mark nodded.

"See ya, Bobby," I said, not expecting a reply.

"Bye," he said. His voice was soft, shy. He sounded like a five-year-old.

Mark picked up a big bagful of fresh corn before we left the farm, and we took it and the fish back to town. Mark, Anna, Lynn, and my folks and I ate fried fish, the sweet corn, and tomatoes from Mark's garden for supper that night. Afterwards, we played lawn games. Mark liked to play killer croquet, an endless version of the game that prized sending the other player's ball as far away as possible over Dad's neatly trimmed lawn. Usually I'd get into it with him, but that night I wasn't in the mood. I tried to send his ball once, but the anticipation of the crack of the mallet against the wood made me flinch. It was just enough of a hesitation to ruin my shot. His ball rolled only about ten feet.

"God, what a pussy!" he said. It was how he and his brothers always insulted each other's masculinity. There was something in his smile that reminded me of Bobby's old smile, though the last time I'd seen it was on the night of their wedding. I realized then that Mark could have been Bobby, or Matthew, that his draft number could have been number one. I wished, with a sharp, painful kind of longing I'd never felt before, that we *were* the kind of touchy-feelie family that I saw all the time now on television. I wanted more than anything right then to tell Mark how I knew I had the best brother-in-law in the world. But I couldn't do it. I'm ashamed to admit that I still can't.

Anna called last week and told me that Matt's wife died, horribly, in childbirth, hemorrhaging to death in the back seat of their car. Since this last war, I've been remembering these years, these scenes, that war, Bobby. For some reason, Anna's news brought it all into sharper focus.

I live in Oregon's Wilamette Valley now. Great fishing country, and I don't mind the rain clouds at all. I don't get back home very often, and I haven't seen Bobby in years. Anna says he's much worse, though I can't even imagine what that might mean.

I don't understand much more about the war now than I did in 1968, when I was fourteen. I'm just a female, and I've been told I therefore have no place writing about this—or any—war, not even from a 10,000-mile-distant perspective. And hell, I don't know—maybe this story isn't about the Vietnam War at all. Or maybe it is; maybe it's me still knitting mittens, sending them to secret-code addresses, trusting that some stranger can find a use for something I made back home.

MICHAEL DORRIS

Shining Agate

THE JOURNAL OF COMPARATIVE ETHNOGRAPHY, Vol. 31, No. 6 (Summer 1989): 118–126.

There was a beautiful young woman named Shining Agate, the oldest of three daughters, and she was very proud. Always, she insisted that her hair flow loose and free of tangles, that her dress be sewn from the most supple skins, that the meat of her soup be tender and cut into very small pieces. To her parents' eyes, Shining Agate could do no wrong, even in the smallest thing, and they never welcomed into their longhouse anyone who suggested otherwise. As a result, Shining Agate grew up convinced of her own perfection, a conviction so powerful and sure that by the time she was twenty almost everyone in the village agreed with her.

Whatever special place Shining Agate preferred immediately became the most desirable spot to visit. Whatever flower made Shining Agate smile became the favorite blossom of every woman, old or still a child. Whatever song, whatever tale, whatever color of the sky pleased Shining Agate, that song or tale or color became for a time the delight of the world.

Now it happened that there was a young man named Left Hand, who was the oldest of two brothers—his younger brother was named Right Hand. For as long as he could remember, Left Hand had dreamed that someday Shining Agate would consent to be his wife, but he was afraid to ask because of course he did not feel worthy of her. Certainly he was a good hunter, an excellent trapper, a weaver of tight, impenetrable fishnets. Certainly he was strong and robust. Certainly the mothers of many young women had invited him to sample the foods their daughters prepared, but none of those daughters interested him. Shining Agate was the only wife Left Hand desired.

"What can I do?" he asked Right Hand. "How can I make her accept me?"

Right Hand was a devoted brother and wanted to help, but to him Shining Agate was too proud, too happy with herself. To him, her beauty was not that *great, her ideas not* that *amusing, her smiles not* that *charming. It was as though Right Hand saw Shining Agate through a mist that obscured her brightness, and because of that, he judged her more clearly than anyone else. He did not find her a bad young woman, but he did consider her vain. Most of all, he hated for his brother to be so unhappy at Shining Agate's expense.*

"She is a woman the same as any other, just as you are a man the same as any other," Right Hand told Left Hand. "Perhaps she will accept you, perhaps not. You will never know unless you inquire."

Left Hand trusted Right Hand and listened to his advice. The next day, when he encountered Shining Agate playing stick games with her sisters, he took a breath and spoke to her.

"I have it in mind to marry," he said softly. "Do you think I can find a wife for myself?"

Shining Agate looked up and noticed Left Hand as she never had before. He was tall and the sun danced on the blackness of his hair. His voice was frightened, his eyes bright, his skin without flaw. For some time she had wondered why no man had yet mentioned marriage to her when even women much younger had found husbands, and she felt a surge of gratitude toward Left Hand for removing this worry from her heart. She smiled on his question, and answered with the words he had hoped to hear.

"Of course," she said without laughter, surprising her sisters. "You must only ask permission of the mother of the wife you prefer and I'm sure she will agree."

No sooner had the news passed through the village—for Shining Agate's sisters were anxious to tell, glad to think of Shining Agate as married and out of their way—than people decided that Left Hand was truly an exceptional young man, even better than they had previously realized. Everyone was glad to celebrate the union, and were certain that it would produce many healthy children. No one was ever happier than Left Hand.

Yet soon after the marriage, Shining Agate experienced a curious change. Now that she found herself with a husband who approved of her every action, who complimented her sixteen times each day, who insisted upon repeating her every observation to anyone who would listen, and who felt so shy in her presence that he dared not touch her or ask anything of her without some prior signal that she welcomed the request, Shining Agate, for the first time in her life, became tired of praise.

Only occasionally at first, but ever more frequently, she intentionally tested her husband's devotion. Some days she would not comb her hair with the hawk's claw that made it smooth, but even then Left Hand would look at her and sigh: "How beautiful you are, Shining Agate. What a sunrise for my eyes." Some nights as they lay together beneath their fur covers she would wait until Left Hand was nearly asleep and then poke him sharply with her elbow or kick him with the heel of her foot. He would wake instantly, but instead of asking her to be still, he would say, his voice low and whispering, "How wonderful to be reminded that you are by my side." Some days Shining Agate would boil the stew meat with salmonberry leaves, making it bitter and sour, but Left Hand would only flatter the taste. Some nights Shining Agate would push Left Hand away when he rolled against her in passion, but he would shut his eyes peacefully and dream of her instead.

"I would do anything for you," Left Hand promised Shining Agate every morning. "No task is too large."

Finally Shining Agate could endure her husband no longer.

"I have heard there is a pure white wolverine deep in the forest," she told Left Hand. "Go seek it for me and don't return until you can bring me the skin for a hat."

Left Hand looked out the doorway. It was early winter and the snows were already heavy upon the ground.

"Surely such an animal will already be asleep deep in its den," he replied. "In the springtime I will trap it and make the hat for you myself."

"Wolverines don't sleep in the winter like bears," Shining Agate reminded him. "And I won't need a hat in the springtime. Go now. Find the pure white wolverine and don't return without it. Was your promise a lie?"

Left Hand gathered up his bow, his snowshoes, and his parka. "It was the truth," he assured Shining Agate as he left the longhouse.

What Left Hand did not know was that Shining Agate had made up the story of the pure white wolverine. No such animal had ever been seen.

Days passed, then weeks, then months, and still Left Hand did not come back to the village. At first Shining Agate was relieved. She visited with her sisters, slept on her back, and ate whatever and whenever she pleased from the ample provisions Left Hand had stored for the winter. Sometimes she did not think even once of her husband between sunrise and sundown, between sundown and sunrise, and tried to convince herself that she was again exactly as she had been before her marriage.

But certain things could not be changed back. When women of the village remarked to her that no wife had ever been so brave at the prospect of a lost husband, Shining Agate could not enjoy their words. When young men began to leave fine pelts and fresh moose meat by her door, she could not receive their gifts as her due. When her parents offered her comfort and sympathy, she could not bear their kindness.

Instead, she sought out the company of the only person who frowned whenever he beheld her, for Right Hand would not forgive Shining Agate his brother's disappearance.

"Sister-in-law," he said one morning as they stood together at the hole in the ice from which lake water was drawn. "Is your head cold today? Would the fur of a white wolverine keep you warmer?"

Shining Agate saw herself through Right Hand's eyes—selfish, cruel, and greedy—and it was as though a heavy cloak had fallen from her shoulders and her arms were free to move.

"No condemnation you can say is bad enough for me," she told Right Hand. The joy in her voice surprised him so thoroughly that he put down his oiled basket and stared at her face.

"Sister-in-law," he tried again. "Have you not been sleeping well? Your face is gray and older than I remember."

"I do not deserve sleep," Shining Agate replied. "I do not deserve to be called sister by the brother of my husband."

"I am too harsh with you," Right Hand apologized. "My brother will be angry when he returns."

"He will not return," Shining Agate said. "You are not harsh enough." And with that she plunged her arm into the icy water, her face bright in pain.

"Shining Agate, stop this," Right Hand cried, and pulled her up. He tucked her dripping arm inside his parka, hugged it against his chest to keep it warm. This touch was lightning in a summer sky, and soon it happened that every night Right Hand slept in his brother's house, and Shining Agate never turned away from his embrace.

Even then the people of the village found nothing to criticize. "How *appropriate," they agreed. "The grieving widow is consoled by the loyal brother-in-law who fulfills his obligation." But Shining Agate paid no attention, and one late night, after Right Hand was too in love with her to hate her, she told him the truth about the pure white wolverine and why he need not worry that Left Hand would come home.*

A year passed, another, a further spring. Shining Agate bore a handsome son whom she named Laughter, and who, like his father, reached only with his right hand. In the summer they moved to a fish camp down the inlet, and guarded by their secrets, the lovers made each day different and better than the one before. Laughter justified his name, and the cabin was filled with his merriment.

On the first day of the last summer moon, however, a rumor flashed through the village: Left Hand was on his way.

"How did he survive?" people asked when they heard the news.

"He almost froze," they were told. "He broke his leg in a fall and had made his death song when he heard wide-spaced footsteps. It was the Sesquatch, the bear people who lived in the world before human beings and who now dwell only in the highest mountains. They took pity on Left Hand and carried him back to their village. They used their ancient magic to set the bone of his leg, but it was a bad break and took many months to heal. Even by the first summer, Left Hand was still too weak to return and so he stayed with the Sesquatch another year, hunted with them, became wise in their ways. When his full strength at last returned, he taught them human skills in gratitude for their hospitality, but their fingers were too blunt to tie sinew dense enough to catch salmon, so Left Hand stayed through the spring and early summer and left behind forty-eight nets of his own construction. The Sesquatch gave him as a sign of their friendship and appreciation a prize of great rarity: the pelt of a pure white wolverine."

When Right Hand heard of his brother's adventures his face turned to stone. Without speaking, he ran from the fish camp. Shining Agate grabbed up Laughter and rushed after him, but by the time she reached the beach, Right Hand had already pushed out his boat and was digging his paddle into the sea, heading toward the sun.

"Take me, take me," Shining Agate called and waded far into the foaming surf. She held Laughter high above her head, but in his shame Right Hand would not look back. "You can't deny me. I will be too lonely," Shining Agate cried, and stumbled farther and farther from

shore. The water passed her knees, passed her waist, and finally it passed her shoulders until only her head and her arms, holding high her smiling son, were visible.

When it became clear to Shining Agate that Right Hand would not come back, that she must face Left Hand without him, her heart turned cold and smooth. She lowered her strong arms, sank Laughter deep beneath the waves, hugged him against her chest until he stopped moving. Then her own legs were caught by the undertow, and she disappeared. The surface of the ocean was once again empty and calm.

—AS COLLECTED FROM SERGEI MISHIKOFF,
SUSCITNA, ALASKA, AUGUST 1970

.   .   .

"Sir," the annoyed flight attendant addressed me. "This airplane cannot move unless everyone is seated."

Everyone was me, and I wasn't, and yet we were. I pleasantly pointed out this paradox to illustrate the capriciousness of codified law: what shouldn't be, nevertheless was.

She was not intrigued. "Sit," she ordered curtly, and, faced with a direct command, I obeyed.

I was on my way to Alaska, propelled by inertia. Three years ago, I had enrolled in a graduate anthropology program, and, having taken the required course work for six semesters, it only remained for me to prove myself in the field. I had no ambitious queries of my own to resolve, so I appropriated one from my adviser, Abraham Wentworth. While passing through a remote subarctic village in 1927, a question arose in his mind that he had never answered to his own satisfaction: Why did human beings remain in this remote, cold, barren environment?

"Find out," he directed me. "It'll be good for at least a major publication or two."

So here I was, my stowed bags packed with painkillers and antiseptics, my sensitive film protected against weather by tied condoms, my future as a respected professional in the balance, aboard a flight diagonal across the continent. My fellow passengers were Japanese businessmen on their way home to Tokyo, healthy hikers, mothers grim-lipped from saying goodbye to their daughters-in-law and knowing, despite protests and promises, that their own solicitous faces would fade within a day from the memory of their drawling grandchildren.

It was one of those endless journeys in which all sense of *from* and *to* is lost, when secrets are confided to seatmates, great thoughts are pondered but not written down, plans are made that will never be carried out. It was a two-meal, two-hot-towel flight, a dislocating hang in the air, and by the hour I arrived I'd be a time traveler: no longer truly from where I'd started but not yet one with where I'd come.

Once in Suscitna, I was given over to the care of small children until I was educated enough to deal with adults without taxing their patience. It took months for me to learn the rudiments of the language—the local dialect varied widely from anything previously published—and so I spent my first days shepherded by reluctant young boys or girls to whom parents had assigned the chore of my improvement. Aimlessly I followed one or another of them along the lanes of the community, pointing at objects and dutifully repeating the name to my instructor's satisfaction before phonetically transcribing it into my notebook.

I had arrived in the early autumn, naively treating my stint of fieldwork as if it conformed to a standard academic calendar. Within weeks the sun all but disappeared from the murky sky, the temperature fell permanently below zero, and my child-hosts returned to their classrooms for hours each day. Time dragged, its waste insufferable whenever I imagined the activities I could engage in elsewhere, the conversations I could carry on, the tasks I could accomplish. Winter was a long, insomniac night, featureless and infuriating, in which events occurred only to vaguely blur together in their recollection. My vocabulary lists lengthened, my hair grew, my connections to the world outside the village frayed and snapped.

One day in March, warmer than most, unable to endure the indoor boredom, I ventured out alone on a path bound high on either side by hard-packed snow. Turning a sharp corner, I saw in the gloom a deeper shadow, tall and menacing. The bear—it must be—hungry from hibernation, out, like me, for the first time. Running was pointless, so I did a thing I'd read about: I dropped to the ground, shut my eyes, and lay completely still. A bear was supposed to believe me dead and therefore unappetizing or unthreatening, anything, to convince it to avoid me. My ears strained for the scrape of paws, the low rumble of a growl. Was it staring at me, transfixed in wonder? Finally I opened one eye and found myself alone, the only spot of color in a vast whiteness.

My immediate terror broadened. I dreaded loneliness, failure, accident. I saw myself drifting within a pointless life, defined by cautious habit, oscillating along the short curve between amusement and annoyance. It was as incorrect to say that nothing mattered to me as it was to claim that something did. At last, the cold penetrated my goosedown parka. I stood up, retraced my steps, went back inside. Two o'clock. In an hour, school would end and perhaps a child would be sent to visit.

I had been resident in Suscitna for eight months before I felt reasonably fluent. Even then, I had no choice but to frequently interrupt my eavesdropping with requests for repetitions, explanations, distinct pronunciations. I fit into no preestablished category within the existing social structure of the village, and so uniquely came to fill my own niche, a role approximately described as "nosy, inept, noncontributory stranger." In the eyes of my informants it must have seemed as though I fairly panted for any scrap of simply expressed gossip, historical or modern, and a few of them took delight in leading me astray, exhorting me to speak inappropriate words. I had no alternative but to become the butt of bad jokes, an irresistible buffoon, a moron who could be counted upon to laugh with the crowd at his own stupidities. How else to ingratiate myself? Anger or resentment would have resulted only in an attitude toward me of indifference or scorn, and the thrust of my work depended upon access. And so I hid my true feelings, reserved my sarcasm and wit for letters that would be appreciatively read thousands of miles to the south, and bided my time. When this exile was over, my voice would be restored.

In the interim, there was the place. Denied the distraction of conversation, I had no choice but to interact with my surroundings, to open myself to their feel and sound, to the salt in the unflagging wind. After the months of darkness, the return of daylight was exhilarating, thrilling. The air smelled brown and green, the sky abounded with calling birds, the ice retreated each day farther from the shore, and beneath its transparent glare could be seen flashes of movement as insects skated the widening pockets. Roads turned to mud, mud to caked ruts. Men heated rocks for sweatbaths and children forgot their coats when they went out to play. At Easter a man, Ivan Kroto, went to church drunk. He sat and knelt and prayed loudly out of tune with the rest of the congregation, and no one minded. His behavior made them smile.

That summer, I moved from the village to an abandoned fish camp, where I lived alone in a tar paper–covered shanty perched high on a bluff, its one glass window fronting the blue-gray of Cook Inlet. From that solitary eye, one July dawn, I spied movement on the rocky beach and quickly descended the steps— planks pushed into the crumbling slope—to find a seal pup the tide had left stranded. It stared up at me, trusting and curious, too surprised at the firmness of land to propel itself back to water, and allowed me to stroke its sleek fur. I kept it safe, protected from the sun by a crate, through the slow revolution of the sea's cycle, and the next day it was gone.

I filled those hours I allotted to myself with projects and assignments. Each night, I would transcribe the notes I had collected, bits of new village trivia, emendations to previously recorded data, chance insights, lines of inquiry to pursue in the future. Most mornings, when the tide was out, I walked the beach, my eyes screening the pebbles for good luck. Among the dozens of locally identified charms, none was more prized than an opaque, soft, orange stone, slightly translucent when held before a light. Encased within, like the grain of sand around which in warmer oceans a pearl is formed, was a dark core of rock, and the smaller the heart, the greater the potency. I kept a collection in a mayonnaise jar on my table.

In winter, I had eaten the charity of others—donated moose meat, muskrat, dried fish. But in the summer, I caught my own salmon with a nylon net I stretched between two barrels and anchored thirty feet offshore. First came the humpies, then kings, and reds, as run followed run. I supplemented my diet with boiled noodles, instant potatoes, Rice-A-Roni, or Hamburger Helper in a rotation of the six flavors stocked by the village all-purpose store. I drank tea, instant coffee, or Kool-Aid, watched the skies for the mail plane. Each night, I listened to country music on KYAK, or to the cassette tapes I had culled from my collection at home and brought north to keep me company. For society, I lost copiously but with forced grace at pinochle or cribbage, the village's twin obsessions. For work, I amassed indiscriminate information from anyone I could persuade to talk to me.

Participant-observation is the name of the game in cultural anthropology, and accordingly I had apprenticed myself to Nikefor Alexan, the experienced fisherman whose one-room summer fish camp lay six miles from the village. With plywood, tar paper, a door, and a window ordered from Anchorage, I constructed a makeshift cabin on a flat, cleared bluff a mile up the beach.

Nikefor, his wife, Madrona, their infant daughter, Mary, and Madrona's father, Sergei Mischikoff, were a quiet family, traditionals who spoke no English and practiced a religion that combined old beliefs with the more recent teachings of nineteenth-century Russian Orthodox missionaries.

I was under no illusion that I was much help to Nikefor with fishing—an extra pair of arms, albeit clumsy and needing constant instruction—but for the group as a whole I believe I provided mild diversion. Though they rarely asked me questions about my background, they suffered my own queries with patience and good humor. In the evenings, during the preparations for supper, the mending of the nets, the sorting of the hooks, I was their excuse to repeat old stories and jokes, a fresh audience who never failed to signify interest and enthusiasm. My tape recorder was always available.

We were not friends, these people and I—too much divided us—but we grew used to each other's presence, began to relax our respective guards. They knew by and large what to expect from me, and I had gauged, more or less, when to laugh. We shared food and labor, weather and isolation, and within the parentheses of the warmer season, we constituted a kind of unit. I felt myself part of a process I had read about in fieldwork courses: the researcher's perspective shifts over the course of his investigation from that of a complete outsider to something approximating an insider's point of view. Oddness is replaced by familiarity, novelty by routine. I had experienced the loneliness I had so dreaded in anticipating my stay in Suscitna, but over time the emotion had evolved and altered. Solitude became my most cherished companion, my trusted friend. After a long day of my own fawning, exhausting smiles, I sought it out.

Silvers are the last salmon to return from the open sea to seek for spawning the streams where they were hatched, and this season, as July turned into August, their appearance was behind schedule. The preference of the canneries, which were our prime source of cash income, an abundance of silvers was directly proportional to the village's prosperity, and so we watched for them impatiently.

"They're smart," Nikefor commented. He sat in shirtsleeves at the table, a hand of solitaire dealt before him. He wore his dark hair long, combed to a ducktail in the back. "They'll come at night when they think we're asleep, or during a storm when they believe we won't take out the boat."

Not sure whether to nod or smile, I lifted Mary out of her playpen and rocked her in my arms.

Madrona stood stirring an iron pot on the woodstove. When the water reached a high boil, she spooned in chunks of fresh fish, a can of green beans, a can of beets.

"Watch for a light," Nikefor addressed me. "If the silvers come when I can't send for you overland, I'll put the lantern on the boat. You come down from your camp and I'll pick you up."

The logistics of my living arrangement were a frequent source of worry for Nikefor. At high tide, the beach between our two camps was swamped under four feet of water, and the danger from bears was too great to permit passage along the top of the bluffs at night. He wanted me to sleep on his floor to ensure my availability the moment the run started. Every day, he tried to persuade me, but I refused to give up my few hours of privacy.

"Stay here tonight, why don't you?" he offered. "Look, the tide is already up to your ankles. You'll get wet if you leave now."

"I have my hip boots," I reminded him. "I'll watch for your light."

"You should listen," Madrona said. She reached her hand into a huge bag of dried potato flakes, came up with a fistful, and then dramatically tossed these into her stew. This technique was her specialty, a conjurer's trick that both thickened the broth and created a skim of tiny dumplings. "This time of year those ghosts you are always asking about will come and get you if they find you walking alone at night."

I looked over Mary's head at Sergei, who made his eyes round in mock fright. My preoccupation with collecting ghost stories was a cause of much teasing. Grown men and women, it was implied, had more important things to think about.

The waves knocked at my knees as I sloshed toward my cabin. The night was moonless, overcast, with a promise of autumn in the chill air. I judged distance by the one constant marker located halfway along my route, a stagnant tidal pool that always stank of rotting seaweed. Once I passed by it, my stairs were only fifteen minutes farther ahead.

By the time I climbed them and closed my door, the Inlet had reached nearly four feet up the bluff. I could imagine Nikefor squinting into the night, frustrated and suspicious, wondering if the silvers would take this murky opportunity to evade his nets. I switched on my battery lamp, dropped a Roberta Flack tape into the player, and finished the day's notes: *N. bullshitting me about believing fish can think? S.'s reaction suggests yes. M. warns me about bogeyman as she would a kid. Cross-check child abduction tales. Function: to keep people inside at night? To instill group dependence?*

Roberta sang "Do What You Gotta Do." I clicked off my lamp, lay on my cot, and zipped myself into my sleeping bag. Four months to go, minimum, before I left this place. I yawned deeply and turned onto my side. A few minutes later, the machine automatically shut itself off and I let myself be lulled by the regular rhythm of the surf, approaching, approaching, approaching.

Suddenly I was alert, listening to light footsteps ascend the planks, reach the narrow porch. I waited for a voice, a knock, but...nothing. An animal, I decided once I thought about it. No one could have crossed the beach after me because of the deepening water. I must have been dreaming.

I recomposed myself, opened a gate for my mind to wander.

There it was again: footfalls, definitely. And there, I smelled the sour odor from down the shore, so it must be Nikefor or Sergei, come to tell me the salmon were making a dash for safe passage. I heard a tap against the wooden door.

"*Tinashdit-ah*," I spoke in Suscitna.

Another tap, soft as a branch moved by an evening breeze.

"*Tinashdit*, come in."

No answer, but wait, I caught the unmistakable sound of stifled giggling. This was a joke, a follow-up to Madrona's imprecation about ghosts. Scare the *bergunidge*, the outsider, with his own research.

"*Aikda*," I called. "I'm already in bed. Pull out the latch string and come in before you fall into the water."

A silence...then a loud rapping—bang-bang-bang-bang—but still no words.

"Please yourself," I said. "But I'm not getting up in the cold to play along."

And all was still, utterly still. No retreating steps, no protests, no whispers. Through the four panes of my window glass, the stars were steady and familiar, balanced in their distant silence. I made a mental note to find out how Nikefor got from his camp to mine and, more importantly, to ascertain his motive. I hadn't realized that my reactions mattered enough that he would risk getting wet to provoke them.

The tide was sufficiently out by 5 a.m., and soon thereafter I sat in my place at the Alexan table, ready for breakfast. Alaska Fish and Wildlife restricted fishing in the Inlet to the hours between seven and four during silver season, and enforced the ruling by sending officers in small planes to overfly the beach in unpredictable patterns.

"*Ya l'ida*, how did you sleep?" Madrona asked me.

"*Ya li aleb*, okay, once I was left alone." I gave Nikefor a meaningful look.

"Left alone?" Madrona was a good actress: her expression seemed genuinely puzzled.

"Ask your husband."

Nikefor had been listening to the radio for the weather report, and glanced up.

"What I want to know," I said, "is how you got from here to my place once the tide came in. How you got back home again. It's a good trick."

"What are you talking about?"

"I knew you'd say that."

I turned to Sergei, expecting a reciprocating grin, but his face was blank.

"All right, all right, if you insist," I said, and with as much sarcasm as I could muster in a language not my own, I told my story.

Nikefor, Madrona, and Sergei had stopped what they were doing and listened closely.

"You should have come in," I finished.

No one moved, no one replied.

"Come on," Nikefor said at last, and walked out of the cabin. Madrona wrapped Mary in a blanket and followed. Sergei splashed water on the fire in the stove and beckoned me to precede him down the stairs to the shore.

"Are we going to fish now?" I asked, surprised that we had packed no lunch.

No answer. Instead, once we were all assembled below, the group began to walk the beach, past the empty boat, in the direction of Suscitna.

"What are we doing? Where are we going now?"

No answer. They were pointedly ignoring me, treating me with what anthropology textbooks termed "ritual avoidance." But why, to what purpose? After a while, we went past the stairs to my shanty without breaking stride, and a mile beyond we reached the next fish camp. Theodore Kroto and his teenage son Max had already loaded nets into their boat and were ready to push off. Wordlessly, the rest of us waited while Nikefor approached them. I couldn't hear what was said, but saw Nikefor gesture back in the direction of our camps, saw the worry in his face. Theodore dug his boot into the sand, nodded once, twice, and finally, in what seemed like an attitude of resignation, threw the anchor from his boat. Max ran to their cabin, and in less than two minutes returned with his mother and younger brother. Quietly excited, they joined us as we resumed our march.

At each camp along the way, a similar sequence occurred. In some instances, boats already launched were summoned back to shore. Laundry was left piled half-washed in rushing streams. Nothing was allowed to delay us, and no one we encountered stayed behind, so that soon we were a ragtag crowd of maybe twenty-five men and women, children, babies, and a few trailing dogs. The only noise was the drum of our feet on sand and rock, the rustle of people in a hurry.

I was confused beyond anything I had ever experienced. To my knowledge, the forfeit of a fishing day was unthinkable, impossible. In Suscitna, what wasn't caught and preserved in August could not be consumed in February—there were no second chances. As I kept pace between Sergei and Madrona, I considered every explanation for this trek, from sudden illness to my own abrupt eviction. Whatever was coming, I was without preparation or defense.

At last, just after noon, the straggling entourage arrived at the entrance to the tiny Russian Orthodox church in Suscitna. Father Peter Oskolov, part Native, though from a different community, listened to Sergei's whispered news and disappeared into the sacristy. He emerged in a purple funerary stole, carrying a gold ciborium in one hand and an ornate metal censer in the other.

I had long since given up asking questions, so I didn't try to catch his eye as we proceeded to the next stop, a log cabin without electricity or running water, the lifelong residence of the oldest woman in Suscitna. Martina Stephan was small and frail, her spine doubled over by osteoporosis. Balding and deeply wrinkled, she was never seen without a black shawl draped over her head. Like the subject of a Goya painting, her hands were forged by arthritis, twisted into attitudes of perpetual supplication. Her voice was harsh, rattling as wind through a gravelly passage, and her eyes were clouded white with glaucoma. She could not have weighed much more than eighty pounds.

"Grandmother," Sergei shouted into her ear as we all stood watching outside the open door. "Bring your hat and come with us. We need you."

Martina gravely dropped her head even farther than its natural posture, then raised it. She shuffled farther into the dark interior, where she rooted among boxes and bags stacked against the far wall. When she moved back into my field of vision, she clutched a small bundle wrapped inside a piece of faded olive-green army blanket. Bunky George, the manager of the store, pulled up in his Jeep, and Sergei and Nikefor lifted Martina into the passenger seat. The rest of us climbed into the beds of what seemed like every pickup in the village, and in a long, jarring procession, we raced the incoming tide back down the rocky beach to the steps that led to my fish camp.

I jumped to the ground, made to go first. I couldn't remember the condition of my room: Had I put away my notes? Straightened my cot? Neatness was a value among the Suscitna and I dreaded further embarrassment.

Sergei touched my arm. "First the priest and the old lady." The fatherly, almost affectionate tone of his voice surprised me. Whatever else he was, he wasn't angry with me.

Nikefor lifted Martina in his arms, carried her like a baby, and matched Peter Oskolov, plank by plank, up the side of the bluff. Madrona, Theodore, Sergei, and I came next, followed by what seemed like most of the population of Suscitna. When he reached the porch, Nikefor gently stood Martina on her feet and stepped back to watch with the rest of us while Oskolov lit his incense and Martina, with jerks and fumbles, unwrapped the blanket. I smelled mothballs as the covering fell to the ground at her feet.

The priest began to chant in Slavonic, the words indistinct and rumbling, to swing the censer in an arc. Martina reached up her arms, pulled off her shawl, and set a hat made of fur on her smooth, shining head. The hat was grayish, fragile-looking, its shape flattened from storage and age, but here and there the pelage bristled magnetic, as if charged with static electricity. Wearing it, Martina seemed to straighten taller.

"I return at last," she said, loud and commanding. "I bring what you asked and now you must be content." With that, unaided, she pushed open my door and walked inside.

All around me, I felt a relaxation of tension. The world rushed back to surround us the way a high wave rolls onto a dry beach: shoulders lost their hunch, mouths loosened into smiles, children whistled, babies cried, dogs barked, the long grass bent in the sea wind.

"Tonight you'll make lots of tea," Sergei whispered in my ear. "I'll explain you your story."

My work in Suscitna was different afterwards, in the six more months I remained. I had crossed a line, joined forces, been validated. People talked to me with less caution, and stopped playing tricks with vocabulary words. I was treated, I eventually decided, like a big, somewhat backward but favored child, a person who had been absent during a crucial time and needed, for his understanding of things, his sophistication, to catch up to where he should be. There was no lack of joking, no forced solemnity, but unmistakably a sense of acceleration. I was in demand, told what questions I should ask, quizzed the next day after an interview to ensure that I had grasped the significance of what had been conveyed. When fishing was over and we all moved back to the village, I had visitors or invitations every night. I absorbed more than I could record, gained impressions that could not be quantified, forgot my notebook more and more often.

And in exchange, my hosts and guests sought but a single courtesy from me, repeated so often it became a refrain: to recount my visit from lonely Shining Agate and Laughter.

"She needed you to let her in," Sergei had pointed out that first night. "She required the door to be opened as her invitation. And just think, you would have seen her, her long hair dripping from the sea, her face beautiful and sad. She would have told you how her son was drowning, asked for your help, and of course you would have gone. Like many before... but see, you turned out to have more power than we thought."

"More power?" I asked him. "Why do you say that? All I did was stay in bed."

"Yes," he nodded, his face lit and pleased. "Think how unusual a thing that was for you. Always you are so anxious to indulge us.

You jump when we call. You laugh at your own errors. You give away your possessions and ask for little in return. But last night, grandson, you were *rude*! That was your power! You are the man who didn't answer, the man who resisted Shining Agate, the man who at last released her by saying no."

A Man of Substance

Marquette Henley's stepson, Lance, had always been a distant boy, dull-eyed and solitary, not at all like the eager young athletes Marquette waited on in his store. Lance spent most of his time watching television with the lights off and the curtains drawn. Blond and pale-eyed, he had skin that seemed to whiten with each passing year. His few friends were sunken-chested boys whose black shirts and stringy hair and furtive whispers floating over the night lawn were as chilling to Marquette as space creatures might have been.

Lance was a bitter disappointment to Marquette, who, as the owner of a sporting goods store, saw himself the gatekeeper to a young man's paradise. For years, boys had come to him for their jockstraps and cleats. He had taught them how to oil and tie their gloves and knew by a sniff of the leather just how long they should leave them tied under their mattresses.

Though never much of an athlete himself, Marquette was a listener, an absorber of lore and tales and tips. "Ted Williams," he enjoyed telling the ones buying new bats, "Ted says you have to look at the ball a very special way." As he spoke, Marquette would lean out over an imaginary plate and widen his eyes so intently that the boys would also lean with their gaze fixed on the imaginary pitcher. "It's coming at you . . . it's coming and all the while it's coming you never even blink—not once, because you have to magnetize it. You have to draw it in with your eyes, with your brain, with your will, with your heart, and then . . . then you can hit it!" he would cry with a click of his tongue and a long wide swing that contained no bat, no ball, but the power to make their eyes glow so openly and purely that sometimes he thought he could see straight through to their hearts.

In the forty years of Marquette's bachelorhood, he had never given much thought to a wife. His constant daydream was of a son—the two of them fishing, canoeing, hiking, tossing the ball back and forth...*I'd like you to meet my son...Hello, son...My son will help you...My son, whom I have taught everything I know...My son...* So on the day that Edna followed her five-year-old son into the store, Marquette couldn't keep his eyes off the child. Lance led his mother up and down the aisles until he found what he had come for, the penknives, which he examined carefully, opening them and holding each one to the light. It fascinated Marquette the way all this was witnessed by the mother, who stood off to the side, waiting, never advising or commenting—but watching.

When the selection had finally been made and paid for, she trailed the little boy outside with a faint, bemused smile. Marquette's heart beat hard. There was so much of himself to give a son, he thought, and his stomach churned with that same old longing, that excess he bore like an undelivered fetus. He wanted a son he could mold and instruct in his own image. Lance had seemed the perfect candidate. Even then, there had been this sense of vastness about the boy, a strange, compelling emptiness.

One day, when the boy was thirteen, Marquette came home from work early and found him watching a show on space flight. The darkened room was closely sweet with a fragrance that reminded Marquette of incense. It made him feel lightheaded and happy. The murky haze of the television's reflection seemed to cloak Lance in an eerie phosphorescence. On the screen, a silver-nosed rocket had just been launched. It cut through a layer of thick white clouds, then screamed into the brightness of space.

"Imagine!" said Marquette, easing down onto the arm of the couch. "Imagine what a feeling, to be so high up and far away from everything!"

"Yeah," Lance sighed.

"Takes your breath away, doesn't it?" Marquette said, leaning closer to the set.

"Yeah," Lance said with a dreamy laugh.

The next day Marquette brought home a book on rockets, a poster of the Apollo astronauts, and three scale models of spaceships. Eventually, these ended up in the same closet with all the unused baseball gloves and skis and soccer balls and fishing rods.

It wasn't long after that Marquette read in the paper that the astronaut Harry L. Baker would be passing through Atkinson on his way north to the state capital. Marquette saw how he might kill two birds with one stone: get a little publicity for the store, and at the same time, do something to impress the boy and fire his lackluster imagination.

A few days later with Lance and the photographer from *The Weekly Crier* beside him in the car, Marquette was pursuing the astronaut's motorcade up the highway. Finally, with flashing lights and frantic hand signals, he got the lead cruiser to pull onto the soft shoulder. There, he presented the bewildered astronaut an oak plaque proclaiming Harry L. Baker an

HONORARY CITIZEN OF ATKINSON, VERMONT
HOME OF THE GREEN MOUNTAIN BOYS
AND FREE MEN EVERYWHERE.
Compliments of
HENLEY'S SPORTING GOODS CO.
MARQUETTE J. HENLEY, PROP.

Lance looked on expressionlessly from the car. When Marquette called him to join them in the picture, Lance shook his head. Then the astronaut gestured for him to come, but Lance looked away.

"He's shy," Marquette said.

"Here," Baker said, scribbling his name on the back of an envelope. "For his scrapbook."

"Most boys would give their right arm for a chance just like that," Marquette complained to Edna that night. "And he just sat there like a lump of cold lard, like a rock!"

Edna had been listening with the intense, quizzical scrutiny that had always puzzled him. "Maybe he was afraid," she said in her slow, thoughtful way.

"He's never afraid. He's never anything," Marquette said.

Edna thought about this a moment. "Maybe he just doesn't like space."

"Maybe he just doesn't like anything," Marquette said. "Including me," he added, and he could tell by the way she blinked and stared past him that she was considering this as a real possibility.

. . .

The blurry, poster-sized picture taken that day of Marquette and astronaut Baker still hangs in the store's front window. It has been the incongruous backdrop for ten seasons of ice skates, and Little League trophies, and ski parkas, and rubber hip waders. It is faded now and sagging and the edges are curled and brittle. But Marquette cannot bring himself to remove it. That picture is as much a part of his store as it is of his life. If the occasion did not impress Lance, the picture has left its mark in the minds of a whole generation of Atkinson's little boys. Even now, ten years later, they still come in to ask about Baker.

"He's a real pioneer," Marquette tells this one, leaning over the glass case of hunting knives and starter pistols. "When nobody knew what was up there, when nobody really knew, Harry L. Baker made it his business to find out," Marquette says with a wink and a nod. "There aren't many men like that left, son."

"He ever show you any stuff?" the boy asks. "Like moon rocks or space food or stuff like that?" His eyes burn eagerly.

"I've seen it all," Marquette says. "All that and more."

"He ever give you anything?" the boy asks.

"Well, this is all I got on me right now," Marquette says, pulling from his wallet a frayed, folded envelope. Carefully, he opens the soft worn squares and holds it out.

" 'Good luck,' " the boy reads. " 'And best wishes, Harry L. Baker.' " He looks up expectantly. "Is this all you got?"

The boy's hair smells sweet, of sweat and soap. Marquette feels perilously lightheaded and dizzy with the sudden closeness of another human being. It has been years since he has been this near anyone.

"Don't!" the boy is saying. His sharp elbows strike Marquette's soft belly. "Cut it out!" he cries.

For an odd, giddy moment, Marquette wonders why he is here in the midst of these strange shapes and colors. The circular rack of red hunting jackets spins round and round, and overhead, the yellow rubber raft sways back and forth on invisible wires. The knife blades glint. The boy is gone. The store is empty. Marquette begins to dust the tackle boxes with the sleeve of his flannel shirt. He rubs and rubs, and his cuff button clicking against the metal tops is the only sound in the store.

That night the boy's father comes to the house.

"Sometimes kids get things confused," he says. His hands are jammed into his pockets, his shoulders shrug self-consciously. "They think you...they think something's wrong that's just...well..." He stretches his neck and grimaces. "How can I say this?"

Over his shoulder, Marquette sees the wife staring at them from the car. Her grim white face curdles with anger.

"...as good a man as you," the man is saying. "But my boy was kind of upset and then the wife got all shook, so I figured I just better come by and see what's what. You know what I mean?" the man asks.

"No," Marquette says firmly, his eyes steady on the man's. "I don't."

The man shifts his weight from foot to foot, then glances back at his car, where his wife's eyes are trained on him like shotgun barrels. The man's face reddens. "Did you hug my boy today? Did you do that, Mr. Henley?"

"Of course not," Marquette says.

"I didn't think so," the man says with an anxious backward shuffle.

Edna was a private woman. Stout and given to fits of nervous giggling and blushing when in the limelight, she welcomed the anonymity of her tiny husband's long shadow. The father of Edna's son had been a welder for the railroad. The first time Edna ever saw him, it was his welding mask and thick asbestos mitts and the mantle of orangey red sparks about his wide shoulders that set her heart afire. His name was Cobbie something. Or something Cobbie. Either *ie* or *y,* she would never be sure. But for her infant son's sake, she would christen him Lance Cobbie. For the first five years of the boy's life, right up to the time she married Marquette, she made monthly trips to Burlington, New York City, Hartford, Boston, Portland, all under the pretext of visiting the boy's father.

These trips ceased when the boy told a neighbor how much he dreaded those long weekends in dreary hotel rooms, the only respite being the walks back and forth to the local train yards, where Edna and Lance would stand on one or another of the huge garaging platforms and watch the trains being repaired. Like great hungry beacons, Edna's small bright eyes would search for Cobbie. With their masks on, all the welders looked alike. Even so, it was a futile mission, because Edna could never be sure exactly for whom she looked.

Her brief relationship with Cobbie had been on a moonlit park bench and, later, that same fateful night, in the garage, in the whispery back-seat shadows of her father's DeSoto.

For the next nine months, whenever Edna tried to picture what the baby would look like, all that came to mind was the crown of a dark bristly head above a welder's fiercely square and pitted mask. It was a strange relief to see the infant's pale hair and squalling red face, looking so wonderfully human and yet completely unlike any other face Edna had ever known.

Of course, Marquette knew nothing of Edna's secret. He knew as much of Edna's past as did anyone in town; of the little known were these fictions and suppositions: that Cobbie was a wanderer or a drinker or both, and that it was to Edna's credit that she had finally come to her senses after the elopement and made the break for the boy's sake.

There had been no elopement, no divorce. And if it hadn't been for Lance, Edna would not have even been certain of Cobbie's existence, so dim has her memory of that night become, so astonished, as the years have passed, is she by her passion.

For the past twenty years, Edna has been a steady, but disappointing, wife. Marquette has no doubt of her love. It is her loyalties that he finds wanting. Whenever he and Lance disagree, Edna, whether by actual assent or just the keen narrow brightening of her eyes, always sides with her son. And yet it bewilders Marquette the way she has always treated Lance, like a guest, like someone she does not yet know well enough to scold or criticize.

Since high school, Lance has worked only once—as a milkman's assistant, a job that lasted five and a half months.

"It wasn't his fault. He just hit the tail end of milk routes," she explains in the dry, somber tones of a sociology professor to whomever is unlucky enough to have inquired. "And then Nixon took such a hard tack on unemployment," she laments, circumferencing Lance's failures with U.S. economic policy. "And the poor boy lost his benefits."

Sometimes, Marquette catches her up short, depending on his own economic condition. Business is way off. Weekdays are dead. Saturday is the one good day left. He blames the discount stores. But what can a small businessman do? And to make matters worse, Flyer's has just come to the mall. Flyer's is a huge discount sporting goods chain from California. They can undersell anyone. All the college football games on TV have Flyer's ads at halftime.

"The poor boy lost his benefits because he wouldn't look for work! Plain and simple," Marquette scoffs, and Edna's bright face shatters inward like a broken headlight.

Somehow, Lance always has money. Marquette suspects that Edna slips it to him when he comes to visit. Lance spends most of his nights in a trailer near the fairgrounds. The trailer belongs to a divorcee named Barb, as do the two children, a boy and a girl Lance often brings to supper after Barb leaves for work. She is a cocktail waitress at the Fairspot.

Tonight, Marquette is trying to read the newspaper. From time to time, he glances at the coffee cup on the wide arm of his easy chair. The little girl's name is Dawn. She toddles from the end table to the television and then drops down on all fours and scurries in a crawl to get to Lance, who sleeps on the couch, facedown, one arm dangling to the floor. She hitches herself up and peers at the crumpled profile that is always too soft, too smooth, boneless, Marquette thinks. Lance's skin is now paler than it has ever been. He reminds Marquette of someone he used to know. Suddenly, he realizes that Lance reminds him of Lance; that if it is possible, Lance has become a ghost of himself, a sourceless shadow.

The little girl's brother is in the kitchen where he waits for Edna to lift him onto the counter top. He likes to sit there and watch her wash dishes. Edna enjoys the children.

They seem afraid of Marquette. He pays them little attention. They make him feel uneasy, soiled somehow. Their trail of crumbs and wet bread crusts and sticky doorknobs remind him of the shallow-chested boys in black shirts. He is as confused as to where these two children fit into his life as he was about those boys.

The little girl is pulling Lance's ear. She wants him to wake up.

"Jesus Christ!" Lance howls, shaking his head so abruptly that she teeters and falls back on her diapered bottom.

"C'mere," Marquette whispers. He moves the cup and saucer and pats the chair arm for her to come. She smiles and the way she comes towards him is frightening. She moves like a crab, determined, yet off-balance, off-center, a fearsome little gust, a blur of hands and feet and bobbing head and eyes that widen eagerly, hungrily.

"Sit down!" he commands, pointing both at her and the floor as she reaches him. She begins to cry then, and Edna, with the little boy on her hip, rushes in from the kitchen. The suddenness of her approach terrifies the child, who begins to wail.

Marquette is startled; his head snaps back, expecting a scolding from Edna. But it is the child over whom she looms. "Sh, sh," she hisses. "Let Lance sleep, now. Sh!"

Marquette has been at the Berwick Hotel for a week. It is almost midnight and he is hungry, but he will not pay the extra charge for room service. For the first week and a half after he left home, he slept in his office at the store. But then the pain began in his chest and shoulders. It radiates down his arms. He feels both weightless and compressed. The whole town knows what has happened and he is ashamed. Most disturbing of all, though, is Edna's reaction; she was surprised, puzzled—at times, almost amused.

In the bluish tint of the television screen, he sits on the bed and holds the remote control straight out in front of himself. Squinting, he pushes the button. He blinks as the channels change and the screen flashes a fireman's head, a blur of racing cars, a can of dog liver, a woman's naked chest...He cocks his head and flicks back just as the woman pulls a sheet up to her chin.

With the remote control still aimed at the set, Marquette waits to see if she will drop the sheet. He has never seen anything like this before. Certainly not on television. He has never seen Edna's breasts, in lamplight or daylight. When the woman does not move, Marquette raises the control and again begins his scan of the channels. He keeps zipping back to the woman with the sheet to her chin, as if he might surprise her, catch her unaware.

The red button on the telephone has been flashing all night. Marquette is not sure what that means. It has been doing it all day long. Marquette has been in bed since last night. Early this morning, he called the store and, pinching his nose, told the bookkeeper that he was too sick to come in.

He pushes the button on the remote control now and nothing happens. The channel stays the same. When he dials the front desk, the clerk is confused by his complaint.

"What's a power source?" the clerk asks.

"For the TV," Marquette almost shrieks. "It's gone! Dead! Kaput!"

The clerk delivers the new remote control himself. Marquette seizes it hungrily through the crack in the doorway.

"Excuse me, Mr. Henley," the clerk says before the door closes. "Your light's blinking, sir." He points and Marquette looks back. "There's a message on the board for you." The clerk reads from an index card. "Please call Mrs. Henley. It is urgent."

Marquette gives him a quarter and closes the door. He turns the power source on the set and eases himself onto the bed with the small plastic box still perfectly aimed.

The trouble began when the police found fifty thousand dollars' worth of cocaine in Lance's bedroom. He was arrested at home. The *Crier* had a front-page shot of Lance, head down and manacled, being led to a waiting cruiser.

Marquette had tried to block the door. But the troopers had a search warrant. While Edna sat in the kitchen, staring numbly at the passing uniforms, Marquette called his lawyer, then Judge Riordan and every other influential person he could think of.

"You're only making it worse," Edna whispered.

He stopped dialing. "I am making it worse? I am trying to do something! You act like it's happening to someone else—like it's none of your business."

A young trooper came into the kitchen then. When he saw Mrs. Henley, he removed his wide-brimmed hat and, as gently as possible, said, "We're having to take a few of the floorboards up, ma'am." He nodded and backed off. "Just so you'd know when the noise—"

"No!" Marquette roared. "You can't do this! I won't allow it!" He picked up a golf club and swung at the young trooper, just missing his chest.

"Put down the club, sir," the trooper said softly.

Marquette blinked. He recognized this young man. Hockey skates and fishing rods. So this was one whose feet he measured year after year, bringing him as surely to manhood as any father.

"Put down the club, sir!" the young trooper ordered, snapping his pistol from its holster.

Still trying to catch the naked woman with her sheet down, Marquette pushes the buttons on the remote control. He searches for her from channel to channel, through the jittery spectrum of images, but she is nowhere to be found. Back again, he goes through a chewing gum ad, *Hawaii Five-O*, a rat being consumed by a wet, writhing snake, an astronaut playing golf on the moon, a false-teeth cleaner, a... Frantically, he clicks back to the astronaut. It is Harry L. Baker in his puffy white spacesuit, teeing up in the barren, dusty center of a moon crater. Baker's long, easy swing makes Marquette smile. Weightlessly, the ball sails into the air, lifting higher and higher into the blackness of space, the small white orb diminishing to a pinprick of light until, like a dying star, it is no more. Now, Harry L. Baker's dimpled, boyish face fills the screen. "Whatever your sporting needs, wherever you are," he grins, holding up a brand-new package of orange golf balls, "there's a Flyer's nearby."

Tears surge in Marquette's eyes. He clutches at the pain in his chest and slides into the slither of sheets. He feels his body enlarging, becoming more than he has ever been; it fills this room, fills all of space.

The dreary courtroom is a blur of rainy windows and the judge's tired voice. Beside Edna, in big white sunglasses and an ill-fitting yellow sundress, is Barb, four months pregnant.

In a way, Edna is relieved that Marquette is not here. Through the years, his constant pursuit of Lance had always alarmed her. Often, when Marquette was lecturing Lance, she would see the boy cringe with such intensity that his eyes would sink deep into his head and his features would begin to dissolve, as if he were turning himself inside out with only the frayed seams showing. It would occur to her at these times that she might lose Lance; that as swiftly and completely as his father had vanished, so could he. When he expressed interest in going to college, she said nothing and was relieved when he changed his mind. When he lost the milk route job, she was again relieved. For too many nights, she had dreamed the same dream. In it, Lance drove the truck delivering milk from house to house along a lengthening street of endless houses. As she watched, he drove and drove, until he was only a speck in the distance, until he was gone forever, like his father, of whom she no longer dreamed, but was certain he mended tracks from coast to coast, from pole to pole, wherever he was needed.

Once on television, she saw the aftermath of a horrible rail disaster in Chile, where a passenger train dangled from the spliced tracks that had once bridged a steep mountain pass. Workmen crawled alongside, attempting to separate the hanging car from the ones still on the track. Among them was a welder. It's him, she almost screamed; him with his fiery cowl and thick, bristled hair and metal face.

When the constables lead Lance into the courtroom, Barb squeezes Edna's hand. "He looks so different," Barb whispers. "Like he's been locked up for years."

He looks back and winks as the constables unlock the manacles on his wrists. The clank of the metal startles Edna. She was remembering the young boy who stood beside her on all those platforms. It had been so noisy; the clanging, banging, coupling of cars. Engines churning, turning full speed; the screeching metal of the brakes; the welder's sparks like fiery rain over all these people, this coughing, shuffling commotion of bodies...

"Is there anything you wish to say?" the judge is asking Lance.

In profile, he is still a stranger to her. Every day of his life, she has watched him, studied him, has even gotten into the habit of coming upon him suddenly as if to disarm him, to discover what he really looked like, who he really was. He has never been a son so much as an ambassador from a strange, exotic land, the emissary of the iron-faced man.

Nothing Lance did ever surprised her. She found him fascinating. As he grew older, she would not punish him for his recklessness. She never lectured him, never nagged or forced him to do a thing he did not want to do. Instead, she observed him as if he were the window through which she might discover the mystery of her dark lover.

When he sang, she heard his father's song, melodious and as deep as dark water. When he broke out in hives, she knew his father was allergic to strawberries. And when a woman as pretty as Barb would love him, she could be flattered that the father had chosen her that night in the park.

"Is there anything you wish to say before sentencing?" the judge repeats.

Barb clenches her hand and presses her shoulder into Edna's. "Dear God," she whispers. Tears run down her cheeks.

Lance has been rubbing his chin, thinking. He lifts his head.

Cool as a cucumber, Edna notes. Even under pressure like this, he is steady and thoughtful and unafraid.

"No, sir," Lance says. "Nothing that would make any difference."

"Three years," the judge says. "Three years in the Windsor House of Correction." He bangs his gavel.

"Three years, it is," Lance says with a shrug. He holds up his hands for the manacles, and as they are snapped shut, Edna marvels at the steely tinges of his flesh without sunlight. It is, she thinks, a priestly pallor.

That very night, she dreams of Lance on his old milk route. The wire case he carries contains no milk, but the diminutive form of a caged man.

A great peace has come over Edna. Every weekend, she and Barb pack a picnic lunch and drive to the state prison to visit Lance.

"Oh!" Barb says, closing her eyes. "It's kicking so hard, my ribs ache."

Edna smiles over the wheel. She passes the road that would take them to the cemetery where Marquette is buried. *On the way back,* she thinks, knowing full well it will be too dark and Barb will be too tired again.

Lovelock

The billboards into Lovelock, Nevada, promised dinner and drink coupons, a roll of quarters, hot showers, cable television, king-sized beds, breakfast coupons, twenty-four-hour free coffee, air conditioning, and a swimming pool, all for only thirty-nine ninety-nine, and Benjamin West, after three nights dozing in rest stops by the side of the interstate, could not help but be swayed. Lovelock came up on the left-hand side in the middle of the Nevada flats, a one-street town with a skyline of gas stations, hotel-motel-casinos, fast-food restaurants, auto dealers, insurance brokers, a combined elementary–junior high–high school, a chamber of commerce. West took the Chevy down Main Street, keeping his eye out for a name that rang true from one of the highway advertisements. The Lickety Split, The Bell Weather, It's Your Night, On the House, Holiday Inn, Motel 6—their signs lighting up in the dusk like struck pinball targets. West pulled into the lot of Lucky Andy's Roadside Hotel-Motel-Casino. That was the one with the five dollars in quarters and twenty dollars' worth of coupons. He parked between a pickup truck with Wyoming plates and a small Winnebago motorhome out of Florida. He had one hundred and eleven dollars left. He got out of the car, slammed the door locked, and crossed the lot through the stolid heat of dusk to the lobby entrance. Through smoked windows, he could see a small casino, with thirty or so one-arm bandits, four card tables, and a horseshoe-shaped bar. In the refrigerated lobby, a slot machine stood to either side of the registration desk. West peeled off two twenty-dollar bills and laid them before a woman with tall blond hair and platinum-painted fingernails. He was too tired to be subtle. "Will that do?" he said.

"Sure will." She smiled at him. "Do you want an upper rack or a lower rack?"

He looked at her in numb confusion.

"First floor or second floor," she said.

"Second."

She gave him a key, a roll of quarters, and a wad of coupons, her fingertips grazing his knuckles. He glanced at her quickly, but she was already occupied with something else.

He walked stiff-legged back out to the car, walked as if he'd been riding a horse for the last four days instead of a car. His right groin muscle ached, so that he almost walked bowlegged. Over the course of the past twenty-seven hundred miles, he had given up trying to get some circulation going throughout his system by stopping every hundred miles, and just drove until he couldn't take the pain and the cramping and the stiffness anymore. When he slept at the rest stops, he slept folded into the front seat, as if afraid that one of the unsavory types who populated these urine-soaked places late at night, all night, would try to steal the car out from under him. He was a tired motherfucker, and he found himself assimilating the personality he projected of every state he passed through. In Iowa, he had been bland and unassuming, slumped low in the car as he drove, like an old man. But by North Platte, Nebraska, where the all-night roar of motorcycles cut into his sleep, he'd begun to swagger and curse, and bought a six-pack for a last two-hour dash down the interstate before sleep overcame him. When he dipped into the tip of Colorado, he felt unaccountably swank, wealthy, a Denver Carrington let loose on Fort Collins, and he tucked in his shirt and nodded gravely at gas station attendants, and touched two fingers to his forehead even though there was no hat there. Now Nevada, where whorehouses and casinos stood as wide-open and brazen as McDonald's and Motel 6. West was ready for it.

He sauntered over to the car, recognizing his own ridiculousness and enjoying his ability to recognize it, reveling in the no small accomplishment of traversing the bulk of the country without a driver's license. From the trunk within the trunk of the Malibu, he pulled out clean underwear, fresh jeans, and a white T-shirt, and hobbled up the fire escape–style stairway to his second-floor room.

In the airless mush of humidity and disinfectant, he undressed and got in the shower. Almost four days without a shower, and he was so ripe with the odor that it seemed to coat him like a second skin, the smell of Iowa corn and pigsties, Nebraska wheat and truck exhaust, Wyoming slag, Utah salt. When he'd driven past the Great Salt Lake, he'd pulled over and gotten out and taken a few steps across to the hills shimmering like quartz in the heat. He felt as if he were walking on the moon, the thick bed of shifting, sucking salt suspending rules of gravity and air. He could barely breathe. He got back in the car and gingerly drove through Utah, the road lined with scallops of tires burst open and shredded by heat and traffic.

Now, in the shower, he held his mouth up to the gush of water and rinsed his teeth first, the four-day grit of fast-food hamburgers and funny sandwiches snatched from the glass refrigerators of gas station convenience stores, the thick, sugary film of two dozen caffeine soft drinks, the occasional chocolate bar for energy and digestion, the odd six-pack of beer drunk on the sly over the last bit of midnight road before fatigue closed in and shut him down at a desolate roadstop in Iowa City, Ogallala, Rock Springs. He enjoyed the taste of the water, its chemical pureness of chlorine and fluoride and Nevada minerals, as if it were actually all chemical and not water at all, but some post-nuclear solution that could cleanse you in and out, above and beyond. He drenched his hair with it, then diligently applied soap to his crotch, lathering the testicles, drowning the pubic hair with foam. He ran the soap down each leg, picked up one foot at a time and worked a coat of white between each toe, soaped up his chest and back, then began in earnest on his underarms. It took a long time to take the smell away, and even then he knew that it would come back. Over drinks later, he would begin to smell it working its way from his pores. His smell, which was now the smell of the country and the car and the interstate and a conglomeration of rest stops.

He changed into the fresh set of clothes and descended the metal staircase, each step pinging under his tired weight, to the parking lot. The place was packed with RVs, station wagons, convertibles, minivans, four-door sedans, two-door economy cars. It was America on vacation, caught in the only town for two hundred miles, the oasis of Lovelock. He passed the outside of the casino again, not at all curious. West had been eighteen when Atlantic City had opened up its massive hotels to gambling, and at first he'd been hooked, driving out every weekend during his senior year in high school with slick-talking friends who convinced him that he only had to *know* he could win, and then he *would* win. After five hundred dollars over a month and a half of weekends, he recognized the myth of it. Now he fingered the roll of quarters in his pocket and counted up how many drinks it would buy.

The restaurant was on the far side of the lobby, a curtain-draped wood-paneled spectacle done up like a Spanish galleon, with waitresses and waiters swashbuckling along in sashes and eye patches and mock swords strapped to their thighs. According to his coupons, he could have the fifteen-dollar salmon steak for five dollars, or the twelve-dollar T-bone for seven. Obviously the T-bone was fresh and the salmon was not. West stood patiently at the entrance, waiting for one of the pirates to seat him. He shivered in the cold of the arctic air conditioning and wished he'd brought his jeans jacket with him.

One of the pirate waitresses finally beckoned, and he walked his athletic, groin-pulled walk to a little two-person booth with a table the size of two plates. He sat and smiled gratefully at the waitress. The seat backs were so high he could see nobody, and he was spared the embarrassment of others observing his solitary eating. He waved off the offer of the menu.

"I'll have the T-bone and a pitcher of Bud," he said, showing his coupons.

She nodded and left to fill his order.

Above the booth backs and all around him swirled the idle but passionate chatter of families and couples eating and drinking after a day of driving across desert and plain. West patted down his damp hair and leaned back in the booth. He wondered if he was allowed to fall asleep. Automatically his legs pumped for the brake, the gas, and he shot awake, his eyes swimming with images of late-night driving, when cars appeared to miraculously jump guardrails and swerve in his path and animals created by headlights and road reflectors and angles of perception crouched in the middle of the lane. Only five hundred miles farther and he'd reach San Francisco. He rubbed his eyes and waited for his dinner.

When it came, he ate slowly. The steak was charred on the outside, rare at each cut. The baked potato looked like and was as hard as an egg laid by some prehistoric bird. He dabbled with the iceberg lettuce, Pollock-dripping an array of dressings but unable to get it to taste like anything. He drank. The meal would be twelve dollars plus tax and tip. He would have fifty-nine dollars left. The drama of money. He would need two full tanks of gas—twenty-eight dollars—and a ten-dollar reserve for tolls. That left about fifteen dollars to have a few drinks at the casino bar, to the accompaniment of the clatter and jangle of the one-arm bandits and the clacking of the roulette wheel. He made himself finish the meal.

He was tired and a little woozy, but this was Nevada and he had to drink. He crossed through the lobby to the casino. He sat at the horseshoe-shaped bar and ordered a bourbon on the rocks. An inlaid video poker game stared up at him from the bar. EASY MONEY! EASY MONEY! He moved down a seat to be away from it. At the slot machines, fifty- and sixty-year-old ladies in blue jeans and neckerchiefs loaded coins in, five at a time, accompanied by the whoops of yet older men in cowboy hats and Levi's. Everybody was from someplace else.

He sipped at his drink. Two seventy-five. He had to go slow. His clean clothes made him sleepy. Twenty-seven hundred miles and he was not even there yet. He just wanted to be there. When he'd finally gotten hold of Bob Fields, he'd felt reassured. "You just take as much time as you need," Bob had said. "The job's waiting for you, it isn't going anywhere. Seven days, eight days. I'd say nine maximum. Can you make it in nine?" West had counted his money. "Would it be a problem if I got there a little ahead of schedule?" "No problem at all," Bob said. "We're on a day-to-day contract with the security company. But nine days maximum. Okay?" The guy was utterly reasonable. He had not even tried to hide his breathing on the phone—a low rattle that occasionally rose to a wheezing. West trusted him instantly.

The job paid room, board, and benefits, plus five hundred dollars a month—a pretty good deal, West thought. It would give him a chance to put some distance between himself and prison, and he could figure out what the next step was. He held up his empty glass and waited to catch the bartender's eye. After a pitcher of beer and a shot of bourbon, he was not really so drunk as he thought he should be. Perhaps Lucky Andy's watered their drinks. What had intoxicated West most about the Atlantic City casinos was that, when he was gambling, they gave him drinks *free*. But that had not helped him in the quixotic struggle to convince himself that he *knew* he would win. Now he was convinced that he had lost five hundred dollars not because the theory was wrong, but because he had failed, ultimately, in *knowing* he would win. He looked at the video poker game and reached into his pocket for the quarters.

"Hey, buddy."

The damn thing apparently talked. He glared at it.

"Hey, buddy. Over here." Someone was knocking on his shoulder as if it were a door. "On your right."

West swirled the bar stool around. His interlocutor, his rescuer, was a man of thirty-odd years and six and a half feet, a white cowboy hat cocked on his head like a second grin, a strong jaw, five o'clock face. An open-lipped toothy smile, waiting for the go-ahead to continue talking. West was delighted to discover that he was drunk, after all, and at the back of his mind he was frightened by it, too, he could feel it coming on like a train through a tunnel, and he was trapped by it. There would be nothing he could do but get up after it had run him over. He wondered if he would have to throw up.

"What," he said uneasily.

The smile drew shut in a line of gratitude, at having been recognized by the chair. The chair nodded for him to go on.

"I've got my hands full, buddy, if you know what I mean," the smile said. "Two ladies." The hat wagged in a direction West could not follow. "I was wondering if you might help me out." He clapped West familiarly on the shoulder. "How about it?"

West looked at him, trying to discern the motivation for such a gift. It was some kind of scam, belied by the easy smile, the white teeth, the open face.

"What the hell," West said. He slouched off the bar stool. "Where are they?"

The smile steered him around the curve of the bar. "Name's

Jack," he said.

"Scott," West lied. It was his favorite of fake names.

"Well, Scott, by the end of the night you'll be thanking me. I just know it."

They pulled up at the far end of the bar, underneath a cold shaft of air conditioning, where two women in their twenties sat stirring their drinks. One of the women looked up. She had long dirty-blond hair waved around a thin face. A smirk spread, which she did not attempt to hide. West had to admit that she was beautiful. "You found somebody," she said.

"This is Scott," Jack said.

"I'm Lisa." The woman frowned at West and gave a sideways nod of her head. "This is my sister, Ana. Don't fuck with her."

Ana looked up at West frankly, with uncautious eyes. Her short brown hair was parted incidentally in the middle, and faint freckles rose with a blush in her face. "Be nice," she said to Lisa. She took West's hand and shook it. Her wrist seemed as thin as his thumb. "I'm pleased to meet you," she said.

"He's a jerk," Lisa said. She jabbed West in the shoulder with her index finger. "I'll repeat myself. Don't fuck with her."

"I'm out of here," West said. He turned to go. Somebody caught his arm and he assumed it was Jack, but when he looked down, it was Ana.

Jack laughed. "Okay, babe. I did my end." He offered the crook of his elbow to Lisa, and she took it and rose off the stool. She was wearing a tank top and very tight jeans, and she undulated in such a way that West instinctively checked to see if his mouth was open.

"You two be good." She smiled fakely at both of them, while Jack began to lead her away. "Honestly," she said. "I don't care what you do."

West watched them go, two tapered backs. Ana still held on to him, and he could not bring himself to move. He shut his eyes and then opened them, expecting to find himself staring down at the video poker game. She let go and patted the empty seat beside her.

"Join me," she said.

Obediently he sat on the stool.

She touched his hair lightly. "I like your hair," she said. "It's clean." He tensed, liking her touch, wanting her to go further. She selected a lock and stretched it unpainfully between two fingers. "Don't you worry about Lisa. She's my younger sister but I frustrate her terribly." She said it in an even way, without irony.

"The way she was"—West felt for each word—"I thought she was older."

"It's because I'm a little slow," Ana said. She let go of the hair and turned his head to face her. "Retarded. Would you mind kissing a retarded girl?"

"No," West said. It was a weird joke, but he'd play along. "I wouldn't."

She pulled his head to her and kissed him, long and tight-lipped, as if she had learned by watching television, her face moving instead of her mouth. It was still a nice kiss. He drew back.

"Did you like it?" she said. Her finger traced his face.

"Sure." West glanced around the casino to see if anyone had noticed. They hadn't. He rubbed the back of his neck. He liked her bangs and how small her nose was. He felt as if the back of his head had been shot off and all the air was rushing in. He reached for the back of his head. It was still there. He wondered if this were the train of his drunk finally coming, to knock him out.

"Can I buy you a drink?" she said. "I have ten dollars." She took out a purse from a little red pocketbook and showed him the money. She handed him a personal identification card that said TENNESSEE in a hologram across her face. She pointed at the birthdate. "I'm twenty-five," she said. "See." Effortlessly she flagged down the bartender. "What are you drinking?"

West shook his head and swallowed to see how close the drink was to overpowering him. It was not close enough. "Bourbon," he said hoarsely.

"Bourbon," she said. The bartender nodded and went off to make the drink. "Bourbon," she said again, drawing out the *r*, tasting the *n* on the roof of her mouth. He could see her that clearly. "What's it like?"

He'd never thought much about it. "It's like," he began. He swallowed. Soon the alcohol would overwhelm him, and he'd be saved. "It's like water mixed with the skin of red apples. Like the very sweet bitterness of apple skin."

"It doesn't sound very good," she said.

"It isn't," he agreed. But it was sure as hell going to stop him, which was lucky.

The bartender returned with the drink. It was straight up, no ice. West nodded at Ana and forced a sip. He hated warm bourbon. He made himself take a gulp. Bile rose halfway up his throat and he was pleased. "Thank you," he said.

"Do you have a room here?" Ana said. She touched his hair again and he froze. "Jack has a room. Lisa and I share a room. I think I'd like to see your room." Her hand fell lightly to the back of his neck, and she squeezed it tenderly between her thumb and index finger. He shivered. He looked at her. The air conditioning fluttered her bangs. She took in his look with what appeared to be mild interest. "Are you ready?"

She was behind the curve but she was not that far behind. But she was far enough behind as to be behind the curve. She was capable of complex thought the way a twelve-year-old was capable of complex thought—serendipitously. It was a long word and he took a dip with it into the bourbon. He wished he did not have a room. He wished he were back at his old seat at the other end of the horseshoe. He wished—almost—that he were back in prison.

"How, exactly," he said. "How exactly did we get into this?" He leaned his head into his hands, her fingers falling down his back, and shut his eyes, saw explosions of light, and opened them again.

"I think you're nice," she said.

"Oh, I'm nice." He sighed. "I'm very nice." He drained his drink. He could feel his train of drunkenness coming through and it was not going to knock him down, it was going to take him with it. He reared off the stool. "Let's go."

She stood, reached for his hand, and caught it. They walked out of the casino, hand in hand, she holding on tight enough so that he knew not to break loose, but loose enough to seem as if she understood he would not think of leaving her. The bright light of the lobby hit him suddenly, and he reeled at it. She guided them to the door and opened it for them, still holding on to his hand.

They were outside, in the night. He hoped the air would help, but it was flat, dry desert air, ineffectual. She led him toward the parking lot, to where the cars sat caged in their heat and grease.

"Where's your car?" she said.

"Don't know." He could see it quite easily, the black vinyl hood, the wide brown body. The Pennsylvania license plate peeking out between the Winnebago and the pickup.

"Ours is over there."

He looked at her arm as she pointed, the way it extended out of her short-sleeved dress in a stunning, naked pureness, the subtle looseness of flesh around the upper arm, the taut forearm with a hint of muscle, the impossible narrow wrist, the fingers long and slender. He wanted to eat them. Their car was a four-door, dull silver Toyota that looked almost blue in the sparsely lighted parking lot.

"We're going to visit our aunt and uncle in San Diego," she said. "Where are you going?"

"Los Angeles," West said.

"Maybe I could see you on our way back. That would be in two weeks." She pressed his hand.

"Sure." He touched her arm, followed it up toward the shoulder, just to see if he could. He certainly could. His fingertips felt for the sleeve opening and he was in and feeling the very light titillating growth of hair at her underarm. And then past and lightly pressing the swell of her breast, touching it at the very base of the bra before the nylon consumed it, measuring its potential size. Already he was hard. He wanted to bring around her hand that so persistently was locked in his and make her touch it. He was aghast to discover that that was just what he was doing.

"Not in the parking lot," she said.

They led each other through the rows of cars and vans and pickups and campers to the metal staircase.

"The second rack," she said.

Up the stairs, the loud pinging like coins dropping down a well, and along the thinly carpeted porch of a hallway to his room. He fought with the key for a moment, wanting it to take long enough to allow her to escape. Instead, she moved out of his light, to give him a better chance to open the door. She strode in without invitation, and he followed, turning on the light and at first hesitating but then shutting the door firmly and flicking on the air conditioning.

"It's just like ours," she said. "I knew it would be."

He started for the television, to get some more noise in the room, but she intercepted him. She caught him and hugged him tightly, her cheek against his, as if they were saying goodbye. He looked forlornly beyond her to the television, which he now realized he had considered his last hope. Against his chest, her breasts seemed to be throbbing, demanding his attention.

The buttons down the back of her dress came easily to him, and he unhooked each of the four discs while her hands slipped down to his buttocks and pressed and then got a grip and squeezed, each hand to its own buttock. Her dress fell from her shoulders to her forearms. In the honeycomb of light—for the overhead lamp had a straw basket shade that released thin sheaves of illumination—he saw the creamy part of her neck, the soft cups of her bra. Without waiting for her to step from her dress, he unhooked the bra. She was undressed in such a way that it looked as if perhaps she were trying to dress. He hesitated, and she came out of her pumps and her dress and her bra all at once.

He fell onto the bed with her and bucked against her, squirming to kick out of his sneakers and jeans and trying to get her panties down her legs. She sighed. He could not tell whether it was a sigh of resignation or enjoyment, and again he stopped. It struck him, taking her in—the incautious eyes, the incidental part in her bangs, the minute nose dotted minutely with freckles, the calm breasts with the inerect nipples—it struck him that it was a sigh of indifference. The bourbon rose in his throat and he shut it down, willed it back to a place he had yet to discover. He was atop her.

"What's that?" she said.

She was fingering a pimple on his right buttock.

"It's a pimple," he said. "I've got a pimple there." He forced his tongue inside her mouth.

"Oh," she said around it. "A pimple." She giggled, it was another word whose sound she seemed to like.

He slid his hand along the inside of her thigh, and at the same time moved her under him so soon her free hand would be where he wanted it to be. He felt the hair between her legs and then probed inside. She was a little wet, not quite wet enough. He was terribly hard. She grazed him, then gripped him. He massaged her wetness.

"I have to ask you something," she said. She was slightly out of breath, holding onto him. "Should you be doing this?"

"Yes." From his perspective, it was just too late, the train had come through and he was on it and he just had to ride it. He just had to follow this through. He pulled against her grip, trying to get loose.

"It's a strange hotel," she said, her face turned to the side so that she appeared to be examining the loud air conditioner and the green curtains that quivered against it.

"You're not kidding." He was finally where he wanted to be. He started.

"You sure you should be doing this?" she asked again.

"Yes." Now retreat was impossible. He had no choice.

"How does it feel?"

He didn't answer her, he kept at it. She clung to him.

"Do you like it?" she asked.

"Yes." He did.

She squirmed. "I think we should stop."

"Soon."

"Are we going to stop?"

"Yes."

She touched his face. "When are we going to stop?"

"Soon." If she would just be quiet, he was almost ready.

"I don't like it."

"I know." He stopped. Through the sheaves of light he could see her eyes, wide open and indifferent. She had certainly had experience in masturbation, but it had not prepared her to understand. He was sure she would be all right. He pulled out.

"Los Angeles," she said.

He came against the bedspread, unable and unwilling to rein it in. It seemed to him that he came for a long time, but he could not be sure. He tried to hide it from her. She was already pulling on her panties.

"Can I use your bathroom?"

He clutched a swath of bedspread around him, began to dry

himself off while he still came. "Of course," he managed.

She moved to the bathroom, picking up pieces of clothing as she went. She shut the door behind her, then laughed, and opened it. He turned his back to the sound of her, felt the light of the bathroom on his shoulders. She hummed and made water at the same time, like a song with instrumentals. He finished drying himself off and began to get into his clothes. She got off the toilet and flushed and washed her hands in the sink. She was fully dressed and he was trying to shimmy into his jeans.

"We leave at seven tomorrow for our aunt and uncle's," she said, touching his back with her clean hand. "Will you come see us off?"

"Sure." He finally had his jeans on. Where was his shirt? Frantically he scanned the room.

"I have to go."

He nodded his agreement. He spied the shirt under the corner of the bed and bent to pick it up. Behind him, she started for the door.

"Won't you kiss me good night?" she said.

Relieved, he stood. They kissed each other on the cheek. She opened the door and was through and shut it quickly behind her. He listened. She did not walk immediately away. She stood at the door and called in, softly, "Don't forget tomorrow morning. Seven a.m." He nodded at the door, even though he couldn't see her, even though he had no intention of making the engagement. Finally, he heard her leave.

He went to the sink in the bathroom and splashed water on his face. In the yellow light, his hands looked green. He felt a little green. He located the toilet, lifted the seat, got down on his knees, and stuck his finger down his throat to help things along. He gagged around his finger. At last, it came, so much liquid, as if he'd not eaten anything in a long time. He let it come, he tried to encourage it to come, he tried to be patient. Sweat broke out on his back. His throat was raw. He stood, went back to the sink, and drank tap water from the cup of his palm. He put his mouth to the tap, rinsed. He considered taking another shower, but concluded he could not spare the time.

He took a last look around the room, gathered up his dirty

clothes, and shut off all the lights. He stood at the door. It was past midnight. He opened the door and slipped through and shut it softly. Lightly he made his way down the metal stairs to the parking lot, the steps almost silent, making only the faintest jangle.

He navigated the rows of vehicles to his car. He unlocked the door, got in, shut the door, and started the engine. He waited a few seconds to make sure it was ready, then backed out of the space and crept to the exit. Only after he had turned right out of the lot and was on Main Street did he switch on his headlights. The road was lined with twenty-four-hour convenience stores, and he was terribly thirsty. Straight ahead and beyond the town, in the blackness of the flats, was the interstate, occasional lights of solitary traffic scudding across the overpass. He did not think he could afford to stop. In his mouth was the taste of tap water and vomit. The still-sunbaked car smelled of it and of his new sweat and of the old sweat that he'd been unable to air out. Once he got on the interstate, he would allow himself to roll down the windows. He would stick his head out the window as he drove, taking in the air like a dog. He laughed at the comparison—it was appropriate.

Now he was up on the interstate, over Lovelock and past it. He could not quite risk rolling down the windows yet. He was terribly paranoid. He deserved paranoia. Almost suffocating with the smell of himself, he drove through the flats.

At three a.m., West pulled into a gas station on the outskirts of Reno, Nevada, with nothing more on his mind than filling up the tank, picking up a couple cans of soda, and getting the hell out of Nevada. By his calculations, it was quite possible to arrive and be already settled in San Francisco before the Tennessee sisters even woke in Lovelock.

West climbed from the car and stretched. His legs and arms felt numb and shaky from lack of sleep and a hangover of indeterminate magnitude. The air smelled of gasoline and money, the dry, papery, handworn, printed odor of stacks of bills lying on a counter somewhere up the boulevard, where in the distance the city glowed like a red hole sunk in the middle of the desert.

West limped his way over to the glassed-in window where an attendant sat hunkered down under a green baseball cap and a rack of cigarettes that appeared to extend from his head all the way up into the ceiling.

"You can't come in," he said via a microphone to a speaker that came out above West's left ear.

"I know it." West took out a twenty and laid it in the projected pocket pushing out from the window. "Can you give me a tank of unleaded and a couple of Cokes?"

The attendant slid the pocket back inside the window, took out the bill, held it up to the light, and sighed. "I'll push in your gas order now, but fetching the drinks will take a few." He pointed behind him at the brightly colored mini-mart that lined the walls—green and orange and red bags of assorted potato chips, pretzels, cookies; a row of glass refrigerators stocked with beer, soda, and fruit drinks; two stunted aisles piled with toilet paper, detergent, dog food. The attendant punched in the unlimited dollar amount for West's pump, and stood up. He nodded down at his hands. They were clutching a walker. He began to maneuver his way out from the cashier's post like a car doing a three-point turn.

"No hurry," West said. He wiped his mouth with his hand and came away with crushed flecks of dead skin. His voice sounded like a rasp. He went back to the car and started pumping.

Across the boulevard was a huddled, shady outline of a trailer park. His hand felt hot and oily around the handle of the pump, and it kept slipping. He had to concentrate to keep the mechanism pressed in, and even then it slipped. He tried to relax. A drop of sweat worked its way from his underarm down the side of his chest. With his free hand, he patted his T-shirt to soak up the perspiration. As soon as he had finished, he felt another drop emerge. The boulevard seemed slick beneath the watery street-light. He touched his hand to his forehead and it came back damp. At seventeen-fifty, the gas pump clicked off.

He screwed on the cap to the tank, replaced the nozzle, and was squeezing back into the car when he realized he had forgotten his change and the Cokes. He righted himself and crossed back to the cashier's window.

"I thought I had me some free Cokes." The cashier grinned from under his cap. He couldn't have been older than thirty. "Or a big tip. Whatever." He stuck the Cokes and West's change into a glass box to West's left, and shut the little door. "Now you can open it."

West reached in and got his sodas and money. He considered leaving the eighty cents as a tip, but decided that would be both weak and self-serving. He clenched the two Cokes in the fist of one hand and returned to the car.

He sat in the Chevy, staring out the smeared windshield. In the hotel room at Lucky Andy's, thin sheaves of light had illuminated aspects of Ana's body, her small breasts, the creamy part of her neck. He'd tasted her nipples, a salty sweetness. He started the car and drove out from the pump. At the end of the gas station, he looked right, studying the boulevard into Reno. The cars on the road appeared to be from a different era, wide bodies with tail fins and brake lights that slanted like eyebrows. He turned left. Within half a block, the interstate arrived, a minor conflagration of on-ramps and overpasses. He stretched against the seat, only to discover that a pool of almost gelatinous sweat had formed at the small of his back. He wiped his mouth, and then cracked open one of the Cokes. Without further consideration, he guided the Chevy up the on-ramp heading east, heading back toward Lovelock.

On his way across the desert, he searched the landscape for signs that he had not been this way before, that he'd only imagined it. The moon lit the bed of rock and sand into shades of blue, and the night sky met the land with walls of depthless black. He couldn't tell anymore what had happened, what she'd said, what he'd said. What they'd done. He took a long swallow of Coke and waited. He could feel it coming. He pulled over onto the shoulder of the road and quickly got out of the car. He walked around the back of it, and descended a soft slope into the flats. The ground was hard under his feet. The crumbles of land that had broken loose felt like marbles against the thin soles of his sneakers. Rocks jutted out across the desert, their points glinting like wrecks in a sea. He could still feel it coming. It bent him at the waist, and the seat of his jeans was suddenly damp with his sweat. He vomited.

Was it what he had done, or what he had drunk? His eyes filled with tears from the effort and pain of puking. Around him, he could feel the dry earth soaking him up. He was careful not to fall. When he had finished, he tiptoed out of the semicircle of it, walked a good distance away, and peed.

Afterward, he climbed the soft slope to the road and walked out onto the middle of the pavement. He could still feel the heat of the sun rising from it. Above and around him, the night was turning, fading, draining into day. Blue crept into the sky. He would still reach San Francisco by the end of this one, provided the sister didn't have him arrested. She did not seem the type. She would dismiss him instead. He could live with that. He did not mind being dismissed. In the distance, he heard something coming, and he turned and saw, about a mile back down the interstate, a truck making its way toward him, the lights atop its cab standing out like a hairline. The truck honked two times, as if it could see him. He crossed back to the side of the road and got into his Chevy. What was left of the first Coke had spilled over onto the floormat, and the car smelled of sugar and caffeine. In a day, he would sell it. He cracked the second can of Coke and took a sip. He swished it around in his mouth like mouthwash, and spit it out the open window. He tried another sip. It tasted better. Up ahead, the truck was still coming, lumbering across the flats toward him. He started the Chevy. He would miss it, when he sold it, but he'd be relieved as well. It was a damned good car.

It moved weightily over the road, through the flats, as if it knew it had been this way before and resented having to repeat it. He laughed and gulped at the Coke. The truck came up from the other direction and shot past him in a clatter of wind and metal and tire flaps. He finished his Coke and tried to lick the film of it from his teeth. Clouds approached in the gradual blueing of dawn. He would arrive in Lovelock on time. A paper bag caromed across the flats. From a great distance, he spied another oncoming truck. It was just him and the truck and the paper bag. He wondered what he would say to her, if her sister knew, what either of them would say to him. He wondered why he was doing this to himself. To leave nothing undone, nothing to chance. To save himself from his conscience. To extend a trip that was bound to end in the hollow disappointment of a crummy job. To stall the onset of the rest of his life. But California, he was going to California! That was *someplace,* by God. He tried the radio. Nothing, not even static. Sparks ought to have had a radio station, but he was too far past it, closing in on Lovelock. The sky around him filled with the flat whiteness of heat and haze. He had somehow missed the actual sunrise, and now the sun had slipped out of view. It was already above the car somewhere. He could feel it through the vinyl roof, but it wasn't even six yet. Yes, it was. It was exactly six. Lovelock in thirty miles. He ought to slow down. He didn't want to get there early, just in case what awaited him proved unpleasant or unfair. He ought to be stretching this out, the passing rockscape, the dry, cracked barrenness, the hot wind coming into the car. This feat of motion. He turned the steering wheel slightly, to see if the car would obey it. He drifted into the right lane, then back to the left and over toward the double yellow line. He could still do whatever he wanted. It was almost mid-June, the steady, relentless, ripening, approaching summer, the sweat of the car mixing with the sweat of the road. Soon he would be in San Francisco, with a job, an apartment, resigning himself to routine, a city, the deadening haul of daily work. He jiggled the steering wheel again, it was still with him, it made the car respond. He adjusted his rearview mirror to see if anyone was coming. There was no one. When he turned his attention back to the road in front of him, the second truck was upon him. He jerked awake, jerking the car with him to the right, then correcting himself. The truck was already fifty feet past, curving toward Sparks. It had not even been close.

He had not slept since the rest stop in Rock Springs, twenty-four hours ago. It was affecting his driving. He shouldered up over the wheel, willing himself to concentrate. The first billboard approached, a blaze of red and orange rising out of the white rock of the flats. He squinted at it. It was not Lucky Andy's. Lucky Andy's colors, he recalled, were the red and black of the pirate sashes and eye patches and pantaloons, with some gold thrown in for the treasure hunters. He thought of the horseshoe-shaped bar and his stomach seemed to stand up and spin against his skin.

His chest still felt tender from the rawness of the vomiting.

Within ten miles of Lovelock, the car appeared to catch a tail wind that made it go faster than he thought it should. He could feel the wide trunk buffeting in the swirl of air. His hands on the steering wheel were greasy with sweat. He braked just to see if he could. The car slowed, but not as much as he had hoped. The billboards were coming fast and furious, as if they'd been held in check for the last hundred miles and were suddenly let free. They gave the flats color and a skyline. Just as he thought that perhaps Lovelock had passed him by, the road opened to his right and the car skated down the off-ramp and he was calmly turning onto Main Street and facing down its procession of gas stations, hotels, motels, casinos, and convenience stores. It was six-thirty. He pulled into the parking lot of a Denny's and turned off the car and got out and stretched his legs and looked up at the sky and kicked at the loose gravel in the lot, to see if he had changed his mind about this. He went into Denny's and bought an iced tea and drank it standing up in the men's room. He urinated, splashed water on his face, and ran his fingers through his hair like a comb.

Outside, at the car, he hesitated about whether to drive the few blocks to Lucky Andy's or walk. He got in and started the car, pulled from the lot, and drove the three and a half blocks. He parked at the curb, got out, and crossed the street to Lucky Andy's. It was six-fifty. The parking lot of Lucky Andy's was still packed with America on Vacation. He found the four-door Toyota with the Tennessee plates and waited next to it, as if expecting a ride.

Lisa came out first, from a door near the ice machine, shouldering a blue-striped beach bag and lugging a tan suitcase. He resisted the impulse to help her. Her face was flushed by the time she reached the car.

"What do you want?" she said, pushing past him to the trunk of the car and dumping the two pieces of luggage on the asphalt.

"I came to see Ana off," West said.

"Well, how about that." She opened the trunk and began to lever the heavy suitcase in, using her knee and shoulder. "Are you going to help me, or what?"

West pitched in with the suitcase, and it thunked onto the floor of the trunk. The car jounced on its shocks. She threw the shoulder bag in, and looked up at him.

"You look awfully guilty," she said. Her tan line showed at the white straps of her tank top. She was wearing shorts, and her legs stretched out of them like swords. He shrugged. "I don't want to hear about it," she said.

"I slept with her," West said. "Last night. In my room."

"In your room," she said, mouthing the words as if they were part of a foreign language. Evidently, Ana hadn't told her. The heat hurtled at his forehead. He'd been up too long. The parking lot glinted with mica chips and car hoods and radio antennas.

"Scott!" Ana yelled. "Scott." In shorts and a pink button-down shirt, she came loping across the sparkling space toward him. She hugged him, her bare legs against his jeans. Even in daylight, she was still nice, her cream skin, the uncautious eyes. "You came."

"I bet he did," Lisa said. She slammed the trunk shut. "What the hell do you want with us?" She stood up straight. She was still not tall enough. "Too bad Jack isn't here."

"Are you all right?" West said to Ana.

"I'm fine." She nodded vigorously. "I know I wanted you to, even if I didn't like it. It's easier by myself. I guess it's the one thing I can do best by myself. Not like I can't do things by myself. I shop for Lisa, you know. I can count change." She held out her hand to him. "Give me some change and I'll show you. I'll count it."

"Jesus," Lisa said.

West stood wavering beside her. He felt very odd.

"You were inside me," Ana said. "I remember that. I remember how it felt. It felt like nothing new. It felt like I could have had my arm inside me. Well, not that big. It didn't do what I needed it to do. Are you going to give me some change so I can count it?"

"I have to sit down," West said. He sat in the parking lot. The heat sealed his mouth. It was awfully hot. He could feel a sunburn coming on, spreading along the back of his neck. Maybe a stroke. He wouldn't mind a stroke. He could feel the dampness of his jeans wedding itself to the stickiness of the lot. He was going to be stuck there. He looked up at the faces of the sisters, blurred by their height and the haze. They were going to need some sort of forklift to get him up. He looked up at them for a long time, his mouth half-open. Their heads bent to listen. The sun was a shoulder above them. It had popped out of the white sky.

"Get up." He could hear Lisa's voice. She pulled at his elbow. "Come on, up with you."

Gradually, he stood up. The parking lot felt like the deck of a great boat, tilting toward the hotel, the street, the hotel again. He righted himself. Now Ana was holding onto his arm. Morning traffic began to flow past on the street.

"Do you know what you've done," Lisa said. It wasn't a question. West nodded anyway, through the thick heat, his neck a lever for the unwieldy emptiness in his head.

"I'm sorry," he said.

"Sorry doesn't do a whole hell of a lot for her," Lisa said. The sun on her face hid her expression. He listened to her, waiting for what she decided. "You think just by showing up you can somehow save yourself from your conscience." She shook her head, the sun holding her eyes. "A jerk like you." She chewed on her lip. "What if," she said, "what if I just left the two of you together like this in the parking lot, stuck here like two posts in cement. What if I did that? What would you do then, Scott?"

"Are we going to call the police?" Ana said.

Lisa turned back to the car, stepping away from the sun, and hitched up her shorts. West saw her clearly, the thinness, the suppleness. "I never wanted to know," she said. "Let's just get out of here." She walked around and unlocked the driver's door and got in and shut it. She started the car.

Ana still held on to West, silently, without expression.

"Ana," he said. "I'm sorry for what I did."

"I wanted you to." She kissed him as the car exhaust rose around them. "And you're coming to see me off. Don't mind what Lisa says."

"Ana," Lisa called from the car. She wouldn't look at them. "Goddamn it."

"Okay." Ana kissed him again, goodbye. Suddenly, but without any kind of accompaniment, she was crying. He could feel her tears on his face. "It's been a wonderful day."

Lisa leaned over and opened the door for her. Ana backed away from West and stepped into the car. Her foot caught and she fell against the seat, her legs sticking out. She curled them up to her chest, those bare legs, and her sister reached around her and pulled the door shut. She stared at West through the window, Lisa did, as if she had something to say to him but she couldn't remember what it was. It could have been *I'm sorry for you,* it could have been *I hate you,* it could have been *I knew.* Instead, she just shook her head and turned back to face the windshield.

West watched them leave, the car rolling out to the street and then turning right and pulling through Lovelock, the bland faces of the always-open convenience stores, to the interstate, where they climbed through the heat onto the road west, the car a silver blur as it raced away from the town. It was seven-thirty. He would have to drive for four hours through the heat, until he reached the Sierra and the temporary relief of the mountains before the sun-boiled stretch of the California central valley. He crossed the street and got into his car, the vinyl hot through his jeans, sweat seared to him. He watched his foot work the gas, felt his hand pop the emergency brake. The car hummed when he turned the key. He looked out the windshield, particles of air shimmering in waves off the pavement, rippling the storefronts of Main Street, the flats beyond it a colorless smear. He pulled a U-turn and headed out toward the interstate. He got on it gingerly, and kept the car to a moderate speed. He would have to be careful for a long time, so as not to overtake the Toyota from Tennessee.

Nerves

How could a grown man with any self-respect sit in the Ghirardelli Chocolate Factory at eleven o'clock in the morning and eat a hot fudge sundae with mint chip ice cream, hold the nuts? It was Charlie's own question; his answer was that he wasn't a grown man, he was a grown boy, or maybe an ungrown man, pre-grown, never-to-be grown. He was in the process of honing his self-pity into a kind of artifact, an arrowhead he could keep in his pocket, its point ever ready. He spooned pure hot fudge into his mouth and told himself it was Linda's fault he was doing this—if he'd had someone to account to he'd never have indulged himself in this way—but it gave him no satisfaction to blame her. Linda was his wife, and fifteen days earlier, she'd taken a suitcase full of clothes and gone to stay with her friend Cynthia "for a little while," leaving Charlie lower than a dead man, as she would say. Maybe *that* was what had gone wrong: she no longer said things like "lower than a dead man" or "Nice play, Shakespeare." Where was that girl? Not, Charlie felt sure, in San Francisco, this meanly cold, this coldly mean city to which they'd moved five months before, from his beloved New York, at her request. Whereupon she'd left him.

Charlie looked at his watch. It was now twelve minutes past eleven, and although that left him thirty-three minutes to walk the ten blocks to his doctor's appointment, he was stricken by a fear of being late—a lifelong fear, one of his many crippling lifelong fears. He forced down the last of his sundae as quickly as he could and stood up. He put on his jacket, but as he was wrapping his scarf around his neck, he felt a sharp pain scorch the surface of his upper arm, and he groaned and sat down again. He rubbed at the sore spot with his other hand, a futile gesture, he knew: the pain was too fast for him, disappearing so quickly he sometimes wondered whether it existed at all. It was the other pain, the one in his elbow, that he could count on. More of a dull ache, he would say to the doctor, a consistent dull ache. He stood up again, and as he headed out of the Chocolate Factory, he patted his back pocket to make sure his notebook was still there—it contained a list of all the symptoms he'd had, back to the first radiating heat from his armpit to his fingers in June of 1988. A few months ago, Linda had joked that he had a sore arm the way other people had a hobby. Sore? he'd wanted to say. I'm in pain. He knew it was a bad sign that he no longer saw any humor in his situation.

Walking along Beach Street toward the Cannery, he saw a cable car filling with tourists. Last to board was an elderly couple, and Charlie watched as the conductor gently helped them up. The conductor wore a dark uniform and a peaked cap, and for a moment, Charlie thought, What a great job! Then he thought, a conductor? He was regressing—first the sundae and now this. And what do you want to be when you grow up, little boy? Charlie worked thirty hours a week at a frame shop on Chestnut, a few blocks from the apartment, and he liked it—he got a discount on framing materials. Linda said she knew it was a good *job;* she wanted him to have a career, but Charlie put careers in a group with pets and lawns—people were always talking about them and tending to them, but they just weren't that interesting.

In his search to discover what, after all, was wrong with his arm, Charlie had been in many New York waiting rooms during the past couple of years, but this was the first in California, and he didn't know what to make of it: it was empty. He was accustomed to a two-hour waiting-room wait followed by a forty-five-minute examining-room wait, sitting there in a paper nightgown. And the New York doctors, who'd never think to apologize for keeping you—Charlie had liked them: their clean, meaty hands, their arrogance.

A tall, red-haired woman in a white coat opened a door and said Charlie's name. He followed her into the doctor's office, and when she circled the desk, sat down, and said, "So, your arm hurts," he blushed and buried his face in his hands. Dr. *Lee* Price. He'd gotten the name from Linda, who'd gotten it from someone in her office, and he hadn't thought—he just hadn't thought.

"Let me guess," she said. "You thought I was the nurse. You assumed Lee Price would be a man. You feel like an idiot—you're really not like this." She smiled at him. "Does that sum it up?"

"You forgot the part about how I'm much more of a feminist than a lot of women I know."

"So I did," she said. "So I did." She unfolded a pair of glasses and slid them on, and her eyes seemed to open up, a delicate pale green. "It's really Leonora," she said. "Big secret. Now tell me about your arm."

She didn't comment as he talked, but every few minutes she held up a finger for him to pause and scribbled something on an unlined sheet of paper. With her head angled toward the page, he was free to stare at her, and he took in her softly curling auburn hair, her clear, creamy skin, her narrow body. Lovely, he thought, and then, *lovely*? It wasn't in his working vocabulary.

"Any headaches?" she asked, still bent over her notes.

"No more than two or three a day."

She looked up and narrowed her eyes. "And Tylenol does the trick, or no?"

"Tylenol or a nap. I've always had a lot of headaches."

She nodded and wrote something. "Do you sleep well?"

"I was all-state in high school. I only wish it were an Olympic event."

"A wise guy," she said, laughing. "Are you married?"

"I—" he said. "My—" There was an answer to this question—it began "Yes, but..."

"I ask because sometimes people can have small seizures in their sleep without knowing it. If you were married, your wife might have noticed if your sleep were disturbed at all."

"I'm married," he said. "But I'm pretty sure nothing like that's been going on."

"O.K.," she said. "Through that door and I'll take a look."

It was the usual neurological thing: she asked him to turn his neck in every conceivable way; she produced a small hammer and tested his reflexes; she took a set of keys from her pocket and ran them along the soles of his feet. Holding his eyelids open with her fingers, she looked into his eyes with a tiny light. Listen, Charlie wanted to say, I've been through all of this.

"Any weakness?" she asked, pocketing the little flashlight.

"I have a little trouble doing this." Charlie held up his forefinger and with his other hand bent the tip forward. "Bending it at the first joint—not exactly life-threatening."

She held her finger up against his. "Push," she said.

He tried to bend his fingertip onto hers, but nothing happened. "I noticed it on my camera, about six weeks ago. I had to use my middle finger to hit the shutter."

"It's odd, but I don't find anything unusual otherwise. When was your last neck x-ray?"

"About eight months ago." They had found something called "change" in his neck, but evidently it had been a red herring.

"EMG?"

"Excuse me?"

"You've never had an EMG?"

"Not to my knowledge," Charlie said.

"You'd know it. Let's see if we can get you in later this week. You have insurance, right?"

"I'm covered by my wife's group policy at work." In his jacket pocket was a claim form that Linda had messengered to him from the office—better than actually having to see him!

Dr. Price nodded and set down her clipboard. "What does she do, your wife?"

"She's an architect."

"And you stay home with the kids?"

Charlie put a finger to his chest. "The kid," he said.

Charlie had met Linda on the first day of their first year of college. They were at freshman orientation week: their college rented a camp an hour's drive from campus, and you stayed in cabins with triple-level bunk beds and met during the day with upperclassmen to discuss College Life. This was in the Seventies, and everyone wanted to *talk*. On the first night, each freshman was given a partner to interview for ten minutes and then introduce to a group of twenty. Charlie and his partner sat at a picnic table, and she launched into her background with such zeal that Charlie didn't have to ask any questions. He sat there staring at her—this blond-haired, blue-eyed girl from Minnesota, who seemed to have had the kind of childhood his parents referred to as "TV mythology"—and he hoped this initial pairing wasn't going to last the whole week. His older brother had told him that the people you hung around with during your first few weeks at college ended up being your friends, whether you liked them or not. Charlie had visions of himself saddled with this girl for the next four years, and he wanted to lean across the table and say, "Neat is the opposite of messy, damn it!"

The girl was Linda. Later that night, after the awkward introductions (she told the group, "This is Charlie from outside of Boston—he likes to read"), Charlie overheard her telling another girl that he had eyes you could drown in. He liked that, and for months, long after the word "saddled" was the last he'd have chosen to describe his feelings about her, he tried to get her to say it to him—eyes you could drown in. Then he woke up one night late in the spring of their freshman year, and looked at her, and he realized it was he who had fallen into her, so deeply into her that he couldn't feel any boundaries. He was the doubter—he hated himself for it, but he tested her in mean, small ways, flirting with other girls, disappearing into silence for days at a time—but he never found the edge of what he was to her; he was contained by her in a way that frightened and exalted him.

Now, fourteen years later, she was gone, and it wasn't so much that he was angry or depressed or even scared: he was adrift.

During hard times, Charlie found it helpful to formulate a philosophy of life, and the past fifteen days had yielded him a particularly effective one: Bob Dylan. What he perhaps liked best about it was that Dylan had so little appeal to women, meaning Linda. He was an anti–sex symbol, or maybe an anti-*sex* symbol. That beard, she would say, shuddering. *That thumbnail.*

When he got home from Dr. Price's, Charlie put "Tangled Up in Blue" on the stereo, turned the volume high, and lay down on the living-room rug. Dr. Price had prescribed yet another anti-inflammatory drug, and Charlie had taken his dose, along with some codeine, and now waited for the customary queasy grogginess to overcome him. He knew that the new drug would help for a while, but that a few weeks after he stopped it, the pain would balloon into his elbow again. The reason he had waited so long to find a doctor in San Francisco was that he was terrified of becoming addicted. Addicted to Dolobid—not a very hip way to go.

The phone rang, and he turned off the stereo and answered it. It was Linda, her voice, and it made him ache.

"How'd it go?" she said. "What'd he say?"

She, Charlie thought. "I have to go back on Friday morning," he said. "For an EMG."

"A what?"

"Electro-something." He paused; this was sure to displease her. "I'm not exactly sure what it is. I forgot to ask."

"You're so funny," she said stiffly.

"A real laughingstock."

"I'm sorry—I just don't see how you could forget to ask something like that."

"My arm hurt."

Linda was silent, and he tried to think of a way to save the conversation. "Sorry," he said finally. "I'm all drugged up."

"Well, guess what? Kiro asked me to work on the clinic in Walnut Creek."

"Lin," Charlie said, "that's great. We should celebrate. Or you should. Congratulations."

She was silent again, and then she said, in a bright, public voice, "I should get going, but I'll talk to you soon, O.K.?"

"O.K.," Charlie said. "Okey-dokey. Till then."

He said goodbye, hung up the phone, and turned the stereo back on. "Oh, shut up," he said to Dylan, and switched the receiver to the radio. He lay back on the rug. Something baroque was playing, and as the violins climbed higher and higher, winding around each other in ever tighter circles, Charlie thought of a string pulled taut, a single translucent nerve stretched end to end, fingertip to brain.

An EMG, it turned out, was really two tests. But just one low, low Price: she was on the floor searching for a pen she'd just dropped. Charlie was lying on a padded table, his arm on a pillow at his side, looking at the pair of imposing machines that would measure the velocity of his nerves and the electric activity in his muscles. He felt queasy.

Dr. Price stood up and smiled at him. "We'll do the nerve velocity test first," she said. "It may be a little uncomfortable."

"I've heard that line before."

Again she smiled at him. She adjusted the position of his forearm, then carefully taped a wire to it. "Ready?"

"Wait," Charlie said. "Is it a high voltage?" He tried to look as if he were kidding. "Could you accidentally give me too much?" Yuk, yuk.

"Don't be scared," she said. She was so close he could feel her breath on the bare skin of his upper arm. "The strongest shock you could get from this thing wouldn't feel much worse than a sharp kick." She held a two-pronged fork to his neck. "We'll start with the worst so you'll know there's nothing to worry about."

The current slammed into his neck, and then it was over. "That wasn't so bad," Charlie said, laughing a little. "That was nothing."

She made a note, then continued down his arm, shocking him here, then there. The worst of it was how she pulled the hairs on his arm when she lifted the tape off.

"What a guy," she said. "Next time I give a demonstration, can I call you?"

She set the wires and the fork on the table behind her. She held up a thin cord, on the end of which was a sliver of a needle, an inch and a half long. "Some people think this is worse," she said, "but it shouldn't give you any trouble. Ready?"

She slid the needle into a muscle in his forearm, and Charlie felt tears pricking at his eyes. "Ah," he said, and then, because it had sounded embarrassingly sexual, "Ow."

"O.K.," she said, "now make a fist."

Such a small, thin needle for such a great, big pain. Charlie's entire arm hurt, not just where the needle jutted out, but in his hand and wrist, too. She moved the needle around, and he thought he might actually cry. He was aware of a strange crackling sound, like a staticky TV, and he realized it was coming from the monitor.

"There," Dr. Price said, "that wasn't so bad, was it?" She pulled the needle out of his arm, leaving him feeling bruised and exhausted. "Just a few more of these."

Half an hour later, the test over, they sat in her office. Charlie rubbed his hand up and down his arm. He was giddy with relief, eager to be terribly funny or audacious.

He looked at Dr. Price—Lee, Leonora, not such a bad name, really—and he willed himself into a crush on her. That red hair, those green eyes, the fetching white coat: he wanted her, or perhaps he only wanted to want her. Did the fact that it was only eleven o'clock in the morning mean he couldn't suggest they go for a drink? He longed to say, "Let's ditch this hot dog stand"—it was a Linda line, but he felt he could use it with aplomb, without the least pang of sentimentality. They could have a drink and then a quick wedding, two or three red-haired kids, and a ranch-style house in the suburbs to which he would repair each evening, loosening the knot in his tie, eager for the martini she would have waiting for him. He only had joke ties now—a tie that looked like fish scales, a vintage tie a full five inches wide, even a tie made of wood—but he could buy one with little white dots, and he would, he would.

"...very useful," she was saying. "At least we've ruled out any denervation."

"What?" Charlie said.

"You passed the test, Mr. Goldman."

"I did?"

"Don't look so morose. Go, take pictures with your middle finger, be happy."

"But my arm," Charlie said. "My arm hurts."

"Take the Dolobid," she said, standing up. "You said you'd worn a cervical collar for a while—do you still have it?" He nodded. "Wear it for a month or two. Sleep in it." She smiled. "You can call me if the pain gets worse."

Back in his own neighborhood, Charlie wandered toward the frame shop, his arm twinging occasionally in memory of the assault it had suffered, and he decided to ask for the afternoon off. He passed in front of a men's clothing store, and after a moment backtracked and stood looking in its window. Men at Work, it was called—the other kind of work. It was a store Linda liked; when they'd first arrived in San Francisco, they'd gone out walking almost every evening, and she'd steered them into this shop several times: she'd held up combinations of shirts and ties for his appraisal, saying he'd look great in this blue or that brown. Charlie was a jeans man, but he hadn't minded—he'd even tried on the odd suit to please her. He understood it: he liked watching her try on clothes, too. It was a way of interpolating his love for her: Linda in the silk dress, Linda in the leather jacket, Linda in the slender gray suit—he loved them all. He thought of going in and buying a tie to wear as a surprise for her the next time he saw her—not one with little white dots, but one he actually liked—but then he thought that it would be much better to ask her to come with him, to help him choose one. It was really a pretty good idea—maybe he'd even let her talk him into a suit. Was it so hard, after all, to imagine himself dressed in a suit and tie, taking the bus downtown every morning? He could see himself carrying a briefcase, could even picture himself passing through a revolving door and standing at a bank of elevators avoiding eye contact with the other people who were standing there. He could see himself stepping into the elevator, facing the doors, could picture the elevator rising smoothly and speedily to, say, the twenty-third floor—but then what? What did people do in those towers all day long? What was *in* the briefcase—a tuna sandwich and an apple? Charlie couldn't get himself out of the elevator.

At the frame shop, he found Kendra, the nicer of the two owners, in the back room, cutting some mats. Cutting mats—now there was work that made sense. He was almost tempted to work his shift, but not quite.

"Poor you," Kendra said when he'd explained about the EMG. "I don't trust doctors at all anymore. Do you know, my gynecologist told me I should have a hysterectomy just because I'm forty-five and I have a little trouble now and then? 'We'll just take it out,' he said. Can you believe it?"

Charlie shook his head.

"If I were you I would go next door and have a nice cup of herbal tea, and then go for a good long walk. You probably just pulled a muscle! An EKG, for goodness sakes. You can't trust them."

He thanked her and left the shop. EMG, he thought. He raised his arm quickly and the pain drilled at him: still there. It was comforting in a way.

At home, Charlie sat down next to the phone. He missed New York, missed his *friends*—they'd never think to mention herbal tea without irony. And as for a good long walk, if he'd been in New York, he'd have been instructed to get into a cab and go straight home to bed—much sounder advice. He longed to call one of his friends in New York, but whom could he call without having to tell about Linda? Instead, he called his brother's office in Boston.

"Chuck!" Richard's voice boomed through the phone. "What's the good word?"

Was there one? Richard seemed to be in one of his increasingly frequent Hail-Fellow–Well-Met moods. "Nothing," Charlie said. "I was at this doctor's—she gave me this test."

"She?"

"Yeah—red hair, green eyes, white coat."

"Uh-oh," Richard said. "Lust alert."

Who was this person? This was not the kind of thing Charlie needed to hear.

"I take it," Richard said, "that Linda is still among the missing?"

"You take it right."

"She'll be back, kid. She will."

"Yeah," Charlie said. "She just needed some space." She'd actually used that word, which had made the whole thing all the worse. "Space." It wasn't how she talked—wasn't, Charlie told himself, how *they* talked.

"What'd you go to a doctor for, anyway?" Richard said. Charlie could hear him moving papers around. "Your arm?"

"Yeah."

"Hmm. You know, I have a theory about your arm. Would you like to hear it?"

"Not really."

"It's nerves, your arm. Ever think of that? Nerves, pure and simple."

Charlie waited in vain for Richard's dumb pun laugh. "It might be *a* nerve," he said finally. "Like I was trying to tell you, I had this test."

"And it was negative, right? Or positive, or whatever, but it didn't show anything, tell me I'm wrong. Have you never wondered why none of these tests shows anything?"

It was true: he'd had x-rays and blood tests and even a CT scan. Would Richard have been happier if there were something terrible wrong? And there *was something* wrong. "I'm glad we had this chance to talk," Charlie said. "Give my love to Kathy and the kids."

"Charlie, Charlie, I'm sorry. I know it's a drag having your arm hurt, I do. But at least you have your legs, young friend!"

Charlie laughed: it was something their mother had said to Richard once.

"Charlie?" Richard said. "She will be back. You two are perfect together. You know what Kathy said a couple months ago? I shouldn't tell you this. She said she wished you and Linda were around more so the kids could see what a good marriage was all about. So there."

"Well," Charlie said. "I guess we showed her." He attempted a laugh. "Is everything O.K.?"

"Yeah, yeah. You know how it is. It's one day, then it's the next day. What can you do? You just go on."

This struck Charlie as immeasurably sad, and as soon as he could, he made an excuse and got off the phone. You just go on and on and on.

He went into the bedroom and pulled open the bottom drawer of his dresser. There, wrapped in a dingy, old plastic bag, was his cervical collar. He put it on and looked in the mirror: the man in the big white doughnut. To hell with neckties—he was taking the idea of the turtleneck to new limits. He felt like calling Dr. Price, but what could he say? Excuse me, but are there any tests to determine whether someone's really in pain? Excuse me, but are you busy tonight? He took a Dolobid and two codeine tablets and got into bed.

Peeling shrimp, Linda had said once, was like giving birth—no one ever told you how horrifying it was, you had to see for yourself. Charlie was peeling a pound of jumbo and not minding it at all: she had invited herself for dinner. As he worked he sang along to "Just Like a Woman" and allowed himself to hope that she, that tonight...But she'd taken her diaphragm with her, he'd checked—she'd probably taken it because she'd known he would check—and while Charlie felt in his heart of hearts that a baby was just what they needed, Linda was unlikely to see it that way.

For that matter, sex wasn't really the issue.

What was the issue?

By seven o'clock, everything was set. The shrimp were ready for sautéing, the snow peas and carrots were ready for boiling, the shockingly expensive raspberry tart was hidden in a cabinet, and the wine, on which Charlie had spent most of an afternoon's pay, was icy cold.

By seven-thirty, everything looked a little wilted.

At eight, Charlie put on his cervical collar and sat on the edge of the bed. He thought of Dr. Price saying, *Go, take pictures with your middle finger, be happy,* and he hoped that she would remember what she'd said to him and be stricken by remorse— preferably tonight. And she'd call him and say, Charlie, I didn't mean it, I want to help you. When the phone rang at eight-thirty, though, it was Linda.

"Charlie?" she said.

He held the receiver away from his ear while she recited her apologies—something about work, something about Kiro. After a while, he broke in. "Let me guess: you'll call me soon. Goodbye." He hung up, and when she didn't call back, he returned to the kitchen and threw away the shrimp and the snow peas and the carrots, forced them into the disposal with a wooden spoon. He took the tart from its hiding place and carefully lifted it out of its box. Holding it with both hands, he leaned over the sink and quickly ate half of it. He was about to have another bite but instead said, "That's disgusting," and let what was left fall from his hands. He could feel the glaze on his cheeks. He started out of the kitchen but immediately turned back and shook pepper over the remains, just in case he changed his mind.

In his dream, Linda was about twenty-three, in blue jeans, but neat in blue jeans—blue jeans that she'd ironed. They were new in New York, living in an apartment that was like one they'd lived in but smaller and darker and dirtier, and she was stacking things: stacks of dishes, stacks of books stacked by subject, stacks of his socks and underwear. He was lying on the naked mattress watching her, and she was babbling, threatening to alphabetize the spices while at the same time relating to him a story about her aunt Marge, the "funny" one—and they were happy, happy.

And when he woke, she *was* there, but not in blue jeans. She was sitting upright on a chair by the door, her purse in her lap, wearing a pair of what she called "slacks" and a blouse and blazer—looking, Charlie thought, like a woman waiting to be interviewed for a job. He propped himself up on his elbows to get a better look, then sank back onto the bed. "Thanks for knocking," he said.

"I did," she said eagerly, seeing that he was awake. "Several times. *And* I rang the doorbell. I guess you're still a heavy sleeper."

"You were expecting major changes? It's only been three weeks."

She came over and sat on the edge of the bed. "I'm really sorry," she said. "Really, really sorry." She touched the cervical collar. "Poor thing."

He ripped open the Velcro fastening and tossed the collar to the floor.

"Please," she said. "Please forgive me."

"O.K.," Charlie said. "I forgive you."

She bent down and kissed him quickly, awkwardly, on the jaw. "I'll make us some breakfast, O.K.?"

When he had dressed, he found her stretched out on the living-room rug, balancing in her lap an old accordion file she kept in a small wooden trunk they used as an end table. She was sipping from a cup of coffee, and it was such a familiar sight that Charlie was moderately cheered: perhaps this was simply another phase of their life together. He got coffee for himself and stretched out next to her.

"Actually, you do look awfully thin," she said. "Have you been eating?"

"Mostly sugar in various forms. It gives me a certain clearheadedness."

"And so good for you." She sipped her coffee. "Did you pour pepper on a tart?"

They laughed, and she leaned over and kissed him again, easily; then she began looking through the file.

"What are you after in there, anyway?" Charlie said.

"My old address book—Kiro wants me to get in touch with Mackenzie about something."

"Oh." Mackenzie was an old professor of hers—it seemed to Charlie that he wasn't supposed to ask about what.

"Oh, look." Linda pulled a postcard from the file. "I can't believe it—remember this?" She held the card up for him to see: it showed a row of tiny cabins and a big sign that grandly proclaimed KENABSCONSETT INN – LODGE, CABINETTES. "Remember our cabinette?"

"You mean cabinet?" Charlie said. He remembered: a dank little bathroom, fringed chenille curtains, a bed like a topographical map. Somewhere in Maine. It had poured rain the entire time they were there, and they'd gone to the "lodge"—a little matchbox of an office with an easy chair crammed next to a fireplace—and bought fifty-two copies of this postcard so he could make them a deck of cards.

Linda turned the card over. "King of clubs," she said. "Remember?"

Charlie took the card. The king of clubs had been the best one: he'd drawn a cave man wearing an animal skin, a long-armed club over his shoulder. He hadn't known she'd saved it. He looked at her, and it seemed to him that she wasn't remembering as much as he was: that it hadn't been just any weekend away, but one organized around a particular date, September 25, 1981, and a particular purpose: the celebration? commemoration? of the fifth anniversary of the first time they'd slept together, their annual marker back in the days before they had a wedding anniversary to observe.

"Remember the lobster rolls?" she said.

He handed her the card and took his coffee cup into the kitchen. He saw the raspberry tart still lying in the sink, and he folded it into the drain. When he looked up, Linda was standing in the doorway, watching him. "Are you O.K.?" she said.

"I'm great. I'd have to say I'm really just thriving."

"Charlie."

He shrugged and turned back to the sink to wash his coffee cup. There was a rule he seemed to be living by: do everything you can to make her want to stay away for good.

"Listen," she said. "Do you want to drive over to Walnut Creek with me today? I was going to go look at the site, maybe do some sketches. Kiro was there yesterday afternoon, and I think he wanted me to go this weekend."

"I guess," Charlie said. Kiro, Kiro, Kiro. "What do you mean you *think* he wanted you to go? Did he ask you?"

"Kiro is amazing," she said, shaking her head slowly. "He doesn't have to ask for things. People just know what he needs, and they want to give it to him, whatever it is."

"Great management technique," Charlie said.

The fog was lifting in the East Bay; by the time they got to Walnut Creek, the sky was clear, the air warm. In New York, it would have been a treasure of a day, a tantalizing hint of spring, an occasion for buying bunches of tulips for your wife—but at least he was with his wife. "God," he said, "you forget you live in a state where it can be seventy degrees in November. It's always so damp and cold in the city."

"It's bracing," Linda said. "I like it."

She led him up a small rise, to a clearing backed by gray-brown hills. "Brilliant," she breathed. She turned to Charlie. "He thinks we should design a kind of medical village, which I think is *genius* now that I've seen this place, don't you? A sort of main house for the information desk and all the administrative offices, and then behind it, conforming to the line of the hills, an S of cottages attached by covered walkways. And everything connected underground, where the labs would be." She touched his arm. "What do you think?"

Charlie shrugged. "Kiro knows best."

Linda took a sketch pad from her shoulder bag, and he crossed the clearing and began to climb the hill behind it, through low scrub and rocks. When he got to the top, he was winded and sweating lightly; his elbow ached. He sat on a boulder and looked down at the clearing. Linda looked tiny and serious—she looked as if she had nothing to do with him. Look up, he commanded her. But she was absorbed in her sketching.

Charlie lowered himself from the boulder onto the ground and lay back. The thing was, he didn't know *how* to think of their marriage as troubled; it had always seemed to him that they got along very well—no fights. He wondered if he could possibly unravel their lives back to the beginning of the trouble, and as he was wondering this another date from their shared past came to him: Halloween 1983.

They were living uptown then, on 113th Street, in one of the nicest apartments they ever had; Linda was getting her M.Arch. at Columbia. Charlie worked at a camera store on 96th Street, and on his way home each evening, he'd go up to Avery Hall to see if she was ready for a dinner break.

Remembering a jack-o'-lantern they'd carved one Halloween in college, Charlie picked up a pumpkin on his way to look for her that afternoon. She wasn't in any of her usual places, though, and none of her friends had seen her all day. He walked back down Broadway under a heavy gray sky and decided that he wouldn't start to worry until he got home and she wasn't there. But she was: the apartment had an unusually large kitchen with a view south, and Linda was standing at the sink washing dishes. She barely looked at him when he said hello. He put the pumpkin on a chair and took off his coat, and when he turned around he realized why it all seemed so strange. The table and the counters were covered with dishes; every dish they owned seemed to be out. He couldn't tell whether she had already washed them or was about to. "What are you doing?" he said.

She turned from the sink, her hands gloved with suds, and began to sob. "You don't care if things are clean," she cried. "It's totally up to me. Do you realize we've never washed our wedding china?" She waved at a stack of the formal, flowery plates; he didn't point out that they'd also never used them. "I don't mind," she said. "I like things to be clean. But you just ought to realize..." Her voice trailed off and she turned back to the sink, plunged her hands into the water, and began to sob harder.

And here was his mistake. He'd said, "Realize what?" He'd stood behind her without touching her and said, "Realize what?" And that evening, he asked her again and again, until she finally told him to stop asking, she was fine. *That* was where they'd taken their wrong turn: into a place where you couldn't tell the difference between polite and happy, to this point, this dry hillside, this separation. When it was so simple, what he should have done: taken her in his arms and said, Darling, darling, please don't, please forgive me for whatever it is I've done to upset you, please, you're my beautiful girl—*my dahling, lovely gehl,* like a character in an old movie—and they'd be wonderful now; they'd be fine.

He found her back at the car, looking over her exquisite sketches—he loved her sketches, had always loved them. "You're very good at what you do," he said.

Once, she would have said, happily, "Really?" Now she laughed a little dismissively and said, "So are you"—and he wondered what it was she thought he was good at.

"Charlie?" she said. "It's getting a little crowded at Cynthia's."

Cautiously, hopefully, he nodded.

"She hasn't said so, but I think she'd like her privacy back."

"It's a small apartment."

"Here's the thing—Kiro's offered me his carriage house for a few months." She looked at him, then quickly looked away.

"Kiro?" Charlie said. "This is all about Kiro? Jesus, Linda—too bad I'm not some fastidious little Japanese architect, is that it? He probably doesn't even have any hair on his chest." He slammed his fist against the car. "I can't believe you."

Charlie had met Kiro once; he remembered him as a small man in a double-breasted suit—a tiny man, really, who smoked tiny black cigarettes and drank a vile drink called a negroni: gin and sweet vermouth and Campari or something. Kiro's philosophy of life was probably cryptic and pretentious, his carriage house full of smooth black stones and thousand-dollar orchids, no furniture. She could sleep on the stones and eat the orchids, and then they'd see.

"Charlie, listen," Linda said. "This isn't about sex, I promise. Kiro is just my friend, my very—my very kind friend. He's not the issue."

"What's the issue, Linda?"

"I just"—she hesitated—"need some space right now."

That word again. He turned away from her, and because there was nothing else to do he got in the car. He watched her standing there, pretending to be looking at her sketches, her beautiful sketches. His *wife.*

She gathered her things together and got in next to him. "Would it help," he said. "Would it help if I got an office job? You know, where I had to wear a suit and tie every day?"

"Charlie, God. Dress up and play a part? That's not how it works." She sighed and leaned against the door. "You're wasting yourself."

He started the car. She had never actually said it before, and while a sour little voice in him was saying, "No, I'm not; I'm *saving* myself," the rest of him had risen to a strange plateau where he felt oddly empowered—he was back on the hill, watching her from a great height.

How could a grown man with any self-respect sit in the emergency-room waiting area of a major city hospital and cry? If he hadn't been in so much pain, Charlie might have asked himself any number of questions, but as it was, he was concentrating on staying as still as possible. He wasn't actually crying so much as tearing up at each involuntary movement of his neck and shoulders, which caused him more anguish than he'd ever known. *At least you have your legs, young friend.* It was true: if it hadn't been for them, he'd probably still be at home in bed, destined to a slow and painful death.

He'd woken up in agony that morning—the day after helping Linda move her stuff to Kiro's, so at first he'd been a bit skeptical: *nerves, pure and simple.* But he couldn't turn his head, couldn't move his arms without unbearable pain; the only way he'd finally been able to get out of bed was to swing his legs up and then use them as a lever to bring his body upright. Picking up the receiver and dialing were excruciating, but he'd finally reached Dr. Price at the hospital, and she'd agreed to see him there, and now it turned out that he had something new wrong: a winging scapula. It sounded like a kind of sailboat, but it was his shoulder blade, unleashed from its mooring.

"That would definitely be uncomfortable," Dr Price had said.

A winging scapula was also Unusual, and while it was probably a fluke (a coincidence that half his upper body was malfunctioning!), some possibilities had to be ruled out. In a little while, he was going to go to Radiology for an MRI, and then later he was going to go somewhere else for an EEG. He was making his way through the alphabet.

Dr. Price reappeared and sat on the chair next to his. "Radiology is going to squeeze you in in just a few more minutes," she said.

"That sounds painful."

She laughed. "After that, I've arranged to have you admitted—just for one night. When you're done there, just come back down to Admitting and they'll have a bed for you, O.K.?"

"I guess so," Charlie said. At least maybe they would give him some morphine; he'd taken some codeine about an hour before, but it didn't seem to be helping much.

"We'll wait and do the EEG tomorrow," she said. "You'll be feeling a lot better by then."

"What exactly are we looking for?" The word in Charlie's mind was "tumor."

Dr. Price was silent for a moment. "Nothing we're going to find," she said, "how's that? I really think it was just moving that new dresser in."

"Right," Charlie said. "The dresser." He hadn't wanted to tell her what he'd really been doing yesterday: carrying twelve boxes of art books down three flights of stairs. He'd strapped together two at a time and carried them over his shoulder, the way the movers had done in New York. "Still," he said, "it's hard to believe this has nothing to do with my arm. What's really wrong with my arm?"

"It hurts," she said.

Thanks a lot, he thought, but then he turned, painfully, to look at her—pretty Dr. Price, whose job it was to know when to say "Don't worry"—and he thought: Well, yes.

She glanced at her watch and stood up. "Listen," she said. "You know who get winging scapulae? Soldiers, from carrying their guns. So you're in good company, huh?" Charlie watched her hurry away, toward people with problems way beyond Unusual. Good company? he thought. He'd rather be alone.

Slowly, carefully, he got to his feet. He had a quarter in his pocket—he'd had the foresight to make sure of this before he left home—and now, walking gingerly to minimize the pain of each step, he started toward a cluster of pay phones. He told himself that what he was about to do wasn't so much calling for help as giving information: she would want to know, she had a right to know—she was his wife. And this time, Charlie had some hard information: he'd already known what an EEG was, and he'd asked and discovered exactly what an MRI was. It was Magnetic Resonance Imaging—formerly, Dr. Price had confided, Nuclear Magnetic Resonance, NMR, but they'd changed the name because people didn't like the word "nuclear." It was like a CT scan, that big washing machine, except they could look at any part of you and it wasn't invasive. Charlie was all for non-invasive.

He reached the phones. She would say: "Charlie, oh my God, no." Or maybe: "Oh, Charlie, no." She would be there waiting for him after the MRI, with flowers and magazines because she was a great believer in brightening a sick room. A sick room—that was another of those terms of hers. It used to be that if he had so much as a cold she'd turn into Cherry Ames, girl nurse—bring him milk shakes and toast, because that's what her mother had brought her when she was sick. Chocolate milk shakes, so thick you had to eat them with a spoon.

Charlie inched his hand into his pocket, and a shiver of pain raced through his neck and shoulder. He knew that lifting his arm to dial would be even worse. And for what? An hour or two. Maybe a day or two. He pulled his empty hand from his pocket. What was that old joke? "Doctor, doctor, it hurts to dial the phone." "So don't dial it!"

If a CT scanner was like a washing machine, an MRI machine was more like a delivery truck. Charlie had taken off "everything," including his wedding ring, and was standing in a paper gown watching the technician prepare the little stretcher he would lie on. And then the stretcher would slide into the machine...

"Got all your jewelry off?" the technician said.

"Yeah," Charlie said, "I left my diamonds in my jeans pocket."

The technician was about Charlie's age, friendly. He laughed. "Metal's the problem," he said. "You know those covered elastic bands women wear in their hair? With a little piece of metal at the joint? I had a woman wearing one of those, and when she came out, her ponytail was on the other side of her head."

Oops. "I guess it's a good thing I don't have any metal staples in my body," Charlie said.

"Good in any case," said the technician. "Ready?"

It hurt to lie down, but once he was in position, he actually felt better. The technician put a wedge under Charlie's knees and then enclosed his head in what Charlie could only think of as a cage.

"The idea," the technician said, "is not to move. It'll take about half an hour. I can take you out at any time, but then we'll have to start over. It'll sound like this." He moved out of Charlie's line of vision and knocked on the side of the machine.

"But what will I feel?" Charlie said.

"Nothing," the technician said. "You'll feel nothing."

He slid Charlie in, and Charlie thought it was a good thing he wasn't claustrophobic: he was lying in a dark tube just wide enough to contain him, his head in a cage, forbidden to move.

"Everything O.K.?" the technician asked. There was a little light down past Charlie's feet, and the technician was in that light.

"Yes," Charlie said. "I guess."

"I'll be going into the control room now," the technician said, "but I'll be able to hear you in there, O.K.?"

Charlie swallowed. Maybe he *was* claustrophobic. There was no reason for this to be any different from lying in bed, but it was. He tried closing his eyes, but he started to spin and had to open them again. Relax, he told himself. If only he had a mantra. He could choose one right now—*field,* maybe, or *stream,* those were peaceful words—but how relaxing could it be to say *field* over and over again, field, field, he feeled really silly with a mantra!

It was cold in the machine, but he could feel sweat trickling down his sides, collecting on his forehead, his upper lip. If he had a tumor it would appear as a blotch on the technician's monitor—a purple blotch, probably. If he had a tumor...

But he knew he didn't. If he did he'd be having dizzy spells, vomiting: he'd be sick. He would have to put his affairs in order, and he didn't have affairs, he had—a sore arm. *The way other people had a hobby.* Or a career. Or a marriage.

The noise started. From inside the machine, it sounded sort of like the clanking of a radiator, but more, Charlie decided, like someone hitting the lid of a garbage can with a hammer, over and over again, arrhythmically. It was actually kind of soothing, in the way bad avant-garde music could sometimes be soothing, and it made Charlie think of his and Linda's last night in New York. They'd been taken out for drinks by their friends Ira and Jeannine, music lovers who chose a little place in TriBeCa where a group called Eponymous was playing: three white guys with dreadlocks and sunglasses, one with a synthesizer, one with drums, and one with a whole battery of weapons, including a hammer and a washboard. Linda was so tense that night—she kept looking at her watch, and kicking Charlie under the table every time Ira ordered another round of drinks—but Charlie had liked it, all of it, even the terrible band. Eponymous—where but in New York could you find a band like Eponymous, a band *called* Eponymous? He wondered what had become of them. He thought that as soon as he got out of here—this tube, this hospital—he would call Ira; Ira would know. He hadn't talked to Ira in almost two months, probably the longest they'd ever gone without talking since they first met. And Charlie *liked* Ira—loved him. And Jeannine, too, and their apartment with all of that overstuffed plush furniture from Ira's grandmother's place. Maybe he *wouldn't* call, he'd just show up at their door with a six of beer and some weird record he'd buy at Tower on his way down Broadway, and they wouldn't ask him any questions, they weren't like that, but they'd know, just as Charlie did, what the issue was: it was I-don't-love-you-anymore, and Charlie knew he'd known that for a long time.

Saving himself? Why talk of saving himself when he could spend himself? All in one place.

My Father's Bawdy Song

Right away, I started meeting people who knew my brother. A bank teller cashing a traveler's check for me was one. At first, she gave me a half-glance when I passed the check through the window towards her, more interested in the amount than my identity. Then she noticed my last name and slowly lifted her eyes as though I was someone she should know. "You related to Owen?" she asked.

"My half-brother," I said. I could have simply said my brother, but I never did. I thought of him only as half a brother, whose features I had forgotten long ago.

"We went to school together," the bank teller continued. "Owen and me. That was ages ago." She shook her head. "I never see him," she said suddenly in an accusing tone. "Tell him I never see him. Tell him he should open an account here."

"Okay, if I see him," I said. I had told my brother I was going to spend my summer weekends in Montauk. My girlfriend, Leslie, and some of her friends were chipping in on the rent of a bungalow for the summer. This was a getaway, a place to relax and swim and walk along the beach. I had sent him a letter, but he hadn't replied, not even a phone call. Maybe I hadn't given him enough time to respond. I wanted to see him, though he didn't seem to want to see me. So I hadn't tried to get in touch with him right away.

"Owen Bonnin," she said slowly. She said this in a mildly surprised way, as though he were now a movie star and invoking his memory was a kind of blessing to her.

For a moment, we looked at each other and smiled. I didn't know what to say. I felt strange that I suddenly existed, that the focus of the bank teller's world had switched, at least temporarily, from the task of transforming my blue piece of paper into a lot of green paper to the more difficult chore of making contact with another human being, of acting like she knew me. My only connection to her was through Owen, whom I hadn't seen in nearly twenty years, since our father's funeral. I say "our," though even now that sounds strange, and I want to say "my father." But standing there I felt a little fraudulent, as though the name on the traveler's check didn't belong to me, at least not in Montauk.

She must have read the doubt on my face because she looked again at the check and then at me. Without any hint of awkwardness, she said, "You know, you don't look like him." After a moment, she added in a more impersonal tone, "May I see some ID?"

A week later, at a party in Bridgehampton, I met a woman who had known my father when he lived in Montauk in the late Forties. The woman, whose name was Ione Perry, swooped out of nowhere, interrupting the conversation I was having with my friends, and led me off to the kitchen in a flutter of reminiscences.

"Someone told me you were here," she said as we stood by a table with hors d'oeuvres on it. "When I heard, I just had to meet you." She stood and looked at me from head to toe. "Stanley's son," she said, and started spreading pâté on Wasa bread.

She laughed and kept on talking as I nodded and tried to follow. The woman was needle-thin and wore a dashiki and long gold earrings in the shape of tuning forks. She flourished the Wasa bread in front of her as though it were a riding crop to point and slice for dramatic effect. She seemed to emphasize at least one word in every sentence, and when she did so, her mouth stretched in a grimace that revealed a tiny set of teeth encased in the most voluminous gums I'd ever seen. "I'll *never* forget the sight of Stanley pushing Owen in his stroller along the beach. Owen must have been two, and the poor boy looked so *baffled,* because, you know, it's not *easy* pushing a stroller through the sand. It kept getting *stuck,* and Owen was holding on for *dear* life, but not crying. He *never* cried. He just looked so *baffled,* as though he was saying, 'Well, I certainly hope *he* knows where he's going.' But really, I'm afraid that *neither* did. *Certainly* not Stanley. A *dear,* dear man. And *absolutely* determined to make headway with that stroller."

Ione held her Wasa bread aloft and balanced against me while slightly caressing my shoulder. "Have you tried the goose liver?"

she screamed suddenly. "Here, you must."

I put my hand in front of my face and smiled.

"No, really, you must," she said, and I knew this was true or she'd never leave me alone. As I took a bite, I wondered what my father must have thought about her. Had she always been this annoying? I wondered what her relationship had been to my father. Acquaintance? Lover? That must have been it. Anyone this persistent couldn't have been anything else.

"Stanley taught me my first bawdy song," Ione told me. "Would you like to hear it?"

I wanted to hear it. I was hungry for any information about my father she might have. Whenever I met someone who had known my father, I could listen to him or her for hours. Whenever I heard some new story about him, I felt like some explorer, like Marco Polo, traveling past the farthest reaches of ancient and distant empires, hearing rumors of coronations and calamity, wondering what these rumors had to do with me.

> Her name was Lil, and she was a beauty.
> She lived in a house of ill repu-ty,
> Gentlemen came from far to see
> Lillian in her dishabille
> Lillian in her dishabille
>
> With branches in Brazil and Haiti
> She decided to incorpora-ti.
> She was the president and she
> was also the secre-tary
> was also the secre-tary.
>
> Then one day our Lil grew skinny;
> The trouble it was endocrin-e.
> Her glands they failed when work was done
> From over stimula-shi-on.
> From over stimula-shi-on.

As people passed through the kitchen for drinks and hors d'oeuvres, Ione sang my father's bawdy song. People smiled and even clapped, but no one stopped for more than a minute. It was clear to everyone this song was meant to be sung to me alone.

. . .

The next day, I called my brother. "Sure, let's meet up," he said without surprise or apology for not answering my letter. "I'll swing by in half an hour."

After fifteen minutes had passed, I went outside and waited.

Leslie didn't like that. As I walked out the door, she said, "Are you embarrassed for him to meet me?"

"Of course not."

"I assume he can walk and talk and get out of his car and knock on the door."

"For God's sake, he's my half-brother," I said.

"Oh no, not that," she said with a horrified look, and put the back of her hand to her forehead. "Not the dreaded half-brother."

"That's not what I meant," I said, "and you know it." I couldn't believe she had such a hard time understanding why I'd like to meet him alone. It had nothing to do with her. I just hadn't seen him in so long. As I stood there, her lack of understanding snowballed in my mind, and I started thinking all kinds of crazy thoughts. I started thinking that this was just like Leslie, that this was emblematic of all our problems. If I chewed my Cheerios on the right side of my mouth instead of my left, she'd be sure to catch the switch, sure she'd said something to make me do it. We hadn't been together long, and neither of us was certain what the other had in mind.

I went outside alone. I waited and fumed, but then the fuming died off and I just waited.

Fifteen minutes, twenty-five, forty minutes passed, and still no one who could pass for a relation of mine drove by. I wondered if something had happened to him. Maybe I'd somehow forgotten to give him the address, but no, I distinctly remembered giving it to him. Three times in the course of our conversation. Maybe I'd said something that upset him. But what could that have been? He might have been upset that I hadn't ever come to Montauk before to visit him. But then he'd never visited me in the city. Maybe he had no intention of getting together with me at all, and had just thought it would serve me right to make me wait. Maybe it would. I started trying to explain myself to Owen in my mind. It has nothing to do with you, I told him. It's just that we've led such different lives for so long. If something could have come of it, wouldn't it have happened before now?

Still, I wanted him to show up. If he didn't, the fraction of our brotherhood would be halved again. I was ready to wait for the rest of my life. No one ever had me in such a powerful grip as Owen had me in then.

As I waited, I thought about my father's life. There was so much of it I knew nothing about, especially from the period in which Owen fit. All I knew about Owen's mother, for instance, was what my mother told me. Whatever my mother said about her was always prefaced with "Oh, she's an awful woman." Despite that, my mother rarely volunteered much more information. She acted as though it hadn't been a marriage at all, but a night in the drunk tank, a boy's first shave with cause and effect. A bad night, no doubt about it, but it could have been worse.

Beyond that, I was able to piece together few facts.

After an hour, a lime-green taxi station wagon pulled up in front of me. It looked like it was from the early Sixties, with tail fins and round brake lights. Written on the door in white paint was the name of a local hotel, The Montalker, and its telephone number. I realized I must have looked like I needed a taxi, just standing in front of a house. Maybe someone nearby had called one to go to the train station.

I bent down and looked into the front seat. "I don't need a taxi," I said.

"Yes you do," the driver said. "Get in."

I stared at him without saying a word. He didn't look exactly like my father, but enough to frighten me a little. For a moment, I had the impression that this cabdriver *was* my father, and that the two of us were now going to go on some strange metaphysical drive along the beach, during which the fare box would click away at a mad rate. Guiltily, I'd know I could never afford it.

"Owen?" I said with a little too much disappointment showing.

If he wasn't my brother, I wouldn't have wanted to share a cab with him. He looked like an aged lifeguard gone to beer nuts, steroids, and LSD. His eyes were large and glassy. He had a bushy black mustache and eyebrows and hair growing out of his ears, but the top of his head was a half-moon of baldness, which he partially covered with a blue beret. He wore flip-flops, baggy white shorts, and a faded yellow polo shirt with a loose mass of threads hanging over his heart where the shirt's insignia should have been.

"I hear you're an architect, too," Owen said as soon as I'd taken a seat beside him.

"Excuse me?" I said, hardly hearing him. It was the face that got me, the roundness of it, that perfect circle I remembered dimly. The scratchiness of his stubble, the warm breath that spoke soft riddles and songs off-key. The eyes also. Blue. Even the same crow's feet. I was astounded how much came back to me.

"You're an architect also," he repeated.

The word "also" worried me, spoken like an accusation.

"Not an architect in the sense you mean," I said, a little flustered.

He laughed. "Oh, an architect in the best sense of the word."

"I'm employed by the state," I said. "I work on low-income housing. It's a misconception that architects are rolling in the money."

Owen nodded through this little speech of mine. He looked at me steadily, his eyes hard, jaw firm, and I realized how patronizing I must have sounded to him. After all, he knew what an architect was. He had lived with Dad longer than I had.

I had a strange thought. I wondered if Leslie was watching me from the window, and if so, what she thought I was doing. In a cab driven by a brother I didn't know. For all she knew, I might have called a cab to take me to the station.

"Where do you want to go?" he asked me like a cabdriver.

"I hadn't thought about it," I told him. "It's your town."

He smiled. "So you want me to show you the sights?"

"Sure."

"Or we could just sit here," he said.

"We could."

"Making small talk. You could ask me what *I* do for a living," he said, and laughed.

I didn't know what my brother had against me, but he apparently didn't like me. We'd established that much. But I was curious about him, and I wouldn't have extricated myself from the situation, even if I could have. He started the car and we headed off towards town, a couple of miles downhill, past Montauk Manor, a sprawling hotel that had been a calamity of the Depression, and had never been successfully developed.

He pulled up in front of a tiny bungalow near the center of Montauk. "Dad and Mom's first house," he said. "All the tourists want to see it. They couldn't care less about Dick Cavett's place or Edward Albee's."

Owen took off his beret. Inside was a photograph, and he handed it to me. It showed my father, skinny and in his early twenties, sitting on a boulder among a set of breakers, and smiling broadly.

"Here," he said.

"I can have it?" I asked.

"No," he said like I was crazy. "It's mine."

Owen popped the photograph of Dad back into his beret.

We drove towards the dunes and parked. We sat like shy lovers, saying very little, watching the gulls hover over the sand. I had no sense of ever having been here before, but knowing that my father had lived nearby, I felt it was in some way my natural home.

"Dad was stationed on Long Island during the war," Owen said, beginning his story. He must have intuitively known that was what I wanted, his story, the places I'd been left out of. "Somewhere near the Shinnecock Indian Reservation."

"I never understood that," I said. "I mean, he was trained as an architect."

Owen laughed. "All he did during the entire war was test ordnance, blowing up fake bridges that spanned the sand, detonating clam beds offshore, and stomping on concrete bunkers with gigantic charges of dynamite. An obscure but needed task for the war effort. I don't know exactly how he met my mom, but I can just imagine her watching his solitary bombing from some sand dune at a safe distance. A courtship dance consisting of the male blowing things up to attract the female's attention, the sand erupting, sending out an invitational spray to all the girls in the area.

"After the war was over, they married and moved here, where my grandfather owned a hotel. They were happy for a while."

That wasn't what I had heard. My mother told me that soon

after they were married, their problems started. My father wanted to return to the city to find work as an architect, but his wife wanted him to stay in Montauk and take over her father's hotel.

"Their marriage ended when I was only six," Owen said.

I was only three when he died.

One of the few things my mother told me about the divorce was that in those days you couldn't just get divorced. Someone had to take the blame. In this case, it was my father. "He agreed to everything she wanted," my mother told me. "He agreed to be the villain, and let her say that he'd been having an affair." A cautionary tale.

"He left her high and dry," Owen said. "Lucky she had the hotel to fall back on."

"That doesn't sound like him," I said. I had to defend him. It was obvious that Owen had absorbed his mother's bitterness over our father, that whatever information he'd received was slanted. Even stranger, Owen was looking as though he blamed me, as though I were his father, not his father's other son.

"How would you know?" he said.

I didn't know how to handle such bitterness. I told Owen that maybe I should be heading back, that Leslie was expecting me to cook that night. "Shrimp curry," I said.

"You have to see the hotel. You can call her from there. It's the main attraction on the tour."

It's strange, but I hadn't even thought about going to the hotel. That didn't seem like my father's territory, and I knew Owen's mother was still alive. She wasn't someone I wanted to meet. But on the drive to the hotel, he didn't say anything about her.

The Montalker was up a hill above a fish processing plant. It needed paint and had an old wooden sign, just the kind of place I would've loved to have stayed in. Inside, there were movie posters all around. It looked like something from the Forties. The windows faced west. A black Naugahyde bar stood in the center, with scratched and scarred wooden tables surrounding it. For a moment, I was sorry that my father had let it go. But what was I thinking?

"You want some chowder?" Owen said. "You should have a bowl. The best thing on the menu."

Owen seemed to be on good terms with the bartender, a woman about ten years younger than him. He leaned over the bar and kissed her. She wore a kind of ruffled, Spanish-looking dress with white and red little embroidered flowers. Her hair was a frizzy cloud around her face.

Owen grabbed a couple of glasses and filled them with beer as he leaned over the bar. The woman regarded him critically.

"Where's Jessica?" he asked.

"Upstairs, asleep, where she should be. Your mother wore her out beachcombing. And the ticks. You know how many ticks I pulled off that child? Seventeen."

"How many were on my mother?" Owen asked. He set down a beer in front of me and clinked my glass with his.

"It's not a contest."

"Okay, I'll talk to her."

"It's just that your mother's getting... well, I'm afraid for *her*."

"I'll talk to her."

The woman shrugged. Then she looked over my way and smiled. "You must be Jack."

"Oh yeah, this is Jack," said Owen.

This was Marie. He hadn't told me anything about her, or his child, and I hadn't asked. Not that he'd asked about my personal life, either. He didn't know about Leslie, and I hadn't felt a need to tell him anything. We weren't strangers. We knew each other in a deeper way. The details didn't matter much.

He wasn't married, but I was impressed that Marie was with him and he had a child. But I wondered where his mother was. I wondered if she was purposely avoiding me. I didn't know what I'd say when I met her. I never was good at small talk, and couldn't imagine it with a woman who probably wished I'd never been born.

"It's June 21st," Owen said to me, sounding in a good mood. He took a sip of his beer. "You know what that is?"

"Something to do with Dad?"

"It's Midsummer Night," he said. Owen set down his beer mug and looked out the window. "Not everything has to do with Dad."

Owen and I sat looking out that window, drinking beer after beer. The jukebox seemed perfect, and made me feel as sentimental as I'd felt all summer. A little sentimentality now and then isn't bad for the circulation. Willie Nelson sang "Georgia on My Mind." And then the Ames Brothers sang "Paper Moon." And Teresa Brewer sang a Tommy Dorsey medley. The sun wouldn't set that night until 8:25, and when Owen told me that, it was only 7:20, and I'd already polished off four beers. We had a ways to go, Owen and me. We sat at the two-seater table, saying nothing, and I observed with fondness all the strange couples at the horseshoe bar. There was one young couple, healthy and tan. She ran her fingers through his hair, which was short and sandy, and then she fondled the sunglasses hanging around his neck. And then she pinched the wrinkles in his shirt.

"You don't look like Dad," Owen told me.

"Everyone says I look like my mother."

"You have his voice, his eyes," he said.

"Where's your mother?" I asked.

"I don't know. Upstairs reading, probably."

"Doesn't she want to meet me?"

"I don't know," he said. "She doesn't know you're here."

I might have thought he'd purposely avoided telling her, that he thought my presence would cause her too much pain. But I doubt it was that at all. I'm sure he just forgot, that it wasn't important enough. I couldn't believe it, that I was that unimportant to him. But then I thought about it. Had he been important to me? I wanted to be significant to him without the necessity of his being significant to me. I had wanted him to feel jealous, but now I felt jealous of him, sitting in his hotel, looking at his girlfriend, his sunset, his Midsummer Night, his sentimental moment.

I made some excuse and stumbled out into the dark and down the hill past the fish-processing plant, and back up another hill by Montauk Manor. All the way home, I tried to remember the song that Ione Perry had sung, my father's bawdy song, but all that came back to me were the words "Lillian in her dishabille." What exactly was "dishabille" anyway? "Lillian in her dishabille," I shouted to the tune of Minnie the Moocher, as though I knew exactly what it meant, and wanted the world to savor its meaning with me.

Maybe it was the influence of the song, or the feelings that had come forth that night, or maybe the worry on Leslie's face when I returned home. She went through the litany of things that might have happened to me, that I might have drowned, or been run over or torn apart by one of the dogs the neighbors never tied up. What was worse, she thought, I might have left her. "I saw you get into a cab. I didn't know where you went."

I was always afraid to marry because of my father's failed first marriage, sure I carried in my blood whatever had caused the problems, some genetic flaw. A werewolf's curse. Leslie knew I was drunk, and so she didn't take my proposal seriously.

All that summer, I saw my brother, usually in his cab picking up tourists at the station. We waved to each other a lot and smiled. "Stop by the hotel sometime," he told me.

I'm still not sure, now that I'm married, though not to Leslie, and have a child. I wonder if my father's blueprint is there, if twenty years after my death, my son will take a cab ride with another half-brother, and he'll come to understand that what he thought of as impossible is happening, that he's meeting me again. "What was that question," he'll wonder, "that I've been dying to ask you all my life? And why does it seem so unimportant now?"

The Life of the Mind

She made some big changes that spring. The first one was moving out of David's house in Beachwood Canyon and into a one-bedroom apartment in Park La Brea.

"Old ladies live there," was David's comment.

"I like old ladies," she said. "Old ladies are quiet and considerate. They don't have car phones, either."

"I'm at the set," he said. "I'll call you later."

She found a new job. For three years, she had coordinated a production office, meeting the demands of actors, drivers, assistant directors, grips. Now she sat alone in a small room on what used to be the Goldwyn lot, reading.

"I am a reader," she reminded herself several times during the first week. "I read for a living. They pay me to read." She repeated this to Bugs when they met for lunch.

"But how much are they paying you, Cecilia?" Bugs asked, over the top of the menu. She was dressed up, for her, in a wrinkled linen suit and high heels. Interview clothes.

"Money isn't the point."

"Then I guess I'm missing it."

Bugs thought Cecilia had made a mistake, leaving production. They'd met as office runners on a low-budget horror spoof called *Killer Fleas*. It was the kind of shoot, rife with tension and disaster, that created good stories and strong friendships, though the film itself went straight to video. As they moved on to other, better jobs, on slightly better movies, Cecilia felt more and more that she was working against her nature. Bugs, on the other hand, came into herself. Production defined her; she seemed stronger, even taller, these days.

"Development is a dead-end field for women—(a)," Bugs said. "And (b), you're what, thirty-two? Too old to be a reader."

"I love the way it sounds. A reader. The life of the mind."

"Oh, please."

"We talked about Kafka when I interviewed with him." Cecilia smiled to herself. What they'd talked about was whether Kafka would have liked *Eraserhead.*

"O.K., he went to college. But what kind of man is named Bayard Buchanan? I bet he made it up."

"He was at Apex. Co-produced *Dry Ice.*"

"Hmm. Interesting film."

"He'll be gone most of the time. I'll just fax him the coverage."

"O.K., I'm beginning to see the potential. You've got your little office, your days practically free. Maybe you can write a script."

"Oh, no."

"Everybody's writing one. It's not hard."

"It should be."

"Excuse me for saying this, but now that you're out of David's shadow, you can make your own moves." As she spoke, Bugs scraped some scattered bread crumbs into a rectangular shape with her fingernail. "He hasn't cornered the market on ideas, now, has he?" she added.

Cecilia hadn't seen David in several weeks, though they spoke on the phone almost every day. He was directing his first feature, an ecological thriller, budgeted at $1.8 million. There were some proposed script changes, and he needed her opinion—what if Ronck (the hero) and Thea (the biologist) were ex-lovers, had a past, as it were?

"It's possible, I guess."

"But is it *better*?"

"Don't know," she said. "Let me think about it."

Cecilia had seen David's picture in "The Great Life" column in *The Hollywood Reporter,* and noticed he'd had his hair buzzed short. They used to laugh at that column—one long string of names interspersed with badly cropped black-and-white photos—faces as small as your fingernail. David was being invited to a few openings and parties now. He was pictured with Minnie Pontesca, a model and bass player. He'd cast her in his film.

"She's very insecure," he told Cecilia. The transmission crackled as he drove through Cahuenga Pass.

"You find that attractive, don't you?"

"Why is everything so personal with you? I don't know, I was hoping we could be friends."

"I think you call me out of habit."

"Want me to stop?"

"Yes, I do."

"No, you don't."

He was right. She didn't want that yet.

They came close to meeting in early April, when Bugs held her annual Academy Awards–watching party. Cecilia felt uncomfortable and exposed, moving among the people who had known her up to now as one half (the less interesting half?) of an established couple. "Why haven't we seen you?" the women asked. The husbands and boyfriends regarded her with sympathy, gave her one-armed hugs and planted friendly kisses on her cheek. Cecilia slipped out before the best actress was announced; Bugs called her the next morning to scold her and inform her she'd won the Oscar pool. David had dropped in late, Bugs said, "with a friend."

"Minnie."

"They came from work. I don't think it means much. He was sorry he missed you."

"How'd he look?"

"Exhausted. He pumped me about your doings."

"Yeah? What did you say?"

"I told him you were an emerging woman."

"That was nice of you, Bugs."

"You know I don't say anything unless I firmly believe it."

"O.K. Don't worry, I'll emerge," Cecilia said.

Her days were quiet. Bayard Buchanan was on location; Cecilia could hear the tension in the coordinator's voice when she called the production office to leave a message for him. That's how I used to sound, she thought. It seemed like a long time ago.

Bugs started work on a new movie, about a clinically depressed country singer, and had no more time to socialize. Not that Cecilia needed to socialize. This was enough—the new, uncluttered apartment, the comfortable little office, the stack of scripts to be read. A nourishing routine.

The first week of May, during one of their cellular chats, Cecilia told David that she'd seen the latest Wim Wenders film, and they argued about it. He couldn't believe that she didn't agree with him that it was bloated, artificial, and sexist in the most insidious way. She told him he shouldn't use words he didn't understand. The conversation took a bad turn, then was cut off when David hit a patch of interference. Neither one of them attempted to call back.

When she'd gone a week without hearing from him, she thought, So that was it. She had wondered how the end would feel, never imagining anything so vague and unsatisfying. She could make herself miss him when she wanted to, by remembering certain tender moments, like the night they saw *Tokyo Story* in Boston and cried and hugged each other for a long time on the sidewalk outside the Brattle. She had been sure she loved him that night, and that he had loved her. She wondered now if it had been a trick she played on herself, a mood they'd picked up from the Ozu film, life imitating art.

The work spilled into her evenings. She would start another script while she ate her dinner, and finish it in front of the TV. She heard that David's movie had finished shooting and was now "in post."

Other than Bugs, Bayard Buchanan, and the kid from the mailroom, the only people Cecilia spoke to on a regular basis were agents phoning in to beg for an early opinion. She kept a list of euphemisms by the phone, things she could say to appease them—phrases like "intriguing setting," "elements out of balance," "needs larger context," "could deepen character of mother/wife/girlfriend."

There was always the chance that some of them would take courage from these phrases and shower her with other, more intriguing scripts with larger contexts and fully developed wives and girlfriends. One such young man, from Rosenthal & Benioff, called her one morning and insisted on sending, that day, by messenger, a script she would not only recommend, but champion, once she cast her eyes upon it.

"What is it called?" Cecilia asked.

"*Succubus.* It's a working title."

"I look forward to reading it." She hung up the phone and

sighed.

The messenger knocked on the door just before lunch. Cecilia signed for the two-pound bundle of words.

"Huh," he said. "Is your name really Cecilia?"

"Well, yes."

"From birth?"

"Soon after."

"Incredible," he said, setting his motorcycle helmet down on the visitor's chair. "That's the name of the girl in my story." He blushed, handsomely. "I'm writing a script."

"No kidding," she said.

"This is truly amazing."

"Well, the name's not that rare."

"No," he said. "It's no accident. I can't explain it now. This is so cool, Cecilia."

He smiled a radiant, young–Gary Cooper smile and handed her a copy of the delivery ticket. She found herself smiling back, enjoying the joke, though she would have been hard-pressed to articulate what that was.

"I'm Sam," he said, picking up his helmet. He paused in the doorway to don his Ray-Bans. "We'll meet again."

It was more a promise than a prophecy, since he turned up the next day with a lighter bundle—the first fifty pages of his own original screenplay.

"You're the one who can help me," he said. "I know it."

Cecilia waved the envelope away.

"Look," she said. "Bayard Buchanan is very strict about unsolicited material."

"I don't want him to see it. It's not ready yet. I thought you might skim through it after work, and we could meet for coffee— maybe Friday. Or how about this: we meet somewhere and I tell you the story. No reading required."

"My time is valuable, Sam."

He sunk into the visitor's chair, script in hand. "I know. I know it's valuable." He exhaled heavily. "I can't argue with that."

She weakened. "Oh, all right. Give me a few days. Then we can talk on the phone perhaps."

"It won't take long," he said, on his feet again. "Half an hour, tops. You just have to listen; you don't even have to think. Then just say whatever pops into your head, or nothing, if that's what pops in. Do you believe in signs, Cecilia?"

Another one of his grins emerged—they were his language, she was beginning to realize, infinitely more persuasive than his actual speech.

"No," she said.

"That's good," he said. "It's good that you don't."

They met the following Monday night at Bob's Big Boy in Toluca Lake, because it was David Lynch's favorite Bob's. Sam insisted they both order Super Big Boy Combos, just to get into the spirit of the place. Then he asked her to please call him Andy from now on.

"Why?"

"Because it's sort of my actual name. The Sam thing was just an experiment."

"Excuse me?"

"You know, like Sam Shepard. I decided I wanted to be Sam Shepard. Some people were telling me I looked like him or something, and he's a writer. Want one?"

When she declined the cigarette, he lit one for himself and exhaled slowly.

"My script's in trouble," he said.

"I guessed that."

"You're so fucking perceptive, Cecilia."

It was a quest, a spiritual story, he explained. If that didn't put her off. She said she'd try to listen with an open mind.

Picture a pilgrim, he said, an everyman. The Poet, the Madman, the Fool. It took place sometime in the near future, in another America—what America will become, in the last days.

"Armageddon?"

"I'm not a born-again, Cecilia. Bear with me."

Our hero, driving a souped-up Chevy Nova, travels from San Diego to Chicago, searching for a baseball card.

"This isn't one of those mystical baseball movies?"

"Not exactly."

Sam/Andy would figure out later which baseball card the hero is seeking. Maybe Gehrig, maybe the Babe. There are very few people left in the small towns; most have armed themselves and taken to the hills, or, where there are no hills, to the caves. In the cities, the rich are on drugs, held hostage in their condos by roving bands of delinquent children. In Kansas, right smack in the middle of the Heartland, Pilgrim meets Cecilia. She is an American shamanness, a woman warrior. They get together.

"They go to bed together?"

"Um, right. So the Pilgrim has broken his vow of celibacy, see, and he loses sight of the quest."

"The quest for Babe Ruth?"

"You think it should be somebody else?"

"I have no idea."

"Because this is where we get stuck. Nick, my partner, thinks Cecilia should be a girl along for the ride, you know? They go to Chicago, find a card, but it's not the card. They're almost killed by the child gangsters. One of the smaller kids gets hurt, and they take him along. You know, a Holy Family kind of thing."

Cecilia stared at the remains of her Super Big Boy Combo.

"It sucks, doesn't it?" He slapped the edge of the table with the hand that wasn't holding the cigarette.

"I didn't say that."

"Is everything all right with you folks?" the waitress asked as she approached their booth with the coffee pot.

"Yeah, hi. Hi, Pat. Tell me, when David Lynch, when Mr. Lynch comes in here, how many napkins does he fill up with ideas? That's how he does it, isn't it? On the napkins?"

"He stares into space, mostly," she said.

They met a few more times, after she'd read his fifty pages. Andy picked the place—always a coffee shop—and they talked, or he talked, later and later into the night. Cecilia, when pressed about the script, emphasized its unique, surreal qualities. She was never required to say very much.

Listening to Andy left Cecilia no room for her own thoughts. He reminded her of the young Richard Basehart in her favorite film, *La Strada*—a beautiful clown. The waitress at Ships said, "Haven't I seen you on TV?" and Andy brushed it off. "This town," he grumbled, but leaning back in his leather jacket, smoke circling his head, he looked like a photograph waiting to be snapped.

After they'd addressed the script from every possible angle, there was his life story, entertaining in its own right. A privileged upbringing in San Diego. Disappointed parents, wrecked cars, vision quests in the desert. A weekend in a Mexican prison, reading *On the Road*. He alluded, in passing, to many romances, as if Cecilia would pick up the references, as if she had been there.

"Who's Tracy?" she'd have to ask. "Who's Carlisle?"

He'd shake his head sadly. "She was a nice girl."

"Did you love her?"

"Love is just a thought, Cecilia."

"Then what's the point of it?" she snapped.

"Whoa. Woman warrior. Are we strung out on some guy?"

She shrugged.

He reached over and rested his hand on her shoulder. "Remember this: it's not about the guy, Cecilia. It's not about happy ever after. There's the good dream and there's the bad dream and then there's no dream. Know what I mean?"

She smiled and shook her head no.

"It's all in the script. The last shot: Pilgrim and Cecilia and the kid head out from the city. It's in ashes. They have nothing left. Zip. No dream. But they keep moving, see? They're alive to tell the tale."

Cecilia got home from these outings at two in the morning and fell into bed, exhausted and relieved. She liked the smell of smoke in her hair the next day, and the way the fatigue distorted her perceptions. "Night, babe!" Andy had called to her in the parking lot at Ships, just before he kick-started his motorcycle. No one had ever called her that before.

It was June. The apartment would be hot and still when she got home, but it didn't seem worth it, turning on the air conditioner for just one person. She found herself craving the presence of a huge, fluffy cat. A few tenants—old ladies, no doubt—were keeping them, secretly, in violation of the lease. Cecilia had looked out some mornings and seen a graceful dark shape brush past the curtains of the window across the courtyard.

"You're just depressed," Bugs said on the phone. Did Cecilia know that depression was anger turned inward? Cecilia said she did. Bugs recommended a self-help book that everybody on the crew was reading: *Depression, The Inner Journey.* Even though she had no intention of reading it, Cecilia felt vaguely uplifted by the title. If she had to endure the diagnosis, it was encouraging to think of it as a form of travel.

It had become her habit to postpone the trip home by bringing some work to a suitable, air-conditioned restaurant and eating dinner there. Bayard Buchanan would be back from location soon, and a flurry of spec scripts had flown in from all over town. She decided to have them read and covered by the time he arrived—not that he'd expect it, but simply to keep herself motivated. She pictured a story meeting, with her and B.B. on one side of the conference table, a team of writers on the other. "I think Cecilia's point is well taken," B.B. was saying.

One night at the Souplantation, she looked up from her script—it was the second one to come in that month about a violent love triangle among real estate agents. She watched the ordinary, low-concept customers, struck for a moment by the gap between life as she was experiencing it and the life contained between the cardboard covers.

A man she'd been watching—tired, fiftyish, raised his head from his plate and met her eyes for a second before they both looked down. In a script, characters often "lost their heads." People locked eyes and passion ignited; they moved towards each other like forces of nature—always that pulling together, hardly ever the slow unraveling that happens down the line. Was that what prevented her from coming up with a script of her own—an inability to lie in this most basic way? Maybe it wasn't a lie for some people. She thought of Andy, whose life was symbol-packed and full of crises, and wondered how such a life would feel from the inside—more immediate, more real?

After dinner, she walked up La Cienega towards the Rexall. A skateboarder with long blond dreadlocks almost ran her down in front of Johnny Rocket's. I'm invisible, she thought. There was a pay phone across the street. She found Andy listed on Poinsettia Place. He picked up before she heard a ring.

"Talk to me," he said.

"Hi, Andy? It's Cecilia."

"Cecilia, what are you doing?"

"Um, I was thinking about your script tonight, and—"

"Where are you right now?"

"I'm at a pay phone, on Beverly and La Cienega."

"Don't move." He hung up.

She waited five minutes, standing by the phone, until she heard the grumbling downshift of a motorcycle engine as Andy approached from the east along Beverly. He swung the bike to a stop in front of the phone booth, with the engine running.

"Hop on," he yelled.

Andy lived in a ramshackle eight-unit building, overgrown with jungly shrubs and painted the color of blood oranges. They stepped over a sprawling, three-toned cat and up a flight of stairs—somebody was playing the Beatles' "Number 9"—to Andy's paper-strewn single apartment. It smelled of cigarette smoke and incense. He cleared a place for her on the futon couch.

"I'll make you some hot chocolate," he said.

"Actually, ice water would be good," she answered, sitting on the edge of the couch. "Is the cat yours?"

"The cat?" She heard pans rattling from the kitchen, then the tick-tick-tick of the gas burner. "That cat thinks he knows everything. But you know what? He's wrong. Dead wrong."

"Are you upset about something?"

There was no answer. She studied the room as if it were a set: an arrangement of crystals twinkled from the top of the television; layers of curling Post-its—sun-dried ideas—covered the entire surface of the ten-inch screen. On the floor near her feet were Egri's *The Art of Dramatic Writing* and the *I Ching*. On the windowsill behind her, an ashtray, a boom box, and a baby cactus in a two-inch pot.

He walked slowly back into the room, carrying two mugs of cocoa.

"What time is it?" He handed her a cup.

"Nine-thirty, maybe ten. I lost my watch this weekend."

"No shit. Cecilia, guess what? I lost my watch. This very afternoon." He sat cross-legged on the couch. "I was in the hell realm when you called. Here—"

Andy touched his mug to hers in a toast.

"We're out of time now, babe." He lifted one eyebrow to emphasize his point as he sipped his cocoa.

"What's happened?" she asked.

"I can't go into it."

Without too much coaxing on her part, however, the story emerged: he had met with Nick late in the afternoon, to discuss the first draft of *The Pilgrim*. They'd argued about the role of the baseball card, which Andy now felt was the key element, the Grail itself. Nick had questioned Andy's sanity, and they came to blows.

"He hit you?"

"Well, not exactly. There was some shoving. He took the draft and told me I was out of it now. He's finishing it himself. Cecilia, a year of my life, maybe my whole life, went into that script."

"I'm sure he'll reconsider, when he calms down a bit."

"You know how the baseball card came to me? In a dream. It was the same dream—I never told you this, but you came to me in that dream."

"What?"

"Your name. Cecilia."

"Oh."

"I'm glad you're here tonight. It's the only good thing that's happened to me today. So what was it you wanted to tell me? When you called, you said you had notes about the script."

"Actually," she said, "I don't have anything to say about your script. I was walking down the street tonight, and all of a sudden I felt totally transparent. Not there. Then I wanted to talk to you. Have you ever felt like that?"

"I like you in glasses. Why haven't you worn them before?"

"I have contacts. They were bothering me."

"You look like Dorothy Parker's little sister, or something."

"Have you ever seen a picture of Dorothy Parker?"

"I think so. Didn't she wear glasses?"

Cecilia removed her glasses and set them on the windowsill. The background blurred. She thought what a relief it was to be in the company of a man with whom there could be no pretense of mutual understanding. Whatever she did couldn't possibly count.

She started to laugh, and Andy joined her, for his own reasons, but it felt for a moment as if they were sharing something.

There was another moment, a half-hour or maybe an hour later—without a watch, who could say?—when they'd kissed for a while and his mouth was soft like a baby's and the stubble on his chin scratched her face. He liked to kiss. His hand moved up under her T-shirt and over her back like the answer to a question, and the answer was warmth and pressure, flesh—all things material.

"Look what we're doing," he said.

Even as their bodies came together, urgently, without any more words, she was conscious of guitar music playing in his neighbor's apartment, footsteps clumping down the stairs, and of a breeze that drifted in through the open windows. She attached no meaning to these sensations. And before Andy untangled his limbs from hers and sat up, reaching for his cigarettes, Cecilia read his second thoughts. She could have gone on for a long while, breathing in salty skin, bearing the weight of another body. She stroked his thigh.

"You're not in love with me, are you, Cecilia?" he said.

She smiled at his fretful expression. "I don't think so," she said.

"That's good." He blew smoke into a long column above his head. "But why aren't you?"

They both laughed at Andy's joke.

"No hard feelings, though?"

She shook her head.

"Cecilia, you're so Zen," he said.

After they had unfolded the futon and turned out the light, Andy said good night and curled up on his side, his back to Cecilia. She tucked her arms behind her head and watched the car headlights stretch themselves one by one across the ceiling as the traffic moved past outside. Her body was wide awake, conscious of its extremities: toes and fingers, elbows, scalp.

Her thoughts rolled by, another kind of traffic. Bits of conversations, Andy's voice, David's voice, lines from the script she'd been reading in the restaurant. She watched the thoughts pass, contentedly, as if she were the surface on which they traveled, vast and self-contained.

In the morning, she would step over the cat who knew everything, ride back to her car on the back of his motorcycle, go to work in the same clothes, though there would be no one there who would remember what she'd worn the day before. She'd call Bugs, who would pump her for the details of the previous evening and reassemble them in her own emphatic way, as a kind of breakthrough. Cecilia wouldn't have the heart to contradict her.

She didn't keep in touch with Andy until, six months later, he sent her a draft of *The Pilgrim* with a note, explaining that he and Nick had patched things up and wondering if she had the time to look at the script again. She had a new title by then—Senior Development Executive—and a new office at Apex, where Bayard Buchanan was now head of production. Andy was very impressed at the news of her promotion, and lifted his coffee mug in toast after toast when they met at Hugo's for breakfast on a drizzly morning in January. They drank to her future, to her mind, to their everlasting friendship. She looked beautiful, he told her, with a smile that spoke of intimacy and regret. She felt herself returning the smile, playing along, though she found the memory of their one night together rather elusive, in fact almost impossible to believe.

"Cecilia, you're so fucking inspiring. You're, like, my muse," Andy said, after she'd given him a few kind notes on the latest draft. He reached across the table and pressed her hand. "What happened with us?"

"I've often wondered," Cecilia said, untruthfully.

"Me, too," he said, giving her fingers another squeeze before they both dug into their omelettes.

How mutable, how pleasant it was, Cecilia thought; this imaginary past of theirs, the what-might-have-happened. Never having begun, it required no development, no second act, no reversal, no catharsis, and no resolution at the end.

Crooked Letter

Mother calls two or three nights a week now, trying to make me come see my father, who is dying of cancer in the hospital in Missouri.

"He asks for you," she says.

"Come on."

"Don't you think he's sorry for things?"

"He's never said so."

"You were hard to handle."

"I was a kid."

I'm in the kitchen, helping my wife, Sue, clean salad. She listens wearily to my end of the conversation. Last week, she took our kids to see my father. They were fascinated by his skull-hollow face, by the coiling IVs.

"You know I'm going to keep bugging you," Mother says.

Sue hangs up the phone for me while I gather the veggies on the cutting board. The kids are in the living room, shedding their coats and snow boots. I hear the TV come on.

"Baby," Sue says, "you should go."

"Don't start." Sue's used to being my good angel. Not this time.

"My daddy used to hit me, too."

"Your dad was a drunk." I put down the knife. My hands are shaking.

"I'll finish that," Sue says. "Check the roast."

When I was a kid, I always wondered why my father hated me. All I knew was that he rarely spoke to me unless I had done something wrong, and then he would say, "Come here, stupid," and knock me down, or grab me by the throat until I couldn't breathe. Mother would tell him to stop, but never tried to stop him. She was afraid of him, even though he never hit her. When he got into one of his real rages, she would take my baby-sister and hide in the bedroom closet. Next day while he was at work, Mother would take me to the doctor. It was always a different doctor, because she didn't want anyone to have a record of how many fractures her "accident-prone" child had had. Once we drove forty miles to Joplin in search of a new doctor. She was crying the whole way, and the sound got on my nerves. By then, I never cried. It was only pain. It was normal.

By the time I started school, I had learned to avoid the man. Mother would give me supper early, before he got home from the mill, and I'd go off to my room in the attic or the tree house in the backyard. When I could, I stayed over at my friends' houses, though I was scared of their fathers, too. By junior high, I was hanging out, going to midnight wrestling down at the Shrine Mosque, smoking pot with older kids in the high weeds by the railroad tracks. At sixteen, I left home, and in the decade since, I have never set foot in my parents' house, nor laid eyes on my father except at weddings and funerals.

After supper, we watch PBS, Sue sitting on the floor between my knees, the kids cradled under each of my arms. Clay asks why the woman on the show is fat, and Stephanie tells him scornfully that she's having a baby.

"I saw fat ladies at the hospital," Clay says. "Is Grandfather going to die?"

"We don't know," Sue says. "He's old. Now shhh. Look what the butler's doing."

"Your grandpa used to make me watch the war news," I say. "He said it would make me tough."

"Shush, Dad," Stephanie whispers. "You're 'sposed to *listen* to TV."

In bed, Sue and I read magazines by the glow of our headboard lamps. Snow piles up outside the bay window.

"Baby," Sue says, "what about your mother?"

"She'll be all right."

"She needs you there, you know. And not going might make the whole thing worse for you." She touches me here, there, her small hands tender. I let the magazine slide from the bed, turn into her arms. She reaches to switch off the lights, and I take hold of her nightgown and draw it from her.

"Here," she murmurs. "Don't tear it."

"Daddy used to hit me and dare me to cry," I say. "I wouldn't do it."

"You wouldn't, would you? This is what you should do, Dave. Just go to the hospital and see him. You don't have to talk about the past."

Sue always says that seeing family is like getting a pelvic: you just look off into space and after a while it's over. But she doesn't know everything about me and my father. No one does.

"You could get free of it, Dave."

"I got free a long time ago."

My sister, Adrienne, calls three times a year, Thanksgiving and Christmas and Easter. It's none of those, but I'm not surprised to pick up the phone the next morning and hear her voice.

"Davy?"

"Adrienne."

"How are Sue and the kids?"

"Okay."

"I'm at the hospital in Springfield. The old man looks bad."

"Okay."

"Please come. For Mom."

Straightforward. It throws me off. In our family, we circle and spar. "I'll come to the funeral."

"Oh, Davy. I know you hate him. But this is for Mom."

"You can't ask this of me, Adrienne."

"Look, I understand how you feel."

"No, you don't."

"I always hated the way he treated you."

"Yeah? First I heard of it. I used to wonder why he was so sweet on you."

"What do you mean?"

"You know what I mean."

"You're nuts, Davy. But that's your business. I told Mom I'd try." The line is quiet for a minute. When I don't speak, she says, "Don't get too hard, bro. You'll end up like Dad."

"I'm not like him." She wants to talk some more, but I tell her I've got to go. I don't want to hear about Adrienne's life. It has nothing to do with mine.

When I was a kid, I slept in the attic. To get to it, you went past my parents' bedroom, then past Adrienne's, to a little closet that had a board ladder nailed to one wall. There was a trapdoor in the ceiling you pushed up. I had my bed up there, and boxes for my clothes and toys. There had been a space heater, but it had a gas leak and Daddy took it out when I was six. After that, it was always cold in the winter, and I slept in my clothes, with the covers pulled up over my head. Some nights, I'd wake up and stick my head out and stare at the barred moonlight on the wall, breathe frost out into the air.

My father kept tools and paint at the back of the attic under the eaves. I always knew when he'd been there because he threw out my junk: jay feathers, fossils, old green pennies I'd collected. I kept my drawings in his tree house. Daddy hated them worst of all. When I was ten he caught me drawing with Adrienne and a neighbor girl I liked. He crunched his boot down on my drawing hand. For weeks, I had to write with my other hand at school.

"You sissy faggot," my father said. "Get on outside and play."

Adrienne laughed and wrote *faggot* across my drawing.

Sue's work is her car, her ledgers, arguing with sales reps all day long. My work is a sun-flooded room with drafting tables, pens and brushes, a Macintosh. Carol is there early, pasting up pages at the light table, sipping at her first cup of coffee.

"Sue told me about your dad," she says.

"What did she tell you?"

"All of it."

I stick down a layout with magic tape, check my pens, start inking the sketch of a top-hatted toff I did last night. I like work. Time goes by.

"Looks good." Carol brings me coffee. She looks pretty in her black skirt and pine-green sweater. I've been noticing her a lot lately. Her clothes and hair, and the way she moves.

"They need an artist where my cousin works," Carol says. "You might want to look into it. It's good money."

"I applied there once. It's run by this old guy."

"So?"

I put down my coffee, pick up my pen. "I don't get along with old guys. Did Sue tell you about our party?"

"Yeah. We had a good talk, you know?"

"She likes you."

"She's a good friend." She pushes back her hair, gives me one of her curious looks. "You don't really have any men friends, do you, Dave?"

"I don't know. Not really."

"Why?"

I hate when people ask why. They say this word, they think they're saying something. "Friends are people you can trust," I say.

Driving home through slush, I keep thinking about my father. He was a gifted winter driver who disdained chains or snow tires, and loved nothing better than to shovel and buck a stranded vehicle out of a ditch. Where we lived, the road ran uphill both ways, and when he heard the rising whir of tires that could get no traction, he would reach for his truck keys and tow chain. If I was around, I had to go with him and help push on the stuck cars while muddy ice caked my jeaned legs.

In the Ozarks, the January ice storms come down out of Tornado Alley and glaze the roads sheer as mirrors. Daddy would take me out with him on winter nights, to cut doughnuts in ice-sheeted parking lots. As he bore down on gas pedal and brake, sending the car skidding in ever-widening ovals, his face became a mask of blissful concentration. He liked to hurl the car head-on at storefronts, then wrench it sideways at the last second. I held on to the door handle, dizzy and filled with terror.

Once, we got out of the car and walked around. I kept falling on the ice. We stood in the open, and the only sound in the vast quiet was the northwest wind's snarl and skirl.

"Listen to that," my father said. "God's got his knife out."

For some crazy reason, I felt close to him for a second. "Why does it blow like that?"

He shrugged. "*Y* is a crooked letter." This was one of his sayings, his answer when anyone asked him why something was the way it was.

That night, we spun till after midnight, and Mother bitched when we got home.

"We can't afford to get a ticket," she said.

Daddy slapped her on the ass, pushed her to the kitchen to fry him a steak. "There's no law in a parking lot," he said.

The night before our party, I make Sue go with me to a meeting, so maybe she can stay sober. She joins now and then, but never for long. She has a lot of white chips. After they read the Steps and the Promises, they go around the room and say their names. I hold Sue's hand under the table, and her nails dig into my palm.

"I'm Susan," she says when it's her turn. She points to me. "This is Dave. He thinks I'm an alcoholic."

Nobody blinks an eye at this, and people start in telling their stories. There's invisible energy in the room, but I don't know what it is, where it comes from. Maybe it isn't really there. When they pass the basket, I slip in a dollar. Sue looks disgusted, shoves her chair back loudly, and walks to the bathroom. Everybody joins hands for the prayer, and I get that tight knot in my throat, the one other people say they get when they cry.

"...forgive us our sins, as we forgive those who sin against us. And lead us not into temptation, but deliver us from evil—"

There. That's where it always gets me. *Deliver us from evil.* I'd like to like God. But where was he when I needed him?

Friday night, we have people over. Come midnight, I'm talking with Sue and Carol at the kitchen table. Sue still thinks I should go see my father.

"Don't you think it would do him good to go?" she asks Carol.

"I think Dave should do what he wants."

"You would."

Carol's a subject changer. "When I was little I wanted to be a nurse," she says, "so I could see guys with their pants down. What did you want to be?"

"I never thought I'd grow up," I say. "I thought my father would kill me."

"He's serious," Sue says.

"I figured someday he'd put his thumb on that cord in my throat and just not let go."

Sue tells how when she was a girl she would walk all over town with her dad on Sundays, trying to find where he'd left the car the night before. I pour more gin. The party is getting hot. Somebody dances in her slip in the living room, cheered on by a ring of clapping hands.

"So who are all these people?" Carol asks.

"Sue's friends from college," I say. "They all fucked each other way back when."

"Asshole," Sue says. "Why do you hate my friends?"

Sue's friends are good people, they really are, but it's hard for me to like people who take for granted things I never had. I don't mean just clothes and contact lenses, but someone to help them with their homework, someone to make them come home at night.

"In a fair fight, I could take them all," I say.

Carol takes my hands in hers. "Don't start any fights, okay?" She saw me fight once. I put my fist in this guy's face a few times, then he laid his face on the bar.

"He will if he wants to," Sue says. When she's tanked, she likes it when things get crazy. Too many times I've had to take a hammer to some guy she led on.

Sue drifts off to empty ashtrays and gets caught up in the crowd. I pour more gin.

"She really wants you to see your dad," Carol says.

"Sue did the big reconciliation thing with her folks. She thinks it's what everybody needs."

"What do you think?"

More gin. Some goes in our glasses and some on Carol's jeans.

Sue comes back. She's very drunk. It hits her that way—sudden. I touch her hair. She pushes my hand away.

"You go there," she says. "You go in the room, make a little small talk. Your mother would be so happy. Tell him, Carol."

Carol's tired of this. "Why don't we leave Dave alone about it," she says.

Sue looks at her, looks at me. "You two," she says. "Why don't you two just fuck and get it over with?"

Carol lets go of my hand.

"I'm sick of you always whispering. Always putting your *hands* on each other."

"Excuse me," Carol says, and starts for the bathroom. Behind her back, Sue grabs a beer bottle and starts to throw it. I lock her wrist and twist. The bottle shatters on the floor. Foam and glass spray Carol's nylons. She looks at Sue with loathing and keeps going.

I think Sue will take a swing at me. She does sometimes. But she just looks down, blinking at the mess of beer froth and broken glass.

"Good job, tiger," I say. "Have another drink."

"Fuck *you*, you cold bastard."

Out by the cars, I find Carol, backing her Isuzu over a curb and around a Porsche.

"Don't start," Carol says. "You can't make this all right. So don't try."

"I'm sorry about Sue. I was real unprepared. She never acts jealous."

"Uh-huh. Does she always drink so much?"

"She's an alcoholic."

"That makes it okay, then? Look, Dave, you and Sue do what you want. But don't put me in the middle. I don't play that game."

I give this some thought. But by the time I've got anything to say, she's driving off.

Some things are easy with liquor. Some you can't do at all. I sit in the kitchen and pour gin. Sue and her friends play a game in the living room, everyone saying *I love you* to everyone in all the tones of voices they can find. They whisper it, shout it, slur it; they butcher it with foreign accents. They say it to the chairs, to the clocks, to the prints on the wall.

When I was little, everyone in Springfield still shopped down on the square. My father would drive round and round till he found an empty meter, rather than use the municipal lot two blocks away. Sometimes we circled for twenty minutes. Then Mother and Adrienne would go into Heers to do her shopping, while Daddy loitered with his buddies at Harmon's Barber Shop. I always wanted to go to Heers and ride the escalators, but Daddy took me with him to Harmon's.

"He's growing," someone in the crowded shop would say. "Going to be a tall one."

"That's a fact," Daddy said, chain-lighting a new Camel and rubbing the old butt out in sand. All the men in Harmon's smoked; the talk was baseball and football in season, civil rights in election years. Over the mirror was a stained banner that read HARMON'S BARBER SHOP: BAPTIST, UNION, DEMOCRAT.

"How 'bout that Lou Brock?" someone would say.

"He's a fleet one," Daddy answered. "He got the call of the wild." And he cupped his hands together and made ape noises through a funnel of smoke.

There was an empty barber chair Harmon never had enough business to need, and Daddy liked to sit in it and spin around. I sat in the last red vinyl chair, by the narrow door to the john, and read the magazines Harmon enclosed in plastic folders, oversized copies of *Life* and *Look*. Every now and then, Daddy would suddenly slap the magazines out of my hands. His buddies waited for this and hooted when it happened. "You're slow, kid," Daddy would say. "They'd skin you alive in Texas." I never reached for the magazine until he looked away.

Daddy was from West Texas, and liked to brag it up. "Hey, Kroger," someone would say, "what about Texas?"

He always answered the same way: "Texas is the floor of Hell." And then he laughed, but it was a laugh I knew. It held his hatred.

Sue's in bed sick all the next day, like always after a party. I clean the place up, then take the kids to the library. In the reading room, a gas fire hisses sleepily in the hearth, and I sit in a big soft chair reading old *New Yorker*s. Christmas stories. Those bittersweet resolutions. Then the kids rush in and show me what they've picked out, square tomes their arms can hardly fit around. I flip through one and see gypsies, pirate ships, a dancing bear.

"Can you teach me how to draw that?" Stephanie asks.

"Sure." My pencil gets into my hand and starts to copy the bear in the margin. Stephanie makes me erase it. All the way home, she lectures me about taking care of the library's books.

I'm in the kitchen making spaghetti when I hear Sue throwing up in the bathroom. After a while, she stumbles in, clutching her robe around her. It's getting dark outside. I make some hot tea.

"There's a beer left in the fridge," I say. "You want it?"

"Jesus, Dave."

I pop it and act like I'm going to pour it on her. She bats at me with hands weak as water.

"Stop it," she whines. "No more parties."

"You always say that."

"Did I do anything bad?"

I used to tell her. She would argue with me. "You were okay."

"You can tell me, baby."

I used to wonder if she really blacks everything out, or if she just pretends. I still wonder. I take a deep breath. "I love you."

"Rub my forehead."

I knead the flushed skin above her closed eyes. "You going to go see your dad?" she asks.

"You really think it will help?"

"It'll help your mother." She starts to stir her tea with her finger, the way she does her drinks, but it's too hot. "Your mom's sweet. Remember the first time I met her?"

"I remember. You got drunk."

"She took such good care of me."

"I heard what my father said about it later. He said, *I've been shot at by better women.*"

Her frown tightens against my fingers. "What are you trying to tell me, Dave?"

I get up and stir spaghetti.

In fifth grade, I had a dry cough that wouldn't go away. My father hated it. "Cut that out," he'd say. "You ain't sick." He and Adrienne would cough when I did, mocking me. Sometimes, he came into my room and bounced me off the wall. Sometimes, he sent me outside so he wouldn't hear it. He liked to send me outside when it was cold. I tried hard to just clear my throat instead of coughing, and my throat got all clogged and raw and I drank lots of water.

When I joined the Army, my chest x-ray showed scar tissue in my lungs. The doc said I must have had TB once long ago.

There's a lot of new construction in Springfield. The roads to the mall are choked with small, shiny cars. But on the west side, where I grew up, it's still the same sleepy, country town. I cruise the square, where the streets have been closed to make a downtown park. Senior citizens stroll past boxed shrubbery, avoiding the eyes of winos at the corners. The giant windows of the old department stores are empty and dark. Harmon's Barber Shop is a Planned Parenthood.

Mother comes out on the porch when she sees my car. She's gotten too skinny. I bend down so she can hug my neck. She's exactly as tall as Sue, something I've never noticed before.

"Long time," I say.

"It's good you're back." She takes me inside and gives me coffee, rattling on about what's happened to neighbors I don't remember. "The Walkers—well, he died, and she went to Arizona." After a while, she starts on my father. First the medical jargon. Then the apologia.

"There's a lot you don't know. Bad things happened to him when he was growing up down there round Amarillo—"

"I've heard all this. All those sad immigrant days."

"You never knew your daddy's father," she says. "He...wasn't a good man..."

Mother goes on talking, but it's like she's speaking in tongues: I can't make out the words. For a minute, I wonder what's wrong with her. Then I know it's me. I go out on the porch to get away.

When something hurts, and you can't make it stop hurting, you want to know why it happens. But there comes a time when pain is bigger than any question. I don't want to know who he was, what bent him. I want him to leave me alone.

After a while, Mother comes out, wiping her face with a Kleenex. "You're a good son," she says.

I want to hit her.

This house is smaller and dustier than I remember. The kitchen faucet leaks, and the top of the stove is black with grease. I poke my head up through the trapdoor in the attic. Nothing there but old tools and rags.

In my parents' room, the bed sags in the middle, and stacks of old clothes cover everything. Voices scratch from the scanner radio.

"That's all he did these last two years," Mother says, "was lay in bed and listen to the police calls. He left it on all night long."

I call Sue. My finger feels funny cranking the dial of the old black phone. Sue is getting ready to go to the movies with her friend Liz. They always get together when I'm out of town.

"Have you seen him?" she asks.

"Not yet... Something happened that was double-weird. Mother was talking and I couldn't make out what she said."

"You're stressed."

I let it go. There's something else on my mind. I try not to say it. But I do:

"Don't get too drunk, honey."

"I won't."

"Is Liz driving?"

"Uh-huh."

"I can come home tonight."

"Whatever you want."

Mother understands that I want to go to the hospital by myself. She's there most of the time, anyway. She's falling asleep on the couch as I put on my tie.

In the bathroom, I run my hand over the cracked tile, the sagging basin. When I was growing up, I would never go in there if my father was in the house; the very idea would throw me into a sweating panic. I've got pieces of memory, though, of being in there with him when I was very small, taking my bath, and he'd come in to urinate. He would run hot water over my head till I cried, then laugh and call me sissy. Then he said I didn't wash good enough and he was going to show me how.

After that, I can't remember anything. I remember the first part happening over and over, but not what happens next. When I was going to the shrink, she tried to make me remember that part. That was when I quit going to her.

St. John's is a rambling castle of cement and stone, less grim and vast than my memory of it. They've raised a new wing and leveled a block of tree-shaded houses for a parking lot. In the marbled lobby, families mingle and fret in low voices, and nurses flex their tired, white-coated shoulders.

Mother's given me the number of my father's room, but I don't go there right away. I sit at a booth in the cafeteria for a long time, staring at the faded mural of the Last Supper that covers one wall. I drink a lot of coffee, paying for each cup. Then I go out and walk the halls. Orderlies push carts of dinner trays, and janitors pace behind their WET FLOOR signs. Through the crack of a door left ajar, I glimpse a young woman, her breasts bare, sitting up among machines. I turn my head and walk a little faster. In Maternity, I watch new babies, their roars muffled by the glass wall, until the ward closes and a patient nun shoos us out. I find the door with my father's number on it, but walk by. Visiting hours are over, and when someone glances at me, I try to look purposeful. There is no end of corridors here. I could walk forever. Like a kid playing hooky, I ride the elevators up and down.

Down one corridor, I find some wheelchairs, racked up against each other like shopping carts. I sit in one for a while, then push off slowly. It glides on the buffed floor much more smoothly than I would have thought, and when I reach back, the rims turn easily in my hands, the chair leaps forward. I roll past a sobbing couple, and the man jumps to open the doors before me. I nod my thanks and he smiles encouragingly.

It's easier, maybe, to be damaged in a way people can see. What would my childhood have been like if I'd been crippled, if Daddy had hurt my spine one time when he knocked me down. Would he have built me a ramp? Given me Adrienne's bedroom? Maybe if I couldn't walk, he would've felt I'd been punished enough.

In a men's room, I stare at my face in the mirror for a long time. It's an ordinary face, but the eyes are blood-raw and afraid. He's dying; he can't hurt you now, I tell my shuddering heart. But my heart answers, He will find a way. For a minute, I press my fist against the mirror and think about putting it through, but there's no point. The world is full of mirrors. Instead, I lay my cheek against the cold glass and close my eyes, and let the memories run around inside my head.

This was a game my father played. He called it Why. He would make me stand in front of him and he'd ask me why I always looked so sad.

"Why so sad, boy?" I wouldn't answer, and he slapped me. "Why don't you cry?" He slapped me with the other hand. It went on and on, the two questions and the rhythmic blows.

Once, when I was ten, I tried to fight him. He got hold of my throat and choked me till my fists relaxed, then dragged me out on the back porch. He made me drop my pants and shorts and then he whipped me with his belt. Across the alley, some neighbor girls were watching. I got teased about it at school all that year.

"Thought for sure you'd cry then," Daddy said as I slowly pulled up my pants. "You're a tough little shit." He got a rag and wiped his belt.

"Why do ya do it?" It surprised us both that I spoke. My voice didn't sound like me. It sounded older.

"What, boy?"

"Why, Daddy? Why do ya hurt me?"

"*Y* is a crooked letter," my father said, and laughed.

Two in the morning. The tiled halls are still, the lights dimmer. Behind the station counter, a nurse sits reading, his broad back turned, and doesn't look up as I slow-foot past. As a boy, I strove to become invisible, a wraith my father would not molest. Now here, at the heart of peril, I have achieved it.

The door is ajar. I slip through, quiet as a thief. A night light glows, and the dials on the machinery blink and crawl. In the shadows, under the oxygen tent, is a man who might as well be a stranger. The hair is gone, the jowls shriveled, the toothless mouth gapes. His breath rasps like a burglar's muffled file.

Light streams in behind me. The dying man's eyes open, rove a little, and close. Nothing flickers in them. I turn to the nurse who stands in the doorway.

"I just got into town. This is my father, and I—" I swallow. It feels like pieces of metal going down. "I had to see him."

The nurse's face softens, but he still has his job to do. "Okay. But you have to go down to the lounge now. At the end of the hall."

He goes out. I stand with the doorknob in my hand, staring back at my father. Once, he was a giant, and had all power over me. But that's been over for a long time, and it's time I came to know it.

His breath rasps. One anorexic shank juts from under the sheet. There are wires that could be unhooked, tubes I could pull. But I don't have to do it that way. He doesn't know me.

Soon I'm out of town, heading west on Highway 60. Snow blows in the beams of my headlights. The night is a black wall, thronged with the wavering ghosts of all our fathers, all our sins, all the carnage we wreak in this world of fear and passion and then have to live with. I think of the woman I love, of the children we've made together, of the fear that chokes me sometimes when I think of the ways I might someday hurt them. This, I think, is my father's last blow against me, his final revenge; and in the drone of the heater I hear his laughter.

A week later, the call comes in the middle of the night. Sue listens, murmurs, hangs up. I lie still in the darkness.

"He's gone," she says.

"I know."

"The funeral's Monday."

"Okay."

"Want to talk?"

"No."

After a while, I hear her slow, even breathing. Headlights outside push the shadows of our elms across the room. And then, slowly at first, my throat tightens, my eyes burn, my chest aches with something I have to get away from. It feels like my face is falling apart. It feels like fighting—but my fists tangle in the blankets, shatter glass across the dresser, pound at the plaster of a wall that won't give me a place to hide. Sue is behind me, holding my shoulders, telling me it's okay to cry.

I pull away. But she hangs on.

Kid Gentle

When she needed to say something just to hear the sound of her own voice, she said "Sam," struck to find his name on the tip of her tongue: she would have reasoned she was so angry that his name would have needed some summoning up, but no.

The stream rilling past Jenny's boots ran, with erosion, the reflectionless soft café au lait of adobe. She waded with what she told herself was caution, fearing a submerged strand of barbed wire. Rain had sleeked her T-shirt to her skin, and each breath was a brief-lived heartache, so cold was the air, so charged with ozone. The arroyo's far wall was washing out in a dangerously deep arch, a red-clay cave marbled with exposed juniper roots and resonant with lapping water. Crouching, she counted twenty or more cigarette butts in a wobbling raft. The Delgado kids played in there, however often she asked them not to. Purely from self-consciousness, Jenny was charming with children, absurd, conspiratorial; in consequence, the dark-eyed, truant Delgados failed to take her seriously. Jenny dragged sandbags back into alignment in the low wall meant to stave off further erosion. The adobe slip that smoothed the burlap weave greased her freezing hands. The wall was useless. Sam needed to assess the damage and come up with their next move. *Sam* needed to warn the Delgados about keeping their three boys out of the arroyo, which flooded fast, often more than knee-deep, after rains like this evening's. The last time she'd talked to them, the two older boys stood pitching stones at a fence post while the smallest, who liked Jenny, stared ashamed at the toes of his sneakers, his unthrown stone in his fist. She was afraid for them: it had made her voice hard, frankly forceful, and of course they'd hated that. And still hadn't—the cigarette butts proved—listened.

Jenny sat heavily on a sandbag that soaked through the seat of her jeans. Her neck was bitten and, though she slapped, bitten again, mosquitoes working air that seemed too cold for them.

From here, a corner of the house was visible, though it was fading fast. The bedroom window, whose blue shutters were the secret reason she'd agreed with Sam to buy the house, wasn't lit. A trick she could have learned in ten days alone: Leave a light on when you go out near dark. A scrap of paper blew shyly past her shoulder, winced and was alive, hyper, a bat after mosquitoes. Echoing back and forth between the arroyo's walls, more bats. Between clouds, the moon emerged, the dazzling white of fireworks, to cast her shadow down running water.

Sam has been sleeping, with his Army surplus bag and a borrowed futon, on the cement slab that will be the floor of a greenhouse, the roof already raised in bright blond two-by-fours. A cat crouches on Sam's chest at dawn, tucking its paws under and purring. The first time the cat's weight landed on his chest, Sam believed he was dying.

"Dying?"

"I wake up thinking *heart attack,* and it takes me a minute: *cat.* No, it's a cat. My heart's going *wham wham wham,* and gradually I figure out this means it's still working." He'd told this to Jenny long distance last night, expecting her laugh, counting on her laugh, and what did Jenny say? "Are you coming home?"

"Ever?" he answered, and she noted the hushed exhale that meant he was smoking a cigarette she would have bitched at him about if she'd been surer of his mood. He was calling from half an hour distant, from the Santa Fe place of the couple whose greenhouse he was building. The greenhouse was ambitious, passive solar, and he'd told Jenny it could easily need another month. *Another month.* "How are you?" he asked. A Sam tactic: Try acting as if nothing's wrong, and see if she'll take him up on it. This disingenuousness got them out of various scrapes, at least those neither of them wanted, or wanted badly enough, to be in.

"I hate the nights."

"You'll be fine."

" 'You'll be fine' is how you blow away whatever serious thing I've just said." She blew across the receiver, vehement illustration, and was surprised by a faint zinging reverberation like a tuning fork's.

"Jenny, all I mean is I know you. You will be fine."

Fine alone? Or fine with you? is what she didn't ask next. *Maybe we need this time apart* is what she didn't provoke him into saying.

Jenny waded back down the arroyo and climbed the skiddy path between drifts of Christmas-tree scent that were wet junipers in the dark. Cascades from the gutters—*canales,* she amended— foamed down the footers for the porch—*portal,* in Spanish—she and Sam had imagined last winter, trading a napkin back and forth across a table homesteaded by their clutter of spoons and saucers, Jenny's gloves, Sam's watch cap, its navy wool glittering with the clear pinheads that snowflakes shrank to in the close café warmth. A hundred futures for their house have appeared on napkins, torn envelopes, the backs of checks for two cups of coffee. However fitful, this was their deepest conversation, these sketches one or the other of them pushed away from the wet ring left by a lifted cup. In this exchange, they played hookie from themselves. Sam grew covetous, ingenious, rash, Jenny sober, calm, calculating, adding up, sometimes aloud, the probable cost of his schemes. They argued more or less softly. When she was pregnant, Jenny began drawing a child into the sketches. The child had an agile, compact body and heavy, fair, straight, stick-straight, bowl-cut hair that couldn't completely hide its too-large ears, but it didn't confront the viewer (her, Sam) directly enough to be definitively boy or girl. Before long, it dawned on Jenny that she kept drawing the same child.

Something else occurred to Sam. "You draw a kid, never a baby."

"So?"

"So you skip the worst helplessness. The first year—entire, total dependency."

"You think I'm frightened." She was more interested than accusing, though she was a little accusing.

"I think you're smart to be frightened."

Just inside the front door, Jenny dropped her clothes in a muddied knot. Her jeans had grown skinny and cold and had to be weaseled out of. She stood pale, even in the dark, hugging herself.

Ah: there was still, despite the storm, electricity. The bathroom
went bright at a touch. She bathed in water so hot it was primally
consoling, a cirrus of steam lolling from its surface, like a hot
spring, with a hot spring's weary mineral taint, which was really
the corroded-iron stink of the old pipes exposed in the wall he
was meditating on. Nearly every project Sam undertook was initi-
ated by a hole in the wall. Jenny towel-dried her hair into strings
and hid her mirrored nakedness in clothes from the floor—leg-
gings, undershirt, sweatshirt, socks, Sam's bathrobe. She remembered marveling at her ignorance after the little stick turned deci-
sive blue. In the mirror, her tongue had gone to the corners of her
mouth, she had tilted her chin this way and that. Her eyelids did
seem subtly fattened, the definition of her hipbones blurred. The
areolas of her nipples had pinked and swollen. In their stems,
openings had appeared, tiny as tear ducts, in a ragged ring. *I can't
believe it:* the vertigo of not having known some grand body
change was taking place, the sense of being dragged forward in
time, *not ready,* victim of a careening loneliness.

From that loneliness, she cast forward. Eventually, her certainty
that she was going to die would be this sharp. Her soul would feel
this tricked, this undercut. *But this is me! Me! You have to listen to
me!* Her body had recognized its chance and closed around it like
some gentle fist. *Tick tock,* Jenny thought, without happiness, and
then, far too fast for any transition, with happiness. She considered her reflection with new regard. It could get pregnant. She
hadn't known that. She knew herself, irresolute and thirty-six and
full of trouble. If she wanted this, if she ever wanted this, now was
the time.

When Sam said, "Do you want it?" she countered, "Do you?"

"Jenny—*Do you?* is the question."

(What did that mean?) (How much would he help?) "Not the
only question."

"The first question."

It was clear from their voices, from the possessiveness of her
arms around him, from the persuasive tenderness with which he
ran a hand down her back to her bottom and up again, her forehead to his chest to hide what she thought, then her chin tipped

up because she couldn't stand not knowing what he thought—but it was already clear, clear what they wanted, what they had learned, that minute, to want.

I, I, I went the fairy tale. You'd been listening ever since you could remember to *Now I'm going to* or *I changed my mind about* or *All I really need is,* absorbed in each twist and turn of the narrative. *I love*—you didn't know how to begin to perceive *I love* for what it was. Distrusting *I* constructions was tantamount to distrusting consciousness. Impossible not to believe the universe—sun and moon and stars—swung around *I love.* "I do want it," in an amazed voice, was meant as an answer, was meant to decide the future.

Miscarriage had taught Jenny: *I* could be so small, could be the magnet for a vast helplessness. *This can't happen to me* never stopped anyone's bleeding. She felt a fool, a freak, not to have known that. She was no longer a fool, a freak, a child.

The kitchen was an almost safe place, *almost* because she was acutely aware of being alone for the night. She set out a cup and saucer.

As a child she'd made a game of passively letting the tears streak where they wanted, slicking her nostril wings, even creeping in, dampening breath, or beading on her upper lip and insinuating themselves into the corners of her mouth until they were a taste, searing fresh salt. Crying's rhythm had been distinct. It escalated, peaked, fell off, and raggedly revived. It finished in clear-eyed calm, even elation. No more. Crying now is ugly, exacting, bitter through and through, monotonous from the beginning, ending only in exhaustion. Sam said, *Unreasonable,* he said, *Come on,* he said, *This can't be good for you, honey.* He said *honey,* and something far, far down inside her went sweet. Whatever else she felt, something went sweet, as if a single leaf in an aspen tree flipped over and caught the light. That's how she keeps herself from crying now. He's not here to say *honey.* He can't seem to say it on the phone. It could be he needed her face to say *honey.*

Was it a change, did it matter, that she didn't cry, was she further along in the course of grief? She was aware there were supposed to be stages, but she'd resisted knowing what they were, or what somebody thought they were. The kettle shrilled. The tea bag bled itself an amber nimbus. Jenny drank, tucking dry cotton feet on a chair rung, newspaper all over the table.

WEDDING DRESS, never been used, size 8 petite. $400. Plus veil. Josie.

Nobody tolerated, in a wedding, any whiff of previous failure, did they? Or could some couple believe their love impervious to the bad luck of a never-got-used beautiful dress? The wind was back, shivering the reflection of the kitchen in the big kitchen window, lofting the page of newsprint a hair's breadth from the table. Sam has said that window needs caulking.

FOR SALE, small six-year-old Paint Mare, Pretty, goes English or Western. Asking $500 or best offer. Call Jim evenings.

Jenny had learned English, but Western was practical in Rio Arriba County's gopher-dug fields, washboarded dirt roads, and eroding badland bluffs. A painter, she liked "paint" used of a horse—liked, too, the cheerfulness of errant capitalization, and the confusion over whether the mare's name was "Pretty" or Jim just thought she was. Evening. This was evening. Getting late. Sam's calls, from the greenhouse couple's place, have been late, evasive, as coded and inconsequential as a boyfriend's. Maybe he became *husband* too young, so that *boyfriend* floated out there, a state whose possibilities hadn't been exhausted. The ring on Jenny's finger was eased on (her friends pretend distress) when she was twenty. He was twenty-two. She will have to learn *girlfriend* all over, the light provocativeness, the essential friendliness. This idea makes her feel tired and sad and heavy-handed.

She reread the ad's last line, finding it simple to lose interest. Sam had said, "*Borrow* a horse, then," sounding like himself again in his impatience with her. She skipped past cords of piñon, ten-speeds, chain saws, tipis, and automatic baby swings to:

FOR SALE, good mountain and pleasure horse, 5 years old, QH type, good disposition and solid dark feet. For an intermediate rider, $700. Leave message for Rick.

Jenny liked this horse for standing so foursquare on his solid dark feet. What she suffered was attraction: Here was such calm. His lip cringed up like a chimpanzee's, elastic, whiskered; his teeth closed on her weed bouquet. He jerked at the leaves with restrained ducks of his heavy head, broad for braininess between the ears—Rocky, his name was. A ten-year-old in a baseball cap had guided Jenny to this field, and was waiting, still straddling his dirt bike, a presence she wished she could ignore, because it was a kind of lie, or at least an act, for her to be here at all. In a fit of blackly descending detachment, she knew she couldn't buy the horse. She lacked the energy to return to the trailer and carry on the nice, vague, glancing negotiation with the boy's father— Rick—that would have shaved some amount from the seven hundred asked-for dollars.

Actually, the boy's father hadn't been alone in the trailer, but with another man, like enough to be his brother or cousin, and they'd been making breakfast, an entire refrigerator's profusion emptied onto the kitchen table—jars of jalapeños, mayonnaise, and salsa, an onion minced right onto Formica, a carton to which the broken eggshells had been returned, a cigarette left burning in a jar lid gleaming the broken-glass purple of grape jelly. "Can you cook?" Rick wanted to know. He'd gestured helplessly with a spatula. *This is a mess.*

"You look like you're doing fine," Jenny said.

Rick studied her up and down. She supposed she looked tense, standing there in her T-shirt and jeans, hands shoved deep in her pockets, a boyish pose, defensive; in fact, she couldn't have said what she was doing there, or how she was going to get out of there, but Rick unexpectedly helped. "If you can find my kid, he can take you out to that horse we're selling."

Now, "Aren't you going to ride him?" the boy demanded. He yanked his bike around and pedaled hard to catch her.

"I just remembered something," she said foolishly.

"What?" he cried. "What?" incredulous as a conscience at what she was doing. She worried he wasn't watching, the dirt road all ruts and stones, but he jarred along gymnastically.

She avoided the trailer stranded on its cinder blocks, but starting her Volkswagen, she had to recognize, through the wind-shield, the boy's disappointment. He didn't wave. She had, obscurely, no right to leave.

A dusk without rain, but growing steadily colder, kindling by the woodstove but no fire lit, tea in its cup by Jenny's elbow. The dark-footed gelding finally disappeared from the want ads a week ago.

> Six-year-old chestnut Quarter Horse mare, nice mover, reli-able. $500. Call evenings.

Not sinful, wanting a horse, but inexplicable, in Sam's view. Or, Sam's code for the irrational, "Not something we need." Their road winds down a hill, two dirt streamers with a central mane of parched grass, and where it passes Delgado's and Salazar's or-chards, it's so narrow Sam's truck is raked by twigs, and he finds apples in with his tools. Sam's gunning of the engine at the foot of the hill is the single familiar sound the night withholds. She knows the phone won't ring. It rang last night, and before they got very far, their mutual evasiveness fell through—did a gaudy col-lapse into tension so flagrant she asked, "What do we do now?"

When he said nothing, Jenny caught herself rehearsing an answer for him: *We try again, O.K.?*

In the space of a held breath, this little inward voice instructed Jenny in her answer to that answer: *Oh, I want to, too.*

Imagine *trying*, knowing what you knew, *trying* deliberately, eyes open.

"What do we do now?" was still waiting, and it was what he answered, obliquely. "You're so angry at me."

She was scared to find herself so alone, and turned on him with consummate scornful patience. "Because you act like this didn't happen, or like it happened only to me, and I'm the only one who has to think about it. I dream about it, did you know that? I dream about you not getting there."

"Jenny. This isn't the time. I can't go into it."

"Of *course* you can't."

She'd meant to hurt. Another wary, hidden-from-her exhala-tion. He smoked more when he was away, and kept the clothes in his duffel neater than in his drawers in their bedroom dresser, and bought lottery tickets. He told her he was tired and when she said she knew that, he said he was too tired to come home.

Six-year-old Thoroughbred mare, race winner at Santa Fe Downs last spring. $400. Call Mack.

The cost of Josie's wedding gown plus veil, and "Thoroughbred" functions as a one-word seduction. *You're not thinking,* Jenny told herself. *Not using your head.* Sam's stress on *using.* Anyone could own a cliché through sheer idiosyncrasy of inflection. Jenny's doctor had warned that they should not rush themselves, but give each other *time.* Boxed, wrapped, ribboned, to be exchanged like anniversary gifts, or did Dr. Chavez mean time was an element they were to share, like the oxygen you both breathed when you lived in the same house, like a bed? The cup rang in its saucer. She couldn't guess how destructive last night was. The injury's dimensions were shadowy because it had occurred in Sam.

The morning after they became lovers, Sam broke two fingers in touch football with his housemates, and because she'd been sitting on the sidelines, barely awake but on the verge of disenchantment, anyway—he'd seemed the silliest, the least familiar, of seven boys—her morning-after doubt abandoned her. She had to drive him to the hospital: he was hers. They waited out red lights with held breath. The doctor told Jenny, "Here's what's going on with your boyfriend." Who was she—girlfriend, after one night? lover?—to be shown his x-rays? Nobody had thought she should be uneasy, seeing inside, seeing irremediably deep, seeing slender bones. He said, "What's come over you?" when they made love that night.

He said "What *is* it?" so tenderly. What had come over her was fear. He was real to her, and she wasn't real to him yet.

He would say that the skittishness with which the mare observed this stranger, Jenny, was proof of the continual high-strung singing of the nerves that wrecks Thoroughbreds. The mare's owner, end of a blond braid showing under her riding helmet, coaxed the mare's nose into the bridle cat's-cradled between her hands, then let the reins drop to the mare's withers, which flinched, even that lightly struck.

"I should warn you," the woman, Lindsay, said. Mack didn't exist; Lindsay hadn't wanted any crazies on the phone. "It took me half an hour to catch her." She rested a palm judgingly on the mare's chest. "Feel."

The slickness was like a wet dog's, muscled, hot, holding a potent faraway heartbeat. Sweat stung a paper cut. Jenny sucked the finger and heard herself: "I haven't been on a horse in so long."

"Really? Is the Bad Girl who you want to start with?"

"Bad girl?"

"Cortez's Shining Daughter, her papers say. Shiny Little Bitch when I can't catch her. The Bad Girl."

"She's beautiful."

"That's the thing." Lindsay was bumped a step forward, butted from behind. "Horse for 'Can we please rock-and-roll?' "

Jenny recollected then that people who hung around horses a lot liked making up dialogue for them. "Why are you selling her?" This wasn't rude, Jenny figured, not given this coyote-fenced paddock, the lap pool in the distance, the architecturally inscrutable house—adobe saltbox?—beyond that. She had parked her VW beside a baking black Mercedes, and felt fraudulent.

Lindsay said to the horse, "Me kiss you goodbye? Can that, can that happen? Is it really a question?"

Jenny assumed the last question meant her. "If you want it to be," Jenny said. "I like her."

"You're still on the ground."

Jenny, given a leg up, hoped this mocking, pitiless person couldn't tell how unsure her seat was. Her hands transmitted an unfamiliar tension, at which the mare's ears flattened. *"Anh-anh-anh,"* Lindsay chided, handing up the black velvet helmet, still warm from her head, a secure fit, Jenny's jaw daintily underlined by the strap. Jenny dug her heels in harder than she meant to, and the mare startled into a canter, ears clicking forward to frame a movie of the ground, sage and junipers reeling past foreshortened, dust acrid on Jenny's tongue, a sly panic rising. The mare perceived mistrust, which was incorporated into her canter as an imprecision, the not-entirely innocent threat that she'd put a foot wrong. Jenny relaxed hands and knees, faking a confidence the mare bought. Her canter settled, the field was crossed, space flung itself out and grandly outward, as if in reaction to them—space set off like rings radiating from a skipped stone—like fast, serial touches of stone across water, and Jenny, remembering it completely as she felt it again, had the sweetly fearless sensation of loving speed. The fence rose before them, the mare cornered neatly, and a magpie flared from a juniper. The mare jarred sideways, dodging the bird and then dodging from haywire momentum, and Jenny was seized by a long, weightlessly pure moment of grief.

Her shoulder smashed first and she rolled, fearing hooves, hoofbeats concussing the ground she was sliding across, her forearm in front of her face, knees and elbows grinding across sun-warmed gritty dust that threw at her a cholla, a prickly pear, before stony gravity fixated on her, before the silently dilating, slowly steadying earth let her lie there. A line of ants wound past her nose in huge close-up, bearing a butterfly wing, a backlit yellow shard carried along, scarcely trembling. The ants that followed carried the butterfly's antennaed head. Jenny sat up, holding her wrist, trying her fingers.

In her bathroom, Lindsay doled out Tylenol before concentrating on the arm Jenny extended.

"I'm a coward," Jenny said.

The thorns were as wickedly elusive as fish bones, translucent but, unlike fish bones, rigid, bristling. Lindsay said tensely, miserably, "Ow," each time she nicked one free. "What's this?" Tweezer tips indicated linked hives.

"Red ants."

"For somebody who didn't get hurt, you got hurt."

"Do you think it needs a doctor?" Jenny asked, a question met somewhat blankly by Lindsay's wide, pale, appraisingly practical face.

"I can do this."

"O.K."

"If you trust me to."

Like all people who ask you to trust them, she was a little offended. "O.K."

"Bear with me. *Ow.* Can you hold any stiller?"

Relief washed through Jenny, seated on the john with nothing more to do. All around them, Mexican tiles sported small blue birds, naively painted, their wings spread wide. Jenny began painting birds. Jenny dashed off wings, curved breasts, swallows' tails in rapid dozens; she lived in a sunstruck Mexican village and she made her living painting exactly the same bird again and again and she was never coming back: it was too nice knowing just what would happen next.

"Done. Now for your face." Lindsay lifted Jenny's chin, Jenny shutting her eyes against the painful glare that was the skylight. Lindsay washed Jenny's face so gently that Jenny felt acutely child-like. She felt shaken by such a dose of tenderness, as only an adult can be shaken.

In her kitchen, Lindsay poured Scotch into tumblers. "Cliché," she said.

"Cliché?"

"Doctor's wife drinks away the lonely afternoon. That was your first ride in how long?"

"I don't really drink," Jenny said. "Years. I'm on her back two minutes, maybe."

"You fell well, you know. Not everybody can, not even good riders. Do you remember Jackie Kennedy calling Jack in a rage because paparazzi caught her landing on her rear? He says, 'Honey, if the First Lady falls on her ass, it's news.' He was what none of them are now—funny."

"I loved him."

"God, I loved him."

"I cried."

"God, I cried."

"Then we find out about Marilyn Monroe."

"Then we find out he's a pig. Well," Lindsay said, "to news," and they chinked glasses.

"You're not telling me to go out there and get right back on."

"Nope. I'm for getting back on when you want to."

Lindsay poured again, talking—the worst tricks Cortie had played on her; other, truly vicious horses she'd known; falls she'd seen. "It's a lot to ask." Lindsay brooded over Scotch barely paled by Perrier. "You're all right, and she's all right."

Jenny grew increasingly dreamy in Lindsay's gleaming, finished kitchen. No holes in the walls anywhere in this house. Maybe this was what Sam got from being away. The details of other people's lives were a distraction surprisingly intense, as if you'd secretly believed your own depression had starved everyone else of vitality. Here was Lindsay, saying, "A bite," scratching at a shoulder, then savaging it with French-manicured nails, here were the blond strands that wavered, buoyed by static electricity, from her loosening braid, and past her shoulder the dishtowel hanging from the oven door, a shadow replicating each fold, farther, infinitesimally scaled shadows cast by each pane in the waffled cloth, like the tranquil iteration of cells across a honeycomb, the compounding of facets in a butterfly's eye, cratering of rain in a stream, the transcendent perfectionism of the world, which Jenny had trusted, which had, in her body, miscarried.

"You have kids?"

"Two of my own—ours—plus one from Kenny's first marriage who lives with us. You?"

"We want one," Jenny said. "I think we want one."

The ambiguity attracted Lindsay. She leaned forward over her own crossed arms. Jenny had found that her friendships with women often began this way, with an ambiguity threaded into small talk. If the ambiguity was taken up, then something would follow. The conversation would make a mutually acknowledged, though small, gain in seriousness. Between women, a neglected ambiguity was a rebuff. Between men, it was a courtesy. Therefore, when you set a man and a woman talking together—

Lindsay touched Jenny's wrist to ask, "Does it still hurt?"

—you laid the groundwork for disappointment—

"Hurt much, I mean?"

—incomprehension, recrimination—

Jenny interrupted her own slightly woozy line of thought. "No. Yes. Not really. You were so patient. I can't thank you." She remembered she was supposed to add *enough*. "I can't thank you enough."

"For a minute I was afraid we'd have to call my husband."

"He's a doctor?"

"The worst, an O.B., gone all the time, and when he's here, he thinks I should be like a patient and adore him. He has trouble with the little daily stuff, and I agree, a lot of what I feel is not adoration."

"What's his name, though?"

"Kenny. Chavez. Do you know him?" She set her tumbler down. "You do. You know him. He's your doctor."

"He's my doctor," Jenny said with a lilt.

"Well—what does he say, about your wanting a baby? He likes to tell women your age—you're thirty-five?—to get with the program. He can be crude."

"He said wait before trying again. He was *kind*. I had a miscarriage at five months."

"I'm sorry, I'm so—" Lindsay shook her head. "Such a—"

"It's all right. It is. It was seven—it was eight weeks ago."

Lindsay said, "But isn't two months what Kenny told you to wait before trying?"

Jenny wasn't disturbed that she'd forgotten; she was disturbed that, under a veneer of forgetfulness, she'd known so exactly. *I want to, too.* "You're right."

To the hospital: Jenny, wearing the paint-graffitied sweatshirt and torn jeans she cleaned house in, had tugged her cowboy boots on over dirty bare feet to go out. In the Pojoaque 7-Eleven, she bought Windex and the newspaper and a Hershey's bar she ate two bites of before clicking off Van Morrison so she could concentrate on the interval of disbelief that followed the first pain, and then—oh, fear took her over, and she let it, because she thought fear might know what to do. One downward-dragging menstrual rush followed another, and Jenny thought, *I can drive, it's fastest,* but she couldn't imagine walking to EMERGENCY, which was red letters through falling rain. She let the wipers sweep their half-moons and the engine idle and the headlights keep pouring into the rain until somebody knocked at her window—an orderly, still in his hospital greens, who'd been taking a cigarette break. He helped her. Dr. Chavez had been in the hospital, making rounds. Alone at last, Jenny found the hostile room nearly dark. Her miscarriage had absorbed the light, like a day's work. They had given her something (a lot of things). She curled up, bare feet and gown and sheets and pillowcases quite clean, curling into herself, into the plush cozening of the drugs. During the night, a slit widened into a doorway, in which her doctor, like a half-dreamed, half-seen father come home late, stood studying her. "You're awake. Good. I'll get Sam."

Sam, illumination from the hallways allowing her to piece together, in quick, slanting takes, the angles and shadows of his face. She was sure she was incoherent, but he answered, "Jenny, you can't believe that."

"I didn't want him enough. Not enough."

"Sweetie, sweetheart, shit, this wasn't about wanting. This was just a bad thing that happened."

"I didn't love him. Not all the time. Not enough."

"You loved him. Let's not do this so late at night. Let's really not. Go back to sleep. I'll hold you, all right? I'll hold you, but you need to *shhhhhhhh. Shhhhhhhh.*"

Dr. Chavez had said the next morning, "We hope we don't get this situation. We like to determine a cause, because that's better all round, so I'm sorry. As far as I know, there's nothing wrong with Jenny, and there was nothing wrong with the baby. That we could find." He'd stopped, anticipating Sam's anger.

"We don't get to know why, and you can't rule out the same thing happening again."

"I'm afraid that's the shape of it. But chances are very—"

He'd gone on, Jenny no longer listening. A nurse, less circumspect, from urgent kindness, than the doctor in this morning's conference, had told Jenny the night before that the baby was a boy.

"I've got to go," Jenny said.

"Oh, I think you need coffee." Lindsay set the kettle on the burner. Jenny knew from magazine ads that the kettle was in a design museum somewhere. Even in her sweaty, horsy T-shirt, Lindsay was fresh, together, somehow visibly rich. Envy, Jenny told herself, that's ugly. Considering Lindsay's concern it seemed a new low point. Lindsay poured coffee into glass mugs transparent even to their handles. "Cream?"

"Yes. Thanks." Cream rolled through the soft explosions of time-lapse roses.

"Know why I'm selling her?"

"Selling her. Liar."

"Kenny expects to happen to me what happened to you, only more serious. He claims it distracts him. Some days, he says, that's what he thinks about, me lying in the field hurt, when his mind has to be on what he's doing."

"There's nobody very nearby if you did get hurt."

"I can tell him I tried to get rid of her. That might help calm him down. Listen, you don't have to be looking for a horse to come back."

"I'd like to." Jenny stood, waiting for her head to clear, and was led through a living room done in Saltillo tile and teak and taupe leather couches. The walls were Rothenberg, T. C. Cannon, a sullen Scholder, the front doors massive and carved, long ago stolen from somewhere.

Lindsay said, "Will you call?"

"Or you can."

"You're in the book? Your last name's—?"

"Small."

Lindsay said, "You're a painter."

"Right." Jenny was confused: they'd talked about her being a painter, in the kitchen.

Lindsay dragged her back through the room, past a grand piano crowned by a vase of calla lilies. How to get your money's worth out of lilies: have them twice, once real, once reflected in the oil slick of a grand piano's lid, Jenny thought, before she was aimed at a wall where there hung a small drawing she'd done two years ago—the bedroom window, the Taos blue of its shutters barely figuring in the composition, which was mostly soft umbers and burnt sienna. The window was open a few inches. You could see, though not far, into the dim interior, the wide planks of the floor, the corner of a bed, the crosshatching that was a nine-patch quilt, and, scarcely there, merest suggestion, the intertwined legs of a couple.

Lindsay said, "It's a tiny daydream, not a drawing. It happens in my head."

"My dealer didn't want it, really. Then, when she sold it, I couldn't ask to who. I missed it."

"Why I bought it—this sounds silly—was because I could cover it with my hand. Make it go away, make it come back, with my hand, and it kept being beautiful." Lindsay paused. "Do you want to borrow it? You said you missed it."

"No. I'm just glad to see it again."

At Lindsay's front door, they said, "Well—"

"Well—"

They parted awkwardly, new friends.

Sam came home that night, tense and formal, ready to be patient with her, but it happened that both of them desired an evening without confrontation. It wasn't as strange as it should have been, by any rational scale, to lie aimlessly talking to him again in bed. It hadn't felt as strange as it should have to make love. Their attraction to each other had often enough seemed simple, precipitous luck. Jenny didn't want to question it.

She said, "I sold a painting." The message had been on her machine.

"Which?"

"The pale green apples on the windowsill with our hill in the background."

"But that's huge." Sam often thought of her work in terms of size—of money, really.

"To a couple from Fort Worth, Callie said, who have lots of brand-new bare walls."

"Walls needing paintings?"

"They like me, Callie says."

"People from Fort Worth like you. *Rich* rich people like you."

"Uh-huh. Oh, you have to talk to the Delgados. They don't like me. They like you."

"Well, I'm more easy-going."

She said, "Will you?"

"I already did. I passed Juan on the road. I said that arroyo keeps flooding. He said he'd get after his kids about it." He lifted her arm from the sheets, and would have run his thumb deftly down the line of rash if she hadn't jerked away. She said, "You have to fix those stairs."

The wooden stairs down the slope to her studio, she meant. He had often wondered if those stairs were all right. Prickly pear grew close against them, and it was a believable scenario. He said, "Jesus. Meanwhile, can you be careful?"

She didn't tell Sam she was looking for a horse, and he was gone in the morning before she was awake enough to be vulnerable to questions. She got kissed, and smelled coffee, and woke again an hour later alone. Leaning to pick his shirt up from the floor, Jenny felt generous and capricious and consumed by curiosity about what would happen next: in love. "We need to talk," she told his shirt. When she held it to her nose, there was a carpenter's day— cut wood, sun, breezy sweatiness.

Jenny in her nightgown, two a.m., read of Chevy pickups, wicker love seats, roof shingles, CD players, sets of encyclopedias and outgrown skis; well drilling, bail bonding, marriage licensing, engine rebuilding; guitars, violins, banjos, and mandolins adrift in the Chagall-like night sky that was the true backdrop of want ads everywhere; vacant spaces for trailer homes with complete service hookups; Sikhs to guard warehouses; child care in my home, Christian atmosphere; Navajo rugs restored to their original beauty.

GREEN broke quarterhorse colt, $550 unfinished, $650 finished. Also kid's pony, make offer.

HORSES: one chestnut gelding, $750. One black filly, halter broke, $200, or deal on the pair. Call Larry after 5 or all day weekends.

What was Sam thinking? It's been two days since their night, and he hasn't called. When she gets in from the studio, PLAYBACK yields a dozen voices, none of them his. Though she was seated in a solid chair, though she could identify every sound the night offered, though she'd washed every dish in this kitchen a thousand times, this was the disorientation of crushed expectations. She cupped her tea's heat between her palms, drank, and found:

PUREBRED, registered Arabian gelding, broke, kid gentle, $800 cheap.

"'Kid gentle' means?" Jenny asked the man, early Saturday, and he had a shy, maybe hungover unkemptness, unshaven. The black hair, combed straight back, still wet from the shower, was a little embarrassing, as if she were seeing him at the wrong time or in a too-intimate way, as only a girlfriend should. She caught herself thinking *girlfriend*, not *wife*. He was the kind of handsome Jenny qualified privately as *almost too*.

"What it sounds like." He hoisted his four-year-old, and the boy, in his loftiness, touched the horse's nose. His fingers got snorted on, and he giggled. He put his fingers into the horse's mouth, its upper lip fluttering accommodatingly upward, then reached for its ear and worked it like a lever. "Jase, you let go now," the man, Carlos, said. "I think you proved my point." To Jenny he said, "You want to ride him?"

"I'd like to."

"Can you keep my kid from getting stepped on a minute, and I get the saddle?"

"Sure."

Jenny sat cross-legged, sun very warm on her back. The little boy took a slice of sugar toast from the plank in the fence where he'd left it balanced. "Let me see," Jenny said, and shook an ant from it, and a brief rain of sugar. "You know that was a red ant, don't you?" she said. "Look. They got me." He considered her garish arm, fascinated, then turned his toast over and over before taking a bite. Jenny felt a rising happiness, the grass blowing around them, level fields running down to a wash brimming with spring cottonwoods, that green, the mesa opposite the red of cayenne pepper, and the boy said, "He's my mom's horse."

"Oh? Your mom's?"

"She wants to live in Albkirky with no room for a horse. We don't know if we go with her or not."

"Hey, are you telling all our secrets?" The father ruffled the boy's hair, leaning slightly, balancing the saddle against his side. "Are you going to be just like I am with pretty women?"

Jenny laughed. The child, confused, serious, laughed. When she was in the saddle, Carlos measured the stirrup leather against Jenny's extended leg, and though she wished she didn't, she liked that. Carlos kept a hand on her knee, pointing. "You can go as far as you want down that dirt road, see if you understand each other. All that's our land, but the neighbors won't mind if you get a little past it. He can't get lost."

"What a good quality." She thought he should probably take his hand off her knee now, and he did.

"This is a good horse I'm selling you."

"What's his name?"

"We never named him. Had him how long?, and never did. It seems funny now, but he was just 'the horse.' It's not like we had twenty. I can make one up for you if you want."

"No, thanks."

The horse had a smart canter, chin down, ears pricked. His style was unassuming and mindful. She gave him a little more leg. His new speed, matched by a fractional gain in interest, was just as judicious. He'd be unlikely to put a foot down one of the gopher holes in the bluffs behind Jenny and Sam's house, or shy at barking dogs. Jenny was under no illusion that the gelding experienced anything like the improbable affection she felt for him—why should he?—but he had sweet manners, willingness, quick wits.

"Can I have some time to watch him?" Jenny asked, when she got back, and Carlos grinned, though this time the grin was a shade conscious in its appeal, before saying, "Buy him. Then you get a lot of time to watch him," taking his son by the hand, and leaving her there. Jenny rested against the fence, following the horse's methodical grazing, the muscled slant of his shoulder, the way he put his nose into the grass and nudged once, twice, so that the small bees were driven out.

"Yes," she said at their back porch. She got high-fives from father and son alike, and sat beside them on the steps to write out the check.

Carlos leaned back on his elbows, his son between his wide-apart knees. "He comes with his tack," Carlos said, "and my feeding him until you come for him, I throw that in for free. He trailers real nice."

"I wonder," Jenny said.

This attracted a slantwise doubtfulness; Carlos thought she

could have changed her mind. "Un-hunh?"

"Can I keep him here?"

"Here?" Impolite to ask, directly, *Why?* "It's a drive for you."

"Twenty minutes. I'll come a couple of times a week. I mean"—the pause was awkwardness—"not for long. Until I find a place closer to home for him."

Carlos said, "That's our field. Nobody's using it. You can if you want to."

"Really?" She didn't know how to sound properly grateful—enough, not too much, not stupidly but gracefully appreciative.

"Sure. Really. He's happy here. Getting a little fat, maybe, but you can work that off him. Want some coffee?"

She raked strands of her hair from the corners of her mouth, where the wind had blown them, as it was blowing Carlos's drying hair, as it was blowing around his son's. She wanted a cup of coffee, a kiss, a life she knew inside and out—wanted, with an absurd passion, this man, this child, this place. Who would she be if she let that show, if she went inside, if she had a cup of coffee?

"No," Jenny said, "I think I'd better go," and she and Carlos shook hands.

That night, unerringly, Sam came home. He sat across from her, the table between them lit by a citronella candle. She supposed that if they ever came to an agreed-on break—separation, divorce—Sam would cook for that occasion, too, and they would discuss it like friends. For a lark, he'd dragged their rickety outside table into the middle of the imaginary *portal*. Beneath their bare feet, warm, turned earth. Stars were out.

"So you went ahead and did it." He didn't want to sound so angry. He was too far in the wrong to carry such anger off.

"It was my money."

"It's not only money." The half-coyote mongrel of their neighbors across the arroyo, the Quintanas, leaped the footer, sat and whined, and Sam tossed him the skin of his grilled chicken breast, gone in a snap, and then a heel of French bread the dog trotted off with.

"We'll have ten dogs here."

"Naw, he can keep a secret." Sam poured more wine. "I don't

want you keeping the horse that far away."

"Oh, you don't want me."

"You'd be gone all the time. It would turn into something."

She said, "Your being gone, what did that turn into?"

"It turned into me right here. Honey, I'm home." He could do this, go from antagonistic to charming, skipping conciliatory altogether. She still expected the concessions she would have made, in his place—the strategies to disarm, to rationalize.

She said abruptly, "How sad were you, Sam?"

"You really want to talk about it?"

"That's just one question."

"And if I wasn't as sad as you, I lose you?"

"If I don't know you anymore, do you have me?"

"All right. How sad was I." His voice was absolutely careful. "I thought, before this happened, that we would always be fine. I didn't know you could be in pain and I wouldn't even know— that I'd only get to you hours later. I never believed in my mind we were exempt, but I'm trying to tell you, I was living as if we couldn't be touched."

"Other things have happened." She didn't want to say, *But that's what I felt,* because it would stop him.

"Not like this. It was finding out I'm not the person who can protect you. I don't know if I thought about the baby as much as I thought about you. Maybe I can't take care of anything, I don't know. I don't know what we do, I don't know what comes next, and you—that's what you want to ask me, isn't it? 'What do we do now?'"

"Yes."

"Maybe we don't plan. Maybe we just see."

And did he mean a baby, or did he mean see what things were like between them? It was their usual accord, spoken only to a certain point, trusted—she feared—only to a certain point, but though they spent their days apart, they went to bed together, and before long she knew she was pregnant. She waited to take the test, she waited to tell him—waited, spending the long afternoons riding, or in Quintana's two-stall shed, long unused, where the gelding was kept, for now. Under the corrugated-tin roof, the straw-fragrant heat formed a room of its own, stifling, luxurious.

Dust fumed from the chestnut flank. The curry comb scoured in circles, the brush followed the grain of the hair. The hoofpick flaked chips of gravel from the massive, upturned bowl of bone weighting her knee, her thigh, her entire side. She rested a palm against his neck—like satin flushed from within by a sunlamp. His neck quaked when flies landed, his head lifted and was shaken irritably, the large eye vulnerable, lashed in languid flies. She swept her hand across it, making the eye blink and flies shoo. She didn't know if anything was changing, if trust could accumulate, or—it seemed far more remote—affection, but she was sure kindness had to be gestural here, consistent, patiently repeated.

One morning, later than usual, she shoved the gate open to find the Delgados' smallest boy under the horse, playing with Star Wars figures in a cave, in shade aglint with motes of straw, anchored at its four corners by immobile hooves. The horse flirted its ears nervously at Jenny, who said softly, "You're doing great. You're doing fine," and bent until the boy granted her his attention. His upward gaze had the uncomprehending felicity of a child getting away with something dangerous. She told him to come out slowly, and he came in a sneakered half-crouch, the crown of his head brushing the horse's belly but not distracting the horse from his deliberate, delicate motionlessness.

Jenny caught the boy's wrist and knelt down. Facing her, he got scared at last and clasped her neck, leaning into her as she leaned her cheek against his hair, and they waited. What could have happened withered and grew incredible and blew away, leaving them alone, her arms around him, and his arms around her.

Photopia

My new wife took very few possessions with her when she left Peru, mostly blouses and books and clumps of the hot pepper *aji* wrapped in cellophane, but she did remember to pack her photograph of her father. It was a cloudy black-and-white shot taken in 1960 on his fifty-fourth birthday, two years before his daughter was born, nine years before his death. Somehow during her first confusing days in the States, my wife managed to lose the picture, frame and all. (It was the one irreplaceable thing she brought, and typically, it was the one thing she lost.)

She instantly wrote to her mother in Lima, asking for another one. Her mother responded with a very stern and disapproving note, warning her daughter that she'd better learn to hold on to things, especially things as precious and rare as photos of her father. And no, she did not have any more pictures to send.

The truth was that there really were just a few solo photos, "portraits," of her father in existence. He had disliked being photographed. He had probably been acutely self-conscious, like most ungainly, unattractive people. My wife would only say that he had had bad eyes, had had surgery for cataracts, and that the afterimage of a camera flash stayed with him for days. But she was sure that her brother Andres—her older, more responsible brother, who had left Peru years before and was now living in Spain— would have a photograph of their father, or else he would know where to get one. Andres had special qualities, including a highly resourceful nature and the twin gifts of survival and serendipity—characteristics my wife claimed he shared with all the men on their father's side of the family, excepting of course their father.

So she wrote to her brother, who was living in Madrid, and gave a long explanation on the events that led to the loss of her one photograph of their father. "Permanently misplaced" was the phrase she used. She was wondering if it was possible that he—Andres—

might have a spare photograph somewhere, it could even be a photo where their father was part of a group, so long, of course, as his back wasn't turned to the camera, so long as he was recognizable. And if he didn't have a photo to send her, did he know, did he remember, someone else she could ask? At the very end, she told him not to send his only photograph, not that she expected him to, but she knew how generous he could be. If only one of them could have him, it should be her brother and not her, the son and not the daughter.

The letter to her brother had to be forwarded a couple of times. He had moved from the Calle de Alcala, and when the letter got to the forwarding address on the Calle Zurbano, it was sent on to a third address on the Calle de las Infantas. So he explained in his reply. His letter was just a letter, with no photograph enclosed. He apologized. He said that he hadn't brought any family pictures with him, just a photo of his old girlfriend, Maria, who had stopped writing to him a long time before and whom he suspected to be engaged or married or maybe even a mother already. To hell with her! As to where his sister might be able to come by a photograph of their father, he wasn't altogether sure, he had been out of touch for so long, but he suggested trying Tía Francesca, their father's first cousin and probably the most likely person other than their mother to be in possession of family mementos and the like.

My wife sat down and wrote him a short note, thanking him for his reply and letting him know that Tía Francesca had died of viral pneumonia two summers before.

She wrote to a long list of people, explaining her search for her father's photograph. Her cousin in Chile. Another cousin in Montreal. Her great-aunt in Miami. She wrote to her mother's friends back in Lima (they must please promise not to tell her mother because this was being done as a surprise for her). She wrote to the Lima newspaper *El Tiempo,* asking for a copy of her father's obituary notice and the accompanying photograph she remembered seeing once (she enclosed twenty U.S. dollars for mailing costs). She even wrote to a nunnery in Arequipa—her father's only sister had lived and died there, back in the 1930s, and he had sent annual donations for Hail Marys to be said—requesting a copy of his photograph she thought they might be keeping in a special donor file.

It was the first time in her life she'd been without a photograph of her father, or without any real prospects for getting one.

His image had been one of the great props of her childhood. She played with his picture, talked to it, slept with it pressed between her knees. He was a living presence, a cross between a guardian angel sitting astride her shoulders and a pen pal who lived in a distant city and communicated through secret subliminal messages. She received "invisible letters" from him that she collected and hid in the mouths of her stuffed animals. She had fantasies in which the picture would come to life—lifting these, probably, from Mexican horror movies that appeared regularly on late-night television—in which the lips would move, the eyes would dance, the whole head would move from side to side. Certain attributes of the baby Jesus she passed on to him, and she mixed the two faces in her mind, her father's face and Christ's, not knowing you weren't supposed to do this until a nun at her parochial school asked her to explain a drawing she had done. Thirty paddle whacks on her right hand every day for a month was her penance.

She even prayed directly to his photograph, asking for toys and very specific wishes to be granted (things like going to the beach, or getting a hula hoop), until her mother discovered it and forbade her from ever praying to anyone but the Father, Son, Holy Ghost, Virgin Mary, or a regulation saint.

Twice during her adolescent years the picture fell. The first time occurred during a minor early morning tremor when my wife was eight. At the first sign of the *terremoto,* she ran out into the street, joined there by mothers hoisting up crying babies, men with shampoo still in their hair, wailing maids clutching crucifixes, dogs paralyzed with fear. When she returned to her room, she saw that the quake had caused the picture to fall off her bureau; the frame stayed intact, but the glass plate had cracked. The maid lectured her nonstop for two days—next time, REMEMBER TO SAVE YOUR FATHER.

The glass was replaced the very next day. Much in the house they were then living in was badly in need of repair, including the oven, the front door, and the part of the roof that overhung the kitchen, but intact housing for her father's photograph was obviously considered a priority.

The second accident was the day of her eleventh birthday. She had just received a shiny new transistor radio, and she pushed the picture back to make room for it on her bureau. The picture hit the wall first, then the edge of a night table, then the floor. The glass shattered and the top of the frame was dented. Worst of all, a sliver of glass somehow sliced part of the photograph, creating a tear just below her father's neck. The maid despaired when she saw it. HOW COULD YOU LET THIS HAPPEN TO YOUR FATHER?—as though not just the sacred preservation of his memory but his actual physical welfare rested with her. But a few days later, the frame was repaired, the photograph restored, and the whole thing returned to its customary place.

All there *was* was his photograph.

Her mother never talked about him. Relatives never referred to him. As she grew older, she sensed more and more the terrible bad luck and the precipitous plunge in the family fortunes that had followed his death. No one ever told her anything, she had to glean bits and pieces from overheard conversations and papers her mother left lying around. She was fourteen by the time she learned the true circumstances of his death, that he had collapsed and died instantly while walking on the Jiron de la Union in downtown Lima, that he had fallen so strangely and brutally that his head split open and had to be sewn up with fishing line so they could prepare him for the wake. It took her four more years to discover that after his death, his business partner appropriated certain assets—including a blind share in a cattle farm—produced certain buyout-in-case-of-death documents and discounted others, asserted that my wife's father owed nearly one million soles he had borrowed from the business (again, there was no record of this), and declared himself the single legitimate executor of his partner's business legacy.

There are contradictory facts, whole years unaccounted for.

The only sure thing was that her father had died and everything seemed to die with him. That was the connecting thread, the central theme. She did find out that in the year right after his death, her mother sold their fifteen-room house to a man who knocked on the front door and asked for it, sold their Packard convertible, sold their antiques, sold jewelry and other assorted valuables, all for a fraction of their true worth.

Through the years, the picture of her father went from bigger houses to smaller houses to cramped apartments on the ground floor of faded avenues, where in the afternoons the dust thickened and coated the windows and mirrors, the way dust dares to be omnipresent in the lesser neighborhoods of a city. It was as though the picture were following her from place to place, sometimes even arriving ahead of her. She'd walk into the new bedroom of their new address, or the bedroom she would have to share with the one maid they managed to retain, and there it was, set in silver, staring ahead resolutely and forlornly, waiting for her.

When I met her at the start of the South American summer of 1981–82, a few days after Christmas, she was barely twenty years old.

I was working for a struggling travel company headquartered in Miami that saw tourism to Peru as its last chance for salvation; she was working for a Lima translation services agency, where her fluency in English put her in contact with a lot of Europeans and, to a much lesser extent, North Americans. I came in every day, at first with real translating work to be done and then with made-up work that gave me an excuse to come by. She was very serious for a long time about not wanting to have anything to do with me. North Americans didn't interest her. Being Swiss or French or German was far more compelling in her eyes.

We slowly began a kind of relationship. I'd sit on the steps of her office building and wait for her to come out, and if I was lucky, she'd let me walk with her a little ways, maybe as far as the bus stop near the Parque Central. She was shy and reserved, and volunteered no real information about herself. After a month and a half, I knew that she lived in a neighborhood somewhere near the national *fútbol* stadium. I knew her brother had gone to Spain and sent her a postcard of the Alhambra Palace from Granada. I knew she liked the Beatles. That was about it. In time, we began going out on official "dates," and I met her mother and her two live-in spinster aunts, Beni and Corazon, and saw the inside of their apartment with its rose-patterned curtains and chair coverings, lace tablecloths, and birds of paradise flowers in a vase in the center of the small sitting area. The air was stale and sweet, and I remember thinking how it seemed such a stifling atmosphere for a man.

One day, I finally asked about meeting her father, and she told me not to worry, there would be plenty of time for that.

It became a kind of running routine. I'd point out middle-aged men on the street and ask her, "Is that him?" I told her she was making me very nervous—couldn't I just meet him and get it over with? Or did he not want to meet me? Did he disapprove of me?

I was going to ask her to marry me—I decided this after knowing her for less than three months—and I knew I needed her father's permission. I had talked to several Peruvians, and they all told me there was no way around it. You must ask the father for the daughter's hand. So one day, I pushed and pushed, and insisted that I had to see her father that night. I would wait no longer.

"All right," she said in English. "Come to my apartment at seven o'clock."

I arrived early, and sprawled on a stone wall across the street from their building, smoking cigarettes, practicing my lines in Spanish. *Yo amo su hija*—I love your daughter. *Soy aplicado*—I am a hard worker. *Tengo una pregunta muy importante para usted*—I have a very important question for you.

At seven *en punto*, I rang the bell, got buzzed in, and climbed the steps to the third floor. She was out on the landing waiting for me. Without saying a word, she took my hand and brought me through the dead silence of the apartment into her bedroom. It was a very small room with one window. There were two beds, with just inches between them: one for her, one for Beni. (The last of their maids had been let go by this point.) There was one antique chiffonier, and standing on its narrow ledge was a framed photograph.

She picked it up and, as though making an offering, held it out for me to take.

"Here," she said in English. "Here he is. He has been waiting the whole day to talk to you."

One day, maybe three months after we'd heard from her brother Andres and no one else, and after my wife began to approach a sense of resignation about the whole thing, an oversized envelope arrived, a warning scrawled on the envelope both in English and Spanish: DO NOT BEND and NO DOBLAR. Inside was a brief letter attached by paper clip to a medium-sized photograph. The letter was unsigned. My wife noticed right away that it was not written in her mother's frenzied script, or by her brother's childish hand, or in any other style she recognized.

The letter simply said that enclosed was a picture of my wife's father from the year 1927. That would make him twenty-one in this picture, the letter writer said, more or less the same age my wife was now. (Whoever it was, they knew her current age.) It was an original photo, so my wife must treat it with the utmost care, she must watch over it and regard it as her most prized possession.

In the photo, a man was standing in front of a stucco wall, and behind that was a blurred dark line that must have been a wrought-iron railing. My wife guessed that this might be somewhere in old Miraflores, on one of the side streets that runs behind Avenue Benavides. She began naming a few of the streets, considering each of them. I told her it didn't matter that much, this whole business of figuring out just where he had been standing that particular day, but she was very determined to settle the matter.

After she had convinced herself of the probable location—the third block of Grimaldo del Solar—she turned her attention to the man in the photo. At first, she declared that it wasn't her father. She was sure. Too thin, too toothy. Wrong expression. Wrong posture.

She put the picture down and walked into another room. Then she came back and leaned over the picture for a long time. Very softly, she admitted that it might be him, after all. She said his long nose and his puffy eyelids gave him away. He was wearing a white short-sleeved dress shirt and pants that were so pale they appeared to have no color. He resembled one of those jungle insects that melts into its surroundings. I even thought I saw a certain look—the shimmer in the eyes, maybe, the romantic attraction to the unknown—that sometimes appeared on my wife's face.

He was still single in the new photograph. He was healthy. He was clear-eyed. He was not afraid of the camera. He smiled agreeably. He invited the photographer to take his or her time, to line up the shot. He had the look very young men tend to have in photographs—confident, undoubting, happily blind to the future.

It was hard for my wife to accept an image of her father as a young man, one that was not in accordance with her finely tuned impression of him. In her mind, he was a much older man; he was born at a certain age, as far as she was concerned. It was too strange to see his face without lines, his mouth so expressive, his hair full and black.

Still, she had the photograph framed and put it on the nightstand next to our bed. At first, she kept her distance. She seemed to be sizing him up, and in fact, the reverse also seemed to be true, that he was wary and slightly afraid of her as well. Many nights, I'd find the frame obscured by piles of books or magazines, or thoughtlessly turned so it faced the wall. It was only gradually that she began to approach him freely, to admire him at close range, to hold him in her two hands and smile at his smooth, untroubled face.

The day her father died, she was sitting in her second-grade classroom, between Balbina Velasco and Alfonso García, in the dead, unmoving air of the afternoon session, when her father's driver, Edmund, appeared at the half-open classroom door. The teacher conferred with him for a moment, and then she calmly and clearly told my wife to gather her things, put them in her satchel, and go with Señor Edmund. He walked her out to her father's car, a big green Packard, and as soon as she saw that no one was sitting in the back seat of that shiny hulk, she knew instantly and intuitively that her father was dead. She started to scream, *Quiero mi papi!* and Edmund had to throw his hand over her mouth and plead with her to stop. He had been given explicit instructions from her grandmother not to say anything to the poor little girl—she wasn't supposed to know yet. When he told her this, she somehow dried her eyes and actually and truly made herself forget her terrible newfound knowledge, suppressing it for what turned out to be a reasonable number of hours, all for the sake of keeping the chauffeur out of trouble.

A couple of days later, they had to fire him. He had no one to drive anymore. At first, my wife missed him much more than her father. She dreamed about him. She heard his voice. If a car stopped at the house, she was sure it would be him, it would be Edmund. If the phone rang, she expected to hear his soothing, familiar voice on the other end.

It took time, almost a full year, before she forgot all about him.

CONTRIBUTORS' NOTES

Ploughshares · Fall 1993

GERRY BERGSTEIN is a Boston-based painter. His work has been exhibited in numerous gallery and museum shows in Boston, New York, Chicago, Geneva, Switzerland, and elsewhere. The painting reproduced on the cover was completed in the spring of 1993, while he was the artist-in-residence at the Camargo Foundation in Cassis, France.

WENDY COUNSIL's fiction and poetry have appeared in *The Amherst Review, The San Francisco Bay Guardian,* and *The Hawaii Review,* among other magazines. Her work is forthcoming in *The Amaranth Review, The Chiron Review,* and *Free Lunch.* She lives in California's Santa Cruz Mountains, where she is currently at work on her second novel.

JANET DESAULNIERS's fiction has appeared in *The New Yorker, TriQuarterly, The North American Review,* and once before in *Ploughshares,* among other publications. A collection of her short stories is forthcoming from Alfred A. Knopf. She lives in Evanston, Illinois.

MICHAEL DORRIS is the author of two novels, *A Yellow Raft in Blue Water* and, with his wife, Louise Erdrich, *The Crown of Columbus;* a children's book, *Morning Girl;* and several works of nonfiction, including *The Broken Cord.* His first collection of short stories, *Working Men,* will be published this fall, and will include both "Shining Agate" and "Earnest Money," which was published in *Ploughshares* last spring.

PETER GORDON's work has appeared in *The Yale Review, The New Yorker, The North American Review, The Antioch Review, Glimmer Train,* and elsewhere. He lives in Framingham, Massachusetts, with his wife, Raquel, and sons, Daniel and Jonathan.

ROBIN HEMLEY is the author of *All You Can Eat,* a collection of stories (Atlantic Monthly Press, 1992), and the novel *The Last Studebaker* (Graywolf Press, 1992). A new volume of short stories, *The Big Ear,* will be published by Graywolf next spring. He is Associate Professor of English at UNC-Charlotte, where he teaches creative writing.

FRED G. LEEBRON's stories have appeared in *The North American Review, The Iowa Review, The Threepenny Review,* and elsewhere. In 1993–94, he will be a fellow at the Fine Arts Work Center in Provincetown.

LAURA GLEN LOUIS received a *Nimrod*/Hardman Katherine Anne Porter Prize for Fiction in 1990 for her story "Verge." She is working on a short story collection.

EILEEN MCGUIRE's stories have appeared in the anthology *Delphinium Blossoms* (Delphinium Books, 1990), *The American Literary Review*, and *Glimmer Train*. She lives in Los Angeles.

T. M. MCNALLY received the Flannery O'Connor Award for Short Fiction in 1990, and is most recently the author of a novel, *Until Your Heart Stops*.

MARY MCGARRY MORRIS is the author of the novels *Vanished* and *A Dangerous Woman*, both of which were published by Viking. *Vanished* was nominated for the National Book Award in 1988 and for the PEN/Faulkner Award in 1989. *A Dangerous Woman* was chosen by *Time* magazine as "one of the best five novels published in 1991," and was named Novel of the Year by the Associated Press Editors.

ANN PACKER's fiction has appeared in *The New Yorker, The Missouri Review, The Indiana Review, Prize Stories 1992: The O. Henry Awards,* and elsewhere. Her collection of short stories will be published by Chronicle Books in 1994. A recent recipient of an NEA Fellowship, she lives in Eugene, Oregon.

G. TRAVIS REGIER has worked as a fry cook, teacher, book reviewer, and technical writer. His literary writing has appeared in *Harper's, The Atlantic Monthly, National Forum, The American Scholar, Amazing Stories, Aboriginal Science Fiction, The Massachusetts Review, Quarterly West,* and other magazines.

ELIZABETH TALLENT divides her time between Little River and Davis, California, and teaches at the University of California, Davis. The author of two collections of stories, *Time with Children* and *In Constant Flight,* and a novel, *Museum Pieces,* her work has appeared in *The New Yorker, Esquire, Grand Street, The Paris Review,* and elsewhere. *Honey,* a new collection of short stories, is due out in November from Alfred A. Knopf.

JONATHAN WILSON's book of short stories, *Schoom,* was recently published in Great Britain by Lime Tree. His first novel is forthcoming next year from Secher & Warburg. His stories and essays have appeared in *The New Yorker, Tikkum, The Boston Review,* and elsewhere.

ABOUT SUE MILLER

Ploughshares · Fall 1993

There is something very reassuring about Sue Miller. At forty-nine, she is a strong, vibrantly intelligent woman at the height of her career. The author of three best-selling, critically acclaimed novels—*The Good Mother, Family Pictures,* and the recently released *For Love*—she is poised, confident, and affable. She is a soothing presence, by all appearances an exemplar for those whose authority and trust must be inviolate: teacher, mother, lover, confidant.

Yet she is apt to reveal, without warning or hesitancy, a well of insecurity that you would never expect of her, and to which few authors would publicly admit. In talking about her writing process, for instance, she confesses that she is disorganized, not a daily grinder who can pound out pages at will, and needs to reach a state of boredom and depression before she can face her desk. For she is trying to avoid the quaking, nearly paralyzing anxiety which grips her whenever she begins a new novel: "I think, *I can't do this, I can't go on, my life is worthless, I don't know where to proceed, I don't understand this material, I should have never started this.* I get to a certain point where I'm so *sick* of myself that I finally just *do* it."

Miller has been living in the Boston/Cambridge area for the past thirty-three years, and now splits her time between her South End apartment and a house in the Massachusetts countryside. The second of four children, she was raised in Hyde Park, on the South Side of Chicago. Both her grandfathers were Protestant clergymen, and her father, an ordained minister, taught church history at the University of Chicago's divinity school. It was an odd upbringing, restrictive and liberal at the same time. "My parents were very judgmental," Miller says. "But their idea was to lay out the precepts that governed their lives, and then let you make your own decision. You had to be able to defend your standing in the universe against theirs. If you wanted to be bad, you had to have a rationale for being bad." What Miller chose to be was studious and, by her own admission, somewhat "overachieving." She was a bookish kid, preferring to read over most other activities, and after skipping her senior year of high school, she entered Radcliffe College as a sixteen-year-old.

She remembers those years as being extraordinarily difficult. "I was really unprepared for college. I learned very little, I was so overwhelmed." Part of the problem was that she had no academic or professional direction. In the Fifties, Miller says, the consensus, as understood and transmitted by her mother, was that "you had to be neurotic to be a woman and want a career." Miller knows now that such limitations had made her mother "miserable," yet at the time, her mother maintained that being a housewife was her proper place. Miller herself married upon graduation, and while her husband attended medical school, she supplemented their income with a series of jobs, teaching high school, waitressing, modeling, and pushing rats through mazes as a researcher in a lab. When she was twenty-four, her son, Ben, was born. Three years later, she was divorced.

She worked in day care centers and parent cooperatives for the next eight years, and, as a single mother, hardly had the luxury to do anything else. Writing fiction didn't become a serious goal until she was thirty-five. She had dabbled, of course. As a child, she had composed poetry and short stories for fun. At Radcliffe, where she majored in English literature, she had taken one creative writing course, but hadn't received much attention for her efforts. She had written a novel in her twenties and then another over a long period of time: "It was so tedious and painful a process, by the time I ended it, I could barely remember what it was about." But for most of her life, she had had no sense that writing could actually be an occupation. (By coincidence, the writer Robert Coover had rented a basement room in her family's Hyde Park home when he was a graduate student, but at the time, he was simply the nice young man with whom they had to arrange the bath schedule, since there was only one tub in the house. Miller recalls being astonished when Coover's first novel was published. "God, *Bob Coover*," she had marveled.)

Finally, in 1977, with her life more manageable, she was able to

PHOTO: JERRY BAUER

give herself to the notion of writing with real commitment and discipline. She took a course through Harvard Extension. Right away, she was tremendously confident about her work. For one thing, she felt she now had something to say. For another, she had learned through careful and attentive reading how fiction works, how to use narrative and to pace drama. Two stories she produced during the semester would lead to her first publications— in *Ploughshares* and in *The North American Review*—and they precipitated a string of happy acquisitions: a scholarship to Boston University's master's degree program in creative writing, a Henfield Foundation award, a couple of teaching jobs at local colleges, a story in *The Atlantic Monthly*, Maxine Groffsky as an agent, and then a residency at Radcliffe's Bunting Institute, where she began *The Good Mother*.

When she finished the novel, she knew it was good. She thought it would be published and well-reviewed, but she had no expectations of anything more. What happened to *The Good Mother* still baffles her: "I always regarded it as kind of an accident." Ted Solotaroff, the venerable Harper & Row editor, enthusiastically purchased the book for a hefty sum; the sales for the paperback and movie rights radically altered Miller's income-tax bracket; the reviews were almost universally effusive in their praise; and the novel sold and sold, and continues to sell—over 1.5 million copies to date. Miller became a literary sensation. Her collection of short stories, *Inventing the Abbotts and Other Stories*, which was published a year later, solidified her standing as a serious writer with a commercial draw.

She chose to look at the success of *The Good Mother* as a "tenure" of sorts. She now had license to move on to different, more ambitious projects, rather than trying to repeat herself. In her next novel, *Family Pictures*, she set out to write a "kind of plotless, shapeless book that was a speculation on the meaning of suffering and the twentieth-century explanations for it—religion and psychiatry—and the floundering we do with those traditions." The generational story of the Eberhardt family, however, proved more difficult than she had anticipated. After extensive research and notes, she wrote two hundred pages over two years, and then showed them to her second husband, novelist Douglas Bauer, the author of *Dexterity* and the forthcoming *The Very Air*. Bauer and her agent both concurred that there was something amiss, the material simply wasn't very strong. Miller has always depended on this pair of readers for guidance, and although often she thinks "they're dead wrong," this time she knew they were right. She spent a few weeks "in the bathtub, weeping and thinking, God, I just don't know if I can do this, maybe I can't," but then began anew. After two more years, she completed the manuscript, and reviewers agreed that she was at the top of her form with *Family Pictures*, which was nominated for a National Book Critics Circle award.

Her third novel, *For Love*, released this past April, came much quicker and easier, and has been called her best yet. With it, a consistent theme in her work has emerged—people's expectation of happiness, of fulfilling the American Dream, and the pain inflicted in its pursuit before they are able to accept responsibilities and disappointments and limitations. "I mark myself as an American writer in my time with this preoccupation," Miller says. "It's something that would seem self-evident to Europeans, not even worth establishing, but I think it's pervasive in American life to see endless opportunities, the possibility of continual rebirths—politically, pyschologically, physically. To me, it's a very damaging part of the American psyche."

Though Miller has no interest in being prescriptive—deeming what is right or wrong—she wants to nudge the reader into speculating about the moral dimensions of his or her life. These convictions sometimes led to frustrations when Miller taught writing. "Often students would be very good writers," she recounts, "but would be clueless as to the importance of tension in fiction, what drama or struggle means." As a frame for discussion, she would cite Flannery O'Connor's belief that every good story is, in some sense, the soul's journey around a dragon. "Although all her stories were Catholic," Miller says, "I do think that stories tend to be about the human spirit, even though they might not be in those religious terms. It seems to me that most writers do, in fact, try to pose a problem for a character that will expose his spiritual crisis, expose him in the moment when he confronts the issues that are central to who he is and what he is doing here on this earth. So I would ask my students: What is the drama that compels this material? What do you think this character's dragon is? What is he running from? What does he need to defeat in order to become fully human? Do you want him to succeed or fail?"

After a total of eight years at Boston University, MIT, and Tufts University, though, Miller acknowledged that she no longer had the energy to teach on a regular basis. "At a certain point, maybe a particular story *was* different than something I'd seen twenty-five times before, but I found myself *saying* the same thing I'd said twenty-five times before—not even shifting my critique over that marginal degree so it was apt to the student's problem, because I'd just gotten lazy." A long hiatus has revitalized her, and she will be teaching next year at Bennington College's new low-residency M.F.A. program, but she still believes that creative writing courses are limited in what they can provide. "You can't help someone who doesn't have it. You can only teach people how to be good editors for themselves. I feel that's what Ted [Solotaroff] has taught me. With each book, I'm a little better at asking myself, What drew me in here? Have I gotten that clearly on the page?"

What is drawing her to the page now? Miller is pensive about the future. She is comfortable with the idea of being out of the literary limelight, having felt somewhat embarrassed by or indifferent to her early celebrity. She has, for instance, never involved herself in the film and television adaptations of her work—has never, in fact, *seen* them. And for her recent *For Love* tour, she asked her publicist to reduce her schedule of readings at large venues—the audiences for which have been diminishing—opting instead to join in on book groups, intimate gatherings of people who read a work and then discuss it. "It's hard enough to write," she says. "To have to hustle your book on top of that adds to the depression about the way literature is regarded in the universe."

Surprisingly, the possibility of retirement is not inconceivable to her. "I feel at a sort of crossroads in my life," she admits. "I've had a lot of family responsibilities, and those are over now. Before, if I could write and take care of my family, garden, play the piano, do a bit of exercise, and also cook and paint my house and patch the plaster, then that was enough. I've been given this gift of tremendous freedom at this point in my life, and I'm not sure what I want to do with it." She adds, "I'd like to think that there was a particular reason to read each of my books—a strong one—and if I felt that I didn't have new territory to write about in some way, I think I would stop."

But one senses that this statement is merely another demonstration of Sue Miller's profound humility. She is a woman in control of her life and her fiction, talented enough to continue providing her many readers with distinctive and beautifully crafted stories—visions of a world that is both cruel and redemptive—and strong enough to persevere, even if it means a little more weeping in the bathtub.

—*Don Lee*

BOOKSHELF

THE PUGILIST AT REST *Stories by Thom Jones. Little, Brown and Company, $18.95 cloth. Reviewed by Kevin Miller.*

Already commercially successful, with half the entries previously in *The New Yorker, Harper's,* and *Esquire,* Thom Jones's debut collection is best described as utterly uncompromising. From his gallery of hard-assed, hard-headed, hard-luck, or simply *hard* cases, to the way these stories are written and sequenced, Jones demands much of the reader—and more often than not gives much in return. *The Pugilist at Rest* isn't quite the "knockout" suggested by some of the advance notice, but like the "brain lightning" experienced by several of his epileptic characters, there are flashes here of memorable and auspicious brilliance.

Three stories narrated by Vietnam vets open the collection; indeed, the first seven of the eleven entries are all told in the first person. Although such sequencing almost invites objection on the grounds of monotony, for the speakers sound very much alike, the voice that does emerge here is singularly compelling. The narrator of the title story is typical. Middle-aged, epileptic from one too many head blows in a Marine Corps boxing ring, and now facing brain surgery, he recalls the battlefield death of his lieutenant in a voice that's direct, ironic, and almost preternaturally focused on the scene's absurd horror: "It [a rocket] took off his whole arm, and for an instant I could see the white bone and ligaments of his shoulder, and then red flesh of muscle tissue, looking very much like fresh prime beef, well-marbled and encased in a thin layer of yellowish-white adipose tissue . . . he stayed up on one knee with his remaining arm extended out to the enemy, palm upward in the soulful, heartrending gesture of Al Jolson doing a rendition of 'Mammy.'" By the next page, the same narrator is quoting Schopenhauer—philosophy being a favorite compass for Jones's tough guys as they try to reason their way through such unreasonable lives.

"Sometimes a bad beating could do a fellow a world of good," opines another of Jones's narrators. And with "philosophy" like that, there's plenty of machismo at play in *The Pugilist at Rest*—machismo that, in the words of several of his narrators, occasionally crosses over into misogyny. The library lizard narrator of "Wipeout," for example, is also conversant with the great thinkers, although he appears to find the likes of Kant chiefly useful in seducing and exploiting women ("The scorpion stings, it can't help itself"). Similarly, in "Unchain My Heart," the collection's sole female narrator sounds as though she could be Mr. Wipeout's dream girl. Speaking of her lover, this New York City magazine editor pleads, "I need him to fuck my brains out."

Irritating as that is, you've got to admire Jones's courage in dishing up first-person story after story featuring characters who are sometimes downright repugnant. He doesn't moralize. He doesn't stack the deck. He simply lets his people talk. Make of them what you will.

At the same time, any suspicions about the *author's* character will surely be allayed by the appearance, near the end of the book, of "I Want to Live," an engrossing and sensitive piece—in the third person, though stream-of-consciousness in effect—about a middle-aged woman dying of cancer. Two more third-person keepers make for a strong finish: "A White Horse" and "Rocket Man." In the former, the most memorable story in the collection, an American advertising man, on a kind of epileptic bender, rescues a diseased horse from a Bombay beach, while the latter approaches a Richard Yates–like pathos in its depiction of a boxer and his alcoholic trainer.

That Jones's stories are apparently drawn from his life isn't especially newsworthy. What is, is the urgency and relentlessness, perhaps because of Jones's life, with which *The Pugilist at Rest* is written. That in itself sets this collection head and shoulders above most recent American debuts. Jones's characters may give out and they may give you trouble, but what redeems them all is that they never give in.

Kevin Miller is at work on a collection of stories. He teaches at Emerson College.

TALKING TO HIGH MONKS IN THE SNOW *An Asian American Odyssey by Lydia Minatoya. Harper Perennial, $20.00 cloth, $11.00 paper. Reviewed by Leila Philip.*

"I am a woman who apologizes to her furniture," states Lydia Minatoya halfway through her engaging memoir about growing up as a Japanese American. " 'Excuse me,' I say when I bump into a chair. My voice resonates with solicitude." Reflecting on her girlhood in upstate New York in the 1950s, Minatoya goes on to explain that while her American peers were learning the rites of individualism—to ask, to demand—Lydia and her sister were being taught the rites of traditional Japanese femininity—to be dutiful, quiet, yet strong, to put the rights of her possessions even before herself.

Such humorous yet telling moments of insight characterize Minatoya's thoughtful first book, which chronicles her struggle to reconcile the opposing cultural forces that have shaped her as a Japanese-American woman. As a young psychologist in Boston, Minatoya suffers from a pervading sense of being out of place, despite early success. When a budget cut eliminates her job, she decides to travel to Asia, hoping to resolve her unhappiness by coming to terms with her Asian roots.

Minatoya's subject—personal identity and its complex relation-ship with culture and circumstance—is always interesting, and as one would expect, her journey is full of surprises. While she may have grown up feeling out of place as a Japanese in the predomi-nantly Caucasian community of Albany, once in Japan she dis-covers that she hardly fits in there, either. In a reunion with her mother's family that had long been estranged because of a shame-ful family divorce, Minatoya is confronted by the family patri-arch. "Remember and be proud," he shouts at her, shaking a scroll that represents some eight hundred years of samurai family history.

Mortified, then deeply moved, Minatoya recognizes for the first time the apologetic attitude of assimilation which she has absorbed from her diligent Japanese parents. She leaves her fast-track career in Boston to teach on an Army base in Okinawa, in the University of Maryland's overseas program, and it is in the strange cultural mix of Army base life that she finds an apt metaphor for her own situation. "It is no accident that I am a psychologist. All of my life I have wondered: who am I? But as I lived in Japan, my anxiety eased. I was a Japanese American, teaching cross-cultural psychology, on American bases in the midst of Japan, and the sheer intellectual tidiness of my situation pleased me."

As the book moves forward, chronicling Minatoya's adventures in Japan and Asia, it also moves backwards through a series of flashbacks to Minatoya's previous professional life in Boston and her early childhood in Albany. Not surprisingly, some of the most poignant writing in the book are the portraits of her dreamy, scientific father and plucky seamstress mother.

Despite the harshness of discrimination they have faced as Japanese Americans, including the outrage of being herded into Japanese relocation camps during the war, Minatoya's parents refuse to abandon the promise of America. In a moving scene, Minatoya describes her father's immense dignity when three years before retirement he discovers that he has only been paid the salary of a high school graduate, even though he has a doctorate degree. Lydia and her sister scream that he should sue his company; he shakes his head and refuses. "My father studied his American daughters. He gently smiled. 'Before I could sue, I would have to review my life. I would have to doubt the wisdom of such loyalty. I would have to call myself a victim and fill myself with bitterness.' He searched our faces for signs of comprehension. 'I cannot bear so great a loss.' "

With this debut, Minatoya joins the fast-growing list of Asian-American authors. Unlike writers such as Maxine Hong Kingston, however, who insist that being Asian American is to be neither Asian nor American, but a third cultural entity altogether, Minatoya identifies and assigns distinctly American and Japanese sides to herself and her experience. For Minatoya, the struggle to come to terms with her identity is resolved through journey—first the journey out to Asia, then back to the United States—and through the experience of writing this moving and graceful memoir.

Leila Philip, currently a Bunting Institute Fellow, is the author of The Road Through Miyama *(Vintage Departures), a narrative account of two years that she lived in rural Japan as an apprentice to a master potter.*

HURDY GURDY *Poems by Tim Seibles. Cleveland State University Press, $10.00 paper. Reviewed by Tony Hoagland.*

Appetite, revenge, and celebration are the animating energies in Tim Seibles's generous-hearted and rambunctious first collection, *Hurdy Gurdy*. As the title implies, this is street music of a kind, alternately plaintive and rapturous as it explores issues of adulthood and desire in late-century America.

In their high spiritedness, and their devotion to invention rather than fact, these poems are more reminiscent of the surreal gusto of the Seventies than the tediously sincere, you-gotta-believe-me tone which prevails in the Nineties. Seibles knows, in fact, that we *don't* gotta believe him, so the tongue is kept firmly in the cheek as he proposes sincerity. *Hurdy Gurdy* is unapologetic in its representations of male desire, as in the delirious "Treatise": "Sometimes I feel my penis / like a prisoner in solitary confinement, / raking his rusty cup against the hard bars / of this life pleading for a woman / whose name I don't even know—a genuine pleading / as though for the secret to a secret / that's been kept ever since the first sperm serenaded / the pinkness of the womb and coaxed an egg / to come out and play."

Such erotic transcendentalism is prominent here, but behind it, less noisy, shadowy chords of anxiety and anger play, connected with the experience of being a black man in white America, "crashing the party, a / coffee stain on the lapel of a white, white / tuxedo, a kinky hair floating in a glass / of milk" ("After All"). Though the speaker, ever amusing and amused, determinedly positive, tells himself, "No big deal, it's cool, no need to / get into a Frederick Douglass kind of thing," historical and cultural unease intrudes on the more pleasant metaphysics of imagination, and the counterpoint adds a gratifying ballast to some poems. In one, the speaker fantasizes assassinating the president of South Africa. In another, he imagines civilization stemming from one African Eve, the mother of humanity, "that slim, short-tempered woman / whose children crawled / all over the planet, then got big and started / hurting each other—with the conquerers / in their bright armor, trying to finish everything. / I know where the blame falls. I know / I could twist my brown skin ... my / kinky hair into a fist. I know..."

Studded with inventive, often hilarious metaphors, these poems offer the reader's efforts a high pleasure return; they are perhaps most serious, though, in their striking and convincing generosity of heart. Employing reality for their imaginative fuel, the poems in *Hurdy Gurdy* comfort and defend the soul.

Tony Hoagland's collection of poems, Sweet Ruin *(Univ. of Wisconsin Press), won the Brittingham Prize in 1992. This year, he is teaching at Colby College.*

THE RIVER AT WOLF *Poems by Jean Valentine. Alice James Books, $8.95 paper. Reviewed by David Rivard.*

There are some poets whose work incites a reader to metaphor. This is especially true of those whose ultimate subject is the unsayable, the numinous—where the risks taken by the poet must provoke her reader into making an equally risky leap of the imagination in responding. Jean Valentine is one of contemporary poetry's preeminent ringleaders of the numinous; and in her moving and fine new book, *The River at Wolf*, she faces head-on the most serious mysteries of desire and death. She does this with a voice that makes me think of the Javanese shadow theater, in which small, handheld puppets—sharply cut, at once simple and intricate—play out the epics of the Mahabarata projected against a large screen. Valentine's poems project strongly into the world that surrounds them, though the flame that throws these shadows comes from a place deep inside, where, she says, "my softness and hardness are filled with a secret light."

Despite their intense, calligraphic lyricism, these poems *are* epic in nature, epics of the inner life: "Here's the letter I wrote, / and the ghost letter, underneath—/ that's my work in life ("To The Memory of David Kalstone"). Letter or epic, the implied story these militantly non-narrative poems tell comes from the place within the poet where a struggle is taking place, between innocence and guilt, love and fear, vulnerability and protection, wholeness and sickness, safety and destruction. One side of the choir sings, "you can't protect yourself, / there is nothing to get" ("My Mother's Body, My Professor, My Bower"), while the other counterpoints with "I want, I want. / I want to become round like you there: like God: reality: / not flat like here, all oil, all pleasantness and heat" ("Lindis Pass, Borage"). Both sides possess flawlessly tuned ears.

Like all poets with God hunger, Valentine's search is for the transcendent. But the grace and power of this book arise out of the denial of transcendence, out of a recognition that transcendence seems impossible in this life, no matter how much desired. So she instead embraces "world-light / and this world company," and out of her attentions transforms that world. And whose work is more attentive than Jean Valentine's? Attentive to the often hidden parts of feeling, feelings provoked here by the death of her mother, by the AIDS epidemic and homelessness, and especially by the shiftings of love. The poems that touch on AIDS or homelessness movingly illustrate not just the great empathy Valentine is capable of, but also the tone of intimacy special to her work: "I remember looking at you, X, this way, / taking in your red hair, your eyes' light, and I miss you / so. I know, / you are you, and real, standing there in the doorway, / whether dead or whether living, real" ("X"). Or, even more poignantly: "Everyone else may leave you, I will never leave you, fugitive" ("The Under Voice").

This intimacy is both unsettling and comforting, as it should be, implying deep familiarity, and trust of the "other" to whom the poems are addressed. That "other" being us. Ultimately, this intimacy is erotic, as are so many of my favorite moments in the poems. Maybe this is because Valentine works in a tradition of poets who tend to fuse religious ecstasy with the sexual. More likely, it's because at so many moments throughout *The River At Wolf* she is as open as we'd all like to be: "Time to taste the round mountains, the white and green, / and the dusk rose of relationship, again, / for the first time, it's time to take off our clothes, / and the fortresses around our eyes, to touch our first fingers, / you and I, like God, across everything" ("The Summer Was Not Long Enough"). It *is* pleasure to read someone who believes so fully that "you must keep seeing: everything / must be turned to love that is not love."

David Rivard's Torque *won the Starrett Poetry Prize from Pitt. He teaches at Tufts University and in the Vermont College M.F.A. in Writing Program.*

NOT WHERE I STARTED FROM *Stories by Kate Wheeler. Houghton Mifflin, $19.95 cloth. Reviewed by Don Lee.*

Since Kate Wheeler was once an ordained Buddhist nun in Burma, an immediate and cynical expectation might be for her first book to espouse some sort of New Age philosophy—a saccharine embrace of everything metaphysical, all in the pursuit of enlightenment and harmony. And while it's true that four of the ten stories in *Not Where I Started From* explore Buddhism and its variants, such an attitude would only expose extreme ignorance and not give proper credit to this fine writer. This particular group of stories—one piece, a foray into Mill Valley, notwithstanding—offers remarkable insights into the practices and frequent beauty of Eastern religions.

In "Under the Roof," a young Thai woman is given charge of an American monk who has been temporarily exiled from Burma, due to visa problems, and they forge a delicate and respectful relationship built on spiritual devotion. In "Manikarnika," a lesbian graduate student journeys to India "to understand emptiness." After learning that her father has died, a probable suicide, she goes to a river burial site: "Four corpses were in various stages of cremation, each releasing a braid of black smoke straight up to Heaven. No wind—intense transparent heat, like vaporized quartz. . . . The dead woman's gastric juice shot up in a bitter, yellow fountain, and fell back hissing on the coals. Reality hits you in the face, Martina thought: What opinion could I possibly have?" And in "Ringworm," a woman cloisters herself in Pingyan Monastery, seeking Nirvana, or the "end of suffering—*cessation,*" but civil unrest in Rangoon drives her out of the country, and a year later, she gives up her vows, despite her love of Buddhism's purity, knowing "I could not stop the whirling of this world."

Indeed, the other stories in the book present characters who are ironic, sometimes deeply jaded, about the prospect of finding any faith in this world. In several, Wheeler uses her own childhood in South America as background—teenage American girls in Columbia and Argentina discovering the divisions between themselves and the nationals. Regardless of their good intentions, they eventually adopt the cultural detachment of their parents'. One of them, the daughter of the U.S. ambassador to Buenos Aires in

"Urbino," befriends a servant who is later killed. Ushered back to the States when Perón makes his return, she guiltily has only one real remembrance of loss: "Of all things, it felt worse to have left my horse alone, a loyal heart defenseless in that place."

The remaining stories in *Not Where I Started From* show a rather breathtaking range, from a woman hiding out with a cocaine dealer in Miami's Little Havana to a couple of sexual misfits in Kansas. As a whole, this sharply written collection is linked by the inexorable motion of its characters and the contradictions inherent in their destinations. They look for transcendence and find moral ambiguity. They attempt fellowship and then abandon friends. They pursue love and settle for indifference. All of them begin to wonder, as does a dancer visiting her former lover in Paris: "How do people ever get along?"

THE PAPER ANNIVERSARY *A novel by Joan Wickersham. Viking, $21.00 cloth. Reviewed by Katherine Min.*

In her first novel, *The Paper Anniversary,* Joan Wickersham writes beautifully and with excruciating honesty about marriage, the sublime and the mundane of conjugal affection, and conjugal brutality. One of the astonishments of the book is the way both partners, Maisie and Jack, are rendered fully and independently, with an even sympathy that allows them their weaknesses— Maisie's self-absorption and need for drama; Jack's uncommunicativeness and passivity—at the same time revealing their greater hopes and more admirable natures.

It begins in trouble. Maisie is living in New York with friends, working as an editorial assistant at a publishing company, while Jack stays in Maine, in the small town where he grew up, to tend his family's ailing french fry factory. Their physical separation soon leads to an emotional one, and Jack, unable to deal with the fickleness of Maisie's affections, finds himself getting involved with Laura, a woman who allows him "the freedom to be dull." Maisie, chafing at her perception of marriage as a narrowing of possibility and the death of passion, realizes it is Jack she wants only when it looks like he has moved beyond her.

It is a long way back from the brink, and the novel spares us none of the pain and bad behavior along the way. Wickersham writes precise, luminous prose capable of great subtlety, humor, and heartbreaking lyricism. Her descriptions are vivid and distinctive, her insights stunningly accurate. In bed with Laura, Jack recalls something Maisie had once said about their cat, Egg. " 'Don't you think he makes all other cats look wrong?' And he wondered, after all his years of staring at Maisie: How long would it take him to get to the point where all other women, even Laura, didn't look wrong?"

Minor characters are memorably drawn: Laura, strong and serene, at ease paddling a canoe or crimping a pie crust, with a self-reliance born of low expectation; Dunnane, the man Maisie briefly, and disastrously, dates, a would-be Horatio Alger, hotheaded and vulgar, full of wild theories and insecurity; Caterina, Maisie's best friend, maternal, aloof, as controlled as Maisie is reckless, keeping her problems to herself rather than spilling them out as Maisie does.

The novel as a whole paints an intimate portrait of a marriage that is as specific as it is universal. Like all of us, Maisie and Jack are admirable and flawed, struggling with their own issues and limitations and, out of their wisdom and their folly, somehow managing to forge a relationship and a life together. Like a pitcher with pinpoint control, Wickersham consistently throws strikes, moving high and low, inside and out, painting the corners, arriving again and again at truth with devastating accuracy. *The Paper Anniversary* is eloquent about the things we cannot explain, even, and perhaps especially, to those we love the most, those we have chosen to love. It is about the extreme risk of deep romantic feeling and the heroic but problematic surrendering of our protective armor; it is about the tenuous, tenacious bond of lifelong commitment.

Katherine Min's fiction has appeared in Ploughshares, Glimmer Train, *and other magazines. A new story is forthcoming in* TriQuarterly. *She has recently completed a novel,* Stealing the View.

BELOVED INFIDEL *Poems by Dean Young. Wesleyan University Press, $10.95 paper. Reviewed by Diann Blakely Shoaf.*

In "The Hive," as in many other of the very fine poems in Dean Young's second collection, *Beloved Infidel*, the slightly cracked and wavy but nonetheless serviceable mirror of contemporary language is held up to our lives, to the thrusts and parries that characterize what is perhaps our age's central obsession: relationships. "None of us are to blame," Young writes, "sitting on the porch, smoking, quitting smoking, / talking about our backs, Italy, finishing / the book on Gertrude Stein, betrayals, talking / about shoes and how we want what everyone wants: / complete devotion and to be left the hell alone." Young's gift for the universal and seemingly irrefutable statement is also felt, as the title perhaps indicates, in "On Being Asked by a Student If He Should Ask Out Some Girl," another of the volume's brightest stars.

The quirky, conversational, self-mocking, and achingly human voice here is well-modulated through the book's four sections. Young plummets into undeniable despair—though always with a kind of stoic humor—in poems like "Shades," where a friend tells him of his lover's suicide. "What can I say," Young asks himself, "that isn't a contrivance of keening and / projection? How twice a woman I once loved / told me gently, almost politely, / sometimes she wishes me dead?" Yet the same section includes a poem Young is able to title, with a straight face, "Pleasure"; he argues for its place in lives carried out in the country that invented the Protestant ethic, its workaholics now laboring in the post-yuppie era. Young's argument is put forth for an entirely unfrivolous reason, one carrying the weight of a moral imperative: "There must be an aesthetic not based on death." In these funny, poignant, spikily intelligent, and unnervingly wise poems, Young makes a real winner of a case for this credo. And in the process, makes a book that's a winner of hearts as well.

Diann Blakely Shoaf's first book of poems, Hurricane Walk, *was published last year by BOA Editions. She teaches at the Harpeth Hall School in Nashville.*

COHEN AWARDS Each volume year, the best poem, short story, and nonfiction piece published in *Ploughshares* are honored with the Cohen Awards. Finalists are nominated by staff editors, and the winners are selected by our advisory editors—comprised of current and former guest editors. Each winner receives a cash prize of $400. The awards are wholly sponsored by our patrons Denise and Mel Cohen of New Orleans. This year, for the first time, all three winners were selected from a single issue—*West Real,* Spring 1992, Vol. 18/1—a testament to the literary vision of the issue's editor, Alberto Alavaro Ríos. The 1993 Cohen Awards for work published in *Ploughshares* Vol. 18 go to:

DINAH BERLAND

RICHARD GARCIA—FOR HIS POEM "IN THE YEAR 1946." Richard Garcia was born in 1941 in San Francisco. Half–Puerto Rican, half-Mexican, he grew up in a house without books, except for one on the meanings of dreams. "Looking back," he says, "that one book seems to have served me well." While still in high school, he had a poem published by City Lights in a Beat anthology. After publishing his first collection in 1972, however, he did not write poetry again for twelve years, until an unsolicited letter of encouragement from Octavio Paz inspired him to resume. Since then, his work has appeared widely in literary magazines such as *The Kenyon Review, Parnassus,* and *The Gettysburg Review.* He is also the author of a bilingual children's book, *My Aunt Otilia's Spirits.* He has received an NEA Fellowship and four California Arts Council fellowships—three as poet-in-residence at the Long Beach Museum of Art. Garcia has lived in Colorado, Mexico, and Israel, and now makes his home in Los Angeles, where he is poet-in-residence at Childrens Hospital, through a program sponsored by the Mark Taper Foundation. The University of Pittsburgh Press has just published a new collection of his poetry, *The Flying Garcias*. He and his wife, poet Dinah Berland, are currently M.F.A. candidates in Warren Wilson College's Program for Writers.

RON CARLSON—FOR HIS STORY "BLAZO." Ron Carlson was born in Logan, Utah. In 1971, after finishing his master's degree in English at the University of Utah, he ventured east to teach, coach, and run a dormitory at the Hotchkiss School in Connecticut. There, while teaching classes six days a week and learning to skate so he could properly coach one of the hockey teams,  Carlson began his first novel, *Betrayed by F. Scott Fitzgerald*, which was published in 1977. After his second novel, *Truants,* was released in 1981, he returned to Utah for a life of writing and periodic teaching engagements sponsored by the arts councils of Utah, Idaho, and Alaska. In 1986, Carlson accepted a teaching post at Arizona State University, where he is now the Director of the Creative Writing Program. His stories have appeared in *The New Yorker, Harper's, Gentlemen's Quarterly, Playboy, Best American Short Stories, Sudden Fiction, Best of the West,* and many other magazines and anthologies. A recipient of an NEA Fellowship, he is the author of the collections *The News of the World* and *Plan B for the Middle Class,* which was published last year by W.W. Norton & Co. He will be co-hosting *Books and Company* next spring on KAET Public Television. He lives with his wife, Elaine, and their two sons in Tempe, Arizona.

DEBRA SPARK—FOR HER ESSAY "THE LURE OF THE WEST." Debra Spark was born and raised in a suburb of Boston. She grew up in a family of professionals—lawyers, doctors, professors—with artistic inclinations: one writes, another is a stand-up comic, and another is an opera singer. After graduating from Yale University in 1984 with a degree in philosophy, Spark attended  the Iowa Writers' Workshop at the University of Iowa, where she received her M.F.A. Her stories have appeared in *Esquire, Prairie*

Schooner, New Letters, and other magazines, and she writes book reviews regularly for such publications as *The Harvard Review, Ploughshares,* and *Hungry Mind.* She also edited the anthology *Twenty Under Thirty,* which was published by Scribners in 1986. Spark has worked as a management consultant, a freelance editor, and a teacher at Emerson College, Tufts University, and elsewhere. In 1992, she received an NEA Fellowship, and she was a 1992–93 Bunting Institute Fellow at Radcliffe College. Currently, she is finishing a novel about a family in Puerto Rico. She lives in Cambridge, Massachusetts.

NOW RECYCLED We're happy to report that *Ploughshares* is now printed on recycled paper, a choice that was precluded in the past by substantially higher prices for such stock.

PUSHCART PRIZES Congratulations to the following writers for the inclusion of their works in *The Pushcart Prize XVIII: Best of the Small Presses 1993–94,* which will be published this fall by Pushcart, with a trade paperback by Touchstone/Simon & Schuster scheduled for next spring: Rick Bass for his story "Days of Heaven" (Vol. 17/2&3); Lynn Emanuel for her poem "The Dig" (Vol. 16/4); Dennis Loy Johnson for his story "Forrest in the Trees" (Vol. 18/1); and Bárbara Selfridge for her story "Monday Her Car Wouldn't Start" (Vol. 18/1).

SOS On October 5, 1993, up to two hundred benefit readings will be held across the country to fight hunger, under the rubric "Writers Harvest: The National Reading." The sponsoring organization, Share Our Strength (SOS), which was behind the publication of the *Louder Than Words* fiction anthologies, is one of the nation's largest nonprofit hunger relief agencies. Since 1984, it has raised and distributed nearly $11 million for domestic and international programs, ranging from food banks in Idaho to emergency relief in Somalia. The Writers Harvest, which strives to unite the country's literary community and raise public awareness about hunger and poverty, was conceived last year by novelist Frederick Busch. This October 5, writers such as Gwendolyn Brooks, Joyce Carol Oates, Calvin Trillin, Scott Turow, Gloria

Naylor, E. Annie Proulx, and hundreds of others will be appearing at bookstores and university campuses in the U.S. and Canada, with one hundred percent of the proceeds going *directly* to relief agencies. We urge you to support this very worthy cause. Call 1-800-955-8278 to find out where events will be held in your area. In and around Boston, readings will be at Waterstone's Booksellers, Boston University, Northeastern University, The Bookstore in Lenox, and UMass/Dartmouth. Tickets will be $10, with a discount of $5 for students.

GOING MADISON AVENUE If you look at the last page of this issue, you'll see that our new subscription ad is much more professional-looking than usual. The reason: Bronner Slosberg Humphrey, one of the most prestigious advertising agencies in Boston, conceived and designed it for us. We were introduced to Bronner by the Boston chapter of Business Volunteers for the Arts (BVA), whose aim is to increase arts advocacy in the business community. Locally, executives from companies such as Digital, Coopers & Lybrand, IBM, Blue Cross, and Fidelity are recruited, trained, and placed as pro bono consultants with nonprofit arts organizations. We're grateful to and heartened by the corporate world's involvement in the arts, and we encourage others to participate in local BVA chapters, either by volunteering as consultants or by signing up as clients. For this particular project, thanks go to Richard MacMillan, Boston/BVA's Executive Director, and the following people at Bronner Slosberg Humphrey: copywriters Martha Connor-VanDyke and Tim Cawley; art directors Greg Sedgwick and Arthur Milano; and Chief Information Officer Clifton Gerring.

—Don Lee

MFA

Writing Program
at Vermont College

Intensive 11-Day residencies
July and January on the beautiful Vermont campus.
Workshops, classes, readings, conferences, followed
by **Non-Resident 6-Month Writing Projects** in
poetry and fiction individually designed during residency.
In-depth criticism of manuscripts. Sustained dialogue with faculty.

Post-graduate Writing Semester
for those who have already finished a graduate degree
with a concentration in creative writing.

Vermont College admits students
regardless of race, creed, sex or ethnic origin.

Scholarships and financial aid available.

Faculty

Tony Ardizzone	Phyllis Barber
Francois Camoin	Mark Cox
Deborah Digges	Mark Doty
Jonathan Holden	Lynda Hull
Richard Jackson	Sydney Lea
Diane Lefer	Ellen Lesser
Susan Mitchell	Jack Myers
Sena Jeter Naslund	Christopher Noel
Pamela Painter	Frankie Paino
David Rivard	Gladys Swan
Sharon Sheehe Stark	Leslie Ullman
Roger Weingarten	W.D. Wetherell
David Wojahn	

Visiting Writers include:

Julia Alvarez	Richard Howard
Brett Lott	Naomi Shihab Nye

For more information:
Roger Weingarten, MFA Writing Program, Box 889,
Vermont College of Norwich University, Montpelier, VT 05602
802–828–8840
Low-residency B.A. and M.A. programs also available.

Other Sides of Silence

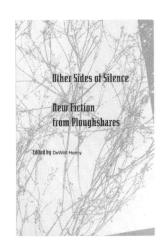

New Fiction from Ploughshares

Edited by

DeWitt Henry

From Sue Miller and Andre Dubus to Stuart Dybek and Joy Williams, *Other Sides of Silence* showcases the best new fiction published in *Ploughshares* since 1984.

DeWitt Henry, Executive Director and cofounder of *Ploughshares,* hails this rich and diverse sampling of short stories as "writing that attempts to confront contemporary experience at the deepest levels." The result is an anthology of remarkable breadth and unusual grace and sensitivity, unrivalled for its selection of writers on the cutting edge of contemporary fiction. Twenty-two stories in all.

$12.95 paperback original
ISBN 0-571-19811-2

Available at bookstores nationally,
or by calling (800) 666-2211.

Linda Bamber
Rick Bass
Ann Beattie
Louis Berney
Gina Berriault
Ethan Canin
Andre Dubus
Stuart Dybek
Tess Gallagher
Gordon Jackson
Wayne Johnson
Phillip Lopate
David Wong Louie
Sue Miller
Joyce Carol Oates
Alberto Alvaro Ríos
Carol Roh-Spaulding
Maura Stanton
Christopher Tilghman
Marjorie Waters
Theodore Weesner
Joy Williams

Faber and Faber

50 Cross Street ♦ Winchester, MA 01890

THE PUSHCART PRIZE XVII

1992 / 1993

BEST OF THE SMALL PRESSES

EDITED BY
BILL HENDERSON
WITH THE
PUSHCART PRIZE
EDITORS

JUST PUBLISHED
570 PAGES
$29.50 cloth

PUSHCART PRESS
P.O. BOX 380
WAINSCOTT, N.Y. 11975

SUBMISSION POLICIES

Ploughshares · Fall 1993

Ploughshares is published three times a year: one fiction issue and two mixed issues of poetry and fiction. Each is guest-edited by a different writer, who will often be interested in specific themes or aesthetics. Postmark submissions to *Ploughshares,* Emerson College, 100 Beacon St., Boston, MA 02116-1596, between August 1 and April 1 (returned unread during April, May, June, and July). The guest editor for the Spring 1994 issue is James Welch, who will be looking for fiction and poetry that explore tribalism. He says, "Tribe: My old *Webster's* dictionary defines this as 'a social group comprising numerous families, clans, or generations together with slaves, dependents, or adopted strangers.' When we think of tribes and tribalism in this country, we think of 19th-century American Indians on the Western Plains, hunting buffalo, tanning hides, performing complex ceremonies to honor the sun. Are there tribes in America today? Perhaps a new definition is in order—one that goes beyond Native Americans and involves gender, political affinities, race, geography, community, spirituality. Who are the strangers today? And what role do they play in tribes? Are they tricksters?" You may call the *Ploughshares* answering machine after 8 P.M., E.S.T., for guidelines of other issues as they are updated. We usually read from August to November for the Spring issue, from November to February for the Fall issue, and from December to March for the Winter issue. You may submit for a preferred issue, but please be timely, as we accumulate a backlog. All manuscripts must first be screened at our office; never send directly to a guest editor. Staff editors ultimately determine for which issue/editor a work is most appropriate. If an issue closes, the work is considered for the next one(s). Overall, we look for submissions of serious literary value. For prose, one story, memoir, or personal essay. No criticism or book reviews. Thirty-page maximum length. Typed double-spaced on one side of the page. For poetry, limit of 3–5 poems. Individually typed either single- or double-spaced on one side of the page. ("Phone-a-Poem," 617-578-8754, is by invitation only.) Always mail prose and poetry separately. *Only one submission of prose and/or poetry at a time, please.* Do not send another manuscript until you hear about the first. Additional submissions will be returned unread. Please mail manuscript in page-sized manila envelope, your full name and address written on the outside, to the Fiction, Nonfiction, or Poetry Editor. All manuscripts and correspondence regarding submissions should be accompanied by a self-addressed, stamped envelope (S.A.S.E.) for reply or return of manuscript, or we will not respond. Expect three to five months for a decision. Please wait five months to query us, then write, rather than call, indicating the postmark date of your submission. Simultaneous submissions are permitted. *We cannot accommodate revisions, changes of return address, or forgotten S.A.S.E.'s after the fact.* We cannot be responsible for delay, loss, or damage. We do not reprint previously published work. Payment is upon publication: $10 per printed page ($20 minimum, no maximum), with two copies of the issue and a one-year subscription.

PLOUGHSHARES BOOKS

1935: A Memoir *by Sam Cornish.* A unique collage of autobiography and poetry, exploring twenty years of African-American experience. $19.95 cloth, $9.95 paper. 1990.

The Ploughshares Reader: New Fiction for the Eighties *edited by DeWitt Henry.* Thirty-three stories from the first fifteen years of *Ploughshares.* $24.95 cloth. 1985.

The Ploughshares Poetry Reader *edited by Joyce Peseroff.* Works by over one hundred poets from eleven volumes of *Ploughshares.* $25 cloth. 1987.

Lie Down in Darkness: A Screenplay *by Richard Yates.* The unproduced screen adaptation of Styron's novel, originally commissioned by John Frankenheimer. $8.95 paper. 1985.

Order with check from:
Ploughshares Books, Emerson College
100 Beacon St., Boston, MA 02116

Phone-a-Poem

617-578-8754

Recordings of contemporary poets reading their work, twenty-four hours a day. A free community service sponsored by Ploughshares and Emerson College.

Please Inform Us When You Move

The post office usually will not forward third-class bulk mail. Please give us as much notice as possible.

"NOW ACCEPTING ENTRIES!!"

The Missouri Review
Editors' Prize Contest 1993

$1,000—Short Fiction
$1,000—Essay
$500—Poetry

Deadline: Postmarked by October 15, 1993

One winner and three finalists will be chosen in each category. Winners will be published and finalists announced in the following spring's issue of *The Missouri Review*. Entries must be previously unpublished, and will not be returned. Enclose a SASE for notification of winners.

Complete Guidelines

- **Page restrictions:** 25 typed, double-spaced, for fiction and essays, 10 pages for poetry.

- **Entry fee:** $15 for each entry (checks payable to *The Missouri Review*). Each fee entitles entrant to a one-year subscription to *MR*, an extension of a current subscription, or a gift subscription. Please indicate your choice and enclose a complete address for subscriptions.

- Entries must be clearly addressed to: Missouri Review Editors' Prize, 1507 Hillcrest Hall, UMC, Columbia, MO 65211. Outside of the envelope must be marked "Fiction," "Essay" or "Poetry."

- Enclose an index card with the author's name, address, and telephone number in the left corner and the work's title in the center of the card if fiction or essay.

Last year's winnners: Fiction—*David Borofka*, Essay—*Tom Whalen*, Poetry—*Jeff Friedman*

Subscription Rates: 3 years–$36   2 years–$27   1 year–$15

Eat, Drink & Be Literary.

HARVARD BOOK STORE
CAFE

Breakfast through Late Dinner
190 Newbury Street at Exeter, Boston • 536-0095

Master's in Writing at

EMERSON

COLLEGE

Develop your writing talent, your knowledge of literature and criticism, your awareness of the literary marketplace, and your skills as a teacher of writing and literature by joining a community of 180 graduate students, who work with a faculty of writers, editors, critics, and publishing professionals at Emerson College, home of *Ploughshares*.

Located in Boston's Back Bay, Emerson offers an M.F.A. program in Creative Writing and an M.A. program in Writing and Publishing.

Current and recent full- and part-time faculty members of the Division of Writing, Literature, and Publishing include:

Theodore Weesner	Jenefer Shute	Melanie Rae Thon
Acting Chair	Lynn Williams	Christopher Tilghman
Jonathan Aaron	Sven Birkerts	Dan Wakefield
Richard Duprey	James Carroll	
Eileen Farrell	Sam Cornish	CONCENTRATIONS
Robin Riley Fast	Christopher Keane	Fiction
Jack Gantos	Margot Livesey	Poetry
DeWitt Henry	Pamela Painter	Nonfiction
Bill Knott	Joyce Peseroff	Playwriting
Maria Koundoura	Elizabeth Searle	Film & TV
Eileen Pollack	Marcie Hershman	Scriptwriting
Connie Porter	Alexandra Marshall	Children's Literature

For more information, contact: Graduate Admissions
Emerson College · 100 Beacon Street · Boston, MA 02116
(617) 578-8610